DARK, IMPOSING
TOWERING BEAUTIFULLY ON THE
CORNISH CLIFFS ...

Adelaide jumped to her feet, her hazel eyes
brightening to burning gold. 'I don't want telling
what to do and how to behave – especially by
you – '

'No, but you damn well need it,' Rupert said
explosively, suddenly losing his temper. 'And
while you're in my house I shall continue to do
it. Understand?'

'I'm sure you will. But let me tell you, Rupert
Hawksley – '

His anger evaporated as quickly as it had
flared up. He got up, took her arm, and forced
her to sit again. 'Addy, Addy,' he said cajolingly.
'Don't scratch so. What's the matter with you? I
told you at the beginning you could make
Trenhawk your home for as long as you wanted.'

'You said I could stay as a guest. That's not
the same thing at all.'

'No,' he agreed, 'I see your point. Let me
remedy it then: let me say, "Cousin Adelaide, if
you want to live here – if that's really your wish,
I'll be delighted".' He waited, watching her
intently, noting the ebb and flow of colour in her
cheeks, the slight tremor of her underlip which
gave her momentarily the vulnerable look of a
child. A flood of tenderness filled him. He'd have
liked to take her in his arms, putting his lips to
her forehead and then her cheek gently pressing
her golden head close against him ...

Trenhawk

MARY WILLIAMS

SPHERE BOOKS LIMITED
30–32 Gray's Inn Road, London WC1X 8JL

First published in Great Britain by
William Kimber Ltd 1980

Copyright © 1980 by Mary Williams

Published by Sphere Books Ltd 1982
Reprinted 1983 (twice)

TRADE
MARK

Printed and bound in Great Britain by
Cox & Wyman Ltd, Reading

I

Mist crept down from the moors to the sea, enfolding the house in a shroud of grey. Only distant turrets and chimneys were clearly defined against the afternoon sky, yet as the carriage wheels rattled down the wind-blown track the girl, sitting pale-faced and rigid behind the driver, knew with sudden conviction she had been right to come to Trenhawk.

From the past a flood of recognitions and half-forgotten memories stirred to greet her, pictures of days long past, incidents of childhood when she'd stayed there for brief periods with her step-cousins David and Rupert Hawksley.

Now, David whom she'd married less than two months ago had been killed at war by the cruel Turks.

She was alone.

But Trenhawk remained. At Trenhawk, despite her grief, she would live as she and her young husband had planned. In time she'd manage to run the estate efficiently, keeping the inheritance intact, letting no one know the bitterness that drove her. Rupert, the elder cousin, was the only stumbling block to her plan because legally he was now sole heir to the house. But Rupert wanted money for the mine Wheal Tansy, which had belonged to his father's family for generations, and she was convinced he could be induced to sell or life-lease to her − whatever it was they called it under such circumstances − for a sufficiently tempting sum.

David had told her that capital was badly needed to explore new levels for copper, and this was where her strength lay. She could make an offer for Trenhawk that would prove irresistible to a man so dedicated to a cause as Rupert was. Even as a boy his interest in the old mine had seemed to her fanatical. She'd never understood; seen no beauty nor anything desirable in the dark gaunt shape of the engine house scarring the wild horizon, or the rhythmic motion of the great pumping rod against the sky. Rupert had never travelled far

from Cornwall, and he lived only a mile from the works, at
Manor Farm, which lay in a fold of the moors some distance
above Trenhawk.

For this reason, she supposed, Wheal Tansy was so important to him, which was lucky for her. She had no doubts of
her power to win him over eventually. Already the deal was
finalised in her mind. Morally the house *was* hers, because it
had been David's, and had already been prepared with additional furnishings as their home.

David's father, William Hawksley, had died only six
months ago; so in the brief period of her marriage to David
there had been hurried arrangements with a 'furnishing
house' in London to have certain equipment sent on to
Cornwall. She and her husband had expected to have at least
a month there themselves getting it in order before he re-
signed his commission in the army. Meanwhile they'd stay a
few weeks at the town house that had been her mother's,
attending parties and theatres, riding and driving in the
Park, and during leisure moments making all the plans of a
young couple desperately in love, with all their future ahead.

Instead had come Sevastopol and David's sudden sum-
mons to the Crimea. In a wave of acute nostalgia the
memory of their farewell at the Port of London returned to
her, rekindling the vivid image of his receding figure waving
to her, so handsome in his scarlet uniform, as the boat sailed
away.

Stupid, stupid war, she thought, to cost so many lives for
such senseless glory. Why couldn't Turkey and Russia have
been left to settle their own troubles? What use was power at
such a price?

She shivered again. The autumn air was suddenly cold,
chilling her body as well as her spirit.

As the gig drew nearer every moment to the house, she
stiffened to a semblance of composure. The caretaker, who'd
been housekeeper to her step-uncle, would surely be there to
receive her. She'd written to Rupert informing him of her
plans, and though they'd never much liked each other – even
as a boy he'd been proud and domineering in a silent kind of
way – she didn't doubt he'd see the polite formalities were
observed.

So she had to appear dignified, as befitting the widow of 'the young master'. There would be all the time in the world later for remembering.

The carriage came to a halt abruptly. Peering through the window she saw they were there. The man opened the door and offered his hand. She stepped out.

Before her Trenhawk stood granite-faced and massive, with turrets towering dark in the sullen light. A few gulls wheeled overhead, circling towards the cliffs beyond, where land and sea merged to uniformity.

She paused for a moment, instinctively glancing up. Was it her fancy, or did a shape move briefly behind the glass of an upper window, – the window of the Tower Room? The impression was vague; a fleeting shifting and curdling of the uncertain light into the semblance of a watchful luminous disc-face that was quickly gone, taken into shadow once more. For an instant she recalled stories she'd heard as a child of Trenhawk's ghost, and realised the impression must merely have been an old memory rekindled through circumstance and her own emotional state. Strangely vivid though, and at that point, compelling.

She sighed, pulled herself together, and waited while the driver deposited her valise at the door. The next moment she was walking ahead – a youthful erect figure in her sombre widow's weeds which were unrelieved by any touch of colour. The black veil falling from her small perched-forward hat, was blown suddenly on a gust of wind, and with it a strand of rebellious fair hair that annoyingly brushed her eyes. She put up a gloved hand to restrain it, and in doing so dropped her vanity-bag near the steps.

With difficulty, because her black crinoline beneath the fitted, short, braided coat was irksome to manipulate, she retrieved it, and holding her head a fraction higher, went on.

There was no need to touch the hanging iron bell-pull. As she reached the door it opened, revealing a dark figure silhouetted by lamplight from the hall.

Not the housekeeper. Not even a man-servant. Before he spoke she recognised the stance, and set of the broad shoulders; the sturdy arrogance she had always resented in the past.

Rupert.

'Come in, Cousin Adelaide,' he said without emotion, 'you must be tired.'

From the way he spoke, his air of possession, she knew with a stab of apprehension that things might not be as easy to arrange as she'd anticipated.

Rupert was in command.

Rupert had already installed himself at Trenhawk.

At first, when she entered the wide front hall, Adelaide felt herself to be moving in a dream. She remembered it so well, yet nothing seemed to register clearly. Emotion had exhausted her more than she realised. The light was shadowed and uncertain, filtering from an upper stained-glass window across the stone flags. The richly woven rugs, worn considerably now from the passing of years, flapped faintly with a whispering sound from the draught of air. Rupert, walking beside her with the valise in one hand, seemed withdrawn and disinclined to talk following his first abrupt welcome. But then 'welcome' was hardly the word, she thought, in a mounting wave of depression. He didn't want her there, and his resentment cast a momentary pall over the house. The corridors that had once rung with laughter and the chatter of children felt deserted – bereft. Her own footsteps had a hollow ring as though ghosts mocked from the past. Then, slowly, she became aware of movement at the far end of the passage, and the emergence of a broad short figure, with a lantern held before her.

The face, shadowed into macabre lines from the transient glow, was thrust forward, peering from creased eye-sockets under a white lace frilled cap. It was years since Adelaide and the woman had met, but recognition was immediate. Except for the thickening figure, slightly bent posture, and ageing features, the housekeeper at Trenhawk had changed little. Her presence conveyed the same instinctive possessiveness Adelaide had known as a child, though her manner was polite when she said, 'Good evening, Mrs – David. How nice to see you again after this long time. I do wish it was under happier circumstances, but you have my sympathies, I'm sure.'

Adelaide stiffened. Perhaps Mrs Pender meant to be kind, but she didn't want her sympathy or even Rupert's if he'd had any to give, which was unlikely. All she wanted was to get to her room and be alone; to accustom herself again to once-familiar surroundings free of formalities and polite conversation – safe behind a locked door, so her tired nerves and body could relax from tightening strain. Her throat ached from the lump of pain threatening to overwhelm her. With an effort she pulled herself together, realising that Rupert was speaking. 'I'm sorry, Adelaide,' he was saying with an awkward show of sympathy. 'About David. But I don't need to tell you, do I – '

'No,' she answered. 'I'd rather not talk about it.'

She sensed rather than heard his sigh of relief. Then he continued in more practical tones, 'We haven't many servants here now – just the man, Carnack, a stable boy, and a daily girl to help Mrs Pender see things are in order. So I'm afraid you won't have the personal attention you're used to. But of course if you want to hire a maid for yourself – ' he paused and shrugged. Was there a hint of derision in his voice? Despite her tiredness she felt a warm flush stain her cheeks.

'I'm not helpless,' she said shortly. 'Things like that can be settled later.'

'Of course,' he agreed calmly, 'if you're proposing to stay for any length of time.'

'If I'm – ' she cut the quick remark short, aware that Mrs Pender's small eyes had narrowed shrewdly, and that beneath her placid exterior her mind and ears were alert.

Rupert turned abruptly, 'You may as well come up with me now. I'll put the case in your room and leave you. When you've had a bit of a rest, and tidied up you can come down any time you like.'

'Thank you,' she said irritated by what seemed to her his condescension, but restraining her emotions. It would be foolish to give Rupert the chance of gaining the advantage before she'd recovered her poise and decided exactly what her best tactics were – to plead with feminine sweetness or to tackle the matter of Trenhawk from a more hard-headed practical angle.

Rupert betrayed no surprise at her apparent meekness, although he was mildly intrigued. The Adelaide he remembered had been so explosively different – as a child rebellious and wayward, and later – at sixteen or seventeen, provocatively self-assured through knowledge of her own increasing beauty and allure. He'd always considered her spoiled and in need of discipline and her marriage to his cousin hadn't altered his opinion. David had seldom been able to resist a pretty face and no doubt before his untimely end had indulged her every whim. Apart from her physical attributes, the wealth she'd inherited on the death of her mother – his step-aunt, two years previously – would have made it well worth his while.

Frederick Drake, Adelaide's late father, had been not only partner in a large shipping concern, but owner of various large warehouses about the country supplying all manner of merchandise including cotton to commercial firms. In the five years following his death the capital which had provided such a tidy income for Richard Hawksley's second wife had expanded considerably, leaving Frederick's daughter sufficiently rich to take her pick from an assembly of discerning beaux in London Society. Not exactly the aristocracy, of course. Adelaide, despite her assets, had originated from, and remained of the middle-class. The division between 'trade' and the nobility was still clearly defined by the élite. And that was one comfort, Rupert thought, as he went ahead of her up the wide staircase. It should prove a safeguard from any possible dallyings on her part with Anthony, St Clare, heir to the neighbouring estate, Carnwikk.

There had been bad blood between the aristocratic Catholic St Clares and the Hawksleys for centuries; ever since 1557 when Charles, son of Jonathan Hawksley, a wealthy protestant merchant, had secretly married Marguerite St Clare. There had been a duel between the sons of the two houses resulting not only in the death of Charles but also of his young wife, when she'd attempted to interfere. Their baby alone had survived, to carry on the Hawksley name. Succeeding generations on both sides had seen to it that the feud continued.

Trenhawk itself, which had been built originally in 1553 as a home for monks but never used for the purpose, had remained impregnable through the changing stages of history, retaining sturdily its stalwart identity as guardian of its own wild coastline. One wall, facing the sea, appeared to rise from the actual granite and gave the impression of being carved by nature rather than by man. The few windows on that side were small and Gothic in design, high up, and well-placed to withstand the onslaught of monstrous waves and winter gales. Round the right-hand jutting corner of the building, a patch of grassland sloped to a ravine where a path cut down to the cove. The gardens were at the other side – and in strange contrast, with assorted flowering bushes and trees brought by former Hawksleys from abroad at various times, and protected by high granite walls and wind-breakers.

Trenhawk, indeed, though retaining its original austere character, had been subjected to a number of conflicting influences through the years which were responsible, perhaps, for the quiet impression sometimes that shadows moved and voices whispered from the past.

As Adelaide followed Rupert that evening round a corner of the staircase leading to the first landing, her senses sharpened.

The very heart of the house felt suddenly alive and responding to her presence.

In former times there had been an arched door opening from a few semi-circular steps on to the grand stone corridor. But now the north wing was open, and in the uncertain light portraits seemed to assume a curious life-like reality as shadows streaked from above.

In spite of her fatigue, Adelaide recalled how, as a child, she'd explored the numerous passages, and secret alcoves; her terrified excitement when some unexpected noise had startled her from behind a closed passage door leading to the servants quarters. At the other end was a flight of steps circling upwards from several landings to the tall tower-room – a place of mystery and enduring legend. The overall plan of the house had obviously been altered and added to with the passing of time, but at certain hours, in certain lights thrown slantwise from the Gothic stained glass windows, imagined pictures from very earliest times could easily be rekindled, until the years fell away, and the shadowy shapes of the monks who'd never lived there seemed to change and take possession of what should have been their inheritance.

There was the face too. The face of the woman the ten-year-old Adelaide had once glimpsed staring down when, against all orders, she'd had the temerity to venture halfway up the stairs leading to the tower. She'd been fascinated, but very frightened, because the face, pale and almost featureless in a cloud of massed black hair, had been somehow without substance, unreal. She'd rubbed her eyes, waited a moment with her heart pounding, and when she'd looked again it was almost gone, taken into the darkening shadows of the afternoon.

A moment later there'd been nothing there at all but the cold narrow stairway and the closed studded door. She'd turned quickly, rushing back to the safety of reality and her cousins' presence.

Afterwards she'd convinced herself the episode had been imagination. But now, walking with Rupert through the half-light, the image returned briefly. She pulled herself back to the present.

The present and its inevitable problem of persuading Rupert to sell.

Rupert.

Through her tiredness she'd almost forgotten him until she heard him saying, 'Mrs Pender's got the small bedroom ready. The one you're used to. It seemed most suitable.'

'Of course.'

He pushed open a door on the left, continuing, 'By the way Adelaide, all the stuff you had sent from town is in store below. The rugs and curtains seemed too delicate for general use, and under the circumstances – ' his voice broke off with a hint of embarrassment.

' – That David and I had chosen them together,' she cut in quickly. 'Don't be afraid to mention David's name. Yes, I understand. Thoughtful of you.'

She passed before him into the bedroom with her head up, her youthful figure stiff and proud. He was not aware of the brief quiver of her under lip or hurt in her green-flecked hazel eyes – only of the exquisite small-waisted figure and the glitter of soft gold hair under the thin black veil.

Her composure was admirable he thought grudgingly, trying and failing to associate her with the Adelaide he'd once known. All the same he was sure that beneath the controlled exterior the fire and spirit were there. Neither was he under any illusions concerning the reason for her sudden visit. She wanted Trenhawk, and assumed he'd be prevailed upon to let her have it without any unpleasant argument, otherwise she'd never have come.

He didn't doubt her grief over his cousin's death – Adelaide and David had always been a united force whenever they were together, not only because of their closeness in age, but because David's charm had the capacity for setting alight the imagination and heart of any feather-brained girl he'd fancied. Feather-brained of course hardly described Adelaide. But even as a youngster she'd had a liking for testing her own feminine allure on the opposite sex, and to have had David so completely at her feet must have been a stimulating experience.

Love? Well, of a certain kind, he supposed. But he doubted it would have withstood the test of time. One or the other would have become bored; and the probability was that David would have been the first to resent the chains. Still, Adelaide was obviously strained and suffering, and a touch of pity softened his voice as he said, 'Here we are then. Everything's aired. You'll find the bed warmed and the dressing room in order – ' he paused before adding tactlessly. 'A pity David had to land himself straight into Sevastopol.'

She turned sharply, and faced him squarely, eyes brilliant with unshed tears and a flash of anger. 'He was brave,' she said, 'and knew his duty. I'm very proud of him.'

'Naturally,' he commented drily, 'and upset. That's why it seems odd you coming here under the circumstances. I should have thought London would have taken your mind off things more – or a trip to Paris perhaps – '

Adelaide flinched. 'That just shows your lack of understanding. But then you never did bother much about people's feelings, did you Rupert – except the miners' and workers'? Do you imagine I *want* my mind diverting? Or to forget David for one single moment? Do you? *Do* you?'

Her voice had risen passionately; the colour was bright in her cheeks, and beneath the tight-fitting black jacket her breasts were heaving violently. For an instant, forgetting she was recently widowed, Rupert's senses stirred, mingled with irritation and a desire to snap back.

'I hadn't really thought about it,' he answered sharply. 'But it won't help you trying to live like a nun, if that's your intention.'

She turned her back on him and walked to the window 'Do you mind leaving me now?' she said coldly, 'I want to unpack and have a wash.'

'Of course. If you'd like something brought up for a meal this evening, I'm sure Mrs Pender would oblige. But I must remind you, Adelaide, she's getting old, so don't expect her to make a habit of traipsing up and down stairs with trays. She'll see single meals are served in the small front parlour at convenient hours while you're here, and sometimes I shall eat with you. But I have the farm as well as the mine to keep an eye on. Other business too. So you'll be on your own a good deal.'

'That won't worry me.'

'No. I didn't think it would,' he said shortly.

'And don't worry about Mrs Pender. I'll see she doesn't suffer on my account.'

He went to the door, but before closing it, asked abruptly. 'And what about tonight? I've ordered a meal for six-thirty, but as I said if you prefer privacy – '

'Oh no I don't,' she answered with a brave show of airy nonchalance and swish of her crinoline as she turned. 'There are things we have to talk about, Rupert. Not tonight perhaps, but some time. Anyway I may as well get used to the domestic routine as soon as possible.'

With the lamplight from the dressing table full on his face, she noted a deepening of his colour and sudden tightening of the well-modelled mouth. There was brief challenge in his glowing fiery eyes that stimulated her for a moment. From a domineering obstinate boy and youth, she thought, Rupert Hawksley had developed into a surprisingly handsome man. Under other circumstances the meeting could have been exciting; but the impact died suddenly when she remembered David. The swift change of mood did not escape him. He gave a brief nod, and went out, closing the door sharply behind him.

Presently Adelaide forced herself to the carved bedstead, where she sat for a minute or two before removing her hat and flinging herself down on the embroidered quilt, hands beneath her head. She closed her eyes hoping for a short rest before unpacking and changing into more suitable attire. But her head and body were too restless to relax. She got up again almost immediately, and went to the mullioned window which looked eastwards over the wild moors stretching to St Rozzan five miles away. Twilight had already faded to evening, and there was no light but a thin glow from the house, throwing the wan, distorted shadows of bushes and wind-blown trees over the drive. As her eyes grew more accustomed to the darkness she discerned dimly the silhouette of the cromlech topping the distant hills. Against her will she recalled an occasion when as children the three of them, Rupert, David and herself, had wandered there, against express orders because of hidden deserted mine-shafts and fog, with the trumped-up excuse of picking blackberries.

A fog had come down, and they'd been lost on the moor for some hours. When they returned her dress – a best one – was torn and muddied, her face and limbs scratched, and one shoe missing. What had happened to the boys she'd not heard, but she'd guessed. Her own punishment had been exceedingly unjustified, and relished no doubt by the strict governess who'd been given permission by her stepfather to whip her soundly, then strap her to a hard straight-backed chair where she was set to work at sewing sheets for a further hour.

How she'd hated the governess and the times she'd accompanied her mother and herself to Trenhawk. Luckily she'd been dismissed soon afterwards, following her stepfather's death, to be replaced by another considerably more indulgent and to Adelaide's liking; her name was Miss Trumper, and Rupert and David had found her an easy target for teasing and youthful jokes.

That period had been brief. When she was eleven Adelaide had been sent to boarding school and David to Rugby. Rupert had continued his education with the vicar of the parish as tutor, and henceforward holidays for Adelaide had become less frequent.

Looking back it didn't appear so long ago, but it was a whole ten years, and during that time much had happened historically, and to the Hawksleys.

Adelaide's stepfather Richard had succumbed to typhoid, and Ellen, Rupert's mother, who'd been widowed when her son was five had died from pneumonia. Winifred Hawksley had been thrown fatally from a horse, which though distressing at the time to Adelaide, her daughter, had compensated her with the freedom and means to enjoy her fortune. David had taken a commission in the Army and at that period was based near London which meant he saw Adelaide frequently. Her mother's sister – Aunt Matilda –who'd moved into the Hawksley town house, was an indulgent chaperone only too pleased to encourage the courtship. There had been no impediment, apparently, to the life they'd planned together. David had soon discovered that in Adelaide's company society's attractions were preferable to regimental duties. Resignation from Army life would mean they'd be free, after they were married, to divide their time between life at Trenhawk and in London.

Meanwhile there were balls, parties, and all manner of events to attend together. A new era of social life seemed to have flowered since the opening of the Great Exhibition of 1851. The wonderful Crystal Palace designed by Joseph Paxton and erected in Hyde Park was taken as a symbol of future prosperity and Prince Albert's rising popularity with the British public. Adelaide, excited and awed by its immense domed roof, pagoda and fountains, had enjoyed flaunting her vivid charms against the background of exotically clad men and women of fashion. She had only been seventeen when she attended with David, but her crinoline had been of pale blue embroidered satin under a fitted coat of the same shade, with a small flowered bonnet.

They had also gone to Kew together, Hampton Court under Aunt Matilda's chaperonage, and ridden in the Row. Adelaide had known they were a striking couple, and secretly enjoyed pretending they were of the Royal élite. This had not been difficult. David, fair skinned, chestnut-haired, strikingly handsome, had a lively distinguished air about him devastating to women and envied by men, and certainly she was quite aware of her own beauty.

Yet at intervals during that heady period she had yearned for Cornwall – for Trenhawk in particular. At heart, being mistress of her own historic private domain, Trenhawk, meant more to her, than the acknowledgement of sophisticated society.

What a world away. And how different her reception from the one she'd envisaged when she'd thought to return there with her young husband. Indignation seized her as she recalled Rupert's unswerving almost bold stare – his air of possessive authority, and dictatorial manner concerning household arrangements. It was harder than ever to accept him as David's cousin. During the years since childhood he seemed to have grown further apart from the rest of the family, and determined now to flaunt his heritage in her face.

She turned from the window abruptly, and went to the mirror, studying her reflection through the lamplight and flicker of logs from the fire. What a wreck she looked – dark smudges of eyes above high cheek-bones, intensified by the shadowed veiling pulled back over the small hat. She wrenched the headgear off and flung it on to a nearby chair, pulling with it a tumble of soft fair hair that broke freely from its chignon. That was better. The new-fashioned bun wasn't really her style at all, she decided, except for the most elegant occasions. When she went down that evening to meet Rupert for the meal she'd see the soft, naturally waving honey masses were arranged becomingly clustered over her ears. Not that she cared what he thought; but instinct told her the more attractively feminine she appeared, the greater her influence would be.

What should she wear?

Most of her wardrobe had been left in London to be sent on by Aunt Matilda when requested. But in her valise was a full grey silk gown, tight-waisted trimmed with black ribbon, with a froth of lace at the neck. It displayed the lines of her figure perfectly, but was dignified, and gave a pearly translucence to her clear skin and gold-flecked eyes.

She opened the case and took it out, shaking it vigorously before returning to the mirror. With it pressed to her shoulders by both hands she turned her head first this way then that, observing the effect critically.

Yes, the grey was the one, she decided. In it she'd feel assured and well able to retain dignity if Rupert took it into his head to start an argument.

Suddenly tiredness returned.

She slumped back on the bed briefly to recover, staring almost unseeingly round the room which had changed hardly at all since she'd known it, although new rugs replaced the old Persian ones. The same ancient chest was pushed against the wall near the window; in the opposite corner was the sturdy stand for ewer and basin. The one spider-legged chair was still upholstered in the pink brocade to match the heavy curtains. All now looked rather shabby, except for the dressing table itself which was new and rather ornately designed in the same wood as the cumbrous wardrobe – mahogany.

Yet the room in a subtle way retained its character of age, despite the varying periods of furnishing. It was as though the oak-beamed ceiling and mullioned window proclaimed – 'Do what you will with new finery and trumpery bits and pieces, the structure and spirit of this place remain Trenhawk; and while the house stands nothing will change it.'

She got up quickly, took off the constricting black travelling clothes, and unlaced her corsets, then seated herself on the dressing-table stool with muscles relaxed and free. She sighed, lifted her arms above her head for a moment before taking the brush to her hair. After this she washed and started the task of redressing, pulling the stays tight again so the tiny waist was emphasised below the gently swelling breasts. On top of the long frilled drawers came three starched petticoats; the last one was black, trimmed with black lace at the hem a little longer than the dress to emphasise the fact she was in mourning. In town of course no grieving young widow would have allowed herself to appear in grey so soon. No doubt Mrs Pender would disapprove. But dead black was so depressing, and David certainly wouldn't have wished her to look drab.

'Promise if anything happens,' he'd said on their last evening together, 'no puffy eyes or stuffy mourning. Keep yourself beautiful – for my sake. My own lovely Adelaide – '

And she'd cried impetuously, 'Oh David – don't. Don't talk like that; if anything happened to you *I'd* die too – '

'Nonsense,' he'd told her. 'And nothing will. I'll live and come back to you, and we'll spend our days at Trenhawk and have lots of children – like you of course. Well, maybe *one* of my sort, poor young devil – ' his smile had suddenly died, and eyes darkened, leaving him looking older and temporarily saddened. 'Honestly darling, you must never let yourself become plain and old with weeping, *whatever* the future is. Now promise?'

She'd nodded and given her word, but it hadn't really made any difference. The war had won, and she and David would have no children, because David was dead.

She drew a hand across her eyes, trying to erase strain from her face; looking miserable only made things worse, and would certainly not help where Rupert was concerned. Presently, feeling more satisfied with her appearance, she took her reticule from the dressing table, opened the door and went out.

The wide corridor and vast stone staircase felt cold after the fire-lit room. As she hurried down the steps she fancied the austere faces of Hawksley ancestors stared at her disapprovingly from their immense frames. They were mostly dark portraits of a puritanical character except for one, on the wall lower down near the hall – that of a laughing red-haired girl whom she'd been told had been David's great-great grandmother. There was a look of David about her, Adelaide thought as she reached the foot of the stairs, so unlike Rupert's rugged features and dark smouldering eyes.

When she reached the small parlour down a short corridor leading off from the main hall, she found her step-cousin already waiting for her by a spitting log-fire. She remembered the room clearly, an unostentatious interior furnished in oak, with an Elizabethan Court-cupboard standing against one wall facing a round Chippendale table near the window. Like most rooms at Trenhawk treasured ancestral relics from different periods intermingled in pleasing harmony. There was a small inlaid rosewood table pushed near the fire, with decanter on it and glasses. Rupert, looking unexpectedly civilised, already had a glass in his hand. He was wearing a thigh-length black velvet jacket, drainpipe dark trousers, and a white silk shirt and white tie. His hair usually so unruly, was carefully controlled, giving him, with the neatly clipped side-burns an air of authority that mildly took her aback.

The round table had already been drawn a little nearer the centre of the room and laid for the meal. Candles flickered from chandeliers one either side of the stone fireplace, casting a fitful pleasing glow over the glass and brown silk upholstered chairs. Another hung from the ceiling.

'Come along and get warm,' Rupert said, as she went in. 'I expect you find this rambling place chilly after London luxury.'

'I was prepared for it,' she said unsmilingly.

'Well for heaven's sake sit down and try to look comfortable, even if you're not,' he remarked edgily. 'We've twenty minutes or so before the meal's due. Time for a drink and a talk if you feel like it.' She didn't reply, but seated herself obediently near the comforting flames.

'What'll you have? Sherry?'

She nodded. 'Yes – yes please. Thank you.'

He unstoppered the decanter, filled a crystal glass and handed it to her. Then he poured one for himself, and took a chair facing her. She felt suddenly at a loss, hoping Rupert would not raise the question of her visit and the reason for it, until the following day. Everything was so different now, from what she'd expected it to be, including Rupert himself who dressed up as he was, resembled more the country gentleman and squire of an estate than the dedicated forceful mining engineer she recalled from her last visit.

But then that was what he obviously meant to be, she reminded herself with a rush of irritation. So she had to be prepared for a considerable duel of wills ahead. They sat silently for a few moments, an interim in which she felt him observing her closely, obviously waiting for her to make the first move in conversation.

When she didn't, he said, 'Well, it's nice to see you again, Adelaide, even under the circumstances.' He paused, adding quietly, 'You've changed.'

'Naturally,' she answered calmly. 'What did you expect?'

'Damned if I know,' he told her rising to her defensive mood. 'But then you were always unpredictable, and if I may say so, a little rash.'

'Rash?'

He nodded.

'You must realise it yourself by now. Oh I don't want to rub things in, Addy. You've had a bad shock. But when you married David you must have realised you weren't aiming for security exactly.'

She stiffened, and said, 'Security didn't come into it. And I don't want reminding of that horrible war or the past.'

Fingering the stem of his glass ruminatively he said half apologetically, half critically, 'That won't be easy will it, as you've returned here? David's name's bound to crop up, and you can't wipe out memories. Tell me, Adelaide – why *have* you come back?'

Taken aback by the question she'd hoped to evade till the next day, she hesitated before replying. Then she said with a burst of reckless honesty, 'To see what you were going to do, Rupert, about Trenhawk. You know very well that David and

I had planned to make it our home. It's only yours legally by chance. I'd still like to live here, if you were willing to sell. David said you needed money for the mine, and I've so much. I could give you what you want. Don't you see, it *could* work out that way? You have the manor farm – you've always lived there – I thought you'd want to go on – '

Taking advantage of the brief hesitant pause he cut in, saying quietly but shortly, 'The farm isn't Trenhawk, Adelaide. Trenhawk's been in the family for generations. What makes you think I'd be prepared to give it up. Sympathy for you? But you'd soon get tired of living here alone shut up with your ghosts. And then what? How do I know what you'd do with it?'

'There could be a deed drawn up or something, couldn't there, stipulating it went to you?'

'Pieces of paper have a way of falling flat under certain conditions,' he told her shortly, 'especially where big money's concerned. Oh I don't doubt you'd act honourably, and that you're rich enough to buy the whole estate up if I agreed. But I don't, and that's definite. As I said, you can stay here for as long as you want as a guest, but that's all. Understand?'

'You've put things very clearly,' she said with a flare of spirit. 'I rather thought you might refuse at first. But perhaps later you'll change your mind. After all the farm doesn't make much profit does it? And if that old mine needs so much doing to it – well? How *are* you going to pay for it, Rupert?'

'That's my affair I think,' he said with the dull colour flooding his face. 'I don't want to quarrel with you, but it's better we should understand each other from the very start. You will *not* get your pretty hands on Trenhawk, Adelaide, simply because I've no intention of selling. So let's end this very unproductive argument, shall we, and keep our digestions placid for Mrs Pender's excellent meal?'

Adelaide did not reply. Her whole being seethed with frustration. She was completely unaware during those few outraged moments how lovely she looked; how the rapid breathing and quickened pulse added to her allure, bringing a deep rose-glow to the pale cheeks, emphasising the translucent brilliance of her clear hazel eyes.

A little termagant, Rupert thought, and a silly chit to have wasted her heart and charms on a young adventurer like his cousin. If he'd lived she'd have learned to regret the day he took her at the altar. But David dead was likely to become a stubborn legend in her mind, and an emotionally dedicated woman could be an upsetting influence about the place. A nuisance too, when he'd so much else on his mind. Her assessment of his financial position was too near the mark for his liking, thanks to his cousin who seemed to have her head screwed on pretty well concerning family affairs. Wheal Tansy was in a tricky position. Reimbursement from some source or other was essential. Under other conditions he might have made a deal with Adelaide. But he was not going to have her assuming that her wealth could buy up anything she chose.

Now if he'd been in David's shoes, or David in his – supposing Adelaide had married *him*? – the passing idea though titivating, was quickly dispelled. As children their temperaments had been in direct opposition and their wills in conflict.

Once, on the moors, when she was about twelve, he'd had a taste of her temper that he'd never forgotten. She'd been pulling elder flowers from a twisted branch, and had half stumbled over a stone. He'd caught her from the back and when she'd twisted her head round to look at him the startled glance of her clear eyes through a tangle of curls was so vivid with changing light, he'd kissed her suddenly on her hot young cheek. She'd broken free, brought one hand hard against his face, with the other clutching a thatch of his wiry dark hair so fiercely it hurt. A tuft of it had been wrenched away, and he'd reached for her arm to teach her a lesson; but she'd been too quick for him, and a moment later he'd seen David standing nearby, half doubled up with laughter. They'd run down the hill, and Rupert, chagrined, had gone morosely in the other direction.

It had always been like that. David to the rescue. David her shining knight in armour. Well – poor Adelaide – it was over now; and a sorry state she'd have been in if it hadn't been for her father's inheritance. David, apparently, had left little more than bad debts. Even his shares in the mine had been sold – mostly to Rupert himself, thank God – though Adelaide probably hadn't taken it in yet. So she really had no claim on the Trenhawk estate whatever, except what he chose to concede morally. And that wasn't much.

Affection?

Studying her face that evening in the firelight following his sharp reminder of how she stood, he found himself softening. Yes, he was fond of her, though not from choice, and under the circumstances he told himself warily, the sooner she took off the better. He had a 'business deal' planned which could be tricky if she somehow poked her nose in.

A Dutch boat with a cargo of spirit and lace was to be unloaded the following Wednesday off Gooly Point. Under cover of darkness the goods would be conveyed by fishing boats to Trenhawk cove and taken by an underground 'run' to the cellars of the house. From there, all in good time, the liquor would find its way to various dram shops, kiddeywinks and inns, where it would fetch a valuable price.

Such ventures had gone on from time to time, even in William's life, generally without dire effect, and, providing all went well, Rupert's share after the participants had been paid would be quite considerable and go a certain way towards providing new mining equipment, and back payment due to workers. Law-breaking for such a cause was in Rupert's opinion a perfectly honorable occupation; a view regarded ambiguously even by the vicar of the parish, and others in high places who turned a blind eye, when it suited them, to such doubtful activities. But this bothersome business of Adelaide! How was he going to get rid of her in a civilised manner without hurting her feelings unduly?

The answer was obvious, he couldn't. He'd have to risk her presence for a time and see to it on some pretext or other that she was well out of the way at crucial times.

His reflections at this point were cut short by Mrs Pender's knock and entrance with dishes on a tray.

The meal, if a strained affair mentally, was appetising to the palate, consisting of roast beef, followed by apple pie liberally topped by cream.

'Whatever else it fails to do, the farm still manages to feed us well,' Rupert remarked at one point, to break the silence between them.

'How many men do you have working there?' Adelaide enquired.

'Just the two and the shepherd. When I've a free hour I give a hand myself.'

'You won't be able to do that much longer, will you, Cousin Rupert? Not with the mine, and living here?'

'I shall manage,' he said firmly. 'I'll divide my time between the two places which will be quite practical with Elizabeth up there and Mrs Pender at Trenhawk.'

Adelaide's heart jumped. 'Elizabeth? Who's she?'

'Elizabeth Chywanna, my housekeeper,' Rupert answered. 'A very capable woman.'

'Oh. And she doesn't *mind* ?'

'Mind what?'

'Never knowing where you'll be, whether she's to cook or not, or if you're going to appear suddenly expecting the table to be laid and waiting, without being told beforehand.' Adelaide said calmly. 'She must be unique.'

Rupert frowned.

'I know how to manage my own affairs,' he said. 'so don't start trying to teach me, if you don't mind.'

'I wouldn't dream of it,' Adelaide told him with a flash of her old spirit. 'But I can't help wondering why you're so determined to take over Trenhawk. And so quickly. After – after David being killed, I mean. I should have thought you'd have waited a bit and considered it. We could've talked things over then. It makes me wonder if – if – '

'Well?'

She paused before answering, then said, 'You were always somehow against me, Rupert, even when we were children. It was as though you resented me and David; and I can't help thinking that you might have moved in at the first chance just so I couldn't get here first. Just for spite.'

Over the candles his dark eyes narrowed. His lips tightened, and one hand clinched the stem of his glass before he took a quick short drink. She waited with a sense of triumph in her, knowing she'd annoyed him. As the glass clicked the table sharply, he sat speechlessly for a moment regarding her unswervingly, his face set and hard. Then he said, 'That was a damned insulting remark. You haven't changed, have you? Still the conceited overbearing little madam.' His breath had quickened under the well-cut coat. 'Well you'd better get this into your head once and for all. I don't resort to playing chase-me games with spoiled young women. You may have twisted David round your little finger and led him a pretty dance into the bargain. But not me, Adelaide. I'm not that kind. So think twice before you decide to remain under my roof. Yes, *mine*. Understand?'

Her cheeks flamed.

'You're so harsh, Rupert. That's your trouble. If you'd only been kinder – ' her voice wavered. She glanced away uncomfortably. 'But yes, I understand. You've made it very clear.' She jumped up suddenly, with a swish of her skirts, toppling a glass and leaving her pie half-eaten on the plate. At the door she turned, lifted her head defiantly and said coldly and clearly, though the tears were bright behind her lashes, 'All the same, I *shall* stay, Rupert. Be as rude and overbearing as you like. I don't care. And if I went to the law you might get a shock.'

'If you went to the law you'd be more stupid than I think you are,' he told her. 'So stop the foolishness and come back to the table.'

She ignored his remark and went out abruptly, slamming the door behind her.

A minute later Mrs Pender obviously having heard something of the sharp interlude, appeared with coffee on a tray.

'Oh,' she said, staring round significantly, 'has Miss Adelaide gone?'

'As you'll observe, Mrs David Hawksley has taken leave of my presence,' Rupert said with heavy irony. 'My company was obviously too much for her. We must be understanding though, and put it down to natural feminine distress.'

The housekeeper sniffed.

'It's not going to be the same with *her* about, Mr Rupert, it never was. But I suppose – '

'We must be tolerant. Yes,' Rupert said before she could finish. 'In time she'll learn to compromise and fit in with arrangements here. So I hope I can rely on your co-operation?'

The woman shrugged. 'Of course. But it won't always be easy, as you must know, sir.'

'We'll get past it,' he said, shortly. 'And in the morning, if I'm not much mistaken, my cousin will be in a gentler mood.'

His prophecy proved to be correct. But it was a long time that evening before Adelaide managed to compose herself, and when at last she undressed and went to bed, her hot indignation relapsed into a sense of futility.

She lay wakeful staring for a long time at the flickering shadows cast across the ceiling from the dying fire, listening to the creakings of the house and soughing of wind against the windows. Once it seemed to her a shadow moved and resolved itself into the form of a man watching from the corner near the wardrobe. But it was nothing. She pressed her eyelids together tightly, trying to induce peace and rest.

But no comfort came. No impression, even, of David's lithe young figure approaching the bed to take her in his arms. Well, how could there be? She just had to accept she'd never see him again.

Slowly, as the creeping shadows became merely part of the old room, she thought she heard footsteps from the landing, soft tip-toeing sounds that paused at her door and moved on again. She stiffened until all was completely quiet, then buried her face under the bedclothes.

At last sleep came.

When she woke daylight already penetrated the curtains, and before she had time to rub the sleepiness from her eyes there was a knock on the door and a girl came in carrying a can of hot water.

'Mrs Pender told me to bring this,' she said, dumping it on the marble-topped wash-stand. 'Do ee want me to pour it out?' Her manner was grudging but curious. She was a well-made young woman with a round shining face under a mob cap, and was wearing an apron over her full blue cotton dress.

'No, thank you,' Adelaide told her. 'I'll do it myself when I'm ready.'

'The winder then? Want th' curtains open?'

'Please.'

The girl walked purposefully past the foot of the bed, and with a rattle of rings pulled the heavy blinds apart. She was wearing boots that thudded heavily from her weight.

'What's your name?' Adelaide asked when she passed to the door again.

'Lucy,' came the answer abruptly.

'Thank you, Lucy, I hope we'll be friends,' Adelaide told her.

The girl turned. '*Friends*? You'n me, maam? That edn' part of my job here to be friends wi' the likes o' you. Got to remember that I have.'

'Who said so?'

After a stealthy peep out on to the landing Lucy put a hand to her mouth and whispered meaningfully, '*Her*, ma'am. Mrs Pender. A real tyrant she es, an' if I do cross her I'll be sent packin' – then we'll all be in the soup, dad an ma an' the little uns, what wi' the mine puttin' men off all the time, and the Lord alone knowin' what'll come next. So please doan' you go tryin' to be familiar. Got to keep to myself I have.'

She didn't wait for an answer, but pulled the door to with a snap and hurried off down the landing towards the back stairs.

As the echo of her cumbrous feet died away, Adelaide's thoughts snapped into order. Obviously what she'd heard previously concerning the uncertain future of Wheal Tansy was true. The girl's words had endorsed the fact that jobs were in jeopardy without further financial ballast. Rupert must have been putting on an act when he dismissed her suggestion of purchase so tardily. An act of defiance meant to keep her on tenterhooks. So if she pretended indifference for a time and did her best not to irritate him unduly she might yet succeed in getting him to accept a tempting offer for Trenhawk.

Although still tired after the previous day's journey and the unsatisfactory meeting with her cousin, she felt sufficiently rested and able to control her emotions to dress carefully and present a comparatively calm front.

When she went downstairs half an hour later, attired in a full black skirt with a fitting bodice adorned only by a cameo brooch at the neck, Rupert was already waiting for her in the hall, near the parlour.

He was wearing boots and knee breeches with a dark coat, and was obviously about to depart for the mine or farm.

'Good morning, Adelaide,' he said, forcing a smile. 'I hope you slept well?'

'Not badly, thank you,' she answered.

'Breakfast's in the parlour,' he told her, 'I've had mine, but I wanted a word with you before I went out –'

'Oh?'

'About last night,' he continued. 'I'm sorry if I appeared brusque and unwelcoming. We shouldn't have attempted any discussion or conversation, especially after what you've gone through. Still – maybe it was a good thing in one way. Now we understand each other things should be easier in the future.' He paused, adding, 'Don't you agree?'

'I'm sure I don't know, Rupert,' she answered. 'We can try.' His smile died. 'I hope you do.'

Walking across the moor towards the farm five minutes later his irritation with Adelaide increased. Why in heaven's name couldn't she make at least a gesture of co-operation, he wondered moodily? What right had she, after all, to assume any claim at all to Trenhawk? He could understand her disappointment. Her love of the place had always been one of the things he appreciated about her. To David tradition had counted far less. An indulgent easy-going life had come first, especially in town at the admiring feet of feminine society. No wonder he'd contemplated leaving the army after such a brief service. Adelaide of course would now never be able to assess the many facets of his character in true perspective. He would remain forever her Sir Galahad and romantic ideal, a symbolic figure putting all other men at a disadvantage.

Not that it mattered to him, he told himself stubbornly. Her languishing at Trenhawk would inevitably come to an end when boredom set in; and not too far ahead either unless he was much mistaken. She'd depart then for more appreciative spheres where her tragic young widowhood would be accepted with the sympathy and indulgent attention she craved for. Perhaps he was being uncharitable, but sometimes this was the only defence against Adelaide's charm. He'd certainly no intention of letting her upset his life now when it was running to his liking in the pattern he'd chosen for himself.

As he cut to the left under the brow of the hill, the sense of uneasy bewilderment in him lessened. In the distance the chimneys and mellowed roof of the farm gleamed gold from the frail glow of the rising sun. A coil of smoke rose grey against the sky, predictive of a fine day ahead. He sniffed the tangy air appreciatively wishing he could have spent the day at the manor instead of the complicated business of straightening matters out at Wheal Tansy. Borlaze – the Captain – was getting difficult. 'Back pay's owing to the men,' he'd said the previous day. 'I can't keep them quiet an' doin' their job for promises alone much longer, surr. You'll have to talk to them yourself. Fear's a killing thing when there's nothin' to ease it. And most of the workers have women and children to feed.'

'All right, I'll do that,' Rupert had said, 'though why there should be such doubt bothers me, Joe. Most of them know very well there's other business ahead and profitable for them. They have something each week in their pockets too, which is more than many Cornishmen have these days with so many mines closing down.'

'I know, I know. That's the problem. It's not you they doubt – it's the state of things.'

'And that's hardly my fault,' Rupert had said shortly. 'I'm not God, Joe. If lodes run thin then I can't wave my hand and have the levels rich with copper again the next moment. But it's there, Joe. William knows it, and he's one of the best engineers I've come across. *I* know it and *you* too.'

'Ah now,' Borlaze said cautiously, 'don't put the onus on me. I've lived longer than any of you, and time has taught me until you've got the ore under your fist you can't be certain it's there. There's always a risk, an' you've got to be prepared to take it. If it doesn't pay off, then you're expected to be able to make up to those who've toiled an' fretted on your behalf. Get my meaning, surr?'

Oh yes. He'd got it. The answer had been clear enough.

'Don't worry,' Rupert had said sharply. 'I'll be over in the morning and put things right. Sorry you're having such a tricky time.'

'Right. Just as long as you know how things stand, Mr Rupert.'

'No worry on that score,' Rupert had said with a tinge of irony in his voice. 'I've got assets besides – the other business – after all. There's always the farm.'

Borlaze had thought at first he was joking. 'But it doesn't pay all that well, does it? When you got rid of most of the herd two years back, I thought – '

'It doesn't pay at all,' Rupert interrupted. 'You know, Joe, I should have concentrated more on sheep, the small and native kind I mean. The grey-faced, short legged breed are hardy, and make good mutton. The wool's profitable, and they thrive on moorland. But then –' he gave a short laugh – 'I'm no farmer, as you well know. It's the mine that matters.'

'I always thought so. What did you mean about the farm then, if you don't mind me asking?'

'I can always sell it,' Rupert had answered abruptly.

'*Sell*? Your father's place?'

Rupert's lips had tightened. 'If necessary. There's Trenhawk now, Joe. I'm a man of property.'

A minute later the two men had gone their different ways, Joe half satisfied but still faintly uneasy, Rupert realising that if it came to the point he'd be extremely reluctant to get rid of the manor.

As he neared the building now his spirits lifted. Elizabeth would be waiting. He hadn't seen her for two days, and following the irritating encounters with Adelaide the thought of her smiling face and warm welcoming presence filled him with desire.

His step quickened.

Elizabeth Chywanna had been his housekeeper since his mother's death; and though five years his senior – perhaps because of it, partly – was the one woman he knew who was content to accept him for what he was, taking and giving without question when she could. Her husband Tom had been completely crippled from a mining accident in 1850 which had left him paralysed from the waist down. Rupert had allowed the couple to retain the cottage on the estate rent-free, provided Tom with a wheel-chair, and also paid Elizabeth a salary for doing what was required domestically at the Manor. It was natural under the circumstances that in the course of time a deeper relationship had blossomed between master and servant. Tom himself was under no illusions about the situation. But he kept his mouth shut. He respected both of them, and if jealousy gnawed occasionally he managed to subdue it through gratitude for the young master's kindness to them both. Elizabeth now in her thirties, at the prime of life, obviously needed something he could no longer give her; and far be it from him, he told himself in his more bitter moments, to deny her the natural physical fulfilment of a normal woman.

So to all intents and purpose the arrangement worked. Every morning after breakfast when she'd seen Tom was made comfortable and a mid-day meal prepared either cold or in the oven for her husband, and the shepherd if required, Elizabeth set off for the farm and hours of further cooking and cleaning. It was sometimes heavy going, but she didn't mind. She was strong, a farmer's daughter. The good pay, combined with the knowledge she was able to keep Tom well fed and properly cared for, and herself able to enjoy a full life, more than compensated for the few drawbacks.

She was busy about the kitchen when Rupert arrived that morning, and the tempting smell of baking already came from the Cornish slab cooking range. She turned when he opened the door, brushing a glistening lock of dark hair from her forehead. Her pleasant rosy face beamed with pleasure, and her dark eyes, brightened before she wiped the flour from her hands on the white apron. Beneath the calico bodice her ample breasts rose and fell invitingly from her quickened heart. She was by no means slender; but her well formed body was in proportion; her waist still neat and provocative above the gently swelling plump thighs.

He strode in and with one arm round her, one smoothing the satin-black hair planted a kiss soundly on her lips.

'How've you been?' he said, with a gentleness in his voice that Adelaide had never heard, 'and how's Tom?'

'Tom's all right, considering,' she said. 'Oh master – I've missed you.'

'Master?' he echoed, 'what a way to talk. You should know by now.'

'Rupert then,' she said quietly, 'although I'll never get used to it.'

He laughed, released her, and flung himself into a spindle-backed chair that creaked under his weight.

'You'll break that thing one day,' she told him.

'Come here,' he said, disregarding the rebuke.

'No, I won't,' she answered, with a touch of coyness. 'Not there.'

He got up and slipped an arm round her waist again. Her body felt soft, warm and yielding.

'You're wanting me, aren't you?'

'I always want you,' she answered. He kissed her again on a hot cheek, and led her upstairs. But unlike most times when their love-making was over, he was not completely at peace. Broken routine, he supposed logically, later. Nothing had really changed between them. Elizabeth was the same glowing devoted creature she'd always been. But something had been lacking.

What?

Fire? Provocation? That certain touch of conflict between the sexes some women unfailingly provoked? His step-cousin for instance – Adelaide Hawksley?

She was a taunting creature, and he wished she hadn't come. Until her unwarranted intrusion life had run on a comparatively even course. The scheming little madam. A faint smile touched his lips. Widow she might be, but she was woman as well; and although he brushed the knowledge aside his instincts told him there was already rapport between them – an unseen fire that one day would inevitably explode or burn itself out.

Which?

At this point he pulled himself up abruptly. There was no point in speculation. He was a man with a goal, an object in life which would permit no diversion through the devious charms of any wayward woman.

The mine and Trenhawk.

II

When Rupert left the farm for his tricky visit to the mine, Elizabeth accompanied him a short way carrying a basket of mushrooms for her husband. The excuse had occurred to her at the last minute, because something in Rupert's manner slightly discomforted her. He was unduly silent, and she could sense he had something on his mind. The day was an exhilarating one, tangy and bright with dew filming the heather and bracken. Below, in its moorland dip, the turrets and roof of Trenhawk were tipped with pale gold; the air was windless and fresh, holding the mingled scents of growing things and brine from the sea.

Yet despondency grew in her. Ever since their relationship had first started she'd known one day things must change. Sometime Rupert Hawksley would inevitably marry or change his mode of life. It was to be expected and she'd steeled herself to be prepared for it. After all, she had no rights. Her real place was with Tom, as Rupert's was with his own social kind. But – the doubt in her suddenly overcame wisdom.

'Something botherin' you?' she asked on the spur of the moment.

Rupert glanced at her quickly, touched her arm briefly, then let it drop to his side again.

'There's always something with what I've got on my hands,' he answered. 'But nothing for you to worry about.'

'Are you sure?'

'What do you mean?'

'Well, I've been thinking. If you mean to spend most of your time at Trenhawk there won't be so much for me to do at the manor, will there? Up to now there's been your meals to get ready, and to have the place nice. But with you away all that won't be needed. I don't want you to think that because of Tom an' everything I'm a sort of duty. No – no, don't say anything, not yet. I can see things as they are, I hope; an' I know without you telling me that you need every penny for the mine, and getting things right there. So if you want me to leave say so, there are always things I can do at the cottage to help out. Tom and I don't need that much to live on – '

'Stop it, Elizabeth,' Rupert cut in sharply. 'What put the idea into your head? It *did* occur to me Tom and you might like to move into the farm as caretakers, and for you to be on hand when the men needed you and for the dairy. But I realised it wouldn't work. Tom needs his own home, and he's got it. As for me – well, it's true I'll be mostly at Trenhawk in the future. But not at the Manor's expense. I shall still keep an eye on things, and produce and food will always be needed for the house. Besides – ' his voice though gentle was a little forced – 'what about us?'

Elizabeth was silent.

'Well?' he insisted.

'Only you can answer that,' she said.

The conversation ended inconclusively. He didn't intend to commit himself. He never had. Neither was he anxious to face the fundamental truth that his need for Elizabeth was daily becoming more of a habit than any consuming desire. He admired and warmly appreciated her. When he wanted comfort from a woman she was there to give it. But latterly he'd felt things were going too deeply with her than they should; he'd no intention of forming a permanent relationship. On the other hand the last thing he wished was to hurt her. She'd had enough of pain in her life already following the shock of the accident and Tom confined to a wheel-chair for life. His instinct was to press her hand when they approached the gate of the small granite cottage garden. But he suppressed it. Whatever happened between them in private was kept secret between them. Tongues might wag occasionally and farm hands pass a knowing wink to each other. But nothing could be proved.

To all intents and purposes Rupert Hawksley and Elizabeth Chywanna were master and servant, no more.

When the door had closed behind her he saw Tom's pale face staring through the window. Rupert lifted a hand in greeting, and then went on, cutting up towards Wheal Tansy. The pumping rod was already visible beyond the brow of the hill, moving evenly against the autumn sky. The Count House, where Borlaze, the manager, had his office, was a mere fifty yards away on the near side of the moor, and Borlaze himself, a stocky figure, was already outside on the watch for Rupert. He was not involved personally in the young master's dubious plans for raising the essential funds for the mine, being a Methodist, with strong opinions of right and wrong. But he had more than an inkling of what went on from time to time, and so long as facts weren't placed directly under his nose, was well content to ignore them if they produced the desired result.

The meeting that day went better than Rupert had hoped, and an hour later, with his optimism re-imbursed, and a feeling that things were going to work out satisfactorily, he did not at once return to Trenhawk, but called on Tom to pass the time of day. Chywanna was still seated in his wheelchair by the window, with newspapers on his knee that Rupert saw were provided weekly. An empty mug stood by his feet.

Hearing the click of the door he looked round. He smiled, but as always Rupert felt a pang of compunction, and saddened by the hopeless stare of the dark eyes which appeared larger than natural in the white face. Somehow that certain look of acceptance and inevitability of his fate was more tragic than any bitterness could have been.

'Well, Tom, how are things with you today?'

'Same as usual, surr, Mr Rupert. Not bad. Not bad at all considering. Lizzy got me a cup o' tay when she called a bit ago. An' thanks for they papers, they help.'

'Good thing you can read, Tom. There are many who can't.'

'Ais.' The short word, brusquely spoken, conveyed so much more than Rupert wanted to hear. It was as though the mind behind the uncomplaining exterior added, 'And there are many sound in mind and limb, who can spend a day working with his mates and come back of an evening to find a woman hungering for his arms round her and feel of her body close. Reading's not all that important.'

Rupert's discomfort deepened. He'd always felt that the tragic accident involving three deaths and Tom's disablement lay in some measure at his door, although inspection of equipment was not his business. The trouble had been due to a faulty rope that had snapped at the top of the shaft when the men were ready for landing, sending the cage hurtling back down. Tom had been quick enough to extricate himself at the first jerk, but both legs had been caught and smashed. At the government enquiry later it was revealed that if the cage had been fitted with safety catches the terrible disaster would never have happened.

Tom, in spite of his injuries, had been honest enough always to insist that the young master couldn't possibly have been expected to know. It wasn't his business. A bad trick of fate – that's what it was.

But since then Rupert had made sure he was kept fully informed of working conditions. In a sense his relationship with Elizabeth, and the knowledge she was not entirely deprived of a natural existence, lightened matters, and he knew Tom mostly felt the same.

That day though, Tom seemed moodier than usual and disinclined to talk.

'Anything on your mind?' Rupert asked before he left, 'If there is – or if there's anything you want, just say and I'll do what I can – '

'No,' Tom answered, 'nuthen. Except it's occurred to me, if you're movin' down to the big place an' not doing so much up here you may be needing more labour for the farm. I s'pose our cottage is safe?'

Rupert gripped the man's shoulder hard and kept his hand there until he'd told him, 'You don't need me to answer that, Tom. I've decided to make the lease over to you for life and for Elizabeth too. All in a proper deed – no rent or rates. I should have done it before but there's been a good deal to think of lately. So forget any worries on that score. Understood?'

'Thanks, Mr Rupert,' Tom said gruffly.

Rupert left shortly after and was soon walking briskly back towards the farm, Polrose. The sun shone full on its cream well timbered exterior and stone roof. It was a cruck house, originally built in Tudor times for a yeoman farmer, and though the chimney and attic dormers were added later, the main structure adhered to the early hall-and-parlour plan of architecture, with a jettied portion at the western end which was unique for Cornwall where most buildings were of granite and

built to a simpler more solid pattern. For this reason and the
fact that his father Richard had gone to considerable pains to
preserve its character, Rupert realised that the last thing he'd
want to do was to sell it. It was as an integral a part of the
Trenhawk estate now as the large house itself and the mine. Be
damned to anyone who assumed he couldn't get through
without giving up any of them – especially his young madam
of a cousin, he thought grimly, setting his jaw tight.

He wondered what she was doing in his absence. Somehow
it was hard to imagine Adelaide being idle or not up to
something she shouldn't be. If he'd known he might have
hurried back instead of calling in at the farm again for a chat
with Brandon, his solicitor, who was due there sometime
around eleven-thirty or twelve.

Adelaide, in fact, was exploring.

With Lucy and Mrs Pender safely occupied in the kitchens,
and the man and boy busy at the stables, she'd managed to
locate the curtains, carpets, and pieces of furniture she and
David had chosen, in a small sewing-room leading off the back
stairs. She was furious. If she stayed for any length of time –
which she was determined to – she'd demand they were put in
their rightful place – not William's large room now presumably taken over by Rupert, but her smaller one.

Wherever *she* slept, their belongings too must be, so she could
close her eyes in loneliest moments imagining David was still
with her. And if Rupert proved difficult she'd get the man and
the other servants in his absence to do the removal. Having
solved the question to her own satisfaction, she closed the door
behind her, and wandered aimlessly up the steps towards the
landing leading eventually in the direction of the Tower
Room.

Once she glanced back, and her senses and body froze. At
the other end of the corridor, illuminated by the strangely
coloured transient light from a stained glass window was a
youthful face watching. Boy or girl she couldn't tell; but the
dark eyes were so intense, the stare so still and concentrated,
she thought at first she must be having a hallucination.
Everywhere seemed uncannily quiet suddenly, enshrouded
with past influences and drifting shadows. Unearthly yet
weirdly compelling.

'Who are you?' she heard herself whisper.

There was no reply. There hardly could be. The corridor was so long and vast; so empty except for the odd portrait or two and tapestries on the walls. And still the curiously intent eyes were upon her. She could sense it, even though the view had become blurred momentarily, but only by a few dancing prisms of light.

She forced herself to move, but at her first step, the young face turned, and was taken round a bend of the steps. Adelaide rushed ahead to the corridor, where the stairs led down to the kitchen quarters. There was nothing there. All appeared quite empty and devoid of human company. Neither was there any sound, but a light tap tap which could have been quickly receding youthful footsteps, or merely the beating of a tree's branch against a window somewhere.

When she reached the curve of the main stairway she glanced instinctively towards the vicinity of the Tower steps, wondering whether to go up. The view from that top small chamber was unique for its panorama of moors covering the whole distance from North to West coast, including the picturesque St Michael's Mount; but the door would probably be locked, and although she didn't believe in ghosts with her brain, the memory of that far distant occasion when she'd glimpsed the shadowed countenance staring down, had a chilling effect on her nerves; especially combined with the experience of a few moments ago.

So she made her way slowly down to the hall, puzzling her mind over the strange interlude of the intruder, wondering perhaps if it was some mischievous little vagabond stolen into the house from the back quarters, or a relative of Mrs Pender's – even a grandchild possibly of the man. Oh, there were a number of commonplace quite practical explanations, but somehow none of them carried conviction to her overwrought imagination. Still, she thought, as she paused uncertainly at the foot of the stairs, she could ask Mrs Pender. She hadn't yet been to the kitchen since her arrival, and the matter would be an excuse to get better relations established with the possessive guardian of domestic affairs.

The cold slabs resounded with the echo of her light feet as she hurried along, and her mind flitted briefly to the past and

her childhood when David had informed her that the foundations of Trenhawk, especially that side of the house were
riddled with tunnels and secret passages through the rock. In
the past, he'd told her, they'd been used for transporting stolen
goods from illegal vessels to different points on the moor.

She hadn't believed him at first, until he'd taken her one
day to a certain holed cavern of a place a hundred yards or so
below Wheal Tansy. They'd climbed in and made their way
for a bit along the dark earthy corridor until it got too narrow
to walk upright. Then Adelaide had been frightened and
scrambled back with David after her.

'Surely you're not a cowardy custard, Addy,' he'd said
afterwards when they stood facing each other with the dirt and
black soil staining their faces and clothes. Then he'd burst into
laughter, and she'd laughed too, knowing she must look as
much of a clown as he did. Together they'd made their way
quickly back to Trenhawk and somehow managed to present
themselves later cleaned up and tidy. They'd escaped punishment that time. David had been an adept at deception with
adults when it suited him. And mostly he'd been believed;
probably because of his shining blue eyes and curly rich hair,
his air of laughter and innocence – and of being – just David.

Her heart lurched again suddenly with the old familiar
longing. She steeled herself to the present with an effort, and
was about to put her hand on the knob of the kitchen door
when it opened revealing the stocky figure of the housekeeper.

'Oh. I thought I heard someone comin',' the housekeeper
said, barring the way. 'Is there anythin' you want, Miss
Adelaide – Mrs David? If so you've only to touch a bell and
me or Lucy will be along.'

'Nothing particularly,' Adelaide answered shortly, 'except
that –'

'Yes?' The voice was faintly belligerent.

'Upstairs just now I saw – at least I *thought* so – yes, I'm *sure*
– a young child playing near the back stairs above. I was
wondering who it could be.'

For a moment the woman appeared faintly flustered with a
tinge of deepening colour staining her cheeks.

'You must be mistaken, Miss Adelaide,' came the abrupt
answer. 'If there was any child about up there I'd know. And

now if you'll excuse me, I've work to do, and I'd be obliged if you'd not worry Lucy in the kitchen just now. We've too much on our hands there as 'tis.'

Feeling both angry and rebuffed, Adelaide lifted her black skirt with both hands and turned hastily to go. But she looked back once saying, 'Certainly. The last thing I want is to be in the way. And you may be relieved to know that I intend – at my cousin's suggestion – to hire a maid for myself whilst I'm here. She may be able to give you a hand too when you're extra busy. 'Another thing – ' she raised her head challengingly, confronting Mrs Pender with eyes cold and unswerving in her set glance. 'At the earliest opportunity I'd like the curtains and all the belongings my – my husband and I had sent down from London removed from their hidey-hole and taken to the bedroom I'm using now. Remeber they were not bought for fun or to be pushed away like rubble into a dark corner. Do you understand?'

Her voice at the end of the brief tirade was sharper than she'd intended it to be. She hurried away before the deepening belligerence in the housekeeper's eyes registered. But when she reached the hall she realised uncomfortably she'd probably gone too far, and made an enemy. Well, she thought rebelliously, if so, what did it matter? The woman could not harm her; she was a servant merely and one in a tricky position if she, Adelaide, related the whole incident to Rupert. The ambiguous answer to her question concerning the child had been mere prevarication. Whatever the whole truth was, the half-glimpsed form and ethereal-looking young face watching from the shadows had been real; she was sure of it. The patter of dying footsteps had been no illusion either, and Mrs Pender knew it.

In a conflict of emotions, and on the spur of the moment, Adelaide decided she must have some air. A few minutes later wearing no hat, she was walking towards the moor sharply with a thin rising wind brushing her cheeks, sweet with the faint scent of heather and gorse.

She recalled days in her early teens when she and David, sometimes accompanied by Rupert, had ridden there bareback on ponies from the stables. For her it had been expressly forbidden of course, as most exciting things were. But the stable-boy had been a willing conspirator, ready to take half the blame if they'd been seen. This had frequently happened, and the usual punishment had been doled out to her. But she hadn't cared; the fun had been worth the indignity. Now she supposed there were only one or two horses in the stables. Rupert, needing money, would obviously have had to economise there. But she intended to take a look sometime when she was safely on her own, and if possible have a ride again over the well remembered wild moors. Rupert would hardly stop her; he had no authority. And if there had to be an argument between them she felt quite capable of facing it, and winning.

Or – did she? There had been something intimidating about him during their brief conversation the previous evening, that had made her uncomfortably aware how very little she really knew about the real Rupert; only that in the past he had sometimes been obstructive in the games she and David had got up to, and that she had enjoyed frequently trying to thwart him; occasions that had generally ended up by a fierce quarrel.

He'd never liked her of course. If he had what a difference it would make now, when she was desperately lonely.

Lost in her own retrospective thoughts she didn't notice his figure above her near the rim of the moor, until a flash of blue in the quivering sunlight arrested her attention. She paused, and stood still, staring. There was no mistaking Rupert's sturdy figure outlined against the autumn landscape. But the woman in the blue dress – who was she? And why did Rupert touch her forearm in that personal way as though he was begging for something, or trying to comfort? The gesture only lasted a second; the next moment the female figure was cutting back to the left, and Rupert making his way sharply down the hill.

For some minutes his form became lost round a raised hump of ground. She walked on leisurely, and almost ran into him suddenly, bringing his steps to a halt.

'Oh,' he said abruptly. 'You.'

'Yes. I felt like a walk.'

'You look – ' his words faded.

'I look – what?'

He shrugged and tore his eyes away from her rose-tinged face surrounded by the sunlit fair hair.

'Much better,' he answered, knowing she was expecting a more direct compliment. 'Did you sleep well?'

'Not exactly. But then that's natural, isn't it?'

'I suppose so. If there's anything you want to make your room more comfortable – '

'Yes,' she cut in before he could finish. 'There is. I've already told Mrs Pender. I'd like the furniture – *my* furniture that was to be ours – David's and mine here at Trenhawk – removed from that dusty little room where it's been pushed – into the one I've got now. If the men can't do it I could get someone from Penzance.' She turned from him and started walking back the way she'd come. In an instant he'd caught up with her and grasped her arm firmly.

'You've a nerve, Adelaide Drake, I mean Hawksley – coming here as an uninvited guest thinking you can have the house – *my* house turned upside down just at any moment you choose, installed with bits and pieces that if I may say so are completely out of character with the place – '

'I don't agree with you,' she said quickly. 'They fit in beautifully. David had taste. We chose them together. And please –' she jerked his shoulder, 'take your hand away, Rupert. Let me go. I'm not that woman up there – on the moor. Who *is* she by the way? Elizabeth? You looked quite – intimate friends.'

Smothering the hot retort on his lips he dropped her arm and managed to answer under a veneer of calmness he was far from feeling; 'Yes, my housekeeper, and incidentally, the wife of a miner who was injured at Wheal Tansy. Though it isn't really your business.'

'No,' she answered more quietly. 'You're quite right, Rupert. But about the furniture – '

'If you really want it moved it can be done,' he told her. 'But remember, Adelaide, manners matter. And so far, since you returned here, you haven't been exactly – tactful.'

She didn't reply; perhaps it was as well, he thought, fighting for self-composure. The interim between them could be explosive, and he didn't relish a quarrel just then. As they walked on together silently he did his best to turn his mind into more charitable channels. She was going through a hard time. Her emotions had always run deep – no half-measures about Ade-

laide. And more was the pity, he thought, with a tinge of regret.
If she'd been less emotionally dedicated and he more flexible
they might have managed a few pleasant hours together while
she was at Trenhawk. She was a lovely creature, even in that
dreary abominable black, and it was an insult to her beauty she
should be doomed by tradition to wear it, although no doubt his
puritanical Hawksley ancestors would have approved.

Many great-grandfathers ago the founder of the Hawksley
dynasty – Jonathan Hawksley, who'd first acquired the house
Trenhawk from Abbey lands – had become impressed with
Lutherism and the New Learning, which though forward-
looking on one hand, seemed, from the records, to have been a
rather joyless philosophy. This stern quality, acquired during
Jonathan's extensive travels abroad, especially through Ger-
many and Holland had softened to a certain extent during the
centuries, although Cromwell's civil war had revived it fan-
atically for a time. William, David's father, had been more
tolerant. If he'd had his way, relationships with the St Clares
would have been adjusted on a friendlier basis. They had after
all, a blood tie through their mutual forbear, Marguerite. But
he had not lived to see the breach healed. To the St Clares the
Hawksleys were not only Protestants, but of peasant stock –
which put them beyond the pale socially, as well as outlaws to
the true Church.

To Rupert the whole affair was childish – a mere game that
he regarded with contempt knowing the contempt was mutual.
He himself was unorthodox. It was people who mattered, and
life he was concerned with – the life of the soil, of the mine –
copper and tin, and the men who worked it. But the house
Trenhawk was in a different category, representing the achievement of generations of Hawksleys who'd striven and accrued
the means to retain it.

Adelaide should have realised this, he told himself as they
neared the drive. Being at loggerheads with her was not
pleasant. He'd far rather it had been the opposite – have had
her in his arms wanting comfort, rather than with narrowed
eyes, and claws ready to scratch if he made the slightest
overture.

As though sensing his trend of thought, she glanced at him
suddenly, and was discomforted by his expression.

'What are you staring at?' she asked.

'You.'

'Why?' Before she realised it the question was out.

'I was wondering why you had to dress up like a black crow when it certainly doesn't suit you. Oh, I know you're in mourning for David, but if you cared for him that much you shouldn't have to be reminding yourself of it all the time. In London I suppose it's different. But *here* at Trenhawk! surely in Heaven's name it would be more of a tribute to him to be the Adelaide he knew – beautiful and tantalising, and damned stubborn into the bargain,' he ended, realising from her flushed cheeks he'd trodden dangerous ground.

She was about to make a hot reply when the sound of hooves diverted her, and looking back from the gates she saw an elegant grey-clad figure in riding kit skirting the base of the moor on a black horse. He was straight-backed, fair-headed, with a quality of lively nonchalance about him that reminded her for a swift instant of her young lost husband. The morning sun was rich on Adelaide's honey-gold hair, the perfectly chiselled features clearly defined in the transient light. The pace of horse and rider involuntarily slowed as the eyes of the girl and the man met. Rupert's figure instinctively tensed. Then the brief interlude was over. The man kicked his mount to a sudden gallop, and the next moment was cutting up the hill to the right.

Adelaide did not ask who the stranger was, but she guessed, and rightly, as Rupert confirmed.

'Anthony St Clare,' he said shortly. 'And if you have any sense you'll steer clear of him.'

'You don't have to tell me what to do,' she answered sharply. 'And what you implied was a little – insulting.'

'In what way?'

'The way you spoke – about steering clear. I'm in mourning for David, remember. It's hardly likely I'd be impressed by the first stranger who came along.'

His tones were cynical when he replied, 'Not willingly perhaps. Not yet. But one day – '

'One day you think I'll be able to put all the past behind me as though it had never existed?' she interrupted passionately. ' – That I'm some sort of light creature with no deep feelings, is that it?'

He would have liked to say, 'Madam, methinks thou dost protest too much?' But he didn't. Instead he remarked coldly, 'Oh, Adelaide, spare me the drama. Do try and have your feet on the ground for a change.'

She said nothing. But her eyes did. Anger, and distress were there, with a childlike bewilderment that nonplussed him.

They walked on together in silence.

He had an uneasy feeling that future trouble between them was inevitable, though just then he couldn't visualise the extent of it, or the pattern it would take.

III

The weekend was a quiet one. Quieter even than Adelaide had expected. Except for a brief time in the evenings she hardly saw Rupert at all. He was either in his study perusing accounts and figures, at the farm, or down in St Rozzan where he apparently had some business on hand. Her time was her own, just as she'd wanted it to be, but lonelier and more boring than she'd imagined possible. Her few lively if aggressive interludes with Rupert at the beginning of her stay, had helped temporarily to subdue the ache over David. But in solitude everything seemed curiously empty and purposeless.

The weather had turned cold, but through the parlour window the moors and hills shone pale gold from the autumn sun.

On impulse she decided to go for a walk, and went upstairs for her cape and bonnet. Bruce, the red setter, was in the hall when she went down. He bounded up barking as she went to the hall door.

'Come on then, boy,' she said, grateful for the animal's welcome.

Rupert appeared almost immediately from the library.

'If you're taking the dog,' he said, 'you'd better have the lead.

Here it is – ' he took it from a peg and handed it to her. 'But don't go the fields way,' he said. 'There are sheep there. Keep to the moors. He's well trained, but not used to women. He might make a dash for it. And in future – '

'Yes?'

'Please tell me when you're thinking of taking him out on your own.'

Trying to hide her annoyance she said, 'All right, I will. I didn't know you were so fussy about him. Anyway – ' she faced him squarely, with a hint of defiance, 'I'm usually good with animals, and I like dogs. They know that and I've never had any trouble so far.'

'There's always a first time,' Rupert said shortly, 'good luck, though, and enjoy your walk.'

As Adelaide had anticipated there was no difficulty with Bruce, and at first she enjoyed the nip in the air, the salty tang of sea and heather, and flying shadows streaking with crying gulls from the cromlech, down the hill. The delighted yelps of the dog, his sniffing and snuffling through the brown heather and furze made her feel young and briefly happy again. At times her steps quickened into a run. But her long skirts got entangled in a thorn bush, and she was caught abruptly to a halt. She sat on a boulder to extricate herself and recover her breath. Then she started remembering – recalling how she and David had raced and ridden there in the past – what fun it had been – so full of excitement; the future so bright.

Now suddenly, everything again seemed meaningless.

She shivered, got up, and started walking back. The dog, as though sensing loneliness, moved sedately beside her, pushing his nose occasionally at her hand.

When she reached Trenhawk the sun had retreated behind a belt of rising clouds, and the interior loomed in shadowed darkness before her. She walked down the hall and let Bruce into the kitchen, then went into the parlour for a few minutes before going upstairs. How quiet it was. No sound at all, but the crackling of logs, and automatic ticking of the grandfather clock – yet in a queer way the house seemed full of whispers. Since her arrival it had been like that, whispers everywhere – in the passages, parlours, library, and especially in the deserted drawing room where the gold velvet curtains were kept closed now against the elements because it was never used. Even the valuable gilt French clock no longer ticked. The gilded Louis Quinze chairs had sheets over them. An ancient smell of camphor and pot pourri hung heavy in the air that was close and thick through no window being open.

Once there had been parties there. As a child she'd been invited to a birthday celebration of Uncle William's, and wine had been drunk from slender-stemmed crystal glasses. David was fourteen then, and she ten. Her stepfather Richard had forbidden her to drink, because he was by nature opposed to alcohol; certainly for children. But David backed by her uncle had insisted and won, and she'd thought how wonderful and clever, and *very* handsome he was. It was then the idea had first taken root in her young mind that she might marry him one day. Only a fleeting dream and vision at the time, but one that had intensified through the years, and unwittingly become a guiding factor in the circumstances that had been moulded to bring their union about.

Now it was over. The drawing room, like the musty library, sitting rooms, great hall, and numerous corridors and closed bedrooms, had become the receptacle merely for memories and brooding pictures of the past. In the conservatory it was no different; flowers and exotic plants bloomed there that had thrived in her childhood. There was the same steamy geranium scent and queer feeling of being trapped in some exotic jungle. David had stolen an orchid for her once, and placed it like a shining white star in her lustrous soft curls. It was just before he'd been sent to Rugby, and he'd been beaten as a taste of what was to come. Luckily she'd escaped punishment because dear silly Miss Trumper was her governess then, and anyway, Uncle William had insisted it was not her fault.

Everywhere she went during those first few days seemed claimed by the past. More than once she wondered if Rupert was right after all and that it would be better for her to go away. But with a rush of her old obstinacy she rejected the idea, and instantly felt a release of tension. She would *not* be dictated to by Rupert or have her rights ignored. Now she was back at Trenhawk she would stay. Though her mind wouldn't admit it, the challenge to Rupert alone was now enough to keep her there.

Sadness began to ease.

But the whispers continued.

At nights when she lay wakeful in the large carved bed, it seemed to her the whole building echoed with the ghostly sighs and murmurs from generations of past Hawksleys. There were creakings and fitful small moans from the wind eddying round floors and walls that to her heightened imagination became the mournful crying of earth-bound spirits asking for release. She stiffened then, clutching the bedclothes tightly under her chin, recalling old tales from Trenhawk's haunting and the strange image of the pale blurred face staring down from the tower room.

The child too. The child who was surely *real*?

Who was it? And why was she, Adelaide, so deliberately barred from entering the kitchens?

These mysteries, however stimulating by day, at night frequently chilled her; and when the tide was high, breaking sullenly against Trenhawk's northern granite walls, its booming penetrated even to her own room facing the moors with threatening sense of disaster to come.

Winter was quickly approaching. Many of the leaves had been torn from the windswept trees and bushes. The unpredictable Cornish weather could turn wild and storm-tossed in an evening following a calm sun-lit day.

On Tuesday night the wind was high and the sea raging sending immense breakers crashing against the rocky coast.

Rupert had appeared edgy and preoccupied all day. His company over the evening meal was so silent and disconcerting Adelaide went up to her room earlier than usual, determined to have an hour or two of reading before properly retiring to bed. She had brought with her a copy of *Jane Eyre* by the woman novelist Charlotte Bronte. Literary critics considered it outstanding, and a rare achievement for someone living such a remote life in wildest Yorkshire. Adelaide, before, had been too busy and preoccupied with David to concern herself much with books. But shortly after her marriage an acquaintance older than herself with a firmly established and accepted social background, had presented her with the edition, saying 'You must read this, Adelaide. It's most educational. And interesting too. Imagine it – the heroine's actually plain. She had to pretend she was a man to get it published – Miss Bronte I mean. And can you believe it – she's married now to some stuffy dreary curate. But the book's exciting. There's a mad wife in it, a thrillingly wicked man – and of course the saintly governess he seduces. Well, not quite seduction, but – '

'Don't tell me,' Adelaide had interrupted, 'you'll spoil the plot.'

At the time wanting to get away from the dreary discussion about books for David's more enlivening company, Adelaide had accepted the novel politely, and forgotten about it until after her bereavement. Then one evening on impulse, she'd glanced into the pages idly and what she'd seen there by chance, concerning poor Jane's suffering, had suggested that in her own sad state she might perhaps gain a little consolation from the tragedy of others. So before setting off for Trenhawk, she'd flung it at the last minute into her valise with the vague thought of dipping into it sometime.

She did try that Tuesday night, but in spite of the intriguing theme, her interest was only spasmodic, and by nine-thirty, she decided to go to bed and try to get the sound sleep that had avoided her recently.

It was no use. She slept fitfully for the two hours, only to wake suddenly, with her pulses racing, head throbbing and alert. Mingled with the ceaseless moaning, sighing, and distant pounding of the sea, she could detect other sounds resembling the thud of giant footsteps or heavy objects being moved somewhere below. The noise was mostly rhythmical, then at intervals it died into all the other turbulent sounds of the wild night. She sat up straining her ears for further confirmation, and presently it started up again with heavy intensity. As her heart slowed and senses registered more calmly, she realised the house itself was probably not concerned, but was a mere structural means – or echo – of what was going on. At one point she fancied the floor of the bedroom shook slightly. The next moment commonsense told her she must be wrong. Trenhawk was an enduring granite erection that had defied centuries of storm against the onslaught of time.

The cellars then?

Suddenly highly agitated and unable to restrain her curiosity, she got up, lit a candle, put on a wrap and slippers, and went to the door. She opened it cautiously and peered out. The rugs on the stone floor were flapping wanly in fitful draughts of wind. Shadows moved faintly as her candle flickered and went out. She went back and lit it again, then shielding the flame by one hand, and carrying the matches in the other she returned to the corridor. There was no sign of human activity; all was wrapt in uneasy darkness. Yet the thunderous sound still boomed from below, lost at times in the monotonous howling of the wind and crashing sea.

She made her way, hesitantly, at first, towards the back stairs leading through the servants' quarters down to the kitchens. When she reached the top of the steps she was startled by an elongated shadow suddenly flung from below in the distorted shape of a human figure. Like a malevolent snake it sneaked across the floor towards her, followed by the distinct thud of footsteps. She blew her candle out, and waited motionless with her back pressed against one wall. But it was too late.

As the shadow resolved into stouter proportions, a face appeared, macabrely lit by the wan yellow flame of a small oil lamp. The scowling countenance of Mrs Pender.

'What are you doing here, Miss Adelaide?' she questioned in a low voice. 'What business have you to be prowlin' about the corridors with nuthen' decent on your back, an' the air so cold. Think I want to nurse you through sickness, do ye? If so you're very much mistaken. Get back to your room now an' have done with such pryin' foolish ways.'

'I heard something,' Adelaide said. 'I've a right to find out if anything's wrong.'

'Nothing's wrong but your own stupid nonsense,' the woman told her. 'What you heard's nuthen' but the wind shrieking and the sea gettin' rough. There's a gale on – that's all 'tis.'

Adelaide was about to contradict her, but realising the futility of an argument, and that now her presence was known, she'd inevitably be prevented from reaching the cellars, she held her tongue, turned suddenly, and walked with all the dignity she could muster, to her room. At the door she paused briefly and looked back. Mrs Pender's shadow was still thrown grotesquely on the walls from a short way down the steps. The quivering shape was somehow far more menacing than the woman's actual presence.

Once back in the bedroom, Adelaide, hardly aware of what she was doing, seated herself before the mirror, and stared listlessly at her reflection. There was no suggestion of movement behind her in the shadows, no longer any feeling of alien presences or whispering voices. The fire had died, and all was quieter below. She could hear nothing but the wind outside and fitful creaking of ancient timber. Perhaps she had been imagining things, she told herself wearily. Perhaps her queer impressions could be explained away by overwrought nerves and a desire on her part to escape from reality and her grieving for David.

She yawned, and realised suddenly she was shivering.

She was about to take off her wrap, then changed her mind and got into bed, still wearing it.

Soon, overcome by exhaustion her body relaxed. The restless beating and surge of the elements became one constant rhythmic murmur, and presently she slept.

The run had been successful, but rough and difficult, owing to the high winds and freak tide. The Preventive had somehow got wind of the Dutch ship's impending arrival and had been on the alert about the area when the *Vanvaal* neared Trenhawk coastline. Luckily the intense darkness had enabled warning to be given. The small boats – mostly fishermen's – had managed to unload the cargo in the cove, where Rupert's half-dozen men waited in readiness for kegs and bundles. The operation had been swift and tense, and not without incident. The brig's retreat, of a necessity had been so speedy, the rush to the small boats such a scramble, that one man – a Dutch sailor – had failed to get aboard. Carnack and one of Rupert's regulars – a farm worker from St Rozzan had managed to drag him ashore to the cave, and from there up the tortuous passage-way and steps to the cellars of the house. By then the kegs of spirit and valuable silk were already safely installed. There was no light at all, not even a candle; only a fitful glimmer of occasional frail starlight when the clouds momentarily cleared.

The great slab barring the entrance to the house was half in place again by the time the foreigner was heaved through, followed by his rescuers.

'Thank God!' Rupert exclaimed feelingly, adding after a

moment, 'were you seen?'

'No, master,' Carnack assured him. 'Not a sign of anyone around. Nor will be now I'm thinkin'.' He chuckled triumphantly.

'Then seal this hole up properly, you men, and we'll see what damage our poor friend's suffered,' Rupert told him.

One by one the small group climbed the slippery steps to the kitchen, hoisting the stranger along with them. There was no one about. Mrs Pender knowing her place, and aware of the business going on, had tactfully withdrawn to her room. But refreshment of ale and heavy-cake had been left on the table.

'You'd better stay here for the time being,' Rupert said, wiping a stream of sweat, mingling with blood from a cut on his cheek, 'don't attempt to get away till the early hours. But you should know the routine by now.' He turned from them to the Dutchman who was slumped in a chair. He was a short broad fellow with a red beard and small bright blue eyes in crinkled creases of flesh. One leg was cut quite badly, and when Rupert examined his arm he gave a wince and groan of pain.

'Hm! Broken,' Rupert told him. 'Damned inconvenient. However we'll keep you here until you're in better shape. Then I'll arrange to get you back to Holland. Understand?'

The man stared at him blankly. Obviously he hadn't taken in a word. Rupert shook his head. 'What we need's a Florence Nightingale,' he said sombrely, wondering for an irrational moment if Adelaide had any experience. But of course she wouldn't have had the time, and even if she had it would have been impractical to trust her. So he did what he could to concoct a satisfactory splint, bathed the ugly wounds, and after a liberal portion of rum, exhaustion and pain mingled with a curious mellow feeling of well-being induced convenient unconsciousness, which enabled them to get the Dutchman settled for the night hours.

'We'll have to get him round to the harness room before Lucy arrives,' he said, 'and preferably before daylight. Can you see if there's a bed there ready?'

Carnack nodded.

'Then I'll fetch Doctor Maddox in the morning. Just to be on the safe side.'

Rupert knew the doctor would keep his mouth shut, simply

because on such occasions he participated in some small share of the spoils.

'And if any prying female gets on the scent,' Rupert added significantly, 'our Dutch friend is a remote cousin of yours from abroad who had an accident with a horse getting here.'

Carnack as usual agreed.

'And what shall we call him, master?'

Rupert thought quickly. 'Porteous, I think,' he said wisely. 'It sounds good, and suits him. He's lived all his life abroad remember – some remote island the other side of the world.'

Carnack grinned, 'I understand, surr. Trust me.'

And so the night ended.

When morning came the only signs left of the previous evening's events were empty mugs in the sink, crumbs on the table, and a trickle of blood on the floor. Even these were dispensed with by the time Lucy arrived.

Rupert was well satisfied. Behind the locked cellar door was rich profit towards reimbursement of Wheal Tansy's needs.

He had no qualms of conscience at all.

The game had paid.

He wondered idly what Adelaide's reaction would be if she knew, and if a time would ever come when he'd be able to tell her.

Probably not, for which he felt faintly regretful.

In the morning the gale had completely died, leaving nothing but a thin shiver of breeze in the chill air.

Adelaide slept later than she'd meant to following her restless night, and when she came downstairs there was no sign of Rupert. She passed Mrs Pender in the hall, and said good morning, but there was no reply. The woman went on towards the kitchen, head thrust forward, muttering something to herself. Clearly she was tired and in a bad mood, which was not surprising, Adelaide thought, remembering the belligerent encounter on the landing.

The house in the grey light seemed desolate that day. A pot of cold tea stood on the parlour table, with only a plate of ham and toast put presumably for her, which looked as though it had been made some time ago. Adelaide's temper flared. She marched out of the room, slamming the door behind her sharply and strode resolutely, with a swish of her black skirts, towards the servants' quarters. Before she reached the kitchen Lucy appeared, carrying a jug of steaming hot water. 'Mrs Pender said I was to bring this ma'am,' she said, 'an' ef there be anything else you need tell me an' I'll be getting et.'

'The fire's low,' Adelaide complained, 'I don't like ham, and the toast looks soggy and cold. Would you please tell Mrs Pender – ' she broke off suddenly, realising the last thing she wanted that day was a scene. 'Oh never mind,' she ended more quietly. 'I'm not hungry. Give me the jug. I realise I'm late.'

The girl handed it to her with obvious relief. 'It's market day in Penjust,' she explained, 'an Nick's takin' the cart to pick up somethin' for the master. We're late as 'tis – ' her voice wavered apologetically.

'Oh. I see' Adelaide's mind worked quickly. 'Who's Nick?'

'The stable boy, ma'am.'

'Yes of course. I remember now. Going into Penjust, you said?'

With a furtive look behind her in case Mrs Pender was on her tracks, Lucy nodded.

'Where's Mr Rupert?' Adelaide asked.

'Away for the morning, ma'am, at the mine, I think,' the girl told her.

'Then go and tell Nick he'll have a passenger,' Adelaide retorted on the spur of the moment. Lucy stared. 'But, ma'am – you can't – not in that thing – '

'Go on, hurry. Do as I say and don't argue,' Adelaide said. 'please.' Her voice had softened. 'There are things I want from the shops, and this is a good chance of getting there.'

She turned, and half running, made her way upstairs, with the full dress lifted well above her ankles in front. A few minutes later she appeared again, wearing a cape over her gown, with a chiffon black veil draped over the small hat and tied under the chin. She went out by the front door and made her way round the side of the house to the stables.

Carnack and the boy were both standing by the vehicle, a rather cumbrous affair intended for the transport of goods rather than passengers. The great shire horse was in harness, and for a moment Adelaide didn't relish the thought of being jerked along the bumpy high moorland road for eight miles in such conditions. The man held the same opinion.

'You shouldn't go, Mrs David, not this way. I'll be probably drivin' the gig myself there at the end o' the week. That'd be different. Mr Rupert wouldn't allow *this* sort of thing, I'm telling you. Could cost me my job allowing it.'

'It will do nothing of the sort,' Adelaide told him, with her decision confirmed firmly again by Carnack's opposition. 'I take full responsibility for my own actions, and if my cousin returns before I'm back, you can tell him so.'

'Very well,' Carnack agreed grudgingly, thinking that if the silly young madam insisted on letting herself in for a very uncomfortable experience, the matter was out of his hands, and he'd be saved having to fret about the possibility of her prowling round the stables and harness room whenever his back was turned. Until Rupert was back and the doctor had seen the Dutchman, it was better no one suspected the presence of 'Cousin Porteous'.

Five minutes later, the cart, with Adelaide sitting beside Nick, was rattling over the stony track towards the high moorland road. Her crinoline was crushed awkwardly; the jerking of the wheels combined with the freshening breeze whipped strands of hair free of veiling. When they reached the main road the course was smoother, but increased speed jolted her muscles, and at one time she gripped the side of the cart tensely, fearing the great animal was getting out of control.

The boy laughed. 'Beauty has a likin' for a bit of a frolic, missis. Don't 'ee fear now. We know each other's ways all right. Country bred. That's us.'

The road twisted this way and that below the brown moors where at odd points ruined mine-stacks stood stark against the grey sky. Some were still working, on the sea side mostly; but many hamlets, due to the mining depression, were half-deserted, leaving only derelict granite and clob cottages as monuments to what once had been a thriving and busy populated district. The natural domain though was mostly unchanged. Standing stones and ancient dolmens and cromlechs remained symbolic guardians of the sweeping hills. Dark under shadowing furze and tangled undergrowth were the bee-hive huts of very early civilisations, having withstood to a miraculous extent the elements and passing of countless centuries.

Penjust, was not large, but more than a village, boasting a town-hall, with penthouses on either side, a fair-sized Church-school, three inns, an ancient coaching house, a police station and a small stannary jail. The church which dated from very early times stood on a hill, overlooking the square which was bordered by most of the official buildings. There was also a grey square Methodist chapel. Huddled in narrow streets leading from the town centre were small shops and granite cottages of fishermen and miners. On market days trade was carried on in the square and penthouses. At other times local people either traded by barter or through one large store owned by a merchant Nathaniel Behenna, who dealt in most wares, including linen, hosiery and groceries. He was also a tallow chandler and stocked an amount of hardware.

The market, that day, was busy.

Special stalls filled the square and even encroached up several streets displaying foods and merchandise of every kind – shoes, boots, and fish in particular. Knitted garments brought in by the country people were placed near a dyer who did a smart trade dipping knitted and hand-woven goods to any shade required. Pedestrians mingling with mules, ponies, and stall-holders, had difficulty in penetrating the jostling throngs, which included a number of girls and women hoping to get hired for domestic service.

Nick turned the cart into the yard of the first inn, the Gipsy Queen.

'Master's got an understandin' with Ted Bossygran,' he said. 'He's the landlord here an' always gives a place for Beauty.'

He helped Adelaide down. Her crinoline, though creased, was secure, but her cape got caught on a nail which left a tear near the hem.

'Botheration!' she exclaimed. 'What a mess I'll look.'

The boy – he was really more of a youth – shook his head solemnly, though his eyes were admiring. 'Carts edn' for ladies,' he said, 'as Mr Carnack told 'ee. An' these crowds edn' gentle either. Be all right, will 'ee?'

Adelaide lifted her head with a dignified air.

'Perfectly, thank you,' she said. 'There's no need at all for you to be concerned about me. What time are you leaving?'

'Bout an hour. Not later 'n twelve,' he said, 'or there'll be the devil 'isself to pay. Mr Carnack's a real fierce one on time.'

'Very well, I'll be here by then, perhaps a little earlier.'

The boy, with a respectful salute, turned to attend the horse, and Adelaide left the yard for the street. The crowd by then was so thick she found it impossible to keep on the pavement. The gathering was more like a small fair than a market, and she decided there was no point in searching through the maze of busy stannins for the lace and black ribbon she required.

On the opposite side of the square she'd glimpsed what appeared to be a haberdashers, so she cut through a narrow alleyway between stalls, trying to ignore the jostling and shouting. But her headgear was knocked to one side, its veiling caught by something sharp, her cloak was disarrayed, and the voluminous outer-layer of her full skirt rent in a slit from the bodice. She glanced down, and saw to her dismay the hem and petticoats beneath had also been caught and torn by a muddied foot, revealing a titivating and highly embarrassing six inches of lacy drawers.

She was furious, knowing she must look a sight. The haberdashery was still some yards up the street, and already her plight had been noticed. As she pushed past a group of amused pedestrians, a rough looking fellow with a red face and lewd tongue made an offensive remark, flipping her skirt suggestively. His breath was whisky-laden, and just for a moment she was panic-stricken. Coarse laughter mingled with the wailing sound of a street musician, dinned in her ears like a nightmare. Her toe caught the hole in her skirt, and she felt herself toppling forwards suddenly to the cobbles below. She'd have fallen on her face if a burly form hadn't caught her in time. Looking up she saw a broad kindly male face, probably a farmer's, staring down at her. 'Hey now, missis,' he said, 'that will never do. Can't have a fine lady like you spoilin' her pretty looks on they dirty stones. Anythin' I can do for 'ee? My name's – '

She never heard it, because another more cultured voice remarked behind her shoulder, 'It's quite all right. I know this young lady. I'll see she's taken care of.'

The large man moved away.

Adelaide turned, holding her skirt discreetly in an effort to disguise the ripped gown and petticoat.

This time the countenance confronting her was different –

fine featured and youthful, with very bright blue eyes under carefully groomed crisp fair hair. For a heady moment she had the impression David was staring down at her. Her pulses accelerated. It was like waking suddenly from a long and painful dream. Then as her heart steadied she knew it couldn't possibly be him. David had been taken from her forever, at Sevastopol. This was just someone bearing an uncanny resemblance to her husband. He was elegantly dressed, wearing a green circular cloak over a lighter green velvet jacket, and white shirt with a high pointed collar. His grey cloth trousers were shapely and well-cut, with straps holding them securely over the shoes.

She had only seen him once, but she knew, before he told her his name, who he was.

'Anthony St Clare,' he said, offering her his arm. 'I hope you remember me – we passed each other briefly the other day, but it was long enough for me to recall your face for ever – '

She blushed.

'You are – Hawksley's cousin, I believe?' he continued. If the name was spoken with underlying contempt he tried not to show it.

'I'm Mrs David Hawksley,' Adelaide managed to say with a brave attempt at dignity. 'My husband was killed only recently, at Sevastopol.'

'Yes. I had heard. I'm sorry.'

'And now if you don't mind – ' Adelaide said attempting to withdraw her arm, 'I have some shopping to do.'

He released her and gave a little bow.

'Certainly. The last thing I want is to delay you. But – after that?'

'I'm returning to Trenhawk,' Adelaide said.

'By chaise?'

The question was so direct, the prolonged stare of his blue eyes so intent, Adelaide's composure faltered.

'Well – not exactly. I had a lift here with – with Nick – '

'Nick?'

'Our stable boy. As he was coming into Penjust this morning I didn't think it was worth using the gig – ' even in her own ears, the words though brave, had a false ring, and she had the uncomfortable feeling he was not deceived.

'So your transport wasn't exactly befitting your beauty,' the cool voice continued. 'Well, I hope you'll let me remedy matters for the homeward journey and join me.'

'Oh but I – '

'Please,' he insisted. 'The St Clare chaise is really a comfortable one, and my man's a good driver. I hope you'll accept, Mrs Hawksley, or may I call you Adelaide?'

Suddenly Adelaide properly found her tongue.

'I don't think I *should* accept, and I don't think you should call me Adelaide. But –' unaware of it, she smiled – 'I *am* a bit bruised from that old cart, and –'

'*Cart*? Good God.'

' – I'd like to get myself tidied up and looking respectable if possible. Then perhaps –' her voice trailed off vaguely.

'Of course,' she heard him saying, as he took her arm again, edging off the crowd. 'I know the very place. A most civilized coffee house, where we can have a little refreshment. I'll see your stable boy gets a message that you won't be returning with him. Where is he, by the way?'

'I'm not sure at the moment, he had business to do. But the cart's at the Gipsy Queen.'

'That will do. Whilst you're having your wash and tidy up maybe, I'll see directions are given here. So don't worry. And now – what about your shopping?'

Adelaide suddenly discovered she didn't want to bother about the lace after all; and a minute later, after admitting it, she was being skilfully manoeuvred from the square to the coffee shop. St Clare stopped once and handed a message concerning Nick to a fisherman for delivery at the Gipsy Queen, then they went on.

Though unobtrusively situated in a side street, with a plain granite exterior relieved only by two bow-fronted Georgian windows, the inside of the cafe was surprisingly elegant in a discreet style, and was as well, a wine-shop.

One or two richly clad women accompanied by gentlemen of fashion were seated in small alcoves each with individual tables, and shadowed from over-prying eyes by delicate muslin side-curtains. As Anthony St Clare led her to a place at the back, Adelaide, glancing curiously at the women, was surprised by the beauty of most of them.

'I didn't realise anywhere in Penjust could be like this,' she remarked, sipping her Madeira which Anthony had suggested would be more of a pick-me-up than plain coffee. 'And upstairs the retiring room was perfect. The attendant was so kind too. She insisted on pinning up my dress herself, and even put in a stitch or two.'

'That's her business,' he said promptly. 'What she's paid for.'

'Do you often come here?'

'Very rarely,' he answered. 'It's seldom such charming company as yours is available. I'm a very spoiled and critical individual. An epicure in feminine beauty, you could say.'

Slightly discomforted by the flattery, but gratified too, Adelaide looked away with her hazel eyes downcast under their fringe of black lashes.

'Please don't speak like that,' she said automatically. 'I'm not in the mood for compliments.'

'Forgive me. I had forgotten for the moment your tragedy. It was thoughtless of me to intrude with personal comments.'

Against her will, Adelaide found herself softening towards her gallant escort, although his strange likeness to David roused a conflict of emotions in her she found hard to understand. Pleasure intermingled with a faint hostility that he could so subtly resurrect memories and desires she'd thought were gone forever.

'It's all right,' she said half absently. 'I realise I've got to live with it – '

'What?'

'Widowhood,' she replied.

He gave her a side-long look that luckily she did not see – a speculative glance of appreciation holding as well, a touch of irony and chagrin.

'You're a very rare young woman, obviously,' he remarked in level tones. 'The faithful type.'

'Yes.'

After this brief interchange, conversation was diverted into less personal channels, and by the time they set off in the St Clare chaise on the return journey, they had conformed to the mere polite formalities of recently-met strangers.

'I hope we may meet again sometime,' Anthony remarked,

as he helped her from the carriage at the gates of the Tren-hawk drive, adding with a touch of malicious humour, 'and that you won't get treated too harshly as a naughty girl for daring to travel in my company.'

Was he joking or not? She couldn't tell. His mouth, then, was grave, his eyes expressionless. But David had looked like that sometimes when he was playing a game; so she took it as such, and answered with a touch of pertness, 'I think it's far more likely *you'll* get into trouble, Mr St Clare.'

He smiled then.

'Anthony.'

She shrugged, 'Just as you please.' But she did not say the name. Already her conscience was niggling for having allowed such quick friendliness between them. She felt in a curious way that she'd betrayed the past. And Rupert, too, as a Hawksley.

Well, what did it matter? she thought, as the chaise turned back to make its way towards Castle Carnwikk, the St Clare home. Rupert didn't know, and if he found out she'd tell him to mind his own business.

The idea of a possible confrontation quickened her foot-steps, and when she reached the house there was a rich colour in her cheeks and a glow in her eyes that for the moment allayed all suggestion of ghosts and hauntings. It was almost as though something young in her was starting to live again. And that, after all, was what David would have wanted.

The trouble was, she knew the feeling wouldn't last. It couldn't. Not without someone she loved to share her life.

If only – once more, when she entered the hall a host of memories returned to torment her.

'Forgive me, David – ' her heart cried, 'forgive me for even one moment letting myself forget – '

She walked upstairs slowly lifting the damaged garment above her ankles. When she reached her bedroom reaction had already set in, and she determined, unless she couldn't avoid it, never to speak to Anthony St Clare again.

IV

Adelaide and Rupert did not see much of each other during the next few days. He was mostly at the farm, or busy at the mine where discussions were taking place with an engineer from Derby concerning the expense and possible output of the new copper levels to be explored. The sum needed had risen. Unexpected snags were possible in such a drive, which would delay output, yet demand additional labour. Even if Tributers were willing to take a chance, the ordinary working miners of Wheal Tansy deserved regular weekly payment. So far most of them had been loyal to the Hawksley family despite the doubtful future. But even in remotest Cornwall the influence of the Industrial Revolution was slowly having its effect.

The Factory Act promoted by Lord Ashley in 1833, followed by the Mines Act some years later forbidding the employment of children and women underground, had woken working men up to a sense of their moral rights. Reforms in the Poor Law were widespread. A period was in being when a half-educated trouble maker could cause disruption in any business concern facing difficulties, and Wheal Tansy had one – Ben Oaks – a stubborn ambitious man who was too ready to talk of 'unions' and miners' demands and rights, given half a chance. Rupert held with many of his opinions, or he'd have got rid of him somehow. It was not the philosophy he questioned, but Oaks' manner of expressing it. And the man was skilled on engineering problems. Difficult he might be, but a stand-by in a crisis.

In view of the financial problem Rupert could not risk alienating him at such a difficult point in the Mine's expansion.

Then what was the answer?

Intermittent adventuring in contraband could provide ballast, but carried to excess would be dangerous. If Adelaide could be induced to take up shares without blackmailing him into surrendering any part of Trenhawk itself, the difficulties ahead could be solved. But would she agree? He doubted it. She'd set her mind on getting the house, and he'd no intention at that point of risking a snub. Pride, if nothing else, put it completely out of the question – not merely because she was a woman, *any* woman – but because she was Adelaide, his tantalising desirable step-cousin. Hurt as she undoubtedly was, she still needed putting firmly in her place and keeping there. And this he was determined on, he told himself every time her image intruded. As long as she remained at Trenhawk it was by his permission only, and on the understanding she behaved reasonably – although the latter he thought wrily was hardly to be expected.

He'd said nothing to her of her trip back from Penjust with Anthony St Clare, deciding to let his temper cool before tackling her. Carnack had informed him of the jaunt, when he'd returned in the early afternoon accompanied by the doctor to see the Dutchman. Rupert's first instinct was to rush upstairs and confront her there, and then. Discretion, however, had steadied his temper, which was as well. Pathetic as the sad young widow might be, he'd no doubt that underneath the delicate exterior there still lurked the wild little tigress of spitting temper and steely claws.

So the incident was temporarily laid aside while he juggled with figures and financial problems.

Adelaide meanwhile was slipping back into a mood of depression and boredom. On Friday the weather changed, becoming rain-swept and grey, enclosing Trenhawk into gloom. The old house seemed to whisper again, only this time the whispers were different – 'Leave – leave – ' the walls seemed to murmur, 'Go back to town, there's nothing for you here – nothing, nothing – ' yet her own obstinacy proved stronger, mingled strangely with a curious inner conviction that there was a purpose and reason for her to remain there.

Once, in desperation, she flung on her black cape, and went out into the rain, making her way from the front door round the side of the house towards the path winding along the ravine. She wore no hat and let her fair hair blow free from her face. The narrow track leading down eventually to the cove was steep and rocky in parts, at others tangled with pricking undergrowth. When she reached the patch of shingle, great breakers rolled and tossed against the rocks, flinging mountains of spray on the keen wind. She stood with chin up, revelling in the wildness and sense of freedom, appreciative of the sting of brine against her lips and tongue. She knew she dare not stay there long; in a quarter of an hour, even less perhaps, the tide would be fully in, and she could be marooned on some rocky ledge or in some dark tunnel until it went down again – perhaps even swept away by some monstrous wave.

For a brief spell of time all that was untamed and primitive in her rose to face the challenge of the storm, and she lived again – a wanton creature of the elements hungering for passion and the sweeping thrill of love. She had an irrational impulse to throw off her clothes and be at one with the rain and wind and ever-restless sea. She was young – young; somewhere, somehow, she must find fulfilment.

The exhilaration lasted only a few minutes. A wave suddenly broke against her; she turned, shocked, and made her way to the path leading past the ravine. As she climbed, she noticed that the stream below was swollen and tumbling in a white cascade of frothing spray where it met the sea. She was breathless when she reached the top of the cliffs; her clothes clung soddenly to her breasts and thighs, her pale hair straggled in a wet mass over shoulders and back. She lifted a hand to eyes that were blurred by rain and foam, smoothing also a few wet locks from her forehead.

When she was ready to go on again, she was startled. Ahead of her distorted by the watery light was the broad squat figure of a man watching. He stood quite still as she approached, and her heart quickened apprehensively. Who was he? What was he doing there? And why was he grinning like some macabre troll in wait for prey. His arm was in a sling, he had a red beard, and small eyes screwed up against the wind. She tried to appear unconcerned and passed by without speaking, but he stopped her, offered his dripping hand which was large and coarsened, then pointing to his barrel chest he said just one word, 'Por*tee*us' which was obviously meant to convey his identity.

'Porteous?' Adelaide echoed. 'You?'

He seemed to understand, and nodded.

She nodded back. He grinned amiably, glanced at her briefly again, then turned his face once more towards the sea.

Adelaide hurried on, with her heart thudding against her ribs. When she was within sight of Trenhawk she was running. It was then she saw Rupert. He had a waterproof cape round his shoulders, and was cutting from the right towards the stables. He paused until she was close enough for him to make himself heard. Then he called, 'Where the devil have you been? Trying to drown yourself?' She didn't reply, but plunged past him to a side door leading down a passage past the kitchen quarters into the main hall. Her drenched clothes and hair left a trail of water behind. At the foot of the staircase he caught her arm and pulled her round to face him.

'My God! What a dismal sight.'

She wrenched herself free abruptly and rushed up the stairs.

'When you've dried yourself and got dressed,' he called after her, 'come to the library; I've a bone to pick with you.'

Of course he had, she thought angrily; he'd probably accuse her of having a liaison or something equally ridiculous with that stupid fat stranger Porteous. Or perhaps he'd just heard about her drive with Anthony St Clare. She rather hoped he had; it would teach her pompous overbearing step-cousin that she intended to do what she liked and was not going to be ordered about by him. And if she wanted to go walking in the rain she would. There was no need for Rupert to worry on Mrs Pender's account. She'd wipe up the wet hall and stairs herself.

As she dressed herself after a good scrub with water from the ewer into which she sprinkled a liberal amount of perfume, Adelaide's nerves and temper relaxed. The rain had stimulated her skin and left a becoming glow in her cheeks. Her hair, even with the most vigorous rubbing, took some time to dry. But its sheen was emphasised, and try as she would it was impossible to control completely the mass of rebellious waves. She twisted a ribbon through it and caught the back portion into combs, leaving clustered curls tumbling provocatively on either side of her face. Then, after stepping into clean underwear she took a gown from the wardrobe, sat on the bed, and pulled it carefully upwards over her feet and delicate thighs, fastening it carefully at the waist. It was not black this time, not even grey, but a soft dark violet silk falling in gathered frills downwards, giving the impression almost of a crinoline, but having a far subtler effect. A demure lace collar encircled her neck. She knew she looked beautiful. Her reflection was proof. Why the knowledge stimulated her so she wasn't sure, except that with feminine intuition she realised Rupert's male arrogance would be reduced when he saw her.

When she stepped into the library however, five minutes later, he didn't smile or appear to notice the care she'd taken over her looks. This subtly affronted her.

'Well?' she said sharply. 'What do you want?'

'Sit down Adelaide,' he said, sounding faintly bored. 'This isn't a theatre.'

'A theatre?'

'For dramatic art,' he said in cold tones that belied his secret admiration. 'You look very charming, and of course you know it. I'm glad too, to see you've discarded your weeds for a change, but I hope you realise Lucy's had to do a lot of wiping up after you.'

'If she'd left it I'd have done it,' she told him. 'I meant to. And please don't talk to me like a schoolgirl, Rupert.'

'Then don't behave like one,' he said. 'The fact is, cousin dear, you're becoming a bit of a nuisance in one way or another –'

'Don't call me cousin,' she interrupted sharply, 'when we're not even properly related.'

'Thank you for reminding me, Addy,' he said with a flicker of amusement or was it desire – in his dark eyes. She flushed, noting for the first time how distinguished looking he was in a strongly male way – wide forehead beneath the black crisply curly hair, straight nose with slightly blunted tip, and firmly set mouth above a square chin with a cleft in it. His full underlip was thrust a little forward now in the characteristic manner he had when he meant to get his own way.

There was a pause between them in which both made an effort to assess the other's potential. Then he continued, with all trace of softening suddenly dispelled, 'Don't ever go driving with that bastard St Clare again. I told you I wouldn't have you mixing with any of them when you arrived. Remember?'

'I shall do just what I choose when I choose,' she told him with her heart quickening angrily.

'I don't think so, because if you give me cause, Adelaide, I'll throw you out of the house by the hair of your head, or put you over my knees for a sound spanking and take great pleasure in doing so. Got that?'

'What a brute you are,' she said, with her eyes flaming. 'But you never were a gentleman. Mama said so, and David – '

'Oh damn your mama,' he cut in shortly. 'She was always a weak lily-livered woman, too rich by half, who'd have seen you were decently disciplined if she'd had any sense. As for David – '

He paused, aware he was going too far.

'Don't talk of my mother like that,' she cried, 'and don't dare to mention David's name. It's an insult – '

'Who to?'

His effrontery staggered her. She got up and rushed to the door, but he was there before her, barring the way. She lifted two clenched fists and beat him on the chest. 'Let me through. You're – you're – ' but what he was she couldn't say, because his lips suddenly were hot and hard on her mouth, and for a moment resistance in her died, swamped by a rush of ungovernable emotions she neither understood or wished to.

Then suddenly it was over. His arms fell away; one hand found the door knob which he turned, stepping aside for her to pass through.

She walked past him, with her head high, but turned briefly to say before moving to the stairs. 'Don't ever do that again, Rupert. I'm not your whore or light-of-love. Isn't Elizabeth enough?'

She did not see his face whiten, or the fleeting look of pain cross his face. But as she mounted the stairs she was ashamed to have spoken that way. Why had she done it? In mentioning Elizabeth she'd somehow demeaned herself and lost dignity.

It did not occur to her she could have been jealous. There was no cause, since David was the one man she'd ever really cared for, and no one in the world could ever take his place.

Even so, her conflict with Rupert had excited her, for which she was mildly ashamed.

Half an hour after his hot exchange with Adelaide, Rupert slung out of the house and walked at a smart pace to the farm. He needed comfort, and he knew Elizabeth was the one person who could give it to him, although not, perhaps, in the way she thought and wanted.

She was busy in the kitchen when he arrived, and one look at his face told her he was upset.

'Sit down,' she said. 'You look a bit done up. Anything wrong?'

Usually at such times, mostly when mining worries were on top of him, or finance bothering him, he would slip an arm round her waist and let his lips linger about the soft curves of her breasts, before taking her to bed. When such intimacies were impractical, he'd draw her on to his knees briefly and relax for a moment, until she'd get up and fetch him a cup of tea or mug of ale.

But this time it was different.

Although she let her lips rest momentarily on top of his head, he did not respond.

'Tell me, master,' she urged. He didn't appear to notice she'd reverted to the old habit of addressing him as 'master', but merely replied, 'Nothing more than usual. Well, nothing much.'

'And what's that?' she asked, trying to shake off the growing feeling of unease and separateness. 'You and me?'

'No,' he said firmly, 'not directly.'

'Indirectly then?'

His dark eyes probed hers, trying to assess how much she sensed or knew.

'Perhaps.'

'Go on, if it's about me I've a right to know, I think.'

'It's not about you, Elizabeth,' he told her. 'It's the house, Trenhawk.'

'Go on.'

'As you know, my cousin's implanted herself there, which makes things a little – complicated. I have to be around more. She has a way of poking her nose into matters that don't concern her –'

'You mean she's found out about – about us?'

Rupert paused before answering. Then he said, 'She knows nothing, and I don't intend she should. She mustn't. Not because of me, that wouldn't matter. My life's my own. But your good name – that's damned important. You know what you mean to me –'

'I know what I used to,' she interrupted meaningfully, 'and I always knew too a time would come when it'd not be right. That's what you're tryin' to say, edn' it? It's over?'

He shook his head, got up, and took her into his arms.

'No no. Not over. We've had something rich and rare. Something that can't suddenly be pushed aside and forgotten. You know that. You've mattered to me, and you always will.'

She nodded, keeping her face averted so he wouldn't notice the rush of tears to her eyes. But she couldn't suppress the knot of pain in her throat,or the quick emotional rising and falling of her ample breasts under the pink calico bodice.

A stirring of the old desire filled him, a longing only a younger man could feel for the warm mothering quality of an older woman.

'Elizabeth – ' he murmured, with his arm tightening round her waist.

She urged herself away firmly.

'No. No – it's better not. Better we should be apart,' she told him. 'After all – there's Tom too. If that cousin of your suspects, it means others know – '

'And do you think Tom doesn't?'

'So long as it's not thrown in his face an' he c'n keep his pride,' she said, 'he'll turn a blind eye. He's a good man. I don't want him shamed.'

'Neither do I.'

'So perhaps – ' her lip quivered. 'Perhaps it'd be better if I left here. I could do with having more time with him. He's alone more than's good for him, just sitting on his own there staring across the moors – '

Rupert with an abrupt movement, strode away from her to the window; then he turned, came back, and without touching her, stood looking into her eyes. Her own did not falter.

'You don't mean that,' he said.

'Yes. I think it'd be best.'

'Well I don't, Elizabeth; not entirely. I've got to have someone here, – part of the day anyway. The farm has to be looked after. The men expect – '

'What isn't theirs by right,' she cut in hastily. 'They're quite capable, any one of them, of making a pot of tea. The harness room's all they need – '

'And me?'

'But you won't be here? Well, hardly at all, will you?'

'I shall be in and out. And there's the dairy –'

'You could get a girl.'

'Who?'

'Dolly, Bill Pengarron's youngest daughter. She's a good hand with butter, an' such like, and's been brought up hard. She'd keep the rooms dusted and floors well scrubbed. An' you'd pay less.'

He shook his head. 'And lose a lot,' he said meaningfully. 'There are things you can't measure in shillings and pence.'

'I know, I know. But – don't rub it in, master. What we've had's been – good. More than that. But it can't last can it? Not for ever?'

He didn't reply. There was no need to. The answer was clear, in his eyes. A sense of regret, longing, mingled with curious relief, filled him. He felt as well a disquieting sense of shame that she'd made the situation so easy.

After that tension eased into a mood of quiet acceptance between them though he was aware that underneath she suffered. The interview was settled eventually by a compromise; for a month Elizabeth would be at the farm every day from eight to eleven, helping the new girl employed to get into the run of things. After that Dolly – if it was Dolly – would be on her own, for mornings only. Rupert was determined to run no further risk of gossip; apart from that, the thought of putting anyone else completely in Elizabeth's place was distasteful to him.

Before leaving he would have kissed her farewell but she automatically turned with the excuse of brushing a cobweb from a corner of the wall and dresser. There was no cobweb; he knew also there was nothing left between them.

They parted as polite strangers.

Watching him walk down the slope towards Trenhawk, she forced herself to think of Tom, comforting herself with the knowledge that he needed her and her rightful place was by his side. A few stray clouds dimmed the pale sky suddenly. Loneliness engulfed her. Ahead the years lay dutiful, yet empty of youth, stretching inevitably towards the onslaught of time and old age.

She felt there would never be anyone else. Rupert had been
both lover and son to her – the son she'd never had, and now
never would bear.

When his figure had disappeared she went to the sink,
washed her hands, then made her way to the dairy, an
upstanding fine-looking woman with a proud face that belied
the sorrow in her dark Cornish eyes. There was work to be
done; only in work, she told herself firmly, was her life justified
– work and through Tom.

When she returned to the cottage later he was seated in his
usual place by the window. His glance was welcoming, but
more speculative than normal.

'You're early,' he told her as she went to kiss him.

'And I'll be earlier still from next week on,' she answered.
'At the end o' the month I'll be leavin' altogether.'

'You will?'

She nodded.

'Why?'

Her heart warmed.

'Because it's time,' she said, 'I'm no chicken, love. I've bin'
thinking quite a bit lately it'd be a comfort to put my feet up
beside you of an evenin' sometimes.'

'Oh. Ah.' He said no more, but she sensed his gratitude.
When she noticed his eyes on her, they were shining and
bright with love.

She knew then she'd been right.

Compassion flowed between them.

Life was not going to be empty after all.

The next few days remained grey and overcast with intermittent showers of thin rain blurring the landscape. Though
Rupert slept at Trenhawk, he was away from the house most of
the time, and when he and Adelaide met relationships were
strained, holding undercurrents of anger and mistrust. She
suggested one afternoon to Rupert that a trip to Penzance or
Penjust would be useful. She had shopping to do; there was
silk needed to adjust the new curtains before they were hung in
her bedroom. Was there any objection to her using the gig? Or
getting Carnack to drive her there? To which Rupert replied
none whatever except that the gig at the moment was out of

order needing a broken shaft repaired.

'When will it be done?' Adelaide asked, not realising the imperious note in her voice.

'As soon as I can get a carpenter round,' he told her abruptly. 'Will Adams from the village is the only one I'd trust to do the job properly, and he's a busy man.'

'A horse then. I could ride.'

'I know that. But it's out of the question. All are in use except the grey which I shall be needing myself tomorrow.'

'You're not very helpful,' she said, with a fiery glint in her eye.

'Well – ' he paused then added, 'you could walk of course. Merely eight miles each way to Penjust. But I wouldn't advise it in this weather. And as our mutual acquaintance St Clare took off to town yesterday it's doubtful you'd get the offer of a lift.'

'Or that I'd have the chance of accepting one even if I did,' Adelaide said quickly, 'since your hawk's eyes would be sure to see.'

He laughed shortly. 'Very well put. Oh, Adelaide, grow up. If you'd mentioned shopping before, I'd have taken you myself. But it's too late today, the shops close tomorrow, and I'm off on Friday to Plymouth on business for a day or two. When I come back we'll arrange it.'

'Thank you, Rupert,' she remarked with cold sarcasm.

'In the meantime Carnack will have orders to see no one rides in my absence. I don't want to get back and find your pretty neck broken or my favourite mare maimed.'

'So I'm supposed to remain incarcerated here – '

'No, no,' he interrupted, quick to seize the advantage. 'No one expects you to remain here, Adelaide. No one asked you to come, if you remember. In my opinion it was the worst possible thing for you. A few days – yes. But grieving and weeping on your own won't bring David back. And as I've told you, Trenhawk's my – '

'Yes, *yours*. You've told me, and you've told me, and you've *told* me, she cried passionately, clenching both hands so the nails bit into her palms. 'It's quite obvious you detest my presence –'

He put out a hand, touching a wrist placatingly.

She tore her arm away, and stood for a moment facing him.

'You're just the same as you always were, Rupert Hawksley, a great domineering bully. And I – I – ' her voice faltered as her throat thickened with sobs. 'I think I hate you. But you won't drive me away from here, and you won't drive David out of my heart either – ' She turned and rushed from the room leaving him staring after her morosely, wondering what the deuce he'd said to so upset her.

It wasn't the horse or missing her shopping spree, he was convinced of that. It was something far subtler and more wounding to her feminine sensibilities; something to do with his not wanting her there?

Maybe. Women, except for Elizabeth, could be highly emotional contradictory creatures when the mood took them. Adelaide most of all. And that remark of hers about not driving David from her heart? What on earth had induced her to think he was trying? He wouldn't waste his time – not yet. But he knew that if she persisted in remaining there anything could happen.

He was not a monk, neither was she a nun destined to spend her days forever worshipping at some obsolete shrine. The response of her warm mouth under his when he'd kissed her, the burning glow of her rain-washed cheek had told him more about the real Adelaide than any of her rebellious words.

She didn't like him, no. The feeling between them on that point was mutual.

But 'liking' was frequently a negative virtue, and however hard she tried to deny it the contact between them was certainly not that; poor Adelaide. One day she'd wake up. Sometime she'd have to. In the meantime let her keep her illusions of eternal love and her adored knight-in-armour intact. Little she'd believe – even if told – how easily he, Rupert, could shatter the dream, and that eventually he might be forced to do so. He hoped not. Such a course would probably destroy for good any possibility of future understanding between them.

When he left later for the stables, he was irritated with himself for allowing any concern about her to intrude and so disturb him. But then he supposed the ending of his affair with Elizabeth had something to do with it. It hadn't been easy snapping the door to on their relationship. He knew he'd miss her. But women, he told himself ruthlessly, were only a part of life. He'd other things on his mind that needed full attention, such as Wheal Tansy, and getting the Dutchman safely off to his own country before too many comments and questions got around. The doctor, John Maddox, had assured him the arm was on the mend, the wounds on the leg weren't as bad as they'd seemed. He was fit enough to travel when a convenient berth could be arranged. The risk was that while he remained in the vicinity of Trenhawk his presence was a danger.

The Preventive might have failed in their business of locating the exact scene and timing of the carefully planned smuggling operation, but their senses would be alert now to anyone or anything likely to give a valuable clue. 'Cousin Porteous' might be acceptable to the household. Most of Rupert's men would be loyal. But in times of poverty, and low wages to feed too many mouths, a bribe could be tempting.

In St Rozzan there were families out of work having to exist on parish relief and what food they could produce by their own hands or other means. Rupert's occasional 'adventures' were no secret, and an obvious unknown foreigner of sea-faring type could be a good lead for the Revenue, and worth a tidy bit in the pocket of anyone likely to give information.

The man, too, blast him, had developed the habit of limping about the moors whenever he'd a chance. Even Adelaide had complained somewhat belatedly of seeing a red-bearded stranger on the cliffs when she'd run from the cove in the storm.

'Why didn't you tell me before?' he'd asked, to which she'd replied, 'I suppose your conduct drove him out of my head. Anyway, he was a rough, unpleasant-looking character. I got away as quickly as I could.'

A 'rough unpleasant looking character'. The description was apt, Rupert thought, as he located the boy grooming the grey; and it was putting a heavy load expecting either the lad or Carnack to keep tabs on the stranger every minute of the day.

'Where's Carnack?' he asked the boy abruptly.

'Just gone to the house for something, master.'

'And Cousin Porteous?'

The boy grinned widely, 'Sleepin' – in the loft master – Mr

Carnack did see he had plenty of cider in 'en – snorin' like a great bull ' ee be.'

Rupert touched the boy's arm in approval. 'Good. I'm going to see he's away in the next two days. In the meantime keep your mouth shut. Understand?'

Nick nodded. 'Oh, ais. Never fear, Mr Rupert.'

Rupert went in search of Carnack, and found him in the kitchen sitting at the table with a mug of ale beside him. Lucy had already left. Mrs Pender was about to retire to her own quarters. The fading light threw only a pale glimmer over the large Cornish range, flagged floor, and freshly scrubbed table. She eyed Rupert shrewdly as he entered. 'I thought it only right Mr Carnack should have a bite and taste to keep him going considerin' the extra work he had to handle,' she said condemningly. 'Things were never like this before – never, not in the old master's time. We'd proper servants to handle things, and no troublesome Cousin Porteous to complicate matters – ' she paused, drew her breath, then continued, 'The sooner he goes the better, pardon me for sayin' so. He's a lusting low character, Mr Rupert, too fond by half of his liquor and women.'

'Women?'

Mrs Pender sniffed, went to the dresser, lit a candle, and before going to the inner door remarked significantly. 'There'll be trouble unless you do something about it.'

'Thank you,' Rupert said evenly. 'That's just what I intend to do. By the weekend he'll be gone, and that's a promise.'

But before the weekend unexpected events took their own macabre trend.

The next day early morning mist turned to fog, which by afternoon had become dense over the lower moors, gradually creeping towards the high hills. Adelaide, feeling claustrophic and slightly ill-at ease, would have gone out if she could have seen a hand before her face. But she couldn't. When she put her head beyond the door the landscape was nothing more than a moist, grey furry blanket taking everything into damp cloying uniformity. In spite of the weather Rupert had ridden over to the mine after the mid-day meal, and Trenhawk itself seemed a shell of a place – desolate, empty. She went up to her room, and made another desultory attempt at reading *Jane Eyre*.

But she couldn't concentrate. The windless oppressive air only seemed to emphasise any small sound of intermittent creaking, and dripping of moisture round the old walls and windows.

At one point, nearing tea-time, she was sure she heard crying from below. Her scalp pricked, and senses were alerted to a sudden conviction her ears had not deceived her. The sounds were real sounds. Somewhere in the maze of corridors and rooms of Trenhawk there was a child – the child she had seen peering from the shadows, by the back stairs leading down to the servants' quarters. Presently the cries died into silence again, and all was uncannily quiet.

Adelaide laid the book down and went to the mirror. How pale she looked against the shadowed background. And how unfair, she thought, that Rupert had not allowed her to have the large bedroom she and David had meant to share. The new pink curtains probably would not have needed altering, the pieces of furniture they'd acquired would have been the right size, and fitted in perfectly when William's old-fashioned wardrobe and dressing-table were removed. The rugs would have given a luxurious touch; whereas here – Rupert had spoken truthfully when he'd said some of the things would not be in keeping with the smaller room she occupied. Much of her enthusiasm for making the necessary re-arrangements before having her possessions brought up, had died. She no longer cared very much whether she had them round her or not. Without David they wouldn't really count much after all. The reality of his loss was gradually sinking in. No ghosts or imagined presence could compensate for his death. He had gone; and yet – what was that? Noises had started up again. No crying or echo of a child's voice, but the distant pattering of light feet, youthful, impatient steps resounding through some trick of the acoustics and structural peculiarity of the building. A moment later all was quiet again.

She went to the door, opened it and glanced out. There was no one about; the air was indistinct and blurred. Fog even seemed to have penetrated into the interior of the house absorbing the shadows in a drab veil of half-light. Yet the portraits on the far wall of the corridor had a certain uneasy life about them. It was almost as though the past centuries were stirring from the forgotten years, and that if she waited long enough, their secrets, ambitions, ancient feuds and dead desires would be reborn again from the dust, making her one with them – the inheritor of Trenhawk. It was easy in that empty lonely atmosphere, to envisage, however, vaguely, history in its making, like a vast tapestry woven from human aims and failures, virtues and mistakes – the dedicated enthusiasm of the monks who'd laid the first stones, only to be defeated by the avarice of a king. The wealthy Puritan merchants of Hawksley blood who'd acquired the building, restored and completed it, followed by the Civil War and failure of Royalist armies to destroy its granite walls. Who would ever know what secret plots and political intrigue had been hatched in the vicinity? How many men faithful to the cause of democracy had been hanged or put to death by worse means?

Adelaide knew little of historical facts. As a child her education had been primarily for the purpose of instilling lady-like virtues that would acquire a rich and eligible husband. The names of Luther and such men as William Cobbett the reformer, meant nothing to her. But she was aware of the atmosphere – of conflicting forces that had never entirely been eradicated from the interior of the old house. It was in itself an identity. Something, like an individual, that had acquired the ageing lines and wrinkles of a single personality through the passing of time.

A personality! As she stood there, with heightened senses, ears keyed to the extreme silence, it seemed the very walls breathed, whispering, 'This is yours – yours.' Then she pulled herself together abruptly, realising that Rupert's claim was legal, his right by blood. Hers was only one of love and desire to possess.

She was going back into the bedroom when she heard the light pattering sound again. And it came from a distance away, in the direction of the Tower Room. Without waiting to get a wrap, she ran barefooted over the cold stone floor to the point where stairs branched off, leading upwards to the mysterious precincts of the forbidden room.

Then, suddenly, she stopped.

Above her, at the bend where the steps took an abrupt turn to the right was the shadowed figure of a young boy. He appeared to be wearing a brown jacket, but nothing else was clear. His features were indefinite, though even through the uncertain light she was aware that he was very fair, and was watching her intently. He could not have been more than five, perhaps even less. She waited for several moments, wondering if she was having an illusion and her overwrought nerves were playing her tricks. Then, as he moved slightly and her sight came into proper focus, she knew he was flesh and blood – the same child she'd seen before.

'Who are you?' she called, gently and quietly so as not to frighten him. 'What's your name?'

He shook his head several times as though he did not understand. She lifted a hand, and took two steps towards him. He made a sudden movement down the stairs and managed to avoid her, tumbled on the lowest step joining the wide corridor, picked himself up, and was off again before she could catch him.

She rushed after his flying figure, and only caught up with him at the entrance leading down towards the servants' quarters. Her hand grasped him by the shoulder. He glanced fearfully up at her face, and she was struck by his beauty which was almost too ethereal for a boy's, with strangely dark blue eyes peering under thick black lashes. His hair was flaxen. He could have been a youthful figure from a stained glass window. When she'd got her breath back and his own breathing had quietened she said, 'Don't be frightened, I shan't hurt you – ' but the very blue eyes had already filmed with tears.

It was then that they were startled by the tread of heavy male footsteps from the main staircase.

Both turned, and were completely motionless as Rupert's figure appeared round the bend of the corridor. He stood statically for a second, then walked purposefully towards them.

'What are you doing?' he said to Adelaide who still had her hand on the child's shoulder. 'Can't you see you're frightening him?'

She dropped her hand immediately. The little boy rushed to the safety of Rupert's enclosing arms, burying his face against the cloth jacket.

'Who is he?' Adelaide asked. 'And I certainly didn't mean to frighten him. Naturally I was surprised to find a child wandering the corridors – '

'Wandering about? Where?'

'Near the tower room,' Adelaide said. 'I heard a sound and wondered what it was, that's all.'

'He's not supposed to go up there, it's dangerous,' Rupert said, glancing down affectionately at the tousled fair head, 'and he knows it, don't you, Julian – ?'

'Julian?'

'My ward,' he told her. 'An orphan. His father was a – great friend of mine. So I hope now you're satisfied.'

'Not quite,' Adelaide replied. 'Why wasn't I told? I mean, it's so ridiculous keeping his presence secret. I saw him once before and asked Mrs Pender who he was. She said there was no child. I was imagining things.'

'Mrs Pender was doing what she thought was right. Julian's only been here a short time, since his mother's – death. She's looking after him temporarily until I find a suitable governess. In the meantime I don't want him upset. The upheaval has been worse for him than it would be for most children. You see, Adelaide –'

'Yes?'

'He's completely deaf,' Rupert answered with a veiled look in his eyes. 'And sensitive. So I must ask you not to go scaring him without reason. He's not used to strangers, and you *are* inclined to be intimidating.'

Before she could think of anything to say he was walking towards the main staircase, with a protective hand on the little boy's shoulder.

Adelaide was not only chagrined, but puzzled. Rupert's concern for the boy was clearly genuine which explained the housekeeper's fierce determination to obey his instructions and keep his presence private. But why? *Why?* It was not as though she, Adelaide, did not like children. She and David had looked forward to having a large family. She would soon have taught young Julian to trust her, and their eventual meeting was inevitable. Perhaps Rupert had foreseen a possible bond between them as just another excuse for her staying at Trenhawk – a link he was determined to discourage in any possible way. Well, she thought stubbornly, his little plot wouldn't work now. He had been – foiled – wasn't that the word? – and it had been unintelligent of him to resort to such melodramatic mysterious means of keeping a young child hidden away like a stowaway on a boat. Unless of course Rupert really had some logical explanation. A guilt complex perhaps?

The idea took root in her mind insidiously, and once there quickly flourished. There had been something faintly familiar about the child's looks – not in features or colouring, but a fleeting expression of stubborn persistence – a gesture, momentary lift of the well-formed proud little chin that held a haunting quality characteristic of the Hawksleys.

Rupert's son?

Rupert was no saint or ever had been. She would not put it past him to father a child out of wedlock, and the boy being afflicted as he was, would naturally make Rupert feel under an obligation, especially since Trenhawk had fallen so conveniently into his hands.

She found the suggestion not only annoying, but extremely distasteful, and one that started up all the old gnawing jealousy in her again. Jealousy concerning Trenhawk.

Back in her room once more she decided her first business the next day would be to locate the boy Julian, and after putting him at his ease make friends. Rupert would have no excuse for refusing, and Mrs Pender would have to comply.

Meanwhile the fog persisted in a thick shroud round the house, though on the hills it lifted showing a rim of greenish twilight under the watery light of a climbing moon.

The woman's figure was strong and comely through the filmed air, as she walked past the front of the cottage, carrying a bucket in one hand. Even the shawl flung round her shoulder could not disguise her proud posture or swelling curves of thighs and breasts. She moved rhythmically, with her head up. Not a young woman, but one ripe for the plucking, the man thought, crouching behind a rock. His small eyes gleamed in their creases of flesh; his tongue lusted behind the thick lips, where a stubble of red beard and moustache sprouted. A man at sea most of his life needed a woman sometimes, and he wanted her. Though one arm was in a sling he knew he could manage her. There was no one about. When she came back from the pump he'd have her in a vice, and it'd be over. He'd be appeased and his loins satisfied and quiet again. She'd make no fuss. The very look of her was asking for it; and no one would see – not with that blanket of fog below and the fitful grey masses still seeping up over the moor from the cliffs.

So he waited, while the moon was taken into cloud once more, and her figure was only a silhouetted shape against the damp air. Then, as she passed only a few yards ahead of him, he made a furtive movement, pushed by a clump of furze, and sprang. She screamed before his large palm found her mouth. There were a few seconds of wild struggle as her skirt was torn upwards from her thighs, revealing a glimmer of pale flesh.

Then the shot came.

One shrill blast of sound that caused a flutter and screaming of whirling gulls above. The man's head fell back, the great body heaved, then all was still. Elizabeth, frozen briefly to a semblance of stone, stared horrified at the blasted face, the distorted jaws revealing broken teeth, and protruding blood-stained tongue. She only moved when the second shot came from the cottage.

'Tom,' she cried, getting to her feet and stumbling to the door, 'Tom – Tom – oh midear, my dear love, – what've you done?'

He was seated by the half open window, staring blankly across the wide expanse of bleak mist-wreathed moors, the pistol fallen from one lifeless hand to the floor. Elizabeth touched his shoulder, and laid her head against his chest, listening. There was no sound of a heart-beat. The blood from one temple was already half congealing on his cheek.

Automatically she smoothed the greying dark hair from his temple, and fetched water and towel to make him clean. She worked methodically as though tidying some muddied child who would presently move and smile again.

Then, only half aware of her actions, she picked up the rug, shook it and arranged it round his shattered stumps of legs. When the sad ritual was over she put on her cape, and tearless still, numbed by shock, started walking down the hill towards Trenhawk.

Rupert was in the kitchen discussing Julian with Mrs Pender, when the outer door burst open and Elizabeth, without knocking, burst in. Her eyes were wide and staring in her pale face; the black hair damp and tumbled over her shoulders. Rupert, shocked, made an involuntary movement towards her. The housekeeper gaped.

'Elizabeth – ' he said, 'what's the matter? What is it?'

At first she tried to speak and couldn't. Then it all came out in a rush. 'It's Tom. He's dead. And another man too. Tom shot 'im. Then 'isself. What do I do, master? What do I do?'

Rupert took her by both arms and made her sit down. Then he got her a stiff whisky, and told Mrs Pender to make some coffee. By then full reaction had set in and Elizabeth was shaking, but still the tears wouldn't fall.

Presently when a little colour had returned to her cheeks and she was dried and warmed by the spirit and hot drink, Rupert said, 'I shall go up and see for myself what's happened. You must stay here. Mrs Pender will look after you. In the meantime – ' to the housekeeper, 'keep things to yourself. If the stranger's whom I think he may well be, there's bound to be talk and a lot of explaining to do.'

Mrs Pender nodded.

'You can trust me, Mr Rupert.'

'And see the child's tucked up in bed,' he said, taking a cape from a peg. 'He's had more than enough excitement for the day.'

'And Mrs David?'

He shrugged. 'If there's anything happening here she's sure to get wind of it. Use your discretion. I'll handle her, when I get back.'

He went out, slamming the door sharply behind him, and with his head and shoulders thrust forward, made his way past the side wall towards the narrow path cutting up over the moor. If he hadn't known the track by heart he'd have found the way difficult. The base of the hill was still dense with fog. Furze and brambles were contorted in the thickened, drifting air. As he climbed higher however, it began to clear, and when he was within sight of the cottage only a thin veil of mist wavered intermittently over the wan moonlight scene. Seven, or perhaps ten yards from the cottage – it could not have been more – he saw the grotesque bundle of humanity crumpled on its back by a boulder. If he'd had less experience of accidents he'd have retched. But after one brief glimpse and a touch on the cold wrist, he turned away, knowing there was nothing he could do, and went on to find Tom.

Except for the dark stain from temple over cheek and chin, Chywanna was sitting as he'd sat for years at the window, but with eyes fixed now, as though concentrated on a world unknown to those in life. One pale hand hung limply over the chair arm; the pistol lay directly below. It had been a gift from William Trenhawk, Rupert's uncle, following the mine disaster that had robbed Tom forever of his working life. 'Keep it by you, Tom,' William had said, 'as a symbol, anyway of my protection. I can't give you new limbs. But it's a wild spot up here, and it'll ease me knowing you and Elizabeth are safe.'

Every day, during the bitter useless years following, it had lain by Chywanna's side waiting. Tom had learned to become an expert shot, and had occasionally got a rabbit or two to supplement their diet. Now, Rupert thought with grim irony, the weapon had provided not only revenge but escape from an existence that must mostly have been little better than a worthless travesty.

On impulse, hardly knowing what he was doing, Rupert touched a dead hand, held it for a moment, then went back to Trenhawk, saddled his horse, and set off for St Rozzan and the doctor.

A double inquest was held the following week in Penzance, when a verdict of manslaughter, under great stress, was recorded against Chywanna who had afterwards taken his own life.

It was not thought necessary, following Elizabeth's controlled and dignified statement of what had happened on the tragic evening, to make other than the necessary formal enquiries concerning the stranger's identity.

All who had been aware, briefly, of 'Cousin Porteous's' existence, kept their mouths firmly shut. The general opinion being that the fellow had been a worthless blackguard who'd asked for 'et.

And so the matter was closed, and the life of the district continued in its normal pattern except for Elizabeth, who after considerable persuasion by Rupert at last agreed to leave the cottage for Trenhawk.

Adelaide was sceptical.

'Won't people think it odd, you having her here?' she asked Rupert when she heard of the arrangement.

'Why should they?'

She flung him a knowing look that momentarily perturbed him.

'Well, I mean, she's quite attractive still. Old – but in a mature way good-looking.'

'Servants' looks aren't my concern,' Rupert answered sharply. 'Mrs Pender needs help, and Elizabeth is qualified. She'll be of great assistance with Julian also.'

'I do hope so,' Adelaide answered, with a tinge of sweet venom in her voice.

Never before had Rupert so longed to slap her. He turned away abruptly and left her staring after him, brows raised mockingly over her lovely eyes.

Indignation filled her, not merely because of Elizabeth Chywanna's future presence in the house, but because she, Adelaide, had not been consulted, and was in no position to object. And Rupert liked the large dark woman. Without admitting it even to herself, she suspected 'liking' fell far short of the truth. Why – a wild idea swept all other considerations aside suddenly – it was possible even that Elizabeth was Julian's mother.

The very suggestion affronted her. She tried to dismiss it, telling herself it was none of her concern. Any secrets Rupert and Elizabeth had were their own business. But the niggle of doubt and suspicion remained in her mind. She resented this new intrusion into Trenhawk – the inheritance that through David should have been hers. She didn't grudge the child shelter. He only deserved sympathy, poor little thing. But Elizabeth! – to have the woman always about, ready to flaunt her hips, and to influence Rupert by her calm soft way of talking and pleasing glance of her dark cow's eyes! – yes. She resented Elizabeth intensely.

As things turned out, Tom's wife only stayed a fortnight. At the end of it she informed Rupert that her sister-in-law had offered her a home in Penzance, which she thought best to accept.

'Having me under your nose all the time isn't going to be comfortable for either of us,' she said bluntly.

'I don't see why not.'

'Then you're not so smart as I thought you,' she told him with a half-smile. 'And I've a feeling Mrs David doesn't approve.'

'Has she said anything? If she has, I'll – '

'Oh, no, no. She doesn't have to, master. We're both women. It wouldn't do. And anyway – '

'Yes?'

'I've a need to get away. A change of scene p'raps will help me put things behind and start again,' she lifted her head an inch or two higher. 'I'm not that old.'

'You don't have to point it out,' he said thinking how handsome she was in a country style. And she was right of course. In all probability she'd meet some healthy man of her own background one day who'd marry her and make up for the past.

He hoped so.

There was no putting the clock back, and he didn't regret the past. But he recognised it had been only an interlude, and one he'd avoid if he had his time over again.

The next afternoon Adelaide watched her driven away by Carnack in the gig, with her few possessions in a case and bundles beside her. She was wearing a tartan cape over a brown cloth dress, with a small bonnet tilted slightly forward, revealing the dark bun of hair on her neck. Her features were not clear through the window, but the general effect was of a well-padded servant or family retainer setting off on holiday or for retirement.

Rupert stood on the bottom step of the terrace waiting to lift a hand in farewell. But she didn't turn, and a moment or two later the carriage was lost to view, taken into the shadows of the networked trees as it neared the bend leading into the main road.

With a shrug of the shoulders, Rupert turned, and walked more slowly than usual up the few steps into the house.

Adelaide was leaving the front sitting room, when he entered the hall. A thin ray of winter sunlight caught her pale hair from the tall staircase window, playing fleetingly about the exquisite features and fine high lines of bone structure. She was wearing the purple dress which fell in voluminous folds from the incredibly small waist. All she needed, he thought, with a touch of appreciative irony, was a flower in her hair, and a cluster of violets at her breast to make her the perfect chatelaine of Trenhawk.

'You're looking quite ravishing, Adelaide,' he said. 'Rather a waste of time, I'd have thought.'

She smiled enigmatically. 'Oh no – no Rupert. You're quite mistaken,' she remarked lightly. 'It's a woman's duty to look her best sometimes, even for her own sake.'

The smile was still on her lips, secretive and subtly seductive, as she passed him to go up the stairs. There was a faint perfume about her, evocative of spring-time and the feminine sweetness which illogically annoyed and irritated him.

He knew she was revelling in Elizabeth's departure, which seemed to him in bad taste. So without another look in her direction he said clearly, walking to the kitchen, 'I shan't be in for the meal tonight, I have things to attend to at the manor, and will probably sleep there for the next two or three days. So enjoy your freedom.'

She went to her room with an unpleasant feeling of having been chastened, like a child. 'Damn, Rupert,' she thought, 'damn, oh, damn him.'

Her eyes glistened bright with anger and humiliation. How could he? When she was lonely and merely trying to keep her end up? And after stealing Trenhawk from her, too.

The image of David returned with sudden overwhelming clarity, she was flooded with remorse at wanting things he could no longer give – warmth and a certain appreciation – especially from Rupert who had such a disastrous knack of infuriating her.

Very deliberately she unbuttoned the purple bodice and drew it over her head, then removed the skirt. Her black dress was lying on the bed where she'd laid it when she'd changed. She put it on and draped its black lace shawl round her shoulders. Then, taking a square of lawn handkerchief from her reticule, she wiped the tinted lipsalve from her mouth, and vigorously rubbed the faint flush on her cheeks till her face was left free of artifice and tinted creams. Her image, through the glass, though still youthful, was over-serious, and still a little strained. She moved the silver framed photograph of David, so it confronted her directly from the dressing table. He was in uniform; smiling, and looking extremely handsome. 'It's so hard being alone,' she whispered aloud. 'So unfair – ' But what was the use? David could neither hear or understand.

There was no point in talking to a dead likeness.

She let a hand stray automatically down a side of her face, neck, and over the gentle swelling breasts, remembering in spite of herself, his kisses, especially those of their last night together before his sailing for the Crimea. The promises he'd given of their future, and the years they'd share, mostly at Trenhawk, but two months every winter in town.

He'd told her she'd be the toast of London, and she'd believed it could very well come true. Then the children they'd have – a boy first, he'd said, followed by a girl, in his own words, 'Just like you, my love.' Such plans, so much looking forward, all of which had come to nothing.

She lifted the photograph, studied it intently for a moment or two, then placed it suddenly face down on the glass-topped table.

Presently she went downstairs, and summoning all her willpower to confront Mrs Pender in her domain, went through to the kitchen. At the same moment Lucy came through from the dairy.

'Is Mrs Pender about?' Adelaide asked abruptly.

The girl hesitated, then replied, 'She's restin', but I'll be takin' her tray in any minute, ma'am.'

'Oh, I see,' Adelaide said, noticing the tray ready laid on the table. 'Well, you can give it to me. I'll do it.'

'Oh, but I don't think – '

Adelaide smiled sweetly. 'I'm telling you, Lucy. Have no fear. You won't get into trouble, I'll make quite sure of that.'

Two minutes later, Adelaide had the tray in her hands, noting that the housekeeper despite her aged dry appearance certainly lived well, and in style. Cream instead of milk, for the tea; finely cut bread-and-butter, with a neat, small jar of strawberry preserve, and on a plate ready to be carried in separately, a slab of Cornish heavy-cake. Lucy held the latter, walking hesitantly behind Adelaide who marched decisively from the kitchen, to the housekeeper's adjoining quarters. The doorway was arched, Gothic style, and in early days had probably led to some priestly retreat.

'You better knock first,' Lucy whispered. 'She c'n be tetchy after her nap.'

Adelaide rapped. There was a creaking followed by a shuffling sound from within. A pause, and a harsh voice calling, 'Come in, girl. Don't stand there.'

Adelaide turned the iron drop-handle, and went through. A wave of hot air greeted her, as Mrs Pender's cumbrous figure confronted her in astonishment. She wore no apron. Her black satin afternoon dress was creased from her long snooze in her rocking chair, the lacy white cap a little askew.

'What do you want, ma'am?' she muttered, as Adelaide put the tray on a small table near a roaring fire, 'an' what d' you mean by this, Lucy girl? Haven' I told you times enough these rooms are private – ?'

'Yes, Lucy told me,' Adelaide interrupted calmly, 'and I overrode her objections. You mustn't blame her. I'm here on my own responsibility.' She paused before adding, 'I think it's time you and I had a little talk, Mrs Pender. In the meantime – ' to Lucy – 'put the plate down, Lucy, and go if you please.'

The girl, obviously scared and shaken, did what she was told. Then Adelaide, to the housekeeper's outraged astonishment, seated herself in a chair. She looked round, observing the antique furniture, thick carpet, and oleograph of 'The Battle of Trafalgar', hanging on one wall. Opposite was a daguerrotype of a bewhiskered elderly gentleman with one hand on a Bible. An air of cosy seclusion pervaded the room.

Before Mrs Pender had found words to comment, Adelaide said, 'You're very comfortable here, Mrs Pender. What a relief it must be to have such a retreat, especially with the heavy responsibility facing you. It must be a difficult task sometimes. And you manage so well.'

Mrs Pender's stare was blank. But from the flush staining the aged countenance, Adelaide knew her tactics were right, and that the housekeeper was flattered.

'Oh, I don't know,' she said grudgingly, 'I do my best I'm sure, but – '

'There's no doubt about it,' Adelaide assured her firmly. 'My cousin has a treasure, and I hope he appreciates it.'

By then quite mollified, Mrs Pender said, 'Can I offer you a cup of tea, Miss Adelaide? Mrs David? Seeing you're here now, and want a talk?'

'Thank you, I'd like one very much,' Adelaide told her, 'if it's not any bother. I wouldn't want to worry you. Your moments of privacy must be precious.'

'As long as people know it, that's all right,' came the answer, rather heavily delivered. 'In the past you weren't too considerate, if you don't mind me saying so. But they say grief is a great leveller and educater of the soul. So we'll forget the past, Miss Adelaide, and try to get things sorted out all right and proper. Cream, do you like, in your tea?'

After that things were easy.

Under the stimulus of Adelaide's flattery Mrs Pender softened agreeably and her tongue soon loosened on the subject of Julian.

'It isn't easy having the care of a young boy at my age,' she conceded when Adelaide questioned her, 'especially one like him, poor little thing, and I can't say I'm lookin' forward to havin' another woman about the place either. But as I pointed out to Mr Rupert, I can't be expected to cope with a deaf child on top of everything else – which is more than enough anyway.' She paused, and drew her breath, giving Adelaide the chance to say sympathetically, 'Of course. I quite agree.'

'So he got this idea of a governess.'

'Well, that should be a help.'

'If she's the right kind, and don't interfere with me,' Mrs Pender agreed grudgingly. 'But there are so many of the wrong sort about, aren't there? Like that – that Elizabeth Chywanna, poor creature. Oh don't think I'm not sorry for her. I'm a human being, Miss Adelaide, with feelings like the rest. But –'

'Yes?'

'It's my opinion she wasn't all she made out to be,' the housekeeper said primly. 'So calm and saintly and kind of quiet. "Still waters", I used to say to myself when she got so thick with the master – still waters run deep.'

'What do you mean exactly?' Adelaide asked after a pause.

'Now it's not for me to say,' Mrs Pender replied, pursing her lips. 'But if you ask me, it's a good thing she's gone. The scandal hasn't been good for the master. And neither would she have been the proper sort to have care of the boy.'

'No, perhaps not.'

'More tea, Miss Adelaide?'

'Yes thank you,' Adelaide answered, seizing the opportunity for prolonging the interview.

'This was my mother's,' the housekeeper said with her glance lovingly on the sturdy earthenware pot. 'Not elegant perhaps like some of those new fangled thin porcelain things from up country and China, but likely to be an heirloom one day.'

Adelaide agreed, then said casually, 'The little boy, Julian, hasn't been here long, has he? He can't have been. Did my cousin bring him?'

Mrs Pender shook her head.

'Oh no. He was just delivered you could say – a few months ago it was – by a grim looking toffee-nosed customer looking for all the world like one of those men hired for funerals dressed in black, and wearing a black stove hat too. "Here he is – ", he said, pushing the poor little thing at me. "Mr Hawksley's expecting him." When he got back an hour later he told me.'

'What?'

'He was his guardian, he said, and if I could look after the child for the present, he'd see I was paid for it, and later on there'd be someone properly qualified to take on the job. Properly qualified! I ask you. I've had two of my own; doing well they are, in America now. As if I didn't know how to bring up a child. Still – I'd no wish to, at my time of life, especially a deaf one like him, and certainly not for money. "I'll do what I can, Mr Rupert," I told him, "but you can keep your gold. Affection can't be paid for, only I'd be pleased to know you were gettin' someone in as soon as possible, and that she's kept well away from not intrudin' on *my* premises." So that's how it was left.'

With the oration concluded Mrs Pender sat back, wiped her brow, then closed her eyes briefly, hands folded over her breast, as though the interlude had been too much for her.

Adelaide got up.

'Well, I've enjoyed talking to you, Mrs Pender,' she said, 'and I hope we'll be friends from now on. By the way – '

'Yes?'

'If I can help you at all with Julian I'd be glad to, really. It's lonely here without – my husband.'

Mrs Pender's small eyes opened. There was a pause in which she regarded Adelaide with shrewd thoughtfulness. Then she asked, '*Why did* you come here? To this great place?'

'Because it was David's,' Adelaide told her bluntly, 'and because I expected it to be mine.'

'Hum. I thought so. But it isn', es it? And it won't ever be, not while Mr Rupert lives. Unless of course – you marry him.'

'*Marry* him? *Him?*'

'Many would jump at the chance,' Mrs Pender said, with cool practicality. 'And I always did think even when you were young, there was a sort of something between you. Forever quarrelling you were.'

'That's because I disliked him,' Adelaide said coldly. 'We never got on.'

'No. But that means nothing,' the housekeeper remarked. 'Where there's fireworks it only needs a match to set things alight.'

'I think you're forgetting I've just lost my husband,' Adelaide said, trying to keep her voice calm.

The woman shook her head. 'I'm not forgetting. But I'm speaking out of place. All this talk began with the boy, didn' it? Would you like to see him?'

'Oh yes. May I?'

'Come with me.'

Mrs Pender led the way through a door on the far left side at the back of the room, to a second, furnished in old-fashioned style which was obviously the housekeeper's bedroom. This, in turn opened into a smaller room that from its structure, architecturally, could have been intended when Trenhawk was first built, as a monk's cell. Now it had been converted into extra sleeping quarters, with a small brass bedstead covered by a patchworked quilt pushed against one wall facing the window. The fading afternoon sky cast a quivering pattern of light and shade through the stained glass over the simple deal furniture. A child's picture book lay open, displaying a fantastic drawing of Jacob climbing his perilous ladder to Heaven. A religious text hung on one wall. There was a woolly rug on the floor, where a wax-headed doll meant to resemble a sailor had been thrown. Though no fire was burning, the room felt warm enough to be comfortable. 'Come along,' said Mrs Pender. 'This way.'

She took Adelaide through a further door which opened surprisingly into a small patch of garden enclosed by a high granite wall. Creepers, now losing their colourful Autumn foliage, climbed over the granite. A square of grass was bordered by flowerbeds which would probably make a brilliant display in the summer.

In the centre of the small lawn was a gold-fish pool. The little boy Julian was on his knees staring into it. He had his back to Adelaide and Mrs Pender, but though deaf, he obviously sensed their presence, and jumped up quickly, turning. At first he appeared so startled Adelaide thought he'd try to run away. But there was no one or nowhere to run to; and presently, with fear allayed by the housekeeper's familiar presence, and Adelaide's quiet smile, he walked slowly forward towards Mrs Pender's outstretched hand, and stood with large eyes raised to Adelaide's.

In spite of the fading grey light, his beauty, for a boy, was astonishing, but not so ethereal as he had appeared before, on the landing. The features, though fine, were quite strongly carved under the thick fair hair. One day, Adelaide realised, with a lurch of the heart, he was going to be a handsome man.

'Hello, Julian,' she said, forgetting for the moment he could not hear. She smiled, and his face relaxed slowly into confidence and promise of future acceptance. Then he pulled himself away abruptly from Mrs Pender's hand, and ran back to the pool where the tiny gold bodies flashed to and fro in the water.

As Adelaide followed the housekeeper back into the small room she wondered for a bewildered moment whose likeness she'd glimpsed so fleetingly on the young boy's face.

And then she knew.

She had to conjecture no longer.

Rupert.

Julian was *his* child, or could so easily be – and for some
unfathomable reason, she resented it, knowing at the same
time she had no cause or right to.

Rupert and she were nothing to each other.

Nothing.

V

Anthony St Clare was bored: bored with Harriet Montmerrick the rich highly born dull girl he was doomed to marry,
bored with his enforced months at Carnwikk with an elderly
father who spent half his days hunting and the other half in a
bemused whisky sodden state in his study; and most of all
bored with his grandmother, Lady Serena St Clare, who despite her ninety-five years held the money bags and tyran-
nised the household. She should be locked up, he thought
moodily every time he saw her in her stupid finery – diamonds sparkling from fingers, ears and wrinkled throat. She
had become a hag, mad as a hatter, but with a mind shrewd
enough to know all that was going on and approve or disapprove according to her mood at the time. The sight of her
malicious face poking round a door under her red wig, confronting him from conservatory, drawing room, or walking
ponderously down the hall or one of the landings – head
thrust forward, bony hand enclosing the silver topped stick –
filled him with distaste and resentment. He had no affection
for her any more. When he looked back he realised there had
never been any, but from childhood he'd had to pretend,
simply because Serena St Clare, the daughter of a duke, had
been born to power and seen to it that the St Clares recognised it.

What she demanded was law; without her wealth Carnwikk would have become badly in debt. When it suited her
she could be generous, but only to have them – the family –
'kneeling at her feet', and for her own comfort. The only St
Clare to escape her machinations – apparently – was Anthony's sister Katherine. Probably because she was such a

gentle creature, without looks or ambition, content to spend whatever free time she had from attendance on Serena, quietly painting in her room. She was talented in an unpretentious way. Her water colours of birds and flowers were detailed and sympathetically executed. Even her grandmother had condescendingly agreed she had a certain aptitude – for an amateur. No doubt one day Katherine also would be forced into a marriage of convenience probably with some elderly suitor of sufficient means to whom in due course she'd produce an heir. He would be of good connections, obviously of Catholic faith, and no doubt she'd suffer her married state uncomplainingly.

But at the moment Katherine was emotionally free of family pressure. She had a year, until her 'coming out' season and presentation at court, before the intrigues and cunning matchmaking plans began.

With Anthony everything was very different.

To Anthony it had been indicated in no uncertain terms that he'd marry Harriet Montmerrick in the New Year – or else!

He'd known very well what the threat implied. The old harridan was quite capable of carrying out her word and leaving the whole of her enormous fortune to Katherine instead of himself, should he thwart her command. He could take himself off, of course, and make a new life abroad somewhere – he had a certain comparatively small income of his own. But Anthony St Clare was not the adventurous type or skilled in making a living. Neither was he interested in the Army or throwing his life away fighting. Tradition and luxury mattered to him. Although wild ideas seethed in his head from time to time, he knew fundamentally, his fate was already sealed.

He'd marry Harriet.

If only she was *different* – smaller, and more feminine with less bosom and behind! Her largeness, when seated on a horse or walking into a ballroom, though magnificent, was decidedly off-putting in any romantic sense.

Her features and skin were good, of course. But the mere idea of bedding her was not only mildly frightening, but distasteful.

Katherine, realising his misgivings, was sympathetic.

'I expect it won't be as bad as you think,' she said once to her brother, 'and anyway you've got months yet – '

Yes. Four at the most. Four months in which the old martinet could die or the massive Harriet ensnare some vulnerable beau more to her fancy.

Neither seemed remotely possible.

In the meantime, Anthony, much against his inclination was incarcerated at Carnwikk, which was close enough to the stately Montmerrick mansion near Braggas for frequent social interludes with Harriet who preferred hunting to the busy whirl of town-life in London.

It was natural therefore, that with his last days of freedom looming so depressingly close on the horizon, his imagination should wander occasionally to more accessible, and glamorous pastures – in particular the pathetic young widow of Trenhawk, who he sensed was not half so fragile as she appeared.

Although Carnwikk was a good eight miles from Trenhawk, the estates met on the wide expanse of Tregarrick moor which stretched from the north coast south-westwards. The valleys below were populated only by isolated small hamlets beneath the rocky hills. The St Clare home, built in Tudor times, commanded the landscape. It stood on the site of an older building and was monumental in design, having six storeys, numerous useless towers fairly characteristic of the great gatehouses of that period, and an intricately carved granite face, with ornate gargoyles and Norman arched windows.

If the mansion hadn't been erected in a gentle dip it would have appeared ostentatious, but it was saved from distasteful predominance by its wooded situation, pleasure gardens of verdant lawns and flower beds, and graceful fountains. The gatehouse and court yard were themselves large. Carnwikk, indeed, was considerably more magnificent than most Cornish stately homes. Only the sturdy grey granite was entirely traditional. Viewed from certain angles it had the appearance of some exotic foreign fortress erected to defy invasion.

Naturally, through the centuries it had become accepted as an integral part of the vicinity, like the St Clares themselves who were treated with deference, though they did not 'mix'. As land-owners of most of the country stretching from their domain to the southern coastline they had power. Gossip and criticism of a political and religious nature were carefully kept at a minimum by dependant tenant farmers and the natives of Nanceverrys and George-Town, the two nearby hamlets. Franklyn St Clare, son of the dreaded Serena, and father of Anthony, was tolerated because of his bucolic good humour. Anthony was not. Although open hostility to him was curbed, he was disliked for his proud airs and roving amorous eye for village maidens. One, the daughter of an ostler at a remote kiddeywink, the Ram and Star, had born a son out of wedlock, now three years old, who showed a remarkable likeness to the handsome fair-haired heir of Carnwikk. Tongues wagged in secret, but nothing was said openly. The ostler and his erring daughter flourished, and apparently lived well. The girl grew stout through her misdeeds, and the boy's paternity was discreetly left to conjecture.

Anthony however, was careful never to visit the Ram. The outcome of his brief alliance, though fruitful, was distasteful to him in retrospect.

A romantic affair with the beautiful young widow of David Hawksley would be a different matter altogether, giving the zest of a tonic during the dreary interlude preceding his marriage to Harriet Montmerrick. Meeting her would not prove difficult. During the last few weeks Adelaide had sent for her riding habit from her Aunt Matilda's, purchased for herself a sprightly young mare, Ebony, and already established the routine of taking a gallop most mornings over the moors which had not escaped his notice. Instinctively or by design, her route invariably took her westward, so it was not entirely by chance that Anthony contrived to meet her astride his stallion Wildfire one day in late November.

The brown hill-turf was crisp with frost, the air heady and keen. Overhead a few gulls hovered silver-bright against the pale sky. Adelaide's cheeks held a rose glow beneath a few strands of tumbled gold hair. Her velvet habit, though not black, was of sufficiently dark a green not to outrage her bereaved state. She was conscious that the social proprieties of London would certainly have condemned her riding at all. But the city was hundreds of miles away. For once, in that lonely, expanse of wild country, she felt free – momentarily justified in allowing her senses to respond to the stimulus of wind and cold moorland air.

When Anthony's figure appeared against the skyline her heart seemed to stop for a second, then bounded on again. But she was determined to remain dignified and aloof.

He reined in a few yards facing her, and said, 'How nice to see you.'

'I didn't expect it,' she replied unsmilingly. 'I'd have thought the other coastline was more convenient from Carnwikk.'

'But not half so adventurous or – surprising,' he told her, without the flicker of an eyelash, adding, 'Of course I wasn't really surprised. I hoped we'd meet.'

'Did you? I suppose I should be complimented.'

'No, the other way round. What I mean to say is – any man would count himself lucky to have a few moments in your company.'

'Please – no flattery,' she said sharply. 'I think you forget I'm –'

'Recently widowed and grieving? No, I'm only too aware of it,' he cut in quickly, 'and I wouldn't presume to think I could cheer you up, but a little conversation can be a help sometimes – ' his smile was merely that of a friend – sympathetic and understanding, although his eyes held an ambiguous assessing quality in them which escaped her because she was once more taken aback by his likeness to David.

'As a matter of fact,' he continued, when she did not speak, 'I was wondering if you'd care to drop in for tea one afternoon. I know my sister Katherine would like to meet you – she leads a lonely life. Also – '

'Yes?'

'You mentioned during our too-short coffee interlude in Penjust that you were requiring a maid. I think the sister of one of our parlourmaids might suit. She's wanting a situation, and I'm sure would be trainable. You could speak to her. At the moment she's helping in the kitchen, but I understand from the housekeeper she doesn't like the work. "Above it" is the term used I think – ' his voice trailed off, caught up in a gust of wind.

The young mare suddenly reared impatiently. 'Stop it

Ebony,' Adelaide shouted with a sharp tug at the reins, and when Ebony had quietened again added, 'Would that be appreciated, by your family? I mean – a Hawksley visiting the St Clares? Especially to steal a maid-servant?'

He laughed. 'No. But you can be – what was your single name?'

'Drake.'

'Good. You can be Mrs Adelaide Drake, recently widowed – I'm sorry, I didn't mean to remind you.'

'It's all right,' Adelaide told him, 'I'm getting used to it.'

'You will come then – one day?'

'I'll think about it,' she said, 'and now, if you don't mind, I must be getting back. Ebony's restive.'

'Shall I see you tomorrow?'

'That rather depends which direction I take,' she cried, kicking Ebony to a canter. 'Perhaps.'

A moment later they were both galloping on their separate ways each well satisfied and exhilarated by the brief conversation, although Adelaide would have been ashamed to admit it, even to herself.

As things turned out circumstance interfered with any plans she might have made the next day. Rupert informed her shortly after breakfast that he was setting off for Plymouth later that morning on business – something she gathered, to do with shipping, and would be away probably for a week. He was about the house until twelve, which meant she had no chance of slipping off on Ebony without causing comment. In any case Rupert would be all ears and eyes, and the last thing she wanted was any risk of his scenting her association with Anthony.

It was a nuisance, but probably for the best, she thought, as Carnack appeared at the front door with the gig to take Rupert to Penzance station. An appearance of being eager to see St Clare again might easily give the young man a wrong impression. And after all it wasn't as though she really wished for his friendship, merely that she was vulnerable to anything or anyone so nostalgically able to revive the living impression of her husband.

So she was looking demure and a little sad in her black dress, wearing jet ear-rings, and a lace collar pinned at the neck with the cameo brooch, when Rupert took his farewell, giving her a 'cousinly' kiss which for a second was a little warmer than mere polite affection demanded.

'Goodbye,' he said, 'take care of yourself, and behave – if you can.' He waited before adding, 'You'll have a chance to get to know young Julian better in my absence. I think Mrs Pender might even be grateful – she's got a lot on her hands.'

'Of course,' Adelaide agreed. 'I'll do what I can.'

His eyes seemed to kindle and darken in a long stare that ridiculously confused her. Involuntarily she found herself squeezing her lacy shred of handkerchief into a tight ball in her hand. Then he turned abruptly, running quickly down the steps, to the waiting gig. He looked a dashing figure in a raglan circular cloak over a dark olive green knee-length coat and grey trousers. He carried his black stove-hat in one hand and briefcase in the other; his crisp black hair glistened bright in the noon light. It occurred to Adelaide that many women must admire him, and she wondered vaguely if his visit to Plymouth was in reality a business matter or concerned with some lady of fashion waiting to fling herself into his arms. If so it was none of her concern she told herself staunchly, Rupert had his own life to lead, just as she had hers. So long as he remembered it, there could be no argument between them. But she knew this was mere wishful thinking, because it was Rupert's nature to want to take command. As a boy he'd been arrogant. As a man – well, she pitied any woman he married. Her life would inevitably be one of servitude and obedience to himself and his wretched mine.

She hadn't realised before how she resented his involvement with copper and tin and endless engineering problems. It was ironic that her one weapon, Wheal Tansy, which she'd believed at first could win Trenhawk had become such a bore. With the passing of the weeks, she'd been forced to recognise that if it meant sacrificing the house Rupert would take no help from her for the mine. Sometimes she believed his obstinacy rose from a deliberate personal grudge against her. If it had been anyone else – at this point she always had to admit that Rupert wasn't a malicious person. His inheritance really *was* important to him. If he'd been less bossy and spoiled her a little, she might even have offered him what finance was necessary on a long term loan. She was desperately in need of affection. Rupert could have helped fill the gap left by David's death – if he'd been kinder.

But he hadn't tried. He'd simply played the martinet, told her what she must do, and what not; done all he could in fact, to get her to leave so she was not in his way or poking her nose in, as he put it, when he was plotting and engaged in his stupid illegal smuggling deals. He thought she didn't know about the latter of course. But careless words dropped by Nick, Mrs Pender's fierce defence of the cellars, the memory of the strange 'goings-on' during the night of the gale, all had pointed only to the one conclusion.

The morality of it didn't worry her one bit. But being kept out of things did, because a little shared excitement could have eased her fretting. It was the same with the child. Until she'd discovered his presence for herself, everything had been done to keep her unaware of him.

And why?

Why had she to be treated as some trespassing stranger, when she bore the family name and had been David's wife? And why under the circumstances, had Rupert kissed her in the way he did after she'd returned from the cove that day in the rain?

Her cheeks flamed at the memory.

She felt confused, and in a queer way ashamed of her own emotional lapse.

Rupert was so sure of himself, she thought, as she turned to go back into the house that morning. He'd been just trying to show her up, prove by his overmastering male charm that he'd only to assert himself and she'd fall in with his every mood. And she was not that kind of person. She was herself, still Mrs David Hawksley.

A month ago recalling the past would have acutely saddened her. Now it was as though true feeling was gradually being absorbed by resentment and indignation. She still loved and fretted for David – of course she did. But what she needed was some form of action to take her mind away from Rupert. Once more the titivating thought of Anthony St Clare returned. But it was almost lunch-time; he'd have returned to Carnwikk thinking most probably she didn't want to see him again; so she dismissed any plan of riding until the following day.

Luckily the next morning was fine, and when she rode Ebony at the accustomed hour over Tregarrick moor towards the high southern horizon, her spirits lifted. The weather was warmer than it had been recently, and the frost had thawed into a thin mist hovering in a grey veil over the landscape. Intermittent jagged shapes of ruined mine-works loomed indistinctly to the west, Penjust way. Ahead, the great standing stones of an ancient Druid circle had the appearance of strange elemental beings conjured from wind and rain and the passing of countless centuries. She didn't consciously expect to see him, but there was no surprise in her when his form took shape from the mist – just awe!

Anthony rode like some legendary young monarch of the imagination through the wraith-like air, drawing his mount simultaneously to a halt with hers.

'If it isn't the lovely Adelaide herself,' he said.

She stared.

His voice, manner, and grey-clad misted figure were so weirdly evocative of David, she could think of no word to say, except, 'Hello, – it's – it's a big foggy isn't it – ?' her tones trailed off into silence. He laughed, gently, lowly and appreciatively, as David had so often done.

'I must be dead,' she thought. 'Surely – surely I've died and David's come to meet me –' even though she couldn't accept it with her mind, the illusion persisted. A hand came out to her, which she accepted, allowing him to help her to dismount. Automatically, with no words between them, because none were necessary, he took both horses by their bridles, and tethered them to trees. Then with his arm slipping to her waist he led her through the thickening air to a dip bordered by furze and drenched shining heather.

Very gently he eased her down and lay close, with his lips on her mouth. She was hardly aware of his hands unbuttoning the constricting bodice, or of their sweet wild coming together; only – as she glanced up at him before the moments of consummation – of David's eyes alight on hers, David miraculously reborn from the dead and come to claim her.

'David – David' – something deep within her cried. Her

head fell back, as her form arched to his. Anguish was dispelled in a spasm of unutterable joy. For a second or two afterwards peace and forgetfulness claimed her. Then, all too suddenly, it was over; and following a dazed pause the bitter truth sank in.

She jumped up, pulling her riding skirt tightly round her body. Her face, white and ravaged, was lifted to the grey sky. All beauty had gone, all warmth faded to death-like chill.

'Go away,' she screamed, 'go – go.'

'But, Adelaide –'

She wheeled on him in a fury.

'How *could* you? I hate you – hate you, do you understand?' Even through the fog the distortion of her features appeared witchlike, inhuman.

'I think you must be mad,' he said with cold contempt. 'But I should probably have expected it – from a Hawksley.'

He jerked his breeches and coat into order, and while a spate of abuse still left her lips, untethered Wildfire and was away.

The little vixen, he thought as he kicked the stallion to full speed, who the devil did she think she was? And what the hell did it matter anyway? Perhaps after all it was a good thing he was off to London next week for a week's social spree with Harriet, who had surprisingly agreed only the previous day to accompany him for once.

Long after Anthony had gone Adelaide sat chilled to her bones, on a slab of wet granite, motionless and static as the rock itself. Her gold hair straggled loose over her shoulders, her eyes were glazed and unseeing. Nearby, Ebony still tethered, waited.

When at last Adelaide forced herself to her feet, a faint glimmer behind the mist predicted that watery sunlight was on its way. She pushed her hair under her hat, and still dazed, tidied herself automatically. Then she freed the mare, mounted, and started back for Trenhawk.

She knew that nothing would ever be the same again.

She had betrayed David.

And Rupert?

She did not dare to think of him.

From her sitting room window old Lady Serena St Clare had watched her grandson riding to the left, towards the stables. He had a savage air about him as he kicked his horse to increasing speed. In one of his tempers obviously. She knew so well the glowering look there'd be on his handsome face, and her old heart quickened with indignation. Spoiled – that's what he was; probably been sent packing by some pert little miss, or an outraged father. If her son had had any spirit in him he'd have taken a stick to his back long before this. But Franklyn had no character. He was nothing but an amiable alcoholic who could no longer even sit his horse properly. A disgrace to the St Clares. They'd be nowhere, any of them but for her. And at her age. How old was she? – Ninety-five? A hundred? What did it matter? – as time passed years counted less so long as the will remained to keep going. And *she* had the will, egad, being born a Ferriell. She'd hang on till the last possible breath, if only to spite them all. Of course her granddaughter Katherine was a nice little thing, but dull; no colour. There'd have to be a tempting dowry for her. But Anthony! drat the boy. She'd no doubts at all, that day he'd been playing ducks and drakes again with some available chit silly enough to believe his soft speeches. Her irritation increased.

In one of his moods there was no telling what stupid situation he'd land up in. Heaven forfend if there was a second Ram and Star affair. She'd cut him off, she would, she would, she decided hotly; – leave all her wealth to Katherine so the young reprobate had to plead with his sister or wife for any extravagance that appealed to him. And that would be a trial to him. Anthony was all extravagance. He couldn't live without his pleasures. Still – she didn't want it to happen. But she decided abruptly the time had come to have a little tour round the district and see what was going on there. Katherine luckily was in Penzance on some Church business – just like her! – and Anthony by then was probably closeted with his father in a drinking session. A malicious touch of irony crossed her ancient features as she thought grimly, 'Good luck to him. Once Harriet's installed there'll be no more of that.'

She reached for her stick, heaved herself to her feet, and touched the bell. Her maid Crawford whose room adjoined her bedroom in Serena's private wing, entered the sitting room after her habitual three short taps. She was elderly, wearing black silk, with a spotless white frilled apron and lace cap on her thinning grey hair.

'Tell that girl – what's her name – Marie, to inform Barnes I want the carriage,' Serena said in her thin voice which though a little shaky was still fiercely imperious. 'Then come back and help me dress. I'm going out.'

Crawford's mouth gaped. 'But m'lady – in this weather?'

'What's the matter with the weather? I shall wear my purple velvet furs, and you heard what I said – the carriage. I'm no weakling, but you can tell them to see the foot-warmer's there, and have Pom-Pom's coat put on. He'll keep my lap warm.' Pom-Pom was Serena's pet dog, a long haired miniature King Charles spaniel.

The maid, who when the time came to retire would be installed comfortably as a family retainer at Carnwikk, hurried to do her mistress's bidding, while Serena leaning on her stick made her own way to her bedroom. This particular private domain in the mansion was luxuriously furnished in a manner providing the maximum of comfort. Fires burned welcomingly in the four rooms; the carpets were thick; chairs and sofas were upholstered in crimson velvet or brocade, and French style elegance was exemplified everywhere by shining gilt, exquisite cut glass, and ceilings and friezes embossed with angels and fleurs-de-lys.

When Crawford returned Serena was already waiting impatiently for her services, pushing her head forward at intervals close against the oval mirror, trying hard through screwed-up eyes, to see if her wig was straight on her head, and sufficient rouge on her cheeks. Of the latter there was more than enough, but Crawford was too tactful to say so. She took the heavy fur-trimmed velvet cape and hood from the wardrobe, arranged it round her mistress's shoulders, after first ensuring jewelled pins and flowers were firmly placed in the ornate head-piece, the diamond brooch securely pinned near the withered throat, and the brandy flask safely installed in the reticule in case of emergencies.

'Now m'lady, shall I get Barnes to help you down the stairs?' the faithful servant suggested when the tedious ritual was over.

'Barnes? Who wants that cumbrous fellow?' Serena half shrieked alluding to the under-footman. 'You'll do. I ain't an invalid. Get down the stairs often enough on my own, don't I? When I can't use them I'll have a suite below. Come along now. Don't waste time, woman. Want to get away before that nosey-parker grandson of mine gets bothersome with his "don't-do-that, Grandmama – where are you going, Grandmama?" Pah! as if he cared! as if anyone cared except for what I've got.'

She was still muttering as Crawford assisted her down the stairs. But once she was seated in the carriage with Pom-Pom on her knees, she lifted her head regally, bowed slightly to Crawford, dismissing her, and before the coachman closed the door said, 'Call at the Pengelly cottage first. A little gift at this time of the year won't come amiss. Who knows – I may not be around that way again before Christmas. Oh – and Watford –'

'Yes, m'lady?'

'There's someone I'd like to see at the Ram and Star.'

Whatever Watford thought he kept to himself. His expression was ambiguously negative when he said, 'Yes, m'lady.'

'Get going then. Don't waste time. Hate hanging about.'

A minute later the St Clare carriage behind its two greys was moving down the drive through the gates of Carnwikk into the lane. As it turned the corner a self-satisfied little smile twitched the corners of the old 'madam's' lips. In the silvered light of sun the wrinkles of her face and mouth were crinkled into a network of tiny criss-crossed lines. No trace remained of the beauty that had once been hers. Her profile, against the window glass resembled more that of some gaudy ancient macaw than a human being's. The little dog on her lap gazed at her in adoration as her old hand by turns stroked and patted him. He was far too stout, and in his old age dribbled. But their affection for each other was mutual. To Serena, Pom-Pom had virtues she no longer looked for in humanity. It was her secret conviction that when Pom-Pom shuffled off his doggy coil the sad event would be herald of her own demise. But before that inevitable occurrence she was determined life at Carnwikk should be well-ordered to her wishes. Anthony would have to inherit, but Harriet, by then, would be in command domestically. It would be made worth her while to keep him as far as possible to the straight-and-narrow. And she was the type to breed well. Good hips, and a lusty appetite beneath her boring exterior. Anthony once married would have no time to go a-whoring.

All the same, Serena's curiosity to see the little bastard at the Ram and Star got the better of her that day. Always put her off in the past they had – that fine family of hers; but she'd heard things. In spite of fitful noises in her head, her hearing was good, and her old eyes saw more than folk thought she did. Oh yes – she'd caught whispers and noticed looks. Well that day she'd learn the truth of things for herself.

The carriage drew up at the Pengelly cottage first – a small clob building where the widow of a farm labourer lived with her two children, a boy and girl. There'd been an elder son who'd stupidly taken himself off from land work on the Carnwikk estate to go to sea. He'd been drowned after a year, and the woman had carried on the smallholding by herself. Serena had heard her reputation wasn't too savoury any more – got herself friendly with a tinner who worked at the Hawksley mine, and Anthony had got Franklyn to cut off the small allowance made. Just like him, she thought as the carriage drew to a halt – overbearing, arrogant, greedy for his own ends and not a whit concerned about anyone else. She'd no liking for the Hawksleys herself, an upstart heretical lot, but women were women and men were men. And whatever the rights and wrongs of the association between Ruth Pengelly and the miner, the children were not to blame, poor little things.

Old and fierce as she might be, deep down Serena had a weakness for children and animals. Salt of the earth they were, as she'd discovered through her long life. No guile about them or treachery. If they liked you they showed it, and if they didn't you soon knew.

So she was already fumbling in her gold chain bag for coins when her coachman walked smartly up the narrow path to the door.

What a hovel it was, she thought, peering ahead, and what a smell came from the cess-pit a few yards away. She took a small bottle of cologne from her bag, sprinkled it liberally over her jewelled front applying it also to a shred of embroidered lawn from a pocket. She sniffed deeply, and fortified herself with a nip from the brandy flask. Then she thrust her head forward, and waited to spring her surprise. After a moment the woman appeared with the boy in front, the girl held tightly by the hand, Ruth Pengelly had a worn, untidy look about her, though she must once have been handsome. Her black hair was now streaked with grey, and her mouth and eyes had a defensive, truculent look. The children appeared shy and un-smiling waifs, too thin through under-nourishment, and more cowed than they should have been. The mother's tongue no doubt was frequently over sharp, and her hand hard, Serena thought with indignation.

'Come here – ' she called in her rasping old voice, pushing the door open a few inches. 'Come here, you two – I shan't hurt you – ' the rings flashed on her gnarled finger as she beckoned.

Ruth pushed the children forward and followed hesitantly.

'Hungry, are you?' Serena asked, affronted by their mute fearful glances. 'Take these then – ' she pushed out a bag of lollipops. 'They were for Pom-Pom, but he's fat enough. Like to stroke Pom-Pom, would you? – ' she pressed the snub doggy nose to the little boy's hand which was already enclosing the lollipops. The little girl came forward and patted the spaniel's head. His tongue came out and she drew back involuntarily.

'Nothing to be afraid of. He likes you,' the old lady said, nodding approvingly. Then she glanced at the woman. 'These children need more to eat. Take this – ' she handed several sovereigns from the mesh bag, 'and see it's spent in the way it's meant – for food. If it's not I shall know. So no games with that Hawksley miner at the Ram and Star. If you behave yourself and look after the children as you should, there'll be more help for you from time to time. If you don't – ' the old eyes narrowed and became slits of fire – 'I'll have you all sent packing to the poorhouse. Understand?'

The woman gave a little curtsey.

'Yes, m'lady. Of course, m'lady. Tedn' that I doan' want things for my chillun. Et's with nuthen' comin in, you see. An the green's edn' s'good this year. The pig took sick and died afore it was ready, and the taties es pore. Then – '

'I know, I know.' Serena's voice was irritable, the temper rising in a flush on her raddled cheeks. 'You needn't explain, woman. Just remember what I said – and unless you want typhus round here see the place is cleaned up. I shall report this smell to my son and see if your slops can't be dealt with differently. Another cess-pit perhaps, away from the cottage.'

Ruth eyed her with a hint of aggressive contempt, though she tried to hide it. What did that painted up old harridan know of poverty, she thought, as the carriage drove away. If she hadn't needed the guineas so desperately she'd have thrown them in her face.

Yes m'lady! no m'lady! of course, m'lady!

Damn her, oh damn her, she cried inwardly, seizing the two children roughly and dragging them back to the cottage. Then her mood suddenly changed. She slumped on a chair by the rough deal table with her head in her hands, knowing that instead of cursing she should be blessing that afternoon and Lady Serena's visit.

It would mean that for the next few weeks they could be sure of food for their bellies.

As for the cess pit – she'd grown so used to the stink it no longer registered. But if the big house was willing to provide another she'd welcome it. She wasn't by nature a drab.

Just tired.

Meanwhile the carriage made its way through the thread-work of lanes to the Ram and Star. The Kiddeywink stood back from the narrow track, near a disused clay pit that had a dusty sad look with its grey mounds and brooding pools. A few cottages were dotted about the forlorn landscape, built of clob, though the inn itself was of granite, with a sign sticking from a post at one side.

The carriage drew up. The coachman got down, walked to the door and rapped sharply. It was opened by a burly middle-aged figure wearing an apron over his portly stomach. His expression was slightly hostile.

'Ais?'

'I have a message from her ladyship – Lady Serena St Clare. You have a young child here. Madam would be much obliged – and it would be to the infant's advantage if they could make brief acquaintance – without the mother, if you please.'

After a few grudging comments the man went to the back of the building and quickly returned with the small child. Serena watched their approach through screwed up eyes behind lorgnettes. He was not badly dressed, and was obviously cared for. Given good grooming and wearing fancy clothes he could pass for any duke's son. And his likeness to that reprobate grandson of hers was chillingly uncanny. She beckoned them. The little boy followed the coachman reluctantly, pushed ahead by the stout figure.

'Open the door,' Serena commanded.

'But, madam – '

'Don't madam me,' Serena shrieked. 'I shan't wilt away.'

The servant bowed respectfully and unlatched the carriage door letting six inches of air blow in. Serena drew her furs half over her face leaving only a beak of a nose visible under the piled up wig which was already toppling slightly. Diamonds winked. Her eyes blazed with fiery curiosity. 'Who are you?' she demanded of the man.

'His grandfather,' came the answer, a trifle belligerently. 'My daughter's his mother.'

'Hm!' Serena considered him with a hint of malicious humour. 'Related by chance, if not by law', she thought acidly, then said peremptorily. 'Show him to me. Here, boy. Want to take a proper look at you.'

The child shrunk back, but was pushed forward purposefully. Serena stared. The young eyes were blue, very blue – Anthony's eyes; the mop of bright fair hair crowned an intelligent forehead and perfectly formed features – the St Clare features of many generations crowding the galleries of Carnwikk. She felt affronted, yet secretly amused at this quirk of nature.

'What's your name, boy?'

He stared at her solemnly. His grandfather shook him. 'Go on then – tell the lady y'r name.'

'Tom,' the little boy said.

'Tom Davy,' his grandfather added promptly.

'Well, Tom,' the old lady said, 'like a peppermint, would you?' she fumbled in the bag once more for sweets, then pushed the whole lot into his hand. 'There you are then, and a guinea or two besides – ' as her fingers struggled with the reticule the thin incredibly gnarled and veined hand spotted with dark patches was visible for a second. The child stared fascinated. 'Take good care of 'em,' she muttered. 'No throwing about now, and you – ' to the man, 'see they're used for his benefit. And be sure he keeps one as a – memento shall we say. Now – go on, off with you. Not so young as I once was; the air's cold – ' she waved her arm in dismissal, and gave a signal to the coachman. The next minute the carriage was moving down the lane, and presently took a curve that eventually joined the main route back to Carnwikk.

'Not a word to anyone, understand?' Serena said, as she was helped from the vehicle. 'Keep your mouth shut or you'll be out before you know it, and with no reference from me.'

'Of course, m'lady. You can trust me.'

'Hm! I hope so. For your sake.' She handed the dog to him, and after he'd helped her up the front steps, insisted on going into the house alone.

All her intentions of secrecy dissolved when she saw Anthony coming down the main hall. He was flushed, and she knew he had been drinking.

'Where have you been, Grandmama?' he queried when he saw her tottering towards him, looking like some ancient crone from a pantomime; she was leaning on her stick, with her chin thrust forward aggressively.

'Where? What's it got to do with you?'

'It's cold outside. You should take care of yourself.'

'Take care of myself, should I? Ha!' she lifted a finger waggishly. 'You're a fine one to talk. Where've I been? As if you cared. But I'll tell you – to see your bastard. That's where I've been. And don't try any lies on me. The living spit of you he is, poor little thing – '

'Why you old – ' Anthony fought with his rage.

She laughed, showing two yellowed fangs of teeth.

'Get out of my way. And you behave yourself in future, or I'll disown you and leave all I've got to him understand? Weak you are. Weak and spineless. Never could abide cowards. If you'd any spunk you'd have acknowledged the boy and been out in the open. A blackguard? Yes. I've respected many a blackguard in my time – but your sort – never – '

She was still muttering breathlessly when Crawford appeared, to help her into the drawing room. Once seated in a chair her breathing gradually eased, and a bluish colour mounted her cheeks beneath the rouge.

'Will you have a hot drink, m'lady?' Crawford asked in practical tones, knowing how her mistress disliked a fuss.

'Not hot, strong.' Serena answered. 'Whisky this time I think. And I tell you what – we'll both have one, together – in your own little hidey-hole. So if you'll just help me upstairs we'll imbibe together.'

'Oh m'lady!' Crawford looked abashed.

Serena leaned forward and gave her an impish dig in the thigh. 'Come along now, I know you. Been together a fair long time. Long enough to let the barriers down occasionally, eh?'

Crawford smiled doubtfully, but didn't make the mistake of arguing.

Presently the two of them began to mount the stairs slowly to Serena's private wing.

Anthony stood glowering at the library door. 'Blast the old witch,' he thought. What a devil she was, reviving antagonism against him in the district. And daring to threaten him.

Obviously the sooner he married Harriet the better. A legal heir would divert her meddling into affairs at the Ram and Star, and also erase for good the taunting memory of Adelaide Hawksley's insulting behaviour.

Harriet might not be a beauty; but a refuge – yes. And at the moment the thought of her was comforting.

VI

The days dragged for Adelaide. With Rupert away try as she would she couldn't help despondency deepening in her. Once or twice she forced herself to make overtures to little Julian. But the child was unforthcoming, and simply stared at her with a kind of questioning wonder in his blue eyes, then turned and ran away. Mrs Pender's glance also was curious.

'You look pale, Miss Adelaide,' she said more than once. 'The weather isn't bad considerin' we're so near Christmas. Why don't you go out for a walk or something? An' what about that horse o' yours? For three days you haven't looked at it –'

Adelaide shrugged. 'I don't feel like riding. I'm all right.'

'Well – you seem wisht' to me.'

'I've told you, I'm all right. Please don't fuss,' Adelaide said more sharply than she'd meant.

Mrs Pender sniffed, turned, and went to the kitchen. She had almost said, 'Don't think you can talk that way to *me*, young woman,' but had caught the words back, remembering that whatever shortcomings the girl had, she was obviously a bit unbalanced by her husband's death. One had to be charitable.

Charitable. Adelaide would have scoffed at the word. Charity was the last thing she'd want under any circumstances. The only thing she needed was the impossible – to have the clock miraculously put back so David could come through the door and tell her everything was all right. She toyed with the idea of returning to town, but the thought of facing the sympathy and determined efforts of acquaintances to distract and amuse her was unbearable. Aunt Matilda, of course, was a dear. But the commiseration in her voice and sad soulful gaze of her eyes would only make matters a hundred times worse. Her gentle, elderly relative was so kind and worthy. So trusting. To meet such trust would strain her to the limit and be sure to end up on a scene of defiance.

Besides, whatever happened, Adelaide was still stubborn about Trenhawk. She had become possessive. It was her refuge – her rightful home. She would stay.

On the evening before Rupert's return from Plymouth, she wandered along the corridors to the stone stairs leading up to the Tower Room. The air was cold there, shivering in icy waves down the spiralling steep steps. Hardly aware of her intention she climbed automatically to the studded door, one hand pressed to the wall for support. She hesitated a moment before turning the iron drop-handle. It opened with a grating sound, sending a shivering gleam of light through the shadows. Adelaide waited a second, then took a step inside. High in the ancient granite wall was a small monastic-style stained glass window. She looked up and it seemed to her golden beams lit with translucent blue, quivered into a blurred eerie shape through the cobwebs and dust of years. No sound penetrated the unearthly silence. Yet for a brief time the small space was vibrant with unseen life; life so compelling Adelaide could not move or tear her eyes away. Then as she stood motionless, the face she had glimpsed those many years before seemed to emerge in luminous clarity.

Dark pools of eyes spread and enveloped her. The massed shadows became flowing hair, and a whisper that could have been merely the wind's sighing from outside stirred the strange quietness. There was nothing frightening in it – only a sensation of troubled yearning. Yet Adelaide was perturbed, and with a sudden claustrophobic urge to escape, turned and rushed from the tower, closing the heavy door behind her.

She leaned against it, breathing heavily until the hammering of her heart eased. Then, as her senses and eye-sight came into focus she turned her head and glanced down. Below her, the narrow staircase coiled and twisted snake-like to the wider corridors below; from there a glimpse of the ground floor could be seen, with a glimmer of light from the fading sky or lamp in the hall.

The effect was like looking from a dark and narrow abyss into another world. How easy, she thought, to slip over the narrow rail into the terrifying empty vortex which would mean inevitable death. No wonder Julian was not allowed there. And how careless that the door should have been left unlocked. Someone must have been up there.

But who?

Puzzling over the question gave her a chance to recover her nerve, and grasping the rail tightly she presently made her way down and along the wide landing to her own room.

When she got there the evening sky was already dark. Candles were alight in their accustomed places, the fire bright and glowing. Though recovered, she still felt in a dream. She remembered stories she'd heard in childhood of Charles Hawksley who'd married Marguerite St Clare, both of whom had died at the hands of Marguerite's brother. The young baby who'd survived as ancestor of both families, had been cursed by St Clare, who'd decreed that every elder son of following Hawksleys should meet an untimely death.

How much of the story was true, and how much fiction, Adelaide had never known.

But sitting on the bed, with the fitful shadows round her, she was comforted by the conviction that if indeed, the Tower Room was haunted, its ghost was benign rather than threatening. She had been frightened merely by the unknown.

Rupert returned late in the afternoon the following day. He was in an optimistic almost ebullient mood, having manipulated a highly successful deal with a rich acquaintance concerned not only in shipping, but as a wealthy merchant in the wool trade. Always a philanthropist when it came to the point, and well able to take a considerable risk without harm to his peace of mind, the ageing magnate had been induced, under the influence of good wine and Rupert's persuasive ability, to invest handsomely in Wheal Tansy, which meant finance from Adelaide would not be necessary for the mine's immediate exploration.

So Rupert emotionally and practically, was off the hook, where feminine blackmail was concerned.

The knowledge instantly made him feel more kindly disposed and sympathetic to her.

'Has everything been all right?' he asked her over the evening meal. 'No worries in my absence?' He thought she looked more strained and tense than usual – even a little less beautiful, with her ringed eyes, and hair drawn back.

She shook her head. 'I'm perfectly all right. Why?'

He shrugged. 'No reason. You've lost your colour. The weather perhaps.'

'Yes,' she answered shortly, looking down at her plate.

'Have you been riding?'

The question took her unawares.

'Once or twice. Ebony needs regular exercise.'

'You can always get Nick to take her.'

'I know that, Rupert. But I don't want to drag him from his regular work.'

Her statement wrily amused him.

'How considerate of you, Addy,' he said drily.

A faint colour rose to her cheeks. 'Was your business trip successful?' she asked, steering the subject from riding.

'Highly. Financially and socially. The problem of Wheal Tansy's solved.'

Her heart bounded and stopped in its beat for a moment. 'What do you mean? Are you going to sell or something?'

He laughed. 'To the contrary. I'm going to work the place like the devil, expand in labour and machinery and be damned to expense. The red streams will see daylight at last. Trenhawk will be rich again, cousin dear. So take that dour look off your beautiful face and celebrate.'

He forced more wine on her than she was used to, or wanted, while her numbed senses fought for an acceptance of the truth. As her heart quickened something like panic seized her. She put her glass down glancing at her portion of admirably cooked chicken pie with sudden distaste. Rupert didn't miss the gesture. 'Lost your appetite? Come *on*, Addy. Surely you don't grudge me my good fortune?'

'Of course not,' she managed to say. 'I congratulate you.'

'Then show it for God's sake. You look – ' he paused contemplatingly adding, 'as if you'd lost a shilling and found sixpence.'

She sighed. 'Rupert, I've a headache. I'm sorry. But I'm glad for you. Of course I am.'

'Then eat your food, empty your glass, and be happy for yourself as well as me.'

'Why should I be?'

'Running Trenhawk will be easier from now on. I'll be able to be generous and even employ a maid for you. That is, of course, if you still intend staying on for some time.'

When she didn't answer he persisted, 'Well, Adelaide?'

'I don't really see why you should,' she told him doubtfully. 'Employ a maid – for me – I mean.'

'No, neither do I. But as owner of Trenhawk I prefer any staff working here to be paid from my own pocket. I'm that kind of man, which you should realise by now. So it's natural I should want to know your intentions before I go to any unnecessary expense.'

Adelaide's flush returned. How pompous he sounded, she thought.

'You always want things your way, Rupert. I'd have thought you could have given me a little time to think. And it isn't easy to get servants. I interviewed two – they were hopeless – '

'You've had weeks, months, to plot and plan. It's been no secret has it? On your very first day here you made it clear you wanted me out of my own place and you in.' He paused. 'I'm sorry to be so blunt, but things just haven't worked out the way you wanted. That often happens in life, Adelaide, and when – '

'Don't preach!' she cried, jumping to her feet, with her hazel eyes brightening to burning gold. 'I don't want telling what to do and how to behave – especially by you – '

'No. But you damn well need it,' he said explosively, suddenly losing his temper. 'And while you're in my house I shall continue to do it. Understand?'

'I'm sure you will. But let me tell you, Rupert Hawksley – '

His anger evaporated as quickly as it had flared up. He got up, took her arm, and forced her to sit again. 'Addy – Addy – ' he said cajolingly. 'Don't scratch so. What's the matter with you, I told you at the beginning you could make Trenhawk your home for so long as you wanted. Well then – why the fuss?'

'You didn't quite put it that way,' she said, calming down. 'You said I could stay – as a guest. That's not the same thing at all.'

'No,' he agreed, 'I see your point. Let me remedy it then: let me say, "Cousin Adelaide, if you want to live here – if that's really your wish, I'll be delighted." ' He waited, watching her intently, noting the ebb and flow of colour in her cheeks, the slight tremor of her underlip which gave her momentarily the vulnerable look of a child. A flood of tenderness filled him. He'd have liked to take her in his arms, putting his lips to her forehead and then her cheek gently pressing her golden head close against him. But he contained himself and queried in matter-of-fact tones after several seconds had passed, 'Well? What do you say?'

'Thank you,' she answered, with an effort at dignity. 'I'd like to stay.'

'That's settled then,' he told her with relief. 'And now let's forget this tedious conversation. You haven't finished your wine. Take it, Addy, drink up.'

'No, Rupert, please. I've had so much already. I shall be quite –'

'Drunk,' he interrupted. 'Good. Then you'll be at my mercy, won't you? Come to think of it I've never yet seen you properly inebriated. Or are you afraid?'

The question acted in just the way he'd anticipated. She lifted the glass to her lips and quaffed the very good Madeira in two quick gulps.

He laughed.

'I'm sure you'll feel better now. And you need have no fears, Addy, I'd never take advantage of a lady under the influence – especially you.'

The significance of the last sentence escaped her. Her senses were gradually responding to the mellowing comfort of the wine. Presently, when they'd retired to the drawing room for coffee, most worries had faded from Adelaide's mind, although the frail shadow of a niggle remained – a distant hazy reminder of a fair young face staring down on her through a swimming sea of fog – David, Anthony? Or – she felt her forehead, already damp with slowly welling fear.

Rupert was concerned to see her hand shaking.

'Addy –' he pressed the coffee to her lips. 'Are you ill? Good God, that wine. I'm a damned fool.'

'It's all right,' she managed to say as the hot liquid revived her. 'I'm really quite all right.'

'You will be, when you're tucked up in bed.'

He lifted her in his arms, and a quiver of desire mingled

with pity stirred him. She was staring at him in a bewildered way. Though strong and taut under his velvet coat, his body trembled and his voice was thick when he said, 'I'll send Mrs Pender to you; she'll see you have everything you need.'

He carried her upstairs, and did not have to go to the kitchens to find the housekeeper; she was already about on the landing when they turned the bend.

Her mouth was tight, her small eyes hostile as she came towards them. 'Has there been an accident?' she asked. 'What's the matter with Mrs David?' Her sniff of disgust implied unmistakably she was in no doubt at all, and that she thoroughly disapproved.

'My cousin was feeling unwell at dinner,' Rupert answered calmly, 'and the wine obviously disagreed with her.' He waited for Mrs Pender to open the bedroom door, then put Adelaide very gently on to her feet. 'Perhaps you'll see everything is made comfortable,' he said, 'and that the fire is ready stacked up for the night.'

'I shall do all that's necessary,' Mrs Pender answered primly, 'an, if I may say so, surr, you look in need of a rest yourself.'

Accepting the rebuke for what it really implied – that he appeared in a perturbed, emotional state, Rupert, without another glance at Adelaide, muttered something under his breath, and went to his own premises.

Before sleep came to him that night, his thoughts which during the day had been so exclusively concerned with plans for Wheal Tansy, had taken an astonishingly perverse turn. Adelaide's face, and hers only, invaded his mind. A damned nuisance, he told himself, and proof that a charming woman could work havoc with a man's routine and ambitions.

But not his, he determined; she'd either come to heel and fit in with life as he intended it to be at Trenhawk, or – the alternative escaped him, because at that crucial moment he drifted into unconsciousness.

VII

Christmas came and went with a show of festivity that
Adelaide was far from feeling. But as a sop to her conscience
and in an attempt to push the memory of her moorland
interlude with Anthony to the back of her mind, she flung
herself with assumed zest into the gathering of servants and
tenant farmers who assembled at Trenhawk for the annual
seasonal party.

Carols were sung first. Afterwards, in the large hall and
parlour Rupert drank the health of everyone from a bowl of
spiced ale which was passed in turn to the others. The scene
was a merry one, lit by candles and the 'kissing bush' sus-
pended by the hall window. It consisted of two wooden hoops
fastened into each other at right angles and covered by ever-
green, fruit, and furze. Inside a single candle flared effectively.

Adelaide could not recall any similar ceremony during the
few Christmases of her childhood at Trenhawk. Uncle William
had been conservative, and except for Christmas morning
when family presents had been taken from the traditional tree,
there had been a good deal of solemn hymn-singing and
Church.

Out of deference to the occasion Rupert did accompany her
to the mid morning service at St Rozzan. She wore complete
black, with her face discreetly hidden behind the black
widow's veil, yet she was conscious of many eyes turned upon
her as she walked to the family pew on Rupert's arm, followed
by Mrs Pender, Carnack, Nick, Lucy, and the Merryns – the
couple installed only recently at the manor in Elizabeth's
place. Rupert had stipulated they must live in and take full
responsibility for the running of the farm's domestic side –
something Elizabeth had been unable to do. So far the arrangement had worked well. Joe Merryn was useful on the
land; Anne his wife was a good cook and quite capable of
managing the dairy.

The church itself dated from the fourteenth century. Its granite porch led through a graceful Tudor arch into a surprisingly spacious interior which was illuminated that day by candles, hanging lamps, and a rich assortment of flowers. Adelaide tried hard to concentrate on the service, but her eyes were tired through too many restless nights and lack of sleep, and she was relieved when the praying and singing were over. She had, as well, a slight headache.

The air outside which was cold, with a flurry of snow in it, revived her a little, enabling her to appear more sociable than she felt. But Rupert was mildly critical of her sombre appearance.

'It's a pity you had to look quite so dreary,' he said on their way home in the gig. 'You appear so conspicuous in all that black stuff.'

'Why shouldn't I?'

'Of course; no reason at all, if you want to draw attention to yourself.'

'Wouldn't it have been more conspicuous if I'd appeared in frilly finery?' she said.

'How you exaggerate. I didn't suggest finery. Just that you should buck up now and make the most of yourself. For your own sake.'

'Why my sake?'

'Well then for others,' he told her. 'There's enough gloom about without having to add to it.'

She stiffened.

'I'm sorry you find me depressing.'

'Oh, Adelaide, stop it,' he snapped, 'you're not sorry at all. Ever since I returned from Plymouth you seem to have lost even the capacity to smile. I could understand at the beginning. Naturally you had to have time to recover. But that was months ago. I'd rather have you spitting and scratching than like this.' He paused, then continued – more quietly, 'What's the matter, Addy?'

'Matter?'

'That's what I said.'

'Nothing more than usual, she told him, turning her face away. 'And I'll try to be more cheerful in future. Even if it's –'

'Only a pretend game?' he prompted, recalling a game she'd

played when a very young child.

'Yes.'

He slowed the gig up, and before she knew what he was about, lifted the veil from her face, pushing it to the back of her small bonnet-hat.

Her face was pale, and vulnerable; her hazel eyes bright in their shadows above the high cheek-bones.

'Tears, Addy?' Rupert queried gently.

For a moment she didn't reply, then she began, 'I wish –'

'What?'

How could she possibly tell him? How could she possibly say, 'I wish I could put the clock back. Oh how I wish you'd never gone to Plymouth, Rupert, and that I'd not met Anthony St Clare on the moor –'

But of course she couldn't. So she shook her head dumbly, and with a shrug and flick of the whip he started the mare up again at a sharper pace, taking the gig rattling along the rough lane to Trenhawk.

January was a dismal month of intermittent rain and mists. Except for occasional visits of Rupert's business acquaintances there was no company at Trenhawk. Adelaide found such occasions not only boring but wearying. Although commiserations and compliments were delivered dutifully on her behalf, the men concerned were primarily occupied with mining or their own private ventures in which Rupert was expected – hopefully – to play a part. If she'd felt in better health she might have found a certain titivating stimulus in watching the subtle by-play, and Rupert's cleverness in manipulating arguments to his own ends; but her own problems absorbed her completely. She dreaded the spring ahead.

'I don't know why you stick here, Miss Adelaide,' Mrs Pender said one day, seeing Adelaide staring out of the hall window. 'January's never a good month in Cornwall, and it seems to me you need a change.'

'Perhaps,' Adelaide agreed. 'I'll think about it.'

'You could always come back for the spring,' the housekeeper continued. 'The house'll be brighter then an' easier to run. The master's gettin' fresh help in, which will ease me, I

must admit. Lucy's all right as far as she goes, but slow.
There are times I remember far back in the past when we
had a butler and footman, and parlour maid *and* a cook. O'
course it was before things went wrong with Wheal Tansy –'

'I remember,' Adelaide cut in shortly.

'Hm. Well, a body my age can't forever shoulder work that
isn't hers by right. I've bin thinkin' for sometime that if Mr
Rupert's set on stayin' here all the time he should see about
getting a cook in right away. There's the boy too. Oh he's a
good little thing, but you can't scold or discipline him like an
ordinary child, not as he is – ' she sighed. 'Oh well, you'll do
what you choose, I s'pose, like you always did.'

'Yes.'

But Adelaide knew her answer wasn't strictly true. She'd
do what she had to. What she'd dreaded for the past few
weeks. She'd somehow have to contact Anthony St Clare.

She was very frightened.

At nights when she lay wakeful in the large bed, listening
to the cold wind beating and whistling round the walls, she'd
been so scared every muscle shook with ague. Not scared of
ghosts this time, but of herself – her own body, and what it
told her. At the beginning, following her first missed period,
she'd managed to shrug the matter off as an attack of nerves,
telling herself fear could easily upset nature's rhythm in such
a way. But now she knew there was no escaping the truth.
She was with child, and Anthony was the father. There could
be no one else. Months had passed since David's death. The
developing baby she carried couldn't by any stretch of
imagination be his. If it had been how different things would
be. She'd have had something she could really care for – a
child born without shame or taint. Looking back to that
fateful meeting with Anthony on the moor, she was shocked
that she'd been so easily able to accept him in passion as
David.

And Rupert? How was she going to explain to him? There
was no answer. She couldn't; because facts to him were facts,
and she could imagine, the inward contempt he'd feel if she
said, 'It was all a mistake – I was so longing for David, and
Anthony was there, looking just like him. It was David I
wanted – '

That, at least, was true. But it was true also that she'd given herself to Anthony. Deep in her heart she'd known it at the time, but blinded herself to the fact. There was no escape. All she could do was to face Anthony so they could share things together.

It didn't occur to her he might refuse, being a St Clare and she the widow of a Hawksley. He'd been kind and gentle to her at their first meeting in Penjust, and though their recent parting had been stormy following their brief lovemaking, it was she who'd abused and taunted him first. *She* who was to blame for the quarrel. He'd marry her surely? He'd have to when he knew. Then the stupid family quarrel could be ended for good and in time they might fall in love properly and have more children. Rupert would probably be pleased to have everything so conveniently settled. As always her mind wandered again to Rupert, and she thought how ironic it was the one person she'd resented in the past was the one now she longed to turn to for advice and couldn't.

Rupert.

On a day in early February she set off on Ebony for a canter over the moors, taking the way intentionally towards Carnwikk, hoping Anthony might be about. Once she saw him again, she'd know where she stood and what her future was to be. At present her mind wavered between doubt and a fear of meeting him, followed by the restless urge to do so. Whatever the outcome, she had to discover if he'd been keeping out of contact deliberately to avoid her; he knew her too little to commit himself as being seriously in love with her, but it was important he should realise she was no light woman to be taken like a serving wench in a moment of passion and then abandoned as though nothing had happened. He must know she was fretting still for her husband and had been over-vulnerable to warmth and sympathy. Or wouldn't he understand at all? Supposing things didn't work out as she hoped. What would she do?

She was rich of course, and as a last resort she could go abroad somewhere and make a new life for herself and the child. But Aunt Matilda would be sure to find out, and although they'd never been particularly close, the idea of hurting her was painful.

Rupert too. How Rupert would despise her. This troubled her more than anything else. He wouldn't turn her away from Trenhawk, but she knew she couldn't bear to spend day after day under his roof having to face his contempt. His own affair with Elizabeth of course just wouldn't count to him. He'd never even think of it. Standards of behaviour for men and women were different. But then Adelaide was merely upper-middle class – a daughter of 'trade' – and Victorian matrons of this kind were shunned for any lapse of virtue.

It was all very stuffy and obsolete, but a part of life; and she knew that she would now never want to return to London even if Aunt Matilda pressed her. What was regarded as an 'interesting condition' in a woman possessing a legal husband, was a sin against God by one without.

So she was under no illusions; her purpose was clear as she cantered that day towards Carnwikk.

The weather had lifted, and the morning was fine, with the glitter of a dew on furze and heather. She gave the mare full rein, and when they reached the rim of the hill pulled Ebony to a sudden halt.

The view was magnificent under the clear sky, with a shiver of pale sunlight tipping the distant towers of Carnwikk to gold. High above, to the right, the cottages of George-Town gleamed like a toy village on the horizon. South and westwards – the stretch of sea glittered, faintly misted by Penzance harbour and St Michael's Mount. She would have liked to gallop ahead to the coast; but her first priority was to locate Anthony. She *had* to see him.

She looked round, screwing her eyes against the quivering light until they focused properly. There was no sign of him; over the whole of that vast moorland expanse, no indication of life stirred but the sudden flap of a bird's wing as it rose from a bush nearby, and the shrill crying of a gull overhead.

She gave Ebony her head, and cut across to the left knowing she must now be riding Carnwikk territory. With anxiety gnawing her, she galloped on, at ever increasing speed, only half aware how near to the great house she was.

She mounted a rough tummock of hill, and had a brief glimpse of the mansion below in its dip, before the mare reared and threw her suddenly, trotting off a second later with a high whinney down the slope.

Adelaide was caught in a tangle of rough undergrowth, and lay for seconds half stunned by shock. Then, she extricated herself and managed to sit up, discovering to her relief she was unharmed except for a sprained ankle that hurt acutely.

'Ebony!' she called involuntarily, ' – Ebony! Ebony!' the last word ended in a screaming wince of pain. She heaved herself on to a rock and made an effort to examine her foot. Beads of perspiration trickled from her forehead, back of the head, and down her neck, bathing her in a flood of weakness. She lay back to recover, and it was then she heard a girl's voice.

'Oh dear. What's happened? Can I help?'

Feeling a touch on her shoulder Adelaide glanced up. The face looking down on her was small, pale, with demurely parted brown hair over large grey eyes and a mouth too wide for beauty. Yet the impression she gave was of great gentleness and sympathy. Her cape was of a nondescript brown shade, and for a moment she appeared to Adelaide more as some gentle fawn-like creature of the moor itself than ordinary flesh-and-blood.

'You've had a bad fall,' the voice continued, as Adelaide pulled herself from threatened faintness. 'I was out looking for berries when your horse – it must have been yours – rushed by. Don't worry, though, we'll find him – '

'Her.' Adelaide said. 'My mare, Ebony.' She smiled, thinking how odd it was to bother about Ebony's sex when she was in such painful plight.

The young woman returned the smile, which quite transformed her from rather nondescript plainness to brief ethereal charm. Then the gravity returned.

'We must get to you to my house, and see what's to be done about your ankle. My name's Katherine. Katherine St Clare.'

Adelaide stared in astonishment.

'You mean – from Carnwikkk? Anthony's sister?'

The girl nodded. 'You know him?'

'We've met', Adelaide replied cautiously.

Katherine smiled again.

'So we're acquainted already – indirectly. Not that it's

important. Anthony has so many friends. But that sprain!' a slight frown pulled her brows together. 'Do you think, with my help, you could hobble to the house? It's only a short way. But if it's too bad – ' she broke off, considering.

'Oh no, it's all right, I'm sure I'll be able to do it. I don't want to be a bother. Really, it's not broken, I'm certain of that. Just a twist.'

'I'm not sure – ' Katherine said doubtfully. 'You'll have to see a doctor. If I got one of our men to help carry you – '

'*No*'. Adelaide was firm. 'And I don't need a doctor. Once I'm back at Trenhawk, Mrs Pender or – '

'*Trenhawk*?' The girl's eyes widened. 'Do you mean you're staying there?'

'I'm Adelaide Hawksley – David Hawksley's widow,' Adelaide said bluntly, half expecting a rebuff of some kind although Katherine did not appear to be that sort of person. There was none.

'I'm sorry about your husband,' the gentle voice said quietly. 'War's a terrible thing. So many lives spoilt. So many brave young men taken unnecessarily. If it was left to women – oh forgive me. Here I am getting on to my pet hobby-horse, and you in such pain – ' she took Adelaide's arm firmly. 'Now, if you lean on me and keep the bad leg as still as possible we'll have a try. Come along now – '

Adelaide clenched her teeth and managed, with Katherine's help, to get up. Once upright a little of her tension eased, although at every slight movement the ankle throbbed acutely. Presently, however, she found it possible to make steady if slow progress in a rhythmic hopping gait, supported on one side by Katherine, and holding her long skirt in the other hand.

In five minutes they'd left the roughest patch of moor behind, and had come to a narrow track cutting immediately down to the back of Carnwikk. The slope was steep, but free of rocks and obtruding undergrowth. Once level ground was reached they went through a gate in a high granite wall. This led into vast enclosed kitchen gardens, and from there through another door that opened on to acres of pleasure gardens laid out in a series of lawns, clipped hedges and flower beds. A fountain – supplied by water from a stream which had been dammed above, at George-Town – cast a cascade of silver against the sunlit sky. As an imperious background of Tudor magnificence, the walls and turrets of Carnwikk rose majestically impregnable against the passing of time.

Ahead, round a bend of drive to the left were the Gate-House and courtyard. The vast frontage of the mansion was at an angle hidden from sight.

Adelaide, in spite of her discomfort, was impressed and speechless at such overwhelming grandeur. She'd always considered Trenhawk imposing; compared with Carnwikk it became a mere country residence of lesser gentry, though not for the world would she have exchanged it.

Katherine urged her to rest on a seat for a moment before continuing.

'Is it much worse?' she asked solicitously.

Adelaide shook her head. 'No. In fact – ' she managed a smile, 'even a little better, I think.'

'Good. We'll go on then. As soon as we have that boot off I'll know more what's wrong.'

Adelaide glanced at her curiously. 'You sound just like a doctor or nurse.'

Katherine shrugged. 'I'm afraid not. I'd like to be. I wish so often I could join Miss Nightingale in the Crimea. It's my greatest ambition. But then women – women like me aren't supposed to do such things. And there's my grandmother. She's rather – ' her voice died.

'Yes?'

'Rather limiting,' Katherine conceded with a sigh. 'Sometimes it's difficult. I suppose that's why Anthony has to get away often. They don't really get on. She's so old, you see – nearly a hundred, and set in her ideas. Still, it will be easier for him now, although I'll miss him.'

Adelaide's heart contracted.

'Miss him? Is he leaving?'

'Oh – hadn't you heard? I suppose not. He got married last week; to Harriet Montmerrick. They're on the Continent now somewhere.'

'Oh.'

Something in that short word and the complete silence following took Katherine momentarily aback. She was puzzled.

'Did you know my brother well?' she asked, noting how rigidly Adelaide sat, as though she was making a great effort to control her nerves.

'Oh no, not really,' Adelaide replied quickly, 'being a Hawksley and he a St Clare.' She forced a smile. 'And that sounds ridiculous, doesn't it?'

There was no answering smile on the other girl's face; she merely said very gravely, 'Yes. I've no patience with old feuds and jealousies. It's only people like my grandmother who keep such old fashioned notions alive. It's a sort of game with her, I suppose, something to give an interest to life.'

Having recovered her poise Adelaide said, 'Then perhaps I'd better not enter your home. If you could find Ebony for me and help me into the saddle, I'm sure I could somehow manage to ride. I wouldn't want to cause an upset with Lady Serena – '

'Nonsense. And you know you couldn't ride as you are. Now come along Adelaide, I may call you Adelaide, mayn't I?'

'If you wish.'

'I certainly do. And remember I'm Katherine – Kate if you like. I prefer it.'

'Very well.'

They got up and slowly made their way towards the drive bordering the side of the house. About fifty yards down they reached an arched entrance. Katherine helped Adelaide up the few stone steps, pushed the door open, and took her in.

The passage was comparatively narrow; but after a short distance it opened into a wider corridor that in its turn joined a large stone-flagged hall with doors and screws indicating an assortment of different apartments. The rugs were mostly rich Persian. Gilded statues were poised at the foot of a wide curving staircase ornately railed. Portraits of long-faced aristocratic St Clares stared contemptuously from carved frames. The hall furniture was mostly Elizabethan, some older. Light from cleverly designed stained-glass windows filtered across floors and walls.

Carnwikk had one thing in common with Trenhawk, Adelaide thought, a character of its own; an identity nurtured through the years to defy the challenge of its equally stalwart though lesser neighbour, the rugged Hawksley house. Reli-

gious ideas and political conflict might divide them; but each
in its own way remained guardian of its individual territory. It
was easy to understand St Clare resentment. In the far past
when Jonathan Hawksley had so shrewdly acquired the
Abbey Lands, the St Clares must have been affronted not to
have stepped in first. No wonder there'd been ill-feeling,
Adelaide thought as she rested again on a carved settle, for a
brief rest.

Then Katherine took her hand, helped her up, and led her
into a sitting room described as a small rest-room. It appeared
to Adelaide very large indeed. Its colour scheme was of blue
and gold, including Louis Quinze furniture, and a good deal of
expensive glass and crystal from abroad. Several inlaid rosewood tables were placed at different angles about the interior.
Chairs were elegant spindle-legged affairs upholstered in blue
brocade, and near the immense white marble fireplace, where
logs flared welcomingly, was a chase-longue also covered in
blue. A square gold-framed French clock with china figurines
on each side ticked on the mantelshelf.

'We can be quiet here,' Katherine said. 'Now first of all we
must take that boot off – and just look at your skirt! It's a bit of
a mess. I'll do what I can to clean it, but I'm not going to risk
trying to get you upstairs, although one of our footmen could
probably carry you, but – '

'No, please no,' Adelaide interrupted, 'and I don't think this
lovely room's the place to bother with my ankle.'

'Sh – she!' the other girl said. 'You're here. Now do as I say.
Heave yourself on to that thing – the chaise-longue. Then I'm
going to send for my maid and see it's bound up properly –
after that we can have tea and talk, and decide what's to be
done.'

It sounded so simple, and yet all, to Adelaide, seemed so
contradictory and out of place; quite ridiculous to be fussed
over in such an exotic setting – she, Adelaide Hawksley in a
bedraggled riding habit with her hair tumbled about her
shoulders, and the lining of her velvet skirt pulled with a twig
of furze below the hem. How odd, she thought, as Katherine
gently eased the boot from her foot, that when Anthony had
met her in Penjust her gown had also been torn, leaving her in
need of help and St Clare assistance.

Anthony!

Whether it was the wrench of pain as the foot was freed – reaction – or the reminder of what Anthony's sister had told her about his marriage, she didn't know. But a wave of faintness suddenly rushed over her. She could feel her face go cold and damp as the room temporarily swam into a curdling void of darkness. Her head fell back. She clenched her fists in an effort to retain consciousness, and as though from a long distance away, heard Katherine saying, 'It's all right, Adelaide. Here – drink this.'

The sting of brandy was forced through her lips, and the hot pungent odour of smelling salts penetrated her nostrils. her brief lapse of semi-consciousness gradually lifted, and normal sight and sound registered.

'Oh dear. What a nuisance I am. Please forgive me.'

'It's not a nuisance at all,' Katherine told her. 'And if I have my way, you'll stay the night –'

'*No*.' Adelaide's tones were almost violent. 'I have to get back somehow. It's important.'

The rest of the interim at Carnwikk held for her more the quality of a dream than reality. When the ankle had been bathed and bound, and she'd been washed and attended like any child in that elegant entirely unsuitable room, tea was brought in by a young butler wearing a maroon and cream uniform. There were thinly cut sandwiches, sweetmeats and an assortment of cakes arranged in silver dishes. The dainty lace napkins alone must have been heirlooms, Adelaide decided idly as she toyed with the food. But in spite of the tempting display and luxury, she was not hungry. All she wanted by then, was to be away again and back at Trenhawk.

'You'll go in our chaise then,' Katherine told her firmly, 'and I shall come with you –'

It was at that moment the door opened and a shaky yet rasping voice shrilled, 'Go with *who*? To whom do you allude, girl, and who – *who* – is this young woman?'

Adelaide, startled, turned her head sharply.

There, with the light from the window striking full on her wrinkled face under its grotesque red wig, was the thin form of Lady Serena. She was leaning on a silver-knobbed stick, bent nearly double. Her strongly carved nose almost met her chin.

Her eyes were so screwed up in their creased network of flesh as to be almost indiscernible. She was macabrely rouged, and wearing an ornate, embroidered gown of purple velvet, liberally bejewelled. Her gnarled fingers as usual, glistened with diamond rings. Diamonds sparkled from her ears and over her corsage. Her whole appearance was ludicrous yet somehow imposing, commanding a certain awe.

'Well?' she queried. 'Are you going to answer me? Answer me girl, do you hear? Or I'll call Hulbert. Hulbert – ' her voice like the screech of some wild angry bird, shrilled through the petrified silence. Almost simultaneously a footman re-appeared.

'It's all right, Hulbert,' Katherine said quietly. 'Everything's under control.'

The footman withdrew, as the gentle voice continued, 'Come along in, Grandmama dear. I want you to meet a friend of mine who's had an accident – '

The old lady hobbled a few steps further into the room, peering ahead almost as though she was blind.

Katherine went forward and took her hand. 'I thought you were resting, Grandmama.'

'Ha! so you did, so you did. It's always the same. As soon as I choose to close an eye you steal off or else get up to some mischief.'

She seated herself next to Adelaide, thrust her hairy chin forward and went on. 'Well, if my stubborn grand-daughter won't tell me your name, perhaps you will. I've a right to know. I hope you understand that. This is my home. I – own everything in it, and when I ask a question I expect a civil answer.'

If Adelaide had seen the warning gesture and look in Katherine's eyes she might have prevaricated in answering, but she didn't.

On impulse she answered unthinkingly, 'Hawksley. My name is Adelaide Hawksley.'

The reaction was electric. There was a brief astounded pause before the old tyrant – the chatelaine of Carnwikk, struggled to her feet and gasped. Then, thrusting her face close to Adelaide's she shrieked, 'Then you'd better leave this instant, hadn't you, miss? This is the first time for more years

than I care to remember that any Hawksley trash has dared to
intrude on my premises or anywhere near it – '

'Grandmama – ' Katherine said placably.

The old woman thumped her stick on the floor viciously.

'Be quiet, girl. Be quiet. If I were a younger woman I'd have
you thrashed as you deserve for thwarting the rules of this
house. Thrash you. Thrash you myself I would.' The paint on
her cheeks deepened to dull blueish crimson. 'You go to your
room this instant, do you hear? and you madam –' to Adelaide,
'take yourself off –'

Adelaide's face had whitened. She got to her feet, wincing.
'Certainly. I never wished to come in the first place.'

Lady Serena's jaw dropped. 'You never –'

'*No.* And I think you're very rude,' Adelaide said clearly. 'I
was brought here because I had a fall from my horse. But if I'd
known what my reception would lead to, I'd certainly far rather
have lain on the moor all day. You grand-daughter was merely
being courteous. But obviously you have forgotten what cour-
tesy is. I must forgive you I suppose, and put it down to your
great age.'

With an air of hauteur, despite her indignation and pain, she
stood for a moment, head high, confronting the incongruous
sight of the raddled ancient creature and a gentle girl so pitifully
in contrast, and yet both so shocked by her outburst. Then she
limped to the door, which was still ajar, and went out. She
waited with her back against the wall, as a faint feeling of
sickness swept over her. A maid, attired in a black starched
dress and white frilled cap and apron, came along with a salver
in her hand, she stopped when she saw Adelaide.

'Is anything the matter, miss – ma'am? I thought – '

Adelaide tried to compose herself. 'No. I shall be all right.'

'I must say you don't look it,' the maid said. She was about to
go for further help when Katherine appeared.

'Oh dear. I'm so sorry.' She eased Adelaide on to a settee.
'Grandmama's so very old. She gets these turns sometimes. In a
minute or two she'll be sorry or have forgotten all about it. Now
if you'd like to stay here you can have a room and I'll send a
message to Trenhawk – '

Adelaide smiled. Colour had already returned to her cheeks.
'I must get back,' she said, 'but thank you. You're kind.'

Katherine frowned. 'Very well, but you'll have to take care. I'd rather you stopped here, but after that scene I can understand.'

'What scene?' Lady Serena's voice came shrilly from the doorway. 'And what's that poor gel doing hunched up on that hard settle?' She thrust her head forward inquisitively. 'Had an accident, didn't you? Upset me when I saw you just now. Hate accidents. You should take more care. Bad riding, that's what I always say. No one's taught properly these days. When I was a young woman – oh never mind. Never mind – ' she waved her ringed hand irritably. 'If you're going, go. If not make yourself comfortable and look pleasant about it. Share my quarters if you like – have a bit of a gossip eh? What's goin' on at the Hawksley place? They say the new heir's a rough character. That true? A farmer. Never heard the like, and calling themselves gentry – ' when Adelaide did not reply she broke off, then continued after a reproving look from Katherine, 'Oh well, I can see you ain't interested. Run on too much, do I? Maybe. Maybe.' She turned and hobbled back into the room.

The door closed. Katherine took Adelaide's arm, and presently when they were both warmly clad and with rugs and footwarmers installed in the chaise, the drive back to Trenhawk began. Adelaide spoke very little, she was still shocked, more by news of Anthony's marriage than the fall. He'd mentioned no girl – no rumour had come to her ears from any source even of his engagement. But then, she, Adelaide, had so few acquaintances. Any St Clare name mentioned at Trenhawk was done so only by chance, and with dislike. If Rupert had any knowledge whatever of Anthony's commitment to Harriet Montmerrick he'd hardly have bothered to allude to it. But Anthony! – Anthony could have told her. It had been his duty – instead of luring her by flattery and deceit into such a disgraceful situation.

Instinctively her hands tightened into clenched fists of outrage.

Katherine must have sensed something.

'Is the pain worse?' she asked.

'No,' Adelaide answered tensely. 'I'm just wondering why you – you fuss so about me. You needn't have bothered to come. I'm not an invalid. I don't want to sound ungrateful but – ' her voice faltered.

'Oh don't let's go over the argument again,' the other girl said more shortly. 'Actually I'm quite enjoying the drive. With Anthony away life gets stuffy at home. I feel so useless sometimes; Grandmama doesn't *really* need me, except to complain to. She's got a place full of servants to bully when she feels like it, which is most of the time.' She paused, then asked, 'Are you going to stay at Trenhawk now?'

'I don't know. I haven't made any definite plans. At first – when David was killed, I meant to. But things change, don't they? You can never be sure of the future.'

'No. Well – ' the other girl's voice brightened, 'if you do, we must see each other sometimes. Make visits. That could put an end to the silly feud business for good.'

'Yes,' Adelaide agreed. But she doubted it. However friendly Katherine might feel she could not see a rift that had endured for centuries being healed simply by the wish of this quiet girl who was so obviously under the tyranny of her fierce grandmother. Neither could she visualise Rupert making a move to comply. It was clear he already disliked Anthony, and would not be slow to show it, if the occasion arose.

'You don't sound convinced,' Katherine remarked.

'No,' Adelaide admitted. 'But – ' her remark was interrupted by a sudden lurch of the chaise at the corner of Trenhawk Drive. A moment later the horses were moving at a more even trot towards the house.

When they got there, Rupert, surprisingly, was standing by the steps. He came towards the chaise while the stable boy dismounted from Ebony. Before the man got there, Rupert was opening the carriage doors. His face had a tight look on it. Even before he spoke Adelaide was aware of disapproval.

'What's happened?' he questioned, holding out a hand to the young woman, 'and you – ' to the boy, 'take the mare to the side there. My man will attend to her.' As he spoke Carnack appeared fortuitously down the side path.

'Miss St Clare has been very kind,' Adelaide said with stiff formality. 'I had a fall from Ebony, and she insisted on helping me to her home.'

'Carnwikk?' The name came out expressionlessly, but

Rupert's eyes were veiled, suspicious.

'Yes', Katherine told him, with a faint smile. 'I'm glad I happened to be about. Your – your sister-in-law was in considerable pain.'

'Mrs Hawksley is my – my cousin, my *step* cousin;' Rupert told her pointedly. 'I'm Rupert Hawksley. No matter. I'm much obliged to you. Perhaps you'll come in for a glass of something – cordial? Or sherry?'

'Thank you,' Katherine answered surprisingly. 'I don't need refreshment, but I *would* like to see Adelaide's ankle hasn't been jerked too much by the drive.'

She took Rupert's proffered hand, alighted and said to her man, 'I shall only be a few minutes, Adams.'

The uniformed figure nodded, touched his tall hat, and resumed his driver's seat.

Rupert led the way into the small parlour. And as Katherine, divested of her cloak, insisted on examining the sprained foot again, he was surprised at such feminine expert handling. He glanced at the young figure with interest, noting the slender almost delicate lines of breast and waist, the thin wrists, and tapering fingers which nevertheless seemed to have such strength.

'Have you had much experience of this sort of thing?' he asked.

Katherine looked up. The clarity of her steady grey eyes beneath the demurely parted brown hair, and calm brow, stirred an admiration in him and feelings he'd never before thought he possessed. She held none of Adelaide's vibrant beauty, but in a strange way she personified beauty itself.

'No,' she answered. 'Except with animals – wild things I help anyone or anything in need when I can. You see – '

'Yes?'

'I would like to be a nurse,' she said. 'If things had been different at home I might even be one now – with Miss Nightingale and her band at Scutari – the Crimea.'

Rupert frowned, then gradually the brows lifted leaving his eyes on her in an astonished stare.

'So you're one of the "new women",' he asked.

She laughed.

'No. Sometimes I feel one of the oldest on earth. Because

that's what they've been from the very beginning, isn't it?'

'What?'

'Born to nurse, and – and cherish I suppose,' she said, with a faint colour staining her cheeks. 'But that sounds pompous, and I don't *mean* to be. It's just – '

'I know what you mean, Miss St Clare,' Rupert interrupted, 'and I admire you very much. The trouble is saints aren't always properly appreciated by menfolk.'

What reply Katherine gave Adelaide did not hear. She was suddenly quite stupidly jealous, though she told herself she had no need to be and certainly no right.

When Katherine had left he returned to the parlour, where Adelaide was still seated with her leg resting, and a glass of sherry at her side.

'Oh!' he exclaimed with a faint sarcastic edge to his voice, 'I *thought* so.'

'What?'

'The sherry, cousin dear. I was surprised when you refused, because – ' his eyes slid over her idly-appraisingly.

'Because what?'

'Unlike your new friend you're no saint. Oh don't mistake me – I don't grudge you your solace, Adelaide. But *please* spare me the hypocrisy.'

Her eyes blazed. 'I don't know what you're talking about.'

'Oh yes you do – and that's what irritates me; the pretence, the lies. You were longing for a drink, then why didn't you say so and take one? Another thing – why were you near Carnwikk when you had that ridiculous fall? It's confoundedly annoying being indebted to the St Clares for anything. But I suppose you were hoping for a glimpse of that young dandy, Anthony?'

She didn't reply. She felt suddenly tired and a little sick under Rupert's scrutiny.

'That's my affair,' she said shortly. 'And now if you don't mind leaving me – '

He shrugged and went to the door. 'I'll send Mrs Pender in. She may be able to do something for you. I only wish – ' his voice was gentler when he resumed, 'I wish you'd be more careful, Addy.'

She wished she had been. But it was too late now. Too late for any plans she'd had simmering that could help her out of

her own tricky situation. There were none. As for Rupert –
obviously one glimpse of the demure-looking Katherine had
gone completely to his head.

This fact, on top of everything else was not only irritating,
but extremely upsetting though she refused to admit it, even to
herself.

VIII

Adelaide saw very little of Rupert during the next few days.
Apart from meetings with mining experts and trips to Hayle
Foundry concerning estimates for new equipment, he was
involved in the tricky business of finding a tutor or governess
for Julian. Once he suggested to Adelaide she might help him
in this matter. But she was not co-operative.

'I hardly know the child,' she said dubiously. 'He's really
fond of you, and you must know the type of person necessary.
I'd think a woman would be best though – until he's a little
older.'

'Yes, you're probably right.'

'If you see Katherine St Clare she might be able to advise
you better,' Adelaide remarked pointedly.

'Why should I see her? You know very well how things are
with the two families.'

'I know how they were,' she replied, 'but since my toss, and
your meeting with her, it should be different, surely.'

'As usual you're romancing.' Rupert told her. 'It's not likely
we'll meet again. And, by the way, what about your ankle?
You're still limping. Wouldn't it be wise to see a doctor?'

'Perhaps,' Adelaide agreed. 'I was thinking of going to
Penzance tomorrow for some shopping. I could call on Dr
Maddox. Would you mind me using the gig? My ankle's not
quite right yet.'

'If Carnack drives you,' Rupert answered.

'You mean you don't trust me handling a carriage?'

Rupert gave her a fleeting smile. 'Not at the moment, Addy.
One day, maybe, when your control's improved.'

She turned away in annoyance, not because of Rupert's

suggestion concerning Carnack, but because he still insisted on treating her like a child whenever he felt like it. True, he was five years her senior, but five years now they were grown up, was not really much. Sometimes, she thought despondently, she felt considerably the elder, especially when she considered the immediate future, which every day presented further emotional and practical problems. Frequently, in dark moments of depression, anger that was almost hatred of Anthony St Clare rose in her. How dared he have used her so shamelessly? And how could she have been so blind and weak as to have thought for a moment he was genuine.

But then she hadn't.

She hadn't thought at all. That was the trouble.

The next day was fine, and her spirits lifted as the carriage took the high road over the moors towards Penzance. The glint of early gorse already spotted the hills with gold. Patches of pale green shone among the furze and springing young bracken. Budding new growth starred the lean branches of wind blown trees. After a time the dark stark shapes of mine works were left well behind, and only grey granite farms crouched in huddled valleys or against the hills. Adelaide realised for the first time how sequestered her life had been during the past weeks at Trenhawk; and with it came another thought – once the doctor himself had confirmed her condition – it was quite within her power to leave for a time until she'd had the baby. Go abroad somewhere, perhaps. She could then have it adopted if she felt like it, and return.

Why hadn't she considered it seriously before? Such things had been successfully kept secret in the past by women of her class and means. And if she found a good home with worthy parents the child wouldn't suffer.

Against her will she instinctively rejected the suggestion. She recalled with a stab of sympathy the wistful glance of Rupert's ward – the pathetic young prisoner of Trenhawk. Prisoner, perhaps, wasn't really the right word; but what chance had a deaf child of enjoying the years ahead? Especially one without parents. Rupert's son he might be, but unacknowledged; and therefore alone. Obviously he was well treated but he mightn't have been. It was unlikely any child she bore would have a similar defect. But she knew she'd never abandon it.

So circumstances remained unchanged – providing the doctor's diagnosis confirmed her pregnancy.

It did.

He was a youngish man, Doctor Maddox's partner, to whom she gave her maiden name of Drake.

After a thorough examination he told her she was in excellent condition. The baby, according to her information and his calculations, should be born in early August, provided she curtailed all horse-riding for the time being.

Adelaide did not mind that at all. Presumably Anthony would be in the vicinity from time to time, and the thought of a chance confrontation with him was now odious to her. Whatever his reaction such a meeting could only mean embarrassment for them both, and revive in her a sense of guilt.

He had chosen to marry the aristocratic Harriet Montmerrick which meant that she, Adelaide, was nothing to him, and that Anthony St Clare was a mere shameful episode in her life, best forgotten.

Perhaps the child would bear no resemblance to him.

She hoped not.

Then she remembered how like David Anthony was.

Instead of depressing her the thought became suddenly in a curious way comforting. She might even be able to persuade herself eventually that the baby *was* David's especially if he was a boy.

Such fancies restored some of her self-confidence, although she found as the days passed it was increasingly difficult to meet Rupert's eyes. They held frequently a reflective and thoughtful look which puzzled her. Did he guess? But why should he? Her figure was not noticeable beneath her full skirts and layers of petticoats. Her waist was still slim. There were no tell-tale dark rings under her eyes. Any sick spells or attacks of faintness had occurred so far only in his absence.

Eventually of course she'd have to tell him, before he learned it second-hand.

But for a week – two weeks – three– she calculated it was safe to keep the knowledge to herself.

Then, on an evening in early March, something happened.

The day had been unusually calm for the time of year. Sunlight had gradually left the grey morning mist behind, and by mid-day was a veil of gold over the countryside. Rupert, as so often happened, set off shortly after his breakfast for the farm, and when Adelaide came down he was already away.

She felt lonely. Except for brief interludes and conversations which mostly had a sharp edge to them, she and Rupert seemed to be growing further apart; this was not as it should be. As David's widow the family tie was there. They should be friends. But he obviously avoided her whenever possible, trying to emphasise, no doubt, she wasn't wanted at Trenhawk. Well, she knew that. But only recently when she'd contrived to 'draw' him on the point, he'd said again, 'I've told you, Adelaide, you're quite welcome here as long as you want to stay. Providing you accept the circumstances of course.'

She'd supposed he'd meant the circumstances of too few servants, no company except occasional dinners for male business acquaintances, and having to keep to her room on evenings when he wished to have the house to himself.

She hadn't, and didn't mind any of that. She'd come there for solitude; in any case, a new parlourmaid, who was also to attend her when necessary, was due to arrive the following week. A governess had at last been chosen for Julian; as for the rare occasions when a suspicious vessel anchored off the coast, and the cellars later resounded with heavy feet and curious thud of barrels and kegs being heaved and dragged up the steps – this she found exciting, although she couldn't help wondering what any new servants would think when they arrived. But perhaps the acoustics only affected her bedroom.

The last time she'd sounded the housekeeper on the 'queer noises from below' Mrs Pender, now more friendly, had said, 'That bedroom of yours echoes funnily. On account of the foundations. Old houses are full of queer noises, as I said before, an' my advice to you, Miss Adelaide, is to keep quiet on what you doan' know but may suspect.'

Adelaide was touched by the housekeeper's loyalty which she guessed was more for the family than to Rupert personally; she was touched also, by the old woman's care and obviously growing affection for the handicapped little boy Julian.

He was a good child, seldom intruding where he wasn't wanted, but though Adelaide did her best to get to know him, he didn't respond. Even that March afternoon when her spirits were so low, he'd run away when Mrs Pender had allowed her into the small charming garden opening from his room. As usual he was kneeling by the fishpond, but when she approached he'd got quickly to his feet, and with his thumb in his mouth stood staring at her. She knew he could speak a little, but he said nothing, and after a moment had run back into the house.

Adelaide returned to her bedroom feeling defeated and bored. Presently she stirred herself, left the room and vaguely wandered along towards the staircase leading to the Tower. She paused at the bottom of the steps, staring up. A golden beam of light spilled from the door above which was half ajar. She forced herself up the steep flight to the top, and went in. The air was very quiet there. The silence absolute. Yet it seemed to her a deep, welcoming influence encompassed her, almost as though some enveloping presence from beyond centuries of time had been recalled to give a moment's peace. She wasn't alone any more. She fancied the shadows moved fitfully into the blurred outline of a waiting form. Giddiness claimed her for a moment and then it was over. Only the cool small room remained, isolated and empty except for a frail lingering perfume weirdly evocative of days long gone.

Adelaide pulled herself together, took a deep breath to steady her nerves, and went out, making her way slowly with one hand on the rail, down the narrow steps. Halfway to the bottom she was startled to hear a sharp rattle and clang of a latch or lock.

She glanced back. To her astonishment the door of the Tower Room had firmly closed. There was no breath of wind or movement of air to account for it. And there had been no one inside but herself, unless – her heart lurched! Up there she had not been afraid, but now she was. She turned and retraced her way quickly down the remaining steps.

Later in the afternoon she brought up the subject of the Tower Room to Mrs Pender.

'I thought I heard something moving up there,' she explained ambiguously. 'I was half way up, and then saw the door was open. I knew it wasn't supposed to be, because of Julian. But –'

The housekeeper frowned and shook her head. 'Always thinkin' you hear things,' she said reprovingly. 'You must be mistaken. That room's always kept locked – *always*, 'cept when I go up to clear out the cob-webs and such-like – an' that's only once or twice a year. I haven' been up for *months* Miss Adelaide, an' I doan' particularly want to, either.'

'But I *saw* it – ' Adelaide persisted. 'And then, when I looked again, it had suddenly shut.'

'Of its own accord?'

'I don't know,' Adelaide replied slowly.

'Well then,' Mrs Pender was obviously relieved, ''tis like I said, you were mistaken. The light can do funny things, especially with all those shadows creeping round. You forget about it; you've had a bit of a turn maybe, is that it?'

'No.' Adelaide's voice was defensive. 'But if you say you locked the door I suppose I'll have to accept it.'

'I didn't say I did. It could have been me, the last time I was up, or Mr Rupert. Nobody else. The key's always kept safe in its own locked drawer in the kitchen.'

'I see.'

'Now if you'd like to go along to the small parlour I'll see Lucy brings your tea,' the housekeeper said, dispelling the subject rather curtly. 'I did some baking today, an' I've some fresh cookies ready still warm from the oven.'

Adelaide did not mention that the idea of warm cookies was at the moment repellent to her. Though she was now on comparatively good terms with Mrs Pender, she knew the balance between them could easily be shaken by an unintentional snub or tactless remark. So she merely replied, 'Thank you, that will be very nice.'

Afterwards, when tea was over, she went up to her room for a brief rest, and to change for the evening meal. She removed her dress and petticoats, and undid the constricting stays which were beginning to feel tighter as the days passed. Oh how pleasant it was to feel her muscles relax and her breathing ease. She studied her figure thoughtfully through the mirror, letting one hand stray over the faintly swelling stomach. Nothing was really visible yet. But soon it would be. Soon she'd have to resort to all manner of devices in order to conceal her condition. Why, she wondered, with a stab of irritation, must women submit to such discomfort merely to disguise what after all was a perfectly natural state? She wouldn't – not for the world, if the baby had been David's child. She'd have been proud to make an exhibition of herself, even if it was considered in bad taste.

But as things were! – her golden-amber eyes darkened in her pale face. The small chin came out defiantly. 'Oh I hate you –' she whispered to herself, thinking of Anthony, 'I hate – hate you–'

Presently she went to the bed and flung herself on it, lying on her back with her arms under her head. She closed her eyes tightly, trying to force sleep; there was plenty of time before she had to dress again. But rest wouldn't come; and after half an hour she got up, wondering what to wear. Aunt Matilda had sent on a trunk of her clothes, so she had plenty of dresses to choose from. If she could have followed her instincts she'd have worn a deep yellow satin with a low neckline dipping to the shadowed hollow above the gentle curve of breasts. But of course it would have been in bad taste, even though David would have approved. Rupert certainly wouldn't. Or at least if he did – he'd have thought she'd contrived the effect just for his benefit. That was the difficulty with Rupert – he had such an annoying habit of somehow making her feel in the wrong. And under present circumstances it was important she was able to face him with dignity and composure.

The blue then? She took a cornflower blue silk, and held it up before her. It had eight flounces falling over hoops from a pointed bodice edged with lace. She remembered painfully the occasion she'd last worn it at a social function with David shortly before he left for the Crimea. All eyes were upon her as she clung to his uniformed arm, head lifted proudly under its massed golden hair, a gracious smile tilting her perfectly modelled lips. She'd heard whispers of – 'Aren't they a handsome couple?' And 'Isn't she lovely? But of course my dear –' she hadn't heard the rest. Women, when they were envious could be the most dreadful cats, and when they were, Adelaide had generally felt flattered.

The memory suddenly saddened her. She threw the dress on the bed in a crumpled mass. Anyway it would be quite unsuitable for dinner with Rupert. She should not yet be out of mourning. The dark olive green then, sprigged with tiny cream leaves? Its neckline was higher, dipping in a discreet V above which she could wear her single string of pearls.

After shaking its few creases out and taking a good look at her reflection with the gown held in front of her, she knew this was the right choice. It wasn't mourning, but dark enough to appear almost black in some lights, and anyway Rupert disliked seeing her dressed as a black crow. He'd said so. Certainly he couldn't criticise her in the green which added brightness to her contrasting hair, and seemed to flood her amber eyes with fleeting emerald sparks.

She was so engrossed in the business of dressing and making the most of her physical assets it didn't occur to her to wonder why she was doing it. If it had, she'd have gulled herself into believing that it was entirely because of the necessity of having Rupert in a good mood from now on. Because of the coming baby, and because, if he turned nasty and told her she would be better away from Trenhawk, she wouldn't know what to do. She couldn't leave now – couldn't and wouldn't. A moment's panic filled her when she considered the possibility. She dismissed the idea almost immediately. Rupert wouldn't send her away. Hard and domineering when he felt like it, yes. But not narrow-minded. Julian for instance – he didn't seem to care what she or anyone else for that matter thought about the child's presence in the house. And then that woman, Elizabeth Chywanna. He hadn't bothered to deny his feelings for her, when she'd taunted him about her once – merely stared at her coldly, and turned away. Why – Elizabeth could be Julian's mother for all anyone knew. Not that it seemed likely. However loyal Mrs Pender might be, a word would have been dropped by someone at some chance moment to give the show away. And the husband – the man who'd killed himself after shooting that horrible Dutchman – he'd not have tolerated such a state of things or been so friendly with Rupert if Elizabeth and Julian were mother and son.

Anyway, she thought, feeling suddenly tired, she was only conjecturing. She hadn't a single fact to go on.

Bringing her thoughts abruptly to the present, she washed, and started to dress. It was a nuisance having to fix herself up again in the stays. She wished she already had the maid Rupert had promised, to help lace her. This time the effort of doing it herself was a breathless business, and the dress, when worn over the layers of petticoats was noticeably tighter than when she'd last had it on.

She'd intended to put a white artificial flower in her hair, but at the last moment discarded the idea, deciding that the all-over effect might appear frivolous. Gloves or mittens were also out of the question. The meal ahead of her was supposed to be no more than a normal ordinary dinner with Rupert, although she fully intended it to be a softening-down occasion for the inevitable confrontation ahead.

When she went downstairs later the light was already fading to the clear greenish glow of spring twilight. She shivered slightly and drew the shawl across her chest. The atmosphere felt weird, as though disaster loomed ahead. She wasn't usually a frightened type of person given to hallucinations, but lately such sensations had been frequent; due to her condition, probably, and the fact that she had not yet told Rupert how things were. When he knew, everything would be different. She wouldn't care a fig what anyone else thought. Once the baby was born he'd have to be accepted. Or a girl – supposing it was a girl? She hoped not. Adelaide was not really very fond of her own sex. By nature she preferred anything male; besides, boys had infinitely more chances in life. Girls of her class had to conform and follow a set pattern unless they were to be regarded askance by society. That rather nondescript and gentle Katherine St Clare, for instance, was obviously dedicated to nursing, but instead of joining Miss Nightingale abroad as she'd wished to, had been forced to spend her time, day after day, at the mercy of that terrible old grandmother's moods.

Adelaide still winced inwardly when she recalled the violent scene at Carnwikk. Rupert probably would have been amused, and one day when everything had been disclosed and put into proper perspective, she'd tell him. But she had to await the right moment.

There was a fire in the parlour, and she went to it gratefully, holding her hands to the blaze. When she was properly warmed she opened an adjoining door which led into the conservatory. It was steamy hot in there. Carnack had probably been busy stoking up at the end of the dark passage leading from the garden. Pipes were fed there for what heating could be utilised for the house.

The strange, leafy smell of earth and growing things so reminiscent of her childhood always mildly disturbed her. But that evening nostalgia was overcome by a sudden bout of sickening faintness. The stays pressed on her ribs and lungs with increasing constriction so she could hardly breathe. She sat back on a latticed seat for a few moments then somehow managed to drag herself to her feet and make her way into the parlour. She lay back in a chair, fumbling at the neck of her gown for air. The walls dimmed and converged upon her. Then, as she fought to retain consciousness, Lucy entered with a bucket of logs.

'Why, ma'am – Mrs David,' she gasped, 'what 'es it? Are you ill?'

Adelaide tried to speak and couldn't. With a gasp, the girl hurried out and returned almost immediately with Mrs Pender. By then Adelaide was recovering. A faint colour was already tinting her pale cheeks and lips when the housekeeper bent down to look at her.

'You can go, Lucy,' the old woman said abruptly. 'Get some hot tea ready, and look sharp about it.'

The girl scurried away, and Mrs Pender stretched her rheumaticky body up. She took a deep breath before loosening Adelaide's clothes and bending again to release the tight lacing of the corsets. Then she placed both hands on her hips, and with a shrewd searching look in her beady eyes said, 'How long have you been like this?'

Adelaide didn't reply at first.

'Well?' The housekeeper insisted, 'you heard me. I said how long?'

'I don't know what you mean,' Adelaide prevaricated.

'Now now,' the relentless homely voice continued, 'I know 'ee well enough to be able to tell when you're speakin' the truth or not – you were never a good liar, Miss Adelaide, an' I recollect many spankings you got in the past because of it. But this edn' a matter for spanking is it? This is somethin' only nature can work out for you. I say – how long? And how dare you lace yourself that tight, the way you be –'

Adelaide refused to answer, until the housekeeper continued. 'Very well then, I'll have to get a word to Mr Rupert.

'Tisn't a seemly thing for any old body like me to have to do. But as you've settled yourself in Trenhawk so firmly it's right he should know what's going on. 'Tisn't *my* business to question or make judgement, but for decency's sake *someone* should be put properly in the picture, an that one's the master – '

Adelaide suddenly came to life.

'No. *No*. I'm going to tell him tonight. As you say I'm not your concern, Mrs Pender. I'm David Hawksley's wife – widow. I've a right – '

'Oh ais. You've a right, miss. But I've a knowledge of such things, and dao'n you forget it. I'm sorry to have to speak this way, but there 'tes. If you don't do the honest thing now, then *I'll* have to.'

Adelaide was about to reply when a door slammed, followed by the heavy tread of footsteps down the hall. Both women glanced round sharply. Mrs Pender was making a fumbling hasty effort to secure Adelaide's corsage respectably when Rupert entered.

He stood briefly, with a puzzled frown creasing his brows before asking, 'What's this? A rehearsal for a play or something – ' his voice faded, then started up again. 'Please explain. I don't generally return to find the women of the house in a state of – what's the word – decolletée?'

Mrs Pender's eyes and mouth contracted primly. 'Miss Adelaide – Mrs David – surr, has something to speak you 'bout. And so if you doan' mind I'll take leave of you both. Presently Lucy will be in with hot tay. If you *must* know, Mr Rupert – Madam has just had a turn.'

The way Mrs Pender said 'madam' and her stiff manner of alluding to 'turn', made Adelaide briefly forget her plight and want to laugh. Then, as the housekeeper with a tremendous effort at dignity, turned and went out, reality swept over her again in a painful rush of nerves.

'Well, Adelaide?' Rupert said, seating himself in a chair opposite to her, 'What's all this about?' She noticed automatically how handsome he was looking in a debonair yet rugged way, wearing a black coat, fawn riding breeches, with a muslin scarf at his neck. His dark eyes, though, were brooding, speculative. There was an unsmiling stern set of the well-cut lips that worried her. It wasn't the right moment, she was sure it wasn't – to confide in him. His mood could be difficult; something could have happened at the mine or farm to put him on edge. If she could have delayed the moment of confession she'd have done so. But that stupid old housekeeper had made it impossible. So she steeled herself to the inevitable, swallowed hard, and then said bluntly and very clearly, 'I'm going to have a child, Rupert.'

There! It was out.

She forced herself to sit rigidly waiting with her eyes half turned from his face so she could not see his expression.

The silence was electric, and seemed interminable, until he said, 'You *what?*'

'I think you must have heard. And it's true. I'm pregnant.' During the pause following she summoned sufficient courage to face him. In the last few moments all colour seemed to have drained from his face leaving it drawn and strained holding the brittle quality of old parchment.

How long it was before he spoke she couldn't guess, she was aware only of her own heart thumping against her ribs and of his eyes burning remorselessly upon her.

At last he said, 'David, I presume, is not the father. No. How could he be?'

'No. I wish he was – oh Rupert *please* understand? I wish he was – '

'I'm sure you do.' His voice was bitter. 'But as David unfortunately was no longer able to oblige your lusting little passions, I'd be *greatly* obliged – ' his tones were heavy with sarcasm, 'if you'd inform me who was.'

'Rupert – ' she begged, 'please don't be angry. Please – '

'Oh for God's sake, Addy,' he said roughly, 'spare the melodrama. Just *tell* me.' He moved forward and took her shoulders with his hands biting into her flesh.

She lifted her head in a sudden flare of temper. 'Let me go, Rupert. You've no right to act this way. You don't own me.'

'No.' His arms dropped away. 'Thank you for reminding me. All the same this is my house, not a retreat for fallen women. So if you'll just give me the bastard's name, I'll – '

'The bastard's name is Anthony St Clare,' Adelaide said very distinctly. 'And I wouldn't advise you to consider fists *or* pistols, because he happens to be away somewhere on honeymoon with his new wife, Harriet Montmerrick. And I wasn't seduced either. I – I – ' her voice faltered.

'Yes?'

'I thought he was David,' she said miserably. 'Just for a moment I really did – however stupid it sounds – '

There was a long pause during which she closed her eyes. When she opened them again he was standing with his back to her, his forehead resting on one hand.

He turned slowly.

'I suppose I should have known you couldn't be trusted to behave yourself out of my sight,' he said. 'Women like you need chastity belts to keep them safe. But – '

'How *dare* you?'

He laughed mirthlessly. 'Oh I *dare*, Addy, make no mistake about that. What I didn't bargain for was you falling for the young reprobate St Clare. I thought at least you'd have the decency to steer clear of that family. But no. You have to demean yourself – '

'Stop it, Rupert, stop it. You've made your feelings clear enough. I thought – I hoped – you might understand, at least a little. But I see now it's impossible. So I shall leave Trenhawk just as soon as I can get packed, and you needn't give me another thought.'

'Really! and where will you go? London? Aunt Matilda's? Oh no doubt she'd take you in, being the kindly soft hearted creature she is. But do you think it would be fair on her? Imagine how her friends, the stuffy matrons, would titter and pity her.'

'Abroad then.'

'Where? France maybe? No doubt you'd find a willing protector on the Continent – some lascivious elderly gentleman with plenty of money in his pocket to swell your own – or possibly a handsome dilettante or confidence trickster who'd fleece you within a month, then take off leaving you penniless in a strange land. Use your head, Adelaide. However cunning you may be in the art of enslaving men, you've certainly no knowledge of the world at all. So – '

'Yes?' Her voice was very low, on the edge of tears.

'After due consideration,' he told her, with the air of a lawyer assessing the pros and cons of some business deal put before him, 'I think the most sensible course would be to marry me.'

Her heart lurched.

'*You?*'

'Why not? It would provide the unfortunate child with a father and establish you beyond question as the rightful mistress of Trenhawk – which is what you've wanted all along isn't it? And from my point of view, should Wheal Tansy ever be in need of further funds, I have legal access to your tidy little fortune remember.'

There was silence before she said slowly, 'You mean – a sort of marriage of convenience? A business deal?'

'If you care to think of it that way, yes,' he answered.

'As – as friends? I mean – '

'I know what you mean,' he replied, with the light that had kindled mockingly, half-desirously in his eyes, fleetingly gone suddenly blank again. 'You mean, with the legal deal completed – the contract as it were safely sealed and signed you'd wish to reign the household as Trenhawk's mistress, but not mine. Is that what you're trying to say?'

She blushed.

'How could I have thought things out in such a – such a cold blooded way?' she asked. 'What time have I had to think at all?'

'Oh you always had a quick shrewd little mind beneath your intriguing exterior,' he told her ruthlessly. 'I'm sorry circumstances haven't permitted a more romantic courtship. You'd have liked that, wouldn't you? To have me on bended knees swearing eternal adoration and fidelity, as no doubt your precious David did – '

'Leave David out of it.'

'But, Addy, how can we? Or that dastardly Anthony for that matter – being so confused in your ever-faithful heart – ?'

She got to her feet and swept past him towards the door, eyes bright with anger, mouth set and hard. Brute! she thought, what a brute he was, to taunt her at such a painful time.

He caught up with her before her hand was on the knob, and turned her round, one hand firmly about her waist, the other under her chin, tilting her face up to his.

'What cat's eyes you have, Adelaide,' he said, a little thickly. 'And what a pity – '

She waited. 'Yes?'

'What a pity you couldn't have liked me more – or even pretended to – '

'But, Rupert, I – '

He put two fingers against her lips.

'No. No protest, no lies now. It's too late. As you said, I offered a business bargain, and if you feel like accepting the risk, it's still on. I'll take you as my lawful legal wife in unholy matrimony just as soon as it can be arranged. Naturally I'll observe the proprieties due to your – delicate state. In other words, Adelaide dear – you need have no fear I shall invade your privacy under the certain circumstances of our union. I shall continue to use my father's bedroom and you can keep the one you've got.' He paused and added after a moment, 'Well? Does the suggestion appeal?'

Her throat constricted nervously. Rupert's face began to swim before her eyes.

'Can't you give me more – '

'Time? No, I damn well can't, and won't. If the idea's so repulsive to you say so, and never again will I so much as touch you with a bargepole.'

'All right – all right,' she managed to say, 'yes, I'll marry you, Rupert.'

His muscles relaxed. She swayed giddily against his chest for a moment; then supporting her firmly he led her back to a chair. When she was settled he remarked drily. 'The next thing I suppose is to tell Mrs Pender. She'll be surprised.'

'Oh no, I don't think so,' Adelaide said, feeling better already. 'She suggested ages ago it might happen.'

'*What?*'

'That you'd marry me,' Adelaide answered coolly.

Rupert didn't answer. The deviousness of women, he thought wrily. They were sly creatures, every one of them, young and old alike. Especially Adelaide. His eyes slid warily to the soft feminine outline of temples and jaw, the swelling breasts under the hastily tidied bodice, and faint curve of stomach in her half reclining position. As yet the full gowns she wore were sufficient camouflage to any unsuspecting eye.

But soon there would be no disguising her condition. For both of their sakes, therefore, the sooner the civil ceremony was over the better. He'd no intention of having any church 'do'. He felt no sentiment, religious or otherwise in marrying Adelaide – only a longstanding repressed desire which he knew must remain unappeased – for a time anyway, queerly intermixed with pity and a brooding anger that could be controlled only by throwing himself determinedly into thoughts of business and the mine.

During the next few days before they were married by special licence at the registry office in Penjust. Rupert at odd moments found himself recalling another face, unlike Adelaide's – the demure gentle countenance of Katherine St Clare.

There had been peace and understanding in the clear quiet eyes – a quality similar to Elizabeth Chywanna's capacity for giving without price.

There would be none of that with Adelaide.

For everything she gave he'd have to pay – with his heart and mind, and torment of indecision.

But he'd see not everything was on her side.

Once the child was born he'd either woo and win her or bring her to heel like a recalcitrant mare. He hoped it was the former, although he doubted it.

They were married a week later with only Mrs Pender and Carnack as witnesses. Adelaide wore her grey dress which the housekeeper had contrived to let out round the waist, discreetly covered by a grey cape purchased at the costumier's in Penzance. She carried a small bouquet of lilies-of-the-valley presented to her by Rupert, and a new grey silk bonnet-hat concocted mostly of artificial flowers, leaves, and flimsy grey veiling.

Rupert was elegantly but soberly attired in a black cloth coat, grey trousers, and a white pleated shirt with a pointed collar and white cravat. Adelaide, feeling dizzy and unreal, could not help a faint stir of admiration. He certainly had an air about him, not romantic exactly, but more that of a man who was both gentleman and buccaneer. For the first time, as

they drove away from the registrar's in the large chaise that
had been William's, Adelaide realised how very little actually
she knew of the real Rupert. She could have married a stranger – he sat so silently and stiffly upright. Yet when she said,
'Rupert' – hesitantly, the look in his eyes became for a moment
deeply and disconcertingly personal.

'Yes?'

She turned her face away. 'Oh, nothing. I was just wondering about – the household.'

'I'd say that was more than nothing,' he replied, 'seeing
you've married for it.'

She winced, and he was instantly apologetic. 'I'm sorry,
Adelaide. I didn't mean it wrongly.' He touched her hand
lightly then withdrew it hastily. 'Go on then,' he said. 'What
about the household? I thought we'd already discussed mari-
tal plans.'

'I wasn't meaning that.' She paused before continuing, 'You
won't mind getting a servant or two in, will you? The maid you
promised me – the governess for Julian, and a cook. A cook's
very necessary, and perhaps – '

'Oh, Adelaide, what's got into you? You've gone over this
time after time. It's all arranged surely. The governess, Miss
Venables, arrives on Saturday. The maid – or maids – are up
to you, so long as you don't run me into bills I've no intention
of paying.'

'As if I would.'

'Oh I think it highly likely,' he retorted, 'given the chance.
But remember, Addy, that from now on that pretty little hand
of yours is not entirely free any more.'

She stiffened, and with amusement he noted the sudden
outthrust of her delicate chin.

'You needn't remind me, Rupert,' she said with an effort at
dignity.

Quite unexpectedly he laughed. 'Adelaide, for God's sake
get off your high horse and make an effort to enjoy yourself. I
suppose it's asking rather a lot on my part. But you might try.'

His hand enclosed on hers again. She let it rest there though
recalling another wedding occasion when another's arms had
been round her – David's. They had been driving from the
church to the grand reception at Aunt Matilda's; she'd been

dressed in a white lace crinoline gown over layers of flounced petticoats, with a wreath of orange blossom on her honey-gold curls. The long chiffon veil had frothed back over shoulders, and David was gazing down on her adoringly, unable to keep his arm from encircling her waist.

It had all been so exciting. The wedding breakfast so heady with wine, speeches, and admiring glances from the fashionable guests present. Adelaide had felt herself a queen, and indeed, for that brief time in Aunt Matilda's élite circle, had been one.

Now, jolting along the Cornish lanes towards Trenhawk in Uncle William's old-fashioned chaise, with Carnack driving and Mrs Pender severe in her best black sitting in front beside him, she felt dowdy and suddenly tired. Her stays were hurting her, and her head ached. The wine she'd had as a pick-me-up before setting off, hadn't suited her, and when they reached the house all she wanted was the solitude of her own room. But she realised to excuse herself would be an affront to the servants, and discomforting to Rupert.

Lucy, with the help of her mother, had a homely spread waiting for them in the parlour, including a two-tiered wedding cake, iced on top, but containing too much fruit, and a liberal amount of saffron that Adelaide detested. Nevertheless, with Rupert beside her she complimented the two women, and smiled artificially, making a pretence of drinking the champagne produced by Rupert at the last moment. Carnack rather farcically gave a toast to the newly married couple, Mrs Pender even allowed the habitual downward lines of her button mouth to curve upwards, though disapproval still glinted in her eyes.

The whole affair, Adelaide thought heavily, was nothing more than a rather ridiculous charade. They all knew – they must, by now – the real reason for the marriage, and if they didn't they soon would. Then why had Rupert to put her through such a pantomime?

After an hour she felt she could stand it no longer. Something in her face – pallor, combined with a tension of manner and exhausted clouding of her eyes, jerked Rupert to sudden awareness.

'Try to hang on a second,' he whispered, 'I promised Julian he could have some cake – ' Mrs Pender caught his eye, disappeared from the room and returned a minute later with the child. He was dressed, rather stupidly Adelaide thought, in a new velvet suit with a white collar, and was wearing silk stockings and his best buckled shoes. His fair hair had been trimmed a little, but it was too long for a boy. Tired as she was, Adelaide decided that at the first opportunity she'd take the scissors to it herself. Then she realised she'd probably not have the chance. Mrs Pender had her hand on his shoulder, proud as a mother hen of her one chick, and the little boy was resting his head against the black silk dress as though she was the one friend he had in the world. Even when Rupert tried to coax him to take a sip of champagne, he wouldn't, although after a moment he suddenly ran from the housekeeper's protection, and clutched 'Uncle Rupert's' hand.

At last to Adelaide's great relief, Rupert took the initiative and put an end to the celebrations. When the few servants were safely dispersed to the kitchen, he held his hand out to Adelaide and said, 'Thanks for your co-operation. You're tired aren't you?'

'Yes. And if you don't mind I'll go upstairs now. It was a – ' she hesitated, then finished, ' – a friendly little affair. I think Mrs Pender enjoyed it.'

'I think they all did – except you perhaps.'

She flushed. 'There's no reason for you to think that, or say it,' she remarked.

'No. Well – ' he glanced at her, 'if you're so weary perhaps we'd better say goodnight. Mrs Pender can bring you something to eat later.'

'I shan't want anything,' she told him, 'I'd rather be left alone.'

His lips tightened.

'Certainly, if that's what you wish. But at least I hope you won't deny me seeing you safely into the bridal chamber.'

His sarcasm could hardly escape her.

'Rupert – '

'Oh never fear, Addy, never fear. I generally manage to keep promises made to fair ladies, however tedious it may be. In short, my dear – wife, you may depend on your nocturnal privacy.'

She bit her lips, with the colour rising in a tide of deep rose to her cheeks and forehead.

He laughed lightly, propelling her by an arm to the door. She followed him upstairs mutely. When they reached the door of her bedroom he opened it, and bowed slightly as she passed through. Just inside, she paused, staring round her in bewilderment. Flowers seemed everywhere – daffodils, narcissus, early roses, lilac – even on her dressing table, an arrangement of exotic orchids in a cut glass vase. How had it been done? And when? How clever he'd been to keep the display private. Everything must have been in wait before they started off to the registry office for Lucy and her mother to arrange in her absence. The scent was heady, overpoweringly sweet and intoxicating. She knew when she was alone she'd have to get the window fully open. But at the moment, touched by Rupert's thought for her, she could only stare and turn slowly, saying with the glimmer of a smile, 'Oh Rupert – how kind of you – how really lovely.'

He stood awkwardly, watching her, trying hard to appear casual.

'No kindness in it, Addy,' he said, 'just customary, I believe.'

'Yes, but – ' her voice faltered. He moved towards her, put both hands on her shoulders, and said gently, 'Good night, Adelaide.'

His lips were on hers. She could feel a quiver of his mouth increasing to slow warm pressure, as she closed her eyes momentarily, waiting for something she didn't understand – for peace, forgetfulness of the past, for anything that would erase the torturing memories of the last year. Not passion or physical appeasement. Either, just then, would be somehow an affront. Then what?

No answer came.

There was none.

Almost immediately the interlude was over. His arms dropped away. He turned abruptly at the door, and before closing it said, 'Sleep well, and don't hurry to get up early in the morning. I'll tell Mrs Pender to get Lucy to bring up a tray.'

'But – '

'I'm going to Truro tomorrow,' he said, 'and will probably stay overnight. Take care of yourself.'

The door closed with a snap.

She walked slowly to the mirror, stared at her reflection with distaste, thinking how plain she looked, then tore the flowery hat from her head and flung it on the bed. She had an absurd desire to cry, and did not know why. It seemed for a few aching moments that her youth was gone for ever, and irrationally she blamed Rupert for somehow failing in making her feel wanted. After all he'd married her, she was his wife, if only in name. Surely he could have said something more encouraging than 'I'm going to Truro tomorrow.'

She hadn't expected that.

Then what had she wanted?

'I wish Aunt Matilda was here', she thought, switching her thoughts elsewhere. 'Aunt Matilda would make me feel all right again – she'd understand.'

But of course she wouldn't. No one would.

She didn't even understand herself.

When he left Adelaide, Rupert knew he wouldn't sleep. His mind was too alert, his senses too stirred and on edge for rest. The contact with her and knowledge she was his wife yet still unobtainable, filled him with irritation mingled with hot desire. Generally he knew his own mind sufficiently to act rationally. But there'd been nothing rational about this marriage. He'd always wanted her. If she'd been less selfish and gentler he could have loved her. Had he been a fool to bind himself so irrevocably to such a self-willed tempestuous woman? Would love ever emerge from their turbulent relationship? He tried to delude himself what he'd done had been philanthropic, for the coming child's sake. But of course it wasn't true. It was simply that he'd lost his head and acted on a wild impulse that had obscured common sense and made him the complete dupe of the situation.

What man in his right mind would marry a woman like Adelaide – then chivalrously leave her to virginal peace on their first night through a sense of honour? Honour be damned. Hadn't she already played fast and loose with that lusting dandy St Clare? She deserved a dose of her own medicine. She deserved – oh God! what had got into him? He could feel himself swelling and hardening physically. He had to have action – somehow rid himself of the need inflaming his whole body and being.

He went out into the cool spring air, and was on the point of going to the stables and saddling his horse for a jaunt to the brothel in Penjust where he could ease his lust with some willing whore, when he abruptly changed his mind and decided on a walk instead. He cut across the patch of moor and made his way down the ravine to the cove. There was a moon, and the black rocks sent dark shadows streaking across the pale sand. Ivan Behenna, a fisherman, was about to put to sea in his small boat. He was a loner – a small dark middle-aged man of half-Spanish ancestry who had a small shack half-way up the headland. In the past he'd been a useful collaborator concerning certain smuggling affairs of the vicinity.

He paused as Rupert approached him, and smiled. There was a flash of very white teeth in the bearded hawk-nosed face. The glint of rings twinkled from his ears.

'Well, maister,' he said, 'fine night edn' et? Lookin' for sumthen' – or someone mebbe?'

'No,' Rupert answered, 'but I'm glad to find you here.'

'Oh?' the man' eyes narrowed, 'business?'

'Could be, could be,' Rupert said. 'But you're the one in the know. If you hear of any little adventure –'

Behenna put a finger to his nose.

'I'm allus hearin' o' things, Maister Rupert,' he said, winking. 'Matter of fact, surr, I bin thinkin for some days of a pretty lil maid – Irish boat – that could do with a spot o' business soon. Interested?'

'If it's practical, yes,' Rupert answered. 'You let me know when you've got things clear – what cargo, when. We'll meet at the usual place a week today. Same hour. All right?'

The fisherman nodded. 'You know me, master. Same kind we are, under the skin – ripe for a gamble when it's waitin ready.'

Rupert laughed. Already he felt better. His muscles had relaxed and sexual fire abated in him to a healthy demand for exercise. After a minute the two men parted. Rupert climbed back up the ravine and hardly aware of what direction he was heading for, cut over the moor above Trenhawk, crossed the lane, and after a time found himself in the vicinity of Carnwikk.

Hours had passed since his session with Adelaide, and

through exertion his mind and body were at last unified. When the great house came into view he didn't turn back, but went on until he reached the top of the slope immediately above.

Only two lights glimmered from the windows. One on the ground floor, the other higher, overlooking the moor. He stood watching, and as he waited perfectly motionless, there was movement behind the glass. The lace curtains parted and a face came into view, pale faintly blurred, but unmistakable. The face of Katherine St Clare.

A conflict of emotions stirred him – admiration tinged with compassion and a touch of awe – feelings he'd not thought he possessed. Even a sense of regret – regret they'd not met before enabling him to consider his future from better perspective.

Involuntarily he smiled and lifted a hand. Her own emerged, rubbing the glass so she could see him more clearly. How long the interim lasted he couldn't judge. But presently her face was withdrawn. He turned abruptly, and walked sharply down the narrow sheep-track towards Trenhawk.

Regrets were useless, he thought. Anyway, he was not certain he'd anything *to* regret.

Adelaide was his; or would be – sometime. And there'd be no pretence between them when that day came, because illusions and dreams would have no part in their relationship. Their marriage would be down to earth.

Real.

When he reached the house it was already past three o' clock, leaving him just four hours sleep before getting up for his jaunt to Truro.

IX

For some time on her wedding night Adelaide lay wakeful in her solitude, watching the shadows of the walls and ceilings that weren't really shadows, but merely darkness against greater darkness, listening as she'd so often listened to the stirrings and creakings of the old house. Her thoughts were a confusion of pictures from the past and present, showing her life in a jumbled sequence of events that gradually became no more than an imaginary ballet in her mind, a revolving kaleidoscope of meaningless shapes taking her gradually to sleep.

When she woke it was morning, and everything suddenly leaped into perspective.

She was married.

Yesterday she'd married Rupert. Involuntarily, as though to prove it, she glanced down at her left hand. The ring shone bright on her wedding finger, replacing David's which now encircled the third finger of her right. She'd insisted on that, although Rupert hadn't really liked it.

'I couldn't – ' she insisted, 'I just couldn't put it away like a – like an old dress. Surely you understand?'

'Yes,' he'd agreed, 'only don't flash it round under my nose too often, if you don't mind.'

That had been some days ago. Now she wondered if she'd been wrong, and decided she had. Wearing David's ring in such a way reduced him obviously to second place; and that wasn't fair. Anyway there should be no comparisons. So on impulse she slipped it off and put it by the bedside table. Later she'd find some secret personal corner where she could keep it hidden with a few other mementos safe from any prying eyes. Not that Rupert would bother to search her things, he wasn't mean in that way. But she wouldn't trust Mrs Pender or Lucy an inch.

She was just about to get up, when there was a knock on the door. The housekeeper came in, puffing and panting, carrying a breakfast tray.

'I thought I'd come myself, seeing it's your first mornin' as Mrs Rupert,' she said, with a certain smug anticipatory gleam in her eye. 'The master's gone; went off early he did, as he told you. "See my wife has all she wants," he said. So I've brought what you usually have – tea 'n' toast, an' a boiled egg. There's bacon too if you do want it, but in your condition – '

'Oh, I only want the toast,' Adelaide said hastily. 'And please don't bother about my condition. I'm not an invalid.'

'No. But you're with child,' the old woman said pointedly.

'An' Mr Rupert's from now on, though who the child come from in first place 'es no concern of anyone's, I s'pose.'

'I hope you remember it,' Adelaide said coldly.

'*Me*?' there was a short strident laugh. 'You can trust *me*, Miss Adelaide. An' what others think I'll see they never speak of – in *my* presence,' She paused, then added with more sympathy, 'You was always a heedless wild one – even as a child. The way you'd be off tearing about like any boy with the young masters. "She'll get into a mess one day", I'd say to myself often. An' you have, haven't you? But then in a way you've bin very lucky, having Mr Rupert to fall back on. He's an unusual fine gentleman, for all his – odd ways – which I doan' always approve of. Still, I hope you doan' hurt him more than's necessary.'

'Why should I hurt him at all?'

Mrs Pender sighed.

'Since you've asked, I'll tell you. Men like Mr Rupert, the strong silent kind, are more open to bein' hurt than the other sort, like Mr David. Oh no – doan' interrupt, you just listen to what I have to say, Miss Adelaide. I've bin' long enough with this family to know what's what. Mr David always had a romantic touch 'bout him – he knew what to say an' how to charm a woman's heart away without needin' to give a thought to et. But Mr Rupert's different. Words doan' always come easy. He's got feelings though – maybe more than he should have sometimes. I'm not sayin' I always agree with him. There've bin times in his life I'd have no truck with. But he's a real man. So jus' you remember that, Miss Adelaide, an' treat him with the respect due – ' she broke off for want of breath. Adelaide, not knowing whether to laugh or to chide, was quick and clever enough to say quietly after a moment, 'I'll not forget what you've just said, Mrs Pender. I'm sure you're right.'

'Oh. Well – ' the housekeeper, half taken aback, looked relieved. 'We'll say no more 'bout it then. So I'd best be going now. You'll be wanting to have your breakfast and dress.' She moved to the door, and as a parting shot remarked, 'Not many men newly married would have such consideration as to leave a young wife at peace, on her own. But then, you being as you are, an' "gentry" as they say, makes a difference. An' that's what I've said to Lucy. "Mrs Rupert's 'gentry'," I said. "the gentry are different." '

'Thank you for explaining,' Adelaide remarked with a straight face.

When the housekeeper had gone, she found to her surprise she felt considerably better, and had even an appetite for the egg and toast.

After breakfast she washed quickly, dressed herself in the grey gown, and went downstairs wondering if Carnack had the free time to drive her in the gig to Penzance. She was in need of new clothes now, and the morning seemed inducive to a spending spree.

The sky was blue with only a few feathery clouds blown intermittently on a light wind across the sun. The air was fresh, holding the mingled spring sweetness of blossom, brine, and young growing things. It would be pleasant to ride over the moors with her hair free, and the breeze soft on her cheeks. But of course it wouldn't be seemly. Some unknown prying eyes would be sure to notice. So instead she decided to go for a walk, and in five minutes had left the house unobserved by the servants, wearing only a shawl over her dress, and carrying a bonnet in one hand.

She cut from the drive to a path leading upwards towards the lane, and from there turned down to a narrow valley locally known as Hook Lane by the natives, presumably named after the man who'd once owned the derelict mine above. The inclines on each side were steep, covered in furze, bracken, and lumps of granite boulders. Yellow gorse flamed between the rocks, with splashes of wild cherry blossom and crab. On the right of the track was a stream cascading past an ancient stamp-house, and ruined mill.

It was a strange lonely vicinity shunned by most locals because of its reputation for being haunted by a farmer who'd killed his wife centuries ago, and thrown her body in the stream.

Certainly the place had an eerie atmosphere which on that spring day was emphasised by slipping shadows thrown through the gaps of hills by the filtering sun. Adelaide, though, was not nervous. Something untamed in her responded to the wild eerie quality of the landscape – to the riot of clutching undergrowth bordering the glint of water beneath the rugged moors, and to the uncanny silence which was broken only by the murmuring of the brook, the chortle of birds, and creaking of twigs when some small wild thing scurried away.

She walked for about half a mile, and when she turned a corner, she saw the house. It was a square granite building, half covered in ivy, enclosed in a thicket of trees and twisted bushes, mostly sloes and sycamores. A thin coil of smoke spiralled from a crooked chimney pot that had several bricks missing. Through the maze of branches Adelaide had a glimpse of something white – probably from a clothes line. She remembered then, hearing tales of a disreputable tinker family who'd taken over a half-derelict house down 'that theer Hook's Lane.' At the time she hadn't been particularly interested, but now she was. Rupert wouldn't approve of course; that didn't worry her in the least. If he chose to take off for a day or two immediately following their wedding, she felt quite entitled to amuse herself in any harmless way she chose.

So she went on, and in a few minutes had reached a tumble-down gate that must once have been white but was now dirty grey. An old woman was seated on the step of the building, smoking a long-stemmed clay pipe. In a patch of long grass almost completely taken up by an ancient appletree with a twisted trunk, a young boy was tethering a white goat to a stake. They both looked up as Adelaide approached, and for a moment bright sunlight caught their faces. The woman's was gnarled and weatherbeaten under a piece of scarlet cloth tied under her jutting chin. Her hawk-like high-arched nose had a predatory look beneath the coal-black eyes. The boy was extremely handsome; brown-skinned, with a mop of black curls half hiding his slant eyes. Adelaide paused, thinking they might speak or smile, but they didn't, simply stared, as if she was some alien creature come to invade their property.

'Good morning,' she said clearly, 'It's a lovely day – ' the boy shrugged and turned away, once more resuming his preoccupation with the coat. The old woman sat up, blew a puff of smoke into the air, turned and shouted shrilly to someone in the house – 'Leesha – ' which was probably meant to be 'Licea' – repeating the cry several times, then returned to her place on the step.

A woman appeared behind her, pushed by, and walked purposefully towards the gate, followed by two small children. She was lean, thin faced with gilt ear-rings glinting through the tangled black hair. She wore a shabby black shawl over a long red skirt showing brown toes poking through a pair of old sandals.

Adelaide forced a smile, thinking the gossip had been right – they were indeed a wild household.

The woman smiled back, showing a flash of very white teeth, but her dark eyes were narrowed and watchful, causing a momentary quickening of Adelaide's pulse.

'Thee's wantin' to know things lady?' she said. 'Thy palm, sweet gorgio lady, for a mite of silver – ?'

Adelaide took an involuntary step backwards, 'Oh, but I didn't – I mean – I was only walking by – '

'Ah now! what a strange talk for such a lovely one as thee,' the woman persisted, and in a harder voice, 'thy hand lady – '

'I've no money with me,' Adelaide told her. 'Nothing at all.'

'That's a pretty brooch you have dear – very pretty,' the woman resumed. 'How nice to be rich an' lovely like thee. And with the world to travel and such things ahead of thee – thy hand lady – '

A man with a sack on his back and a gun appeared round the corner of the house, but after one glance from his swarthy face towards Adelaide, he crossed the patch of grass to a copse and field down a dip at the far end of their garden. The woman still stared at Adelaide intimidatingly. Feeling it might be wiser to comply, she grudgingly offered her hand, telling herself the brooch pinned at neck was luckily of no particular value, just a trinket she'd seen and purchased from a London shop. The mount was not even gold.

As things turned out she need not have worried about its worth. The woman took only a minute at most to scan the lines of her hand, then she dropped it abruptly, and said shortly. 'Thy fortune's thine own, gorgio. Keep it, an' thy fancy bauble. I want none of it.'

'But – '

There was no touch of friendliness or subterfuge in the lean face, only a grudging furtive fear when the grating voice rasped, 'The elder son of the son before, and the one to come – there's doom there, and a curse, lady. Darkness I see, and a long long road. Get thee to thine own place, gorgio one, and leave the likes of us to our own – ' she turned abruptly, and with the two children tugging her trailing torn skirt went back into the house.

The old woman was still seated on the step smoking her pipe when Adelaide started to walk back the way she had come. The boy was watching her, hands on hips, with a proud contemptuous half-smile on his lips. She quickened her pace, feeling chilled with a slow creeping sense of doom. The sky had clouded, and shadows snaked over the narrow lane from the huddled bushes and twisted trees. She was relieved to turn the bend and see in the distance the glimmer of the brook and square dark shape of the stamp-house and ruined mill outlined dark against the moor.

As she hurried on she was surprised to find how quickly her heart was racing. What was it the wild character had said that was so disturbing? Something about the elder son of the elder son and the one that was to come – darkness, and a long road, and something about a curse? A *curse*! how ridiculous.

But *was* it?

She recalled, uncomfortably, the old feudal business between the Hawksleys and the St Clares; how in very early times two had died because of it.

That was history. Fact. But any curse surely could survive only as a story, or because it was sufficiently believed. It was preposterous to imagine that the ill-wind of some far distant St Clare ancestor could work havoc with the Hawksley family so far ahead.

Yet the tinker woman had known and sensed something when her strange shrewd eyes had searched the lines of her own – Adelaide's –

She tried to dispel the increasing insidious dread, but it was difficult. The wind had risen bringing thickening cloud to the spring sky. A magpie rose with a flap of wings from a clump of trees, flying low over the furze towards the moor. Automatically Adelaide recalled the old superstition, 'One for sorrow, two for joy', and watched for the second; there was none. She drew her cape close to the neck, and once or twice looked back over her shoulder with the odd sensation that someone had followed from the cottage, and was watching her. But there was no one to be seen; no sign of human life. Only the grey stream flowing beneath the now leaden sky, and the patterned dark shapes of bushes and willows crouched over the water.

When she reached the house it had already started to rain.

Mrs Pender was busying herself about the hall, and from the heightened colour in her face Adelaide guessed she was bothered about something.

'Where have you been, Miss Adelaide?' she said, resorting to her old manner of addressing a child. 'Here I've bin searchin' for you, an callin' you, an no sign anywhere. I do think you might tell me when you're taking yourself off to heaven knows where –'

She broke off to get breath, enabling Adelaide to say, 'I'm sorry. I merely wanted exercise. And I really don't see why I've got to explain myself every time I leave the house for five minutes –'

'Oh don't you? Don't you indeed. And five minutes! I ask you! – 'Twas more like an hour. An' that – that woman here too. Come to bring –'

'What woman?'

The housekeeper drew herself up with an effort. 'The one that was at the farm – Chywanna's wife, he that killed his'self. Elizabeth Chywanna.'

Adelaide stared, and paused before answering. Then she said, 'What does she want? I didn't know she was coming, or anything about it.'

'No. Maybe not. But Mr Rupert did – he must have, although I don't say he knew when. She's got someone with her – a girl, says it's her niece an' she's bin offered a place here as maid – to you, Miss Adelaide, among other things.'

Adelaide was angry.

'So she said that did she? And without my knowledge at all. Indeed. We'll have to see about it.'

Mrs Pender's eyes were briefly triumphant. 'They're in the small parlour,' she said more quietly. 'So while you get yourself tidied and ready to interview them, I'll go through and tell them you're back. I had to get them coffee – ' she added as a parting shot. 'They got a lift part way from Penzance station, but walked the rest. An' if you take my advice, Mrs Rupert, you'll think twice 'bout taken' that young wumman on. She looks a bit of a hussy to me.'

When Adelaide confronted Elizabeth and her niece five minutes later, she saw what the housekeeper meant.

Lilian Tregurze was a tall black-haired, cream-skinned girl of seventeen, with narrow greenish eyes fringed by short thick dark lashes, a wide full-lipped mouth, and a pert manner that suggested she was fully aware of her good looks and meant to use them to her best advantage. Yet when Adelaide questioned her, her answers were given demurely in a quiet voice. She'd been primed well by Elizabeth, Adelaide guessed, and instantly wondered why. Was it that Rupert was anxious for her to employ the girl? And if so for what reason? Did he really think her suitable? Or had the idea occurred to him simply as an excuse for Elizabeth to visit from time to time?

The suggestion affronted and angered her.

'I shall have to think about it,' she said, 'I hope you understand – both of you, that situations like this need just a little consideration. I'm sure – ' to Elizabeth – 'that your niece, Lilian, looks strong and capable. But seventeen seems rather young for my requirements. You say she's been working in a public house – '

'Only for two hours each day – ma'am – ' Elizabeth said quietly. 'Never in the bar. Her mother, my sister-in-law would not allow that. And she's already quite a good cook.'

'I don't need a cook,' Adelaide said shortly. 'What I – '

Before she could finish Elizabeth interrupted still in her calm controlled way, 'Oh but, forgive me, Mr Rupert mentioned cooking when he saw me. But he must have been mistaken.'

'Yes.' The word fell curtly from Adelaide's lips. Against her will she was filled with jealousy that Rupert, all unknowing to her, had consulted Elizabeth and practically promised the position to her young relation. As for the cook business – they had already decided to have one full time. So whether the girl was handy with recipes or not didn't apply.

'I'm sorry, then, we'd better be going,' she heard Elizabeth saying in her controlled placid way. 'Come along, Lilian, you heard what Mrs Hawksley said, she'll let us know.'

The girl stared very directly into Adelaide's face, a trifle insolently though only another woman would have recognised the glance.

'I should like to work here, ma'am,' she said. 'I'd do the very best for you possible, I'm sure.'

Adelaide nodded.

'Thank you. I won't forget.'

When they'd gone there was a rap on the door and Mrs Pender entered. 'Well?' She questioned, 'what did you think – if I may be so bold?'

'I think you were right,' Adelaide answered. 'She seemed hardly the type.'

'And you told her so?'

'Not definitely. As Rupert – as my husband – had made the suggestion I naturally had to agree to consider it.'

'Hm. Well I shouldn' take too long 'bout it,' the house-keeper retorted sharply. 'In another day or so the master'll be back, an' then you'll quite likely find 'tis settled for you. There's a weakness in him for them Chywannas, as you must well know, Miss Adelaide – 'specially for that there Elizabeth. Oh I've nothing against her personally. But – well – there 'tis. "Let the past be" they say, and most probably would. Still – when it concerns the future as well, you can't be too careful. There now!' She took a deep breath. 'If I've bein talkin' out of my turn, you must excuse me. It's only you I'm thinkin' of, Mrs Rupert. I should say "ma'am", I know, as things are now, but to me you'll always be the young headstrong miss I knew as a child. So you must be understandin' with an old body who's not got too many years ahead of her.'

Adelaide smiled, 'Don't worry. I don't mind being called either Mrs Rupert or Miss Adelaide; it makes things – friendly, somehow. And there are times when I feel I haven't got much of it round me. That's a silly thing to say, isn't it?'

Mrs Pender shook her head.

'No. Not under the circumstances. But you've got to take care of yourself now for the child's sake as much as your own.'

Yes, Adelaide thought with a touch of wry sadness – the child.

And she remembered with sudden disquiet the recent scene down Hook's Lane when the strange wild woman had prophe-sied doom for the elder son and the one to come.

X

Rupert was away for three days. On the morning before his return Adelaide told Mrs Pender she was going to drive herself in the gig to St Rozzan to get stamps and reels of cotton from the village shop. 'Do you want anything?' she asked the housekeeper. 'If so I'll bring it for you.'

Mrs Pender stared at her for a moment thoughtfully, then said, 'I don't think I'd go if I were you.'

'Why? Do you think I'm not capable?'

''Tisn' that at all. It's – the rest, Miss Adelaide.'

'What do you mean?'

'Folk talk, you know. Gossip; that's what I'm tryin' to point out. For your own sake you should keep quiet – lie low for a bit so folks round here get a chance to forget what's bin' goin' on. Do you really b'lieve you can be widowed an' marry agen so quickly without causin' a stir? Why, most young women in your position would've bin wearing proper mourning for a whole year or more. But here you are – gallivantin' round and gettin' thrown from a horse into the bargain, – expecting to be treated like any God-fearing body observing the proper decencies. You haven' even kept to black; not in the house anyway. An' then as you are! – ' the old woman sighed and threw up her hands. 'Oh, I've tried to be charitable, for Mr Rupert's sake. But – '

'My husband doesn't wish me to appear like a black crow,' Adelaide interrupted. 'And I don't want reminding of other things.'

'No. I don't suppose you do. An' I doan' intend pokin' an' pryin'. But there are plenty who will, when the truth comes out. If you was living in a town like Penzance or – '

'I'd probably be stoned or beaten or put on show in the Market Place as a Scarlet Woman,' Adelaide exclaimed bitterly. 'You needn't tell me. I know how society feels. According to the rules I should still be wearing a black veil to my

169

knees, still be red-eyed from weeping, and smothered in horrible black clothes looking like death warmed up. I should have hidden in my room at Christmas, instead of trying to appear cheerful, never smiled, and certainly never let any man so much as touch my hand. Well – as you know, the rules haven't interested me. Grief doesn't mean putting on a show of things, Mrs Pender. You're trying to tell me I've sinned. You needn't. I'm married again now, and I'm going to do the best I can to make it work. If Rupert wants me to wear pretty clothes I'll wear them, and be damned to the rest, the busy-bodies you're talking about. But don't ever suggest I didn't love David. For weeks and months, I've done my best to forget it. It's been hard. But I'm starting again now and it's going to be a new start, with a new me. Do you understand?'

She broke off, breathless.

Mrs Pender shook her head slowly, then answered in a curiously quiet voice, 'Yes, I think I do; part of it anyway. But you mark my words. You'll have to put your heart into it – both of you. And when the babe comes – ' something in Adelaide's face stopped her finishing the sentence.

'When the baby comes it will have good parents and a happy life I hope,' Adelaide interrupted in steady tones. 'In any case that's my affair. Please remember.'

Mrs Pender's face flushed. 'Certainly, Miss Adelaide – Mrs Rupert – I should say ma'am, shouldn't I? I'll try an remember that too. I can see you've got everything worked out and put in its place. Well, it's your home now. You're mistress. It's just that I had to let out things that've bin' ranklin' an' gnawing at me for quite some time. So I won't be bothering you further.'

She lifted her chin and walked to the door.

Adelaide suddenly softened.

'Oh Mrs Pender, let us be friends. I need you. I don't always agree with you. But you're part of the past. Of David's as well as mine.'

'Yes, Miss Adelaide, that's true. And of Mr Rupert's too. Very well – I'll do what I can for you. But – '

'Yes?'

'Give the village a miss for the time bein'. B'lieve me, I'm speaking for your own good.'

Adelaide didn't reply, but five minutes later, when the housekeeper had gone to her own premises, she decided the old retainer was probably right. Anyway the stamps and the cotton had merely been an excuse for taking the gig. The time would probably be more usefully spent in trying to communicate in some constructive way with Julian.

The little boy was in his garden planting some seeds that Carnack had given him in small earthernware pots. He was wearing an apron Mrs Pender had made him from a strip of green baize which obviously made him feel a real gardener, and quite important. His face when he glanced up at Adelaide was brighter than usual, and his manner more confident, although he didn't smile, just stood there with a pot in his hand waiting for her to make the first move. Adelaide took it from him and nodded. 'Flowers?' she said, forgetting for an instance he couldn't hear. But he understood and shook his head. Then he spoke. Just one word in a rather light voice. 'Beans.'

'Oh.' She nodded. 'Like Jack and the Beanstalk!'

He may or may not have known that time what she meant; she rather thought he did. But it didn't please him. He drew his brows together and muttered 'silly', then turned away to scoop more earth into another pot.

Adelaide stayed there a little longer, but she'd quite clearly put her foot in it with the boy and realised if he could lip-read that well, he'd probably got the impression she was being condescending, which was disastrous with children.

So presently she went back into the house, and after wandering about aimlessly for a bit went upstairs thinking she might just as well wind some wool she had, as bother to go out. The sky had clouded, and the lanes and moors looked unwelcoming in the grey light.

Rupert returned about twelve. She was in the small parlour when she heard the sound of a carriage outside, followed by the slam of a door. There was a brief sound of voices from the hall, and a moment or two later he came in. He was wearing a dark thigh-length overcoat with a velvet collar, and looked debonair except for his thick rebellious hair which was ruffled from the wind.

He paused, staring at her, then strode to the window where

she was sitting, and planted a kiss on her cheeks. 'How's my lady wife?' he said lightly striving to ease their mutual embarrassment.

'I'm all right, thank you, Rupert,' she said. 'And you? How did the – business go?'

He hesitated then replied, 'As well as could be expected.'

'Oh. I see. You mean you were disappointed?'

'I didn't say so. I never accept things on face value where business is concerned. There's always a risk, if it's worth while at all.'

'Oh well, as I know nothing about it there's no point in talking,' she said, dismissing the subject.

He laughed. '*Addy*! don't say you're *annoyed*. You surely don't want to be involved in my dry-as-dust ventures –'

'No. But –'

'Yes?'

'Something's happened while you've been away, Rupert. Something rather irritating. That woman Elizabeth Chywanna –'

He was taking a decanter and glasses from the chest when she spoke, and at Elizabeth's name he turned quickly.

'Elizabeth? What about her?'

'She came here with her niece obviously expecting me to engage the girl as personal maid on the spot. She implied you'd already arranged everything, which seemed very odd as I'd not been told.'

He frowned. 'Why odd? You want someone, don't you?'

'Yes. But not as cook too. And we'd agreed to have a proper one. But they said –'

'What are you so bothered about, Addy? Lilian's a very capable young woman, I can vouch for that. Or can't you take my word?'

Adelaide jumped up from the chair. 'Why should I? What do you know about women's maids? Except – well –'

His lips tightened. 'Yes, well? Go on say it –'

'Oh nothing.' With reddened cheeks she caught back her hot retort just in time, and answered firmly, 'I didn't like the girl, Rupert, she seemed a bit precocious and above herself.'

'Too attractive, you mean,' he commented drily.

She swirled round with a rustle of skirts. 'Of course not.

That's nothing to do with it at all.'

His eyes when he put his hands on her shoulders, forcing her to look at him were not only penetrating and warm, but held a hint of laughter in them, which puzzled her.

'Sure?'

'Of course I'm sure,' she answered with her heart racing. 'It's no concern of mine how a girl looks if she's well mannered and – and –'

'Plain, and good, and extremely virtuous. Naturally, naturally,' he said, in a maddeningly teasing way. Astonished, because this was an entirely new Rupert from the one she'd thought she'd known for so many years, she pulled herself away and went to the window. 'It isn't only Lilian,' she said, 'it's Elizabeth.'

'What do you mean?'

She turned again and faced him. 'Why have we got to have her about now she's already gone? You know very well she'll take every excuse to call if once her niece is there. And after what's happened I'd have thought you'd not have wanted it, especially as you were so – friendly. Or is that the reason? Can't you do without her? Tell me, Rupert. I've a right to know.'

'My dear Adelaide,' he said, with a look on his face that suddenly confused her, 'you've no right at all in this matter, which you'd do well to remember. We made a perfectly legal practical deal as you pointed out very clearly before accepting the – proposal. But that doesn't give you the right to interfere in my personal life. If I desire a mistress to comfort my chill marriage bed I shall take one. But it won't be Elizabeth. I wouldn't so demean her. As for Lilian –'

He paused. She didn't speak.

'You'll damn well take her, my dear, and be grateful for the chance. And no bullying or tantrums, understand?'

Adelaide swallowed nervously. Then she said, 'You're just the same as you always were – hard and unfeeling. I thought just now you'd changed. But you've not. You've never properly liked me. I don't think you ever will.'

He poured a glass of wine, then another one, and handed her one.

'You don't give me much chance, do you, Addy?' he said

more quietly, with a touch of regret in his voice. 'There. Drink it up. It may ease your jealous little heart.'

'I don't know that I should – as I am,' she answered, sounding slightly prim, even to herself.

He laughed.

'My dear delicate little flower, I'm quite sure you've the constitution of an ox, despite your frail condition. Still, you know best, of course.'

His words – the sarcasm – not only angered but hurt her. She turned impetuously, unwittingly catching his arm. The wine spilled, splashing his cravat. She stood for a moment staring miserably, watching him wipe the stain with a handkerchief.

Then she rashly rushed towards him and grasped a hand.

'Oh Rupert – it was an accident. What a mess. I'm so sorry. Here – let me do it.' She pulled the silk from him and stretched up, trying rather ineffectually to make amends.

Her body was close; he waited tensed and stiffening, looking down on her, noting the changing lights of her hazel curiously green-flecked eyes. The cheeks were flushed above the half parted rosy lips, the soft hair fragrant against his face. Her nearness inflamed him. Suddenly his mouth was on hers, draining it seemed, all the sweetness of life into his being. She didn't resist, but whispered as her head fell back, 'Please – please!'

Mistakenly thinking she was begging for release he let go suddenly and went to the door.

'I'll take care that doesn't happen again,' he said. 'Don't worry.'

She was still standing with one hand to her cheek when the door closed. She rushed to the chaise-longue and flung herself down on it, wondering why every contact between them seemed to end in misunderstanding and distrust. She knew she'd probably handled the Lilian affair badly. But it wasn't her nature to think before she spoke. And certainly Rupert had no tact. So different from David.

She waited for a rush of the old grief, but it didn't come. It was as if the unfortunate little episode in a strange way had wiped out the past.

For that she realised she should have been grateful.

But she wasn't.

Her chief reaction was disappointment and a determination that the next time she had an argument with Rupert she'd keep her poise and dignity. It had been a mistake to bring Elizabeth Chywanna into things. But a time was sure to come when she'd manage somehow to get rid of her and her saucy niece cleverly, without Rupert knowing.

During the days following, Rupert did his best to make her feel contented and wanted. If she'd not made it so clear to him the memory of David was so important to her he'd have found it easier. But in every chance conversation between them his name at some point would crop up and he'd be filled with irritation and a sense of failure. The feeling he was being 'used' gnawed and ate into him with increasing persistence. Damn it, he thought frequently, she could at least stir herself occasionally to show some interest in him as an individual. He kept to their bargain – which was not always easy – never intruding on her privacy or forcing unwelcome attentions on her. He gave her what she wanted in reason and could afford. He brought her flowers whenever he was away for more than a day, tried to cheer her when she was low and despondent. Occasionally he'd take her chin in his hand, force her to look up at him, and say searching her face, 'What is it Addy? What's worrying you?'

Her lips might be tight or tremble when she answered, 'Nothing, Rupert, nothing at all.' But in her eyes he'd see just one thing mirrored – her love for the dead.

Those times for him, were the worst of all. Once he saddled his horse and rode wildly to Penjust where he drank himself under the table and later to his astonishment, found himself in a room at the elegant brothel known as Ye Old Coffee House, with his head on the lap of a perfumed prostitute who was wiping his forehead with eau-de-cologne. Her full white breasts were bare, her ripe lips curved and inviting. The room seemed pink – all pink and cushiony and heady with scent. Somehow he extricated himself, and with his coat over his arm plunged out of the room and down the stairs, confusedly aware of doors opening and young girls giggling, and a stout fashionable figure, Madam herself, pushing him through to the back of the establishment into the cobbled yard.

His horse still saddled, had been tethered there. He'd loosed him, mounted, and galloped away unthinkingly taking the road to the high moors, past Castle Tol, the ruined stone erection dating from several centuries BC. From there he'd turned southwards, until the turrets of Carnwikk were visible in the distance far below. He drew up for a moment. His body and mind still fired from liquor, yet sharpened and clear from the sting of moorland air, felt a sudden urge and need for conflict. If that swine Anthony St Clare had appeared just then, he thought savagely, he'd have knocked him flying, and be damned to the consequence. But there was no sign of the lusting reprobate. So he rode on again a little more casually, while his temper gradually cooled, and desire for revenge eased.

He'd been about to turn and cut downwards in the direction of Trenhawk when the figure of a girl on a colt appeared on the rim of the moor. As she drew nearer he recognised the slight form. She wore no hat, but the sheen of the demurely parted hair above the wide forehead, pale heart-shaped face, and slim neck rising from the cravat of her riding jacket were unmistakable. Katherine St Clare.

He brought his horse to a halt and waited. She cantered towards him and then stopped. He straightened himself, drew a hand over his brow in an effort to smooth the unruly hair, fastened the top button of his coat, and striving for dignity and composure, said, 'Good afternoon, Miss St Clare.'

She smiled. 'Can't you call me Katherine? You – your cousin does.'

'My wife,' he told her, bluntly. 'We were married quite – recently.'

Was it his fancy, or did the faint colour suddenly drain from her face fleetingly?

'Oh,' she said, 'oh – I didn't know. I hope – I hope you'll be very happy.' There was no resentment there, no tinge of envy or regret. From the clarity of her eyes he knew she meant it.

'I hope so,' he agreed. 'Although I rather doubt it. The Hawksleys are not, by nature, a happy breed.'

'Then you must try,' she said. 'I'm in the same boat you know, in a way – oh not *married*, I didn't mean that – But things aren't always easy at Carnwikk.'

'What about the nursing?'

She shrugged. 'That's not possible at the moment. I've other obligations.'

On impulse he said, 'I wish things were different – '

'Different?'

He flushed. 'For you, I mean,' he added hurriedly.

A tentative smile crossed her face. 'So do I. But then, we have to make the most of what we've got, haven't we?'

'How right you are.' His lips tightened as he recalled the recent stormy months at Trenhawk. How pleasant life could have been if Adelaide had possessed even a vestige of the sweet gentleness of this quiet fawn-like creature.

'Well, goodbye, now, Mr Hawksley – Rupert – ' he heard her saying. 'I hope we may meet again sometime.'

'I hope so too,' he said, thinking ironically as she rode away, that by blood, as the coming child's aunt, she'd have every right to come visiting. It would not be wise of course. There was something too disarming about her for comfort. A quality of innocence beyond Adelaide's comprehension, that he would not for anything in the world put at risk.

When he reached the house Adelaide was upstairs resting. He was grateful for small mercies and the chance to get himself fully under control for when she came down later.

He had a wash, changed, then went into his study for a look at some accounts handed to him by Borlaze the following day. They were not entirely satisfactory. Tin output was still low, and though work had already been started on the new levels, not so many Tributers had been encouraged to invest as had been expected. Of course time was young yet. Driscoll, a mining engineer from Birmingham, had seemed pretty certain of future yield. But from experience Rupert knew, like his manager, that there was no certainty of these things. They could strike water or the ore could pinch out. Worst of all, men could be thrown out of work and the rest slaving for a mere pittance. He didn't expect such disaster to happen; but it could. It was happening everywhere. Throughout Cornwall families were still emigrating to the States. And it was all the more worrying that Adelaide, just at this period of uncertainty should be demanding more servants, and expense to be laid out on Trenhawk.

He didn't want to touch her money. But he realised grudgingly that if the worst came to the worst she might have to draw on her income to pay for her own maid's wages.

The maid! a wry touch of curiosity lightened his anxiety when he recalled the scene over Lilian. She'd obviously been jealous, which should mean she felt something for him. But it could be no more than characteristic possessiveness. That brief interlude when he'd held her body warm and pliant against him – the momentary desirous response of her lips under his had so quickly passed, dispelled by her own cry begging him to release her.

Frustration welled up in him. If only she could guess a slight part of what was happening to him – even *begin* to understand her own need. But circumstance had been against them from the beginning. David had held all the cards. David, the flatterer and master of words and beguiling ways. 'He is to the manner born', William had said once of his son. 'A throwback, or chicken returned to its roost from former days I shouldn't wonder. You're more of a Hawksley than he'll ever be, Rupert my boy. St Clares don't die; they merely sleep and linger in the blood until a propitious or unpropitious moment for setting the cat among the pigeons. When poor little Marguerite died those centuries ago she left a germ of trouble behind. And I don't mean the family curse. Curses have got to be believed to work. But what's in the blood will out one day. And I tell you, Rupert, I fear for my son.'

'Why should you, Uncle? He has all the advantages.'

William had shaken his head. 'No. There's a taint of weakness in him – instability if you prefer it – that I'd rather not have trusted with Hawksley tradition. But I've no alternative. He's my son. You'll keep an eye on him, won't you, when I'm gone? He respects you, y'know.'

Rupert had promised, though he doubted if it came to the point of argument he'd have any influence with his younger cousin.

It seemed strange to him, thinking back over this past conversation, that he was now doing what his Uncle had wished – watching over David's interest, or rather the interest of his young widow Adelaide; whether she admitted it or not, Adelaide needed him. With him it was different. He'd got on perfectly well before she thrust herself into his life. And if she took off tomorrow he knew he'd survive. But life without her would not be the same. There'd be something missing; a zest? A colour? Oh more than that. A man of his kind could find colour elsewhere – in some daring contraband scheme or battle of wits with the Revenue. He had the mine to work for and expand; always a challenge ahead. But this new core of tenderness in him – the developing passion for his wife was something he'd not counted on. If it hadn't been for that dastardly St Clare he might have won her eventually, in spite of her girlish yearnings for David. But the seed of treachery would now forever stand between, causing disquiet and doubt in his own heart and a longing in her own for the shadow Anthony had left behind.

He'd have liked to tackle the bastard with fists, and hoped to God they never met again face to face. No punch-up would exorcise the damage already done, or allay the inward pain caused by Adelaide's falseness. She could have waited. Surely to God she could have waited, before expending her passion so wastefully. He still couldn't accept her puerile explanation that she'd thought the fair-haired philanderer was David. Pretence or lying didn't come easily to him. But whatever her failings one thing was clear.

He loved her.

Other women, like Katherine St Clare might arouse his admiration, affection – even veneration. But it was Adelaide he longed for with his heart and loins and senses. Adelaide he wanted to crush in his arms feeling her warmth and sweetness close against him, fused in the richness of mutual giving and taking.

She had spoiled all other women for him, though he doubted he could endure monastic celibacy for ever.

As always at such moments his mind turned to Elizabeth's capacity for easing torment into peace. Thinking of her reminded him of Adelaide's jealous dislike of having Tom's widow visit the house, and his spirits lifted a little. To wonder and fret for a bit would do Adelaide no harm. Most women had a perverse habit of wanting what was hard to get. He didn't flatter himself love came that way, but interest was the first step, and he meant to play any card he had.

As for Lilian – she would come to Trenhawk, and whenever she felt like it Elizabeth would be free to visit.

If his young madam of a wife chose to make another scene he'd be well prepared for it, and enjoy immensely putting her in her place.

Such sentiments roused him from moody gloom to mischievous anticipation.

Fireworks ahead?

There would be, one day, he thought.

Once the baby was born he'd see they both understood each other clearly. The outcome might mean fulfilment or disaster. Either way he was prepared to gamble on the risk.

Rupert's planned meeting with Ivan Behenna took place at a remote kiddeywink on the outskirts of St Rozzan. The dram shop was an ancient building situated on the sea-side of the moor where a disused mine track led down to the old village harbour. It had a shady reputation, and many illegal deals had been hatched there in the past. But due to its ill-name it was now mostly avoided by those interested in serious contraband, and the revenue had concentrated their attention elsewhere. Those who patronised the place now were mostly farm labourers, fishermen, and small time rogues out to fleece any chance caller ready for a hand of cards.

The cramped bar parlour with its one swinging lamp and shadowed interior was a favourite haunt of Ivan's who always had his ears sharp for a yarn or useful hint of possible trade.

Rupert called very infrequently, and when he did it was on the pretext of buying a young pig or two from the landlord Sammy Trewartha who had piggeries adjoining his yard. That evening when he went in Behenna was waiting for him with his mug of ale in his hand by a corner of the bar. Rupert first concluded his business with Trewartha, then took his pint over to join Ivan. The black eyes gleamed welcomingly; the white teeth flashed. 'Et's on,' he muttered through his whiskers. 'An Irish boat, *The Mary Dean*, landin' in three days time 'ef you're interested – brandy.' He paused, watching Rupert's face, with his tongue licking the frothy moustache.

'Go on,' Rupert said.

Ivan glanced round to make sure no one was listening.

'Trewartha will be in 'et', he said. 'It'll be third shares after the drivers bin paid – maister, – you'n me, an Sammy.'

'I'm not sure I'm interested,' Rupert told him. 'Third? what's that to me? If I take the risks I – '

'But you doan'. You doan'. Not this time,' Ivan assured him, in a whisper. 'The liquor'll be stored in fishin' boats by the quay the night before, then tek by waggon t' Redruth th' next evenin'.'

'I don't see where I come in,' Rupert said.

'One o' they waggons carries a perfectly legal keg or two o' spirits signed an paid for to be tek to Trenhawk, another's filled wi' young slips, you understan? A foil, maister. Cos I tell you this – there's that nosey revenue man Capn' Day bin pokin around lately. Let him get a sight o' the fust lot an' he'll have his men after et proper quick, more fule him.' He paused, and when Rupert didn't answer, began again, 'Where's the danger to you then? There edn' any. Just a red herrin' you be.'

Rupert was doubtful at first. 'Oh I don't know. Is it worth it? The gain won't be much.'

'Not much? With all them kegs? I tell you, maister, there'll be one o' the best hauls we've had for donkey's years. Course ef you edn' interested – '

But Rupert found he was interested.

The plan was properly laid, and on the appointed night the liquor was unloaded from the fishing boats on to the wagons, and the trek up the old track to the main high moorland road began. There was no moon, and the stars were hidden by low cloud. But the sound of wheels and horses' hooves were unmistakable, and as the two first wagons took the turn at the top of the hill well ahead of the others, the Preventative, led by Captain Day had appeared on horseback from the opposite side of the road and were speeding after them. Rattling away, the two wagons had already turned into Trenhawk drive when they were surrounded and stopped at pistol point. The real contraband meanwhile was safely on its way to Redruth with little danger of being halted by coastguards or police.

Rupert, in readiness for the confrontation, appeared nonchalantly from the house.

'What's this?' he said facing Robert Day squarely. 'Any

trouble with my men, Captain?'

Day, a shrewd-eyed officer with a keen assessment of men eyed him speculatively, with suspicion.

'I'd like to see in these waggons if you don't mind, sir.'

'I do mind,' Rupert answered. 'You've an infernal nerve if I may say so. But since you insist – ' he turned to the drivers. 'Let the officers inspect our cargo,' he said ironically.

When the order was completed, following a screaming smelly interlude with the young pigs and inspection of the receipted bill for the brandy, Day turned once more to Rupert and remarked, 'It seems an odd time of the night for conducting business, Mr Hawksley. I should have thought daylight would be easier and safer. Is this the usual procedure?'

Rupert's eyes held a challenging light in them when he replied, 'Goods are delivered at any time I think fit. And I'm sure there's no law concerning hours. If there is I didn't know, and I shall rely on you to keep me informed of any changes in the rules.'

There was a brief battle of glances between the two men. Then without another word the Preventive were mounting their horses, and a few minutes later were away.

Rupert laughing to himself, shortly followed the two wagons which were already on their way to the back portion of the house. When the young pigs had been despatched squeaking to their new quarters, and the liquor taken to the cellars, he went in.

He already felt better for the little duel with the Law. Whether the exercise had been worth it financially was debatable. But the interlude had certainly taken his mind for a time from Adelaide, which he found curiously relaxing and a relief following the turbulence of their recent relationship.

The following afternoon Rupert was at the stables about to set off for the farm and mine when he noticed Mrs Pender's broad figure beckoning him from the side door. He left his horse with Carnack and went to meet her. 'What is it?' he asked. 'Anything wrong?'

She shook her head. Her beady eyes held a touch of awe. 'I shouldn' say wrong, surr. But – ' she glanced behind her shoulder meaningfully. 'Tes vicar, Mr Rupert.'

'Carncrose?'

'The Reverand Carncrose, as I did say,' the housekeeper emphasised. 'Wantin' to have a word with 'ee.'

'I see,' Rupert answered, with a shrewd idea of what the word might be about. Joseph Carncrose, spiritual guardian of the parish, was an amiable custodian of village welfare, generally willing to turn a blind eye to any harmless legal offence, providing it caused no human misery and was of mutual benefit to his flock and to himself. A keen eye, and quick ear were habitual with him, and very little went on in the district without his knowledge.

Mrs Pender had already shown him into the library, when Rupert entered the house. The short portly figure was standing by the window and turned quickly at the sound of the door opening. He was about sixty with a broad rosy countenance that beamed benevolence.

'Good afternoon, vicar,' Rupert said. 'This is a surprise.'

'Ah well!' the Reverend Carncrose stepped forward taking Rupert's hand in a firm grip. 'Having a bit of a breather, sir – hardly any sleep last night. Zacky Daniel's mother was ill. So I thought it my duty to be with her in what looked to be her last hours.'

'And were they her last?' Rupert enquired politely.

'Happily no. But it was a miracle, indeed it was. And by the way – '

'Yes?'

'As my horse was nearing a certain curve in the road it was a wonder I wasn't taken myself.' There was a short pause before the Reverend gentleman continued. 'Wagons sir – just missed us by a hair's breadth.'

'Indeed.'

'Yes, yes. Curious thing was – ' the bland voice hesitated as one eye half closed in a wink ' – two went in the opposite direction to the others. And would you believe it – the Law was waiting.'

'The Law!' Rupert echoed with no trace of expression on his face. 'No trouble, I hope.'

'Come, come, sir,' the vicar remonstrated, 'one does not, I think, expect trouble at Trenhawk.'

Rupert shrugged, relaxed, and gave a short laugh.

'All right. I understand. Well, I mustn't be mean. Sit down,

Vicar, and when you've had a sip of brandy – my best vintage I assure you – I'll be honoured to know you have a keg in your own cellar.'

'Mine's the privilege,' came the reply with a return of the bland smile. 'A united community's a happy one. And no one can say we're not united in St Rozzan, can they?'

Rupert threw his companion a shrewd glance.

'You're trusted and respected, Vicar. It's hardly likely anyone would doubt your integrity. Now – what about that drink?'

'Splendid. And then I must be on my way. I hope I've not inconvenienced you. Your time, I know, is precious. And I must look in on Zacky's poor mother.'

'Give her my wishes for a quick recovery,' Rupert said, as he poured the liquor and handed a glass to Carncrose.

'I will most certainly. And may I wish you and your good lady the best of health and future prosperity.'

A plump hand was raised as Rupert echoed the sentiments on the vicar's behalf.

Five minutes later the sturdy clerical figure was riding leisurely back towards St Rozzan having been assured the keg of brandy would be delivered by Carnack at the vicarage within a week.

XI

Jane Venables, a spinster in her thirties, plain faced, but with a pair of fine dark eyes, duly arrived at Trenhawk, followed shortly afterwards by the pert Lilian. To her surprise, after the first few days Adelaide's attitude to the girl changed, and she began to find her company quite stimulating. She had a sister working as housemaid at Sir Melford Rickson's establishment in London, which meant that Adelaide gathered titivating news items of current society, concerning Lady Rickson in particular. It was said she had captivated the interest of a foreign prince, and already had an apartment of her own in some discreet district where intimate meetings took place.

Sir Melford, considerably older than his wife was something in politics, so Lilian said, Tory with a great dislike and mistrust of Mr Gladstone who was too concerned with the welfare of the trouble-making Irish to be 'quite a gentleman', although he had been to Eton and Oxford.

She spoke of a strange looking MP whom Sir Melford admired in principle because he had nice manners and was 'an up and coming' politician. His name was Benjamin Disraeli, and although he was Jew, he had been to dinner at the Melfords – which should show how clever he was. He had made quite a hit with Lady Melford, and she with him. But, according to Lilian's sister, it was all sly ambition on his part. A maid servant of Mrs Disraeli's had told her he was happy with his wife, and that she adored him.

'If you ask me' – the letter had ended, 'm'lady should steer clear of getting mixed up with her husband's friends. One day, if she goes too far he'll give her her come-upings'. He shuts his eye to his wife's liaison with the prince. But then it wouldn't do, would it, to snub royalty?'

Lilian, relating the letter almost word for word, was a graphic talker, and Adelaide enjoyed such conversations.

'Your sister and you seem to have been well educated,' she

said one day to the girl. 'Not many in your position can write letters.'

Lilian's lips tightened. 'We were brought up to have ambitions, ma'am. My da had a small store of his own and until he was took ill it was never thought either of us girls would have to go into service. When Aunt Elizabeth married Uncle Tom he said she'd lowered herself – him just a worker down a dark dirty mine. And so she had, too. It was all wrong. Well I mean – look what happened.'

'How *is* your aunt?' Adelaide enquired politely but coldly.

'She's all right. The choirmaster at our Church there's got his eye on her already.'

'You mean they're – they're fond of each other?'

Lilian shrugged. 'Oh I wouldn't say that. Not *her*, anyway. It's my belief she's got hopes in another direction.'

'Where?' asked Adelaide pointedly.

'I've no idea. And I may be wrong. But you can't expect a woman like her to go on without a bit of love in her life for ever, can you?'

'I suppose not,' Adelaide agreed, pretending indifference. 'But I hardly know her. She certainly seemed a capable woman.'

Lilian laughed.

'But that's not the same thing is it? Men don't always go for a good housewife. There are other things. And since she came to us, Aunt Lizzie's sort of blossomed if you know what I mean. Well, you'll see for yourself soon, I expect. Ma's sure to send her over to find out how I'm shaping.'

'I don't think there's any need for that,' Adelaide retorted promptly. 'If I wasn't satisfied I should say so. And it isn't always advisable to have relations calling on servants. I tell you what I'll do, I'll write a note to your mother myself, saying how efficient you're becoming.'

'Oh but – Mr Rupert – the master said – '

'The master has nothing to do with it,' Adelaide interrupted sharply. 'Domestic arrangements are *my* affair. But I've no objection at all to you having an extra afternoon off occasionally – a whole day perhaps, which should give you ample time to see your family. Will you please remember that, Lilian?'

'If you say so, ma'am.' The girl's voice had changed, become sullen with a hint of underlying rebellion in it.

Adelaide turned her head away, as a signal of dismissal.

She wished the subject of Elizabeth Chywanna had never arisen. She supposed it was her condition that made her suspicious and so unreasoningly jealous of the other woman – that, and Rupert's refusal to see her point of view. He could so easily have been nicer about things. Even a marriage of convenience like theirs surely entailed certain obligations and show of politeness over certain matters.

But Rupert had never been polite to her and she recognised that under present circumstances he could hardly be expected suddenly to turn into a man of fine manners and gallant speeches.

Shortly following Lilian's arrival in the household the cook was engaged, having first been vetted by Mrs Pender who'd assumed she had the right to choose the proper person to work under her. The woman was a widow, Mrs Dorcas Cole. She was amiable middle-aged, plump and clean looking, obviously capable, with two excellent references to her credit, one of ten years standing with a Lady Mildmarsh who had recently died.

Mrs Pender, though endeavouring not to show it, had been impressed. 'Think you'd like it here, do you?' she'd enquired. 'It's a cut off place – not much company, and plenty to do. Not fancy cookin' generally, you understand – but those who come here have to fit in with the ways of the house an' there are other little things you'd have to be prepared to take on in an emergency.' She'd paused, adding, 'There's something else that has to be understood too. I'm housekeeper here, and getting on. Peace of mind, I have to have, such as knowing when I take my rest you'd keep an eye on the others. We've a new girl, Lilian, and I've a fancy she'd be a flighty one, given the chance.'

'I understand,' Mrs Cole had said. 'I've dealt with many of that sort in my time. You've explained things perfickly, ma'am, Mrs Pender. and make no mistake about it, I know my position in a properly run place, an' that the housekeeper is always top. As for being quiet – ' she gave a little laugh – 'I was born a country woman, and will be glad to return to it. High society isn't really "my cup of tea", as they say; only being fond of Lady Mildmarsh made me stay longer in Bristol than I would've in the ordinary way.'

Mrs Pender thought a moment then said, 'And you don't mind workin' for less money, Mrs Cole?'

The woman shook her head. 'I wouldn't be here if I did. When I first saw Mr Hawksley he put me in the picture right away.'

'There's another thing you'll have to know, an' no questions asked,' Mrs Pender added. 'Sometimes the master gets called out at nights. He has shipping interests, you understand, and it's not for us to be about then. He's very set on keeping business private.'

Mrs Cole nodded.

'I'm not the curious sort, Mrs Pender, nor interfering either. If you think I'll suit, I'll see your word's law and keep to my own place. As a matter of fact –'

'Yes?'

'I have a feeling you and I might get on very well together, Mrs Pender.'

Mrs Pender thought so too, and Dorcas Cole was engaged forthwith as cook.

Adelaide meanwhile, at times lethargic, at others restless and still irritated that she'd not been given a more free hand in the choice of staff, turned more and more to Lilian for company and a little lighthearted stimulus.

In April France's new Emperor, Napoleon III had gone with his Empress Eugénie to visit Queen Victoria at Windsor. There had been gossip, Lilian's sister's last letter had implied, that the Queen was not half so prim and truly virtuous as the public thought. Word had got round that she was besotted by the dashing and dangerous Napoleon, and that he was always whispering romantic notions into her ear. He had ambitions of course – everyone knew that. His wife was very beautiful, and had been a Spanish Countess, Eugénie de Montigo before her marriage. She had red hair in which she often wore flowers, and looked very elegant driving through the London crowds in delicate coloured gowns with small feathered bonnets on her fashionably coiffured lustrous hair.

The epistle, of course, was worded more simply, but in language sufficiently graphic to stimulate Adelaide's interest and set her planning her new wardrobe for when the baby arrived. Expense at that time did not enter her mind, and if it had she would have dismissed it as of no importance. She had her own money; she would enjoy it.

Being completely ignorant of financial affairs she was unaware that a certain shipping organisation in which half her capital was invested was on the verge of complete collapse, and that dividends from other of her holdings were at a low ebb. Rupert took care not to enlighten her, but he was secretly worried, which made him more withdrawn than usual and liable to take off by himself to the mine or farm. Sometimes, glancing at Adelaide over dinner in the spring twilight, with only candles lighting the pallor of her face and glistening fair hair, it seemed to him morosely he was facing a stranger. She appeared so remote from him, yet completely self-satisfied and at ease now everything had been practically rounded off to her own satisfaction. Most men, he thought moodily, would insist on certain rights. She was no weakling. If it had not been for her precious David or that dastardly Anthony – !

Always at this point he caught himself up abruptly. Hot blooded he might be, but such violation under the circumstances, was to him unthinkable. So he contained himself, trying to be content with her dutiful response to his good-night kiss, and occasional brief visits when he went to her room for a chat before retiring to his own premises.

It was a lonely life. What with doubts of the mine, increasing expenditure, less in the bank, and a wife who did not love him, existence frequently appeared decidedly fruitless and unrewarding. So he forced his mind to other matters and the problem of finance which seemed once more to demand a tricky exercise in contraband, something he'd thought to put behind him for good.

Adelaide's child, a girl, was born on the evening of 17th August. The delivery was easy, without complication or much pain. When she came round and first looked on the new born infant, hoping to find a miniature David in the curve of her arm, Adelaide had a shock. The minute scrap of humanity had a wrinkled cross little face under a thatch of red hair.

She appeared in fact to be the image of her great-grand-mother by blood – Lady Serena St Clare.

Adelaide turned in momentary disgust. 'Take her away,' she said to Rupert who was standing nearby. 'I don't want her.'

'But, Adelaide – '

'Take her away,' she repeated. 'That's not my child.'

The nurse shrugged.

'Your wife's shocked and tired, Mr Hawksley,' she said. 'Later everything will be different. You'll see.'

But Rupert, having seen Adelaide's expression, doubted it, and from that moment decided doggedly, that whatever love the little girl lacked from her mother, he would repay twice over. The child's parentage was not her fault, poor little thing. Bastard in blood she might be, but not in name. She bore his own, and he'd see she'd benefit by it.

And so a bond was sealed between them, stronger than any tie of blood, which the little girl was quick to sense as the days passed.

Adelaide's indifference continued. Even when Rupert sounded her on a choice of name for the child, she said coldly, 'Call her what you like, it's no matter to me.'

'What about Genevra?' he persisted. 'Genevra was my grandmother's name.'

She shrugged. 'All right. Genevra.'

And so it was.

The christening took place at St Rozzan Church with a small congregation including Carnack and Mrs Pender. Adelaide had been surprised at Rupert's insistence on a religious cere-mony. 'I didn't know you were so conventional, Rupert,' she'd remarked with an edge to her voice. 'I should have thought under the circumstances –'

'What?' The look in his eyes had been dangerous.

Displeased she'd answered, 'Oh nothing. But – well, it isn't as if – '

'She was *my* child? Be careful, Adelaide,' he'd warned her. 'From now onwards she *is*, and you'd do well to remember it.'

She hadn't replied, except to ask icily, 'And what about Godparents?'

'I'm sure the vicar's wife would oblige,' he'd said drily. 'I could get Bob Staines, my solicitor, and his wife for the other two – or Aunt Matilda?'

'Oh no,' quickly. 'Aunt Matilda mustn't know until – until later.'

'Quite,' he said drily, 'late enough to arrange a conveniently fictitious birthday.'

Adelaide had had the grace to blush. She already felt guilty at not having informed her trusting aunt of the birth, which Rupert knew very well. News of the marriage itself had come as a shock to the good lady who had felt it a little unseemly that her niece could remarry so quickly following upon dear David's death. She had been hurt also not to be invited down but a bad attack of influenza followed by bronchitis had luckily spared the embarrassment of contrived and devious explanation from her niece.

Adelaide meant to delay any encounter with her elderly relative for as long as possible. When the time came there would be sure to be an endless stream of questions, congratulations, and fussy remarks concerning likenesses and characteristics. A point would most certainly be made of the child's astonishing crop of red hair.

'Red hair! Imagine it!' she could already almost hear her aunt exclaim! 'Whoever heard of a Drake or a Hawksley with red hair? Quite remarkable.'

Yes, 'remarkable' was certainly the word, Adelaide thought, visualizing the scene and remembering with a stab of dislike the macabre hateful face of old Lady St Clare who had been so proud of her own red locks in youth, that like Queen Elizabeth she'd resorted to artifice in her ageing years.

If only Genevra could have had a look of David.

But there was none.

It seemed to her the child was some wilful trick of fate sent to torment her.

During the weeks following Genevra's birth Rupert was forced to spend much of his time away from the house, due to increasing worry that Wheal Tansy's expected new lodes were going to be far less than expected. Further consultations with Borlaze and engineering experts, confirmed Rupert's own opinion that a new shaft would have to be sunk to a final depth

of 500 fathoms. The operation might involve serious risk of
ground collapses, which could endanger the mine itself, but if
the venture was not undertaken the working life of Wheal
Tansy had only a limited time left.

So it was decided to go ahead, with Rupert putting on a
front of optimism that lulled the men into a temporary sense of
security.

'And s'posing after all this expense an' work the ore's not
worth it?' Borlaze enquired one day. 'What then, master? I'm
not saying things'll work out that way. We know tin's there –
but how much, Mr Rupert? Those last levels were quick
enough to run out. Too quick by half for my likin'. It's a
gamble. You've got to face it – all mining is, if you're not
prepared to sink a fortune as well.'

'I'm sinking all I've got,' Rupert told him bluntly. 'And I'm
contemplating doubling that with what I take out. Cheer up,
Borlaze. We're on to a good thing – you, me, and all the men.'

But inwardly the slight fear niggled, especially when he
considered Adelaide's extravagance. It was then at such
moments, resentment gnawed at him. She took everything,
but offered nothing in return. Almost two months had passed
since Genevra's birth, yet so far she'd given no sign of allowing
the slightest intimacy between them.

It was now a year since the routine of life had been dis-
rupted by her intrusion into his affairs. A year of upheaval and
restless emotional change. Looking back he was amazed to
find how remote his association with Elizabeth now seemed.
At times, though, he would have given a great deal for a chat
with her husband and a glimpse of his loyal figure seated at
the window of the cottage. Tom Chywanna had been one of
the old sturdy type of workers – uninterested in talk of unions
and 'rights', though God alone knew if ever a man had excuse
to grumble, it had been Tom. Elizabeth, he knew, was getting on her feet again. He'd discovered she had ambitions to
take over a small bakery near her sister's, and he was himself
thinking of loaning her the sum required as down payment for
six months rent ahead, and the goodwill of the business.
Financially it would eventually be no loss to him; he had
complete faith in Elizabeth's capacity to pay back at a future
date, and the amount required, even as things were at the

mine, would neither break or make him. All the same the niggle of it, combined with his wife's disregard for economy and determination to have matters entirely her own way at Trenhawk, added a restricting sense of frustration demanding outlet and release from tension.

The outcome was inevitable.

On an afternoon in late October when he was locked in his study pouring over business problems with a decanter of Williams very old and excellent brandy beside him, domestic matters were brought to a head. He'd told Mrs Pender that he was not to be disturbed unless Mrs Chywanna called. But the housekeeper, now completely deaf in one ear, had misunderstood, believing he'd said, '*even*' Mrs Chywanna.

So when about four thirty, Mrs Pender poked her head round the parlour door and told Adelaide Elizabeth was there and wanted to see the master, she ended by asking, 'What am I to do? Shall I tell her to wait or not, Miss Adelaide? – ma'am, – the master said –'

'Where is she?' Adelaide asked sharply.

'At the back, in my sitting room,' Mrs Pender said. 'She's got a cab waitin' at the side door. All smartened up she is, jus' as though she was some duchess going her rounds. I told her Mr Rupert wasn't available – that's the word I used – but she said she'd wait. Is that all right, Miss Adelaide?'

'No,' Adelaide replied promptly. 'Leave her to me, Mrs Pender, I'll see her myself. You won't mind me using your room, will you? There are a few things I must make clear to Mrs Chywanna.'

'Oh no, ma'am – there's plenty for me to get on with in Master Julian's room. An' I've got to see that Lilian's properly tidied up for Miss Venables.'

'Where *is* Lilian?'

'She went to St Rozzan 'bout ten minutes ago to take the mail, must've gone the field way or they'd have met –'

'Oh.' Adelaide thought for a moment, then said, 'Well, that makes it simpler, doesn't it? I don't want my husband bothered with anyone just now. He's seemed tired lately.'

The old housekeeper flung her a shrewd glance that told more than any words could have done what she thought. Then she remarked, 'Ais. I agree. Best get rid of her – ef you can.'

'We'll be as quiet about it as we can then,' Adelaide said, 'You go, Mrs Pender. I won't be a minute.'

As the door closed she went to the mirror, smoothed her hair, pushing a rebellious golden lock behind her ear, straightened the narrow velvet bow in the froth of lace at her neck, and quietly left the room, making her way down the hall to the housekeeper's quarters.

She turned the knob of the door and went in. Elizabeth was still standing, with her plump shapely figure outlined against the window. she was wearing a short fur cape – probably rabbit, Adelaide thought scathingly – over a high-necked blue cloth bodice and blue skirt not full enough to be fashionable. Yet as always her appearance was comely, and when she turned, with the light from the hall striking across her pleasant countenance, Adelaide noted that her skin was still excellent, surprisingly fresh and young for her age.

'Well, Mrs Chywanna,' Adelaide said, with polite cold formality, 'I understand you have come all the way from – Truro is it – to see my husband. If so I'm extremely sorry. He isn't in.'

'Not *in*?' Elizabeth's voice was puzzled. 'But I – he's *expecting* me, Mrs Hawksley. We have business to talk over, and it was arranged for today.'

'Then I'm afraid there's been some mistake,' Adelaide told her firmly. 'You must have misunderstood. My husband won't be back for some hours yet. Is there anything I can do?'

Her tones was haughty, but her own deliberate lie combined with the steady stare of the clear blue eyes confronting her were inwardly disconcerting.

Elizabeth picked up her gloves – so obviously meant to imply gentility, Adelaide told herslf scathingly – and lifting her head an inch or two higher replied, 'If you wouldn't mind telling Mr Rupert I called, I'd be obliged. I'm sorry to have bothered you, I'm sure.'

Adelaide smiled with false sweetness. 'No bother at all. Your niece, I'm glad to say, is getting on very well here, and you have no cause to make enquiries. She's quite a treasure.'

'Oh. I'm glad to hear it.'

'And now, Mrs Chywanna, if you'll excuse me – ' holding the door open, 'I have things to attend to. We are in the throes of re-organising the household. I'm sorry Lilian too is absent, but I'll see she has a day off to visit you as soon as possible.'

Recognising the dismissal Elizabeth went out, followed by Adelaide who took her to the side door and the drive where the cab was waiting. Almost immediately there was the rattle of wheels and sound of horses' hooves dying into the distance.

Adelaide breathed a sigh of relief and relaxed. She was not proud of herself for the role she'd played, and she knew she'd taken a risk. Rupert, in spite of his study being so well tucked away, might have heard something of the activity going on, or taken it into his head to leave his snug little private domain at an inopportune moment. Then the fat would have been in the fire.

As things turned out everything had apparently been settled satisfactorily. So Adelaide went upstairs to her bedroom, had a wash, wiped her forehead with cologne, and slipped off her dress to change for dinner. Her own reflection through the mirror was pleasing following the uncomfortable months previous to her confinement. Although she'd had to accept the unwelcome process of breast-feeding the baby for a time her figure was gradually assuming its youthful elegant lines, and as she released herself for a brief interim from a newly designed corset, she told herself with a stab of vanity that her skin was more fair than Elizabeth's, having a creamy milk-white quality that emphasised the honey-gold glints of her lustrous hair. Instinctively she let a hand stray to the combs and pins that confined it, allowing its waves to cascade over her firm young shoulders and breasts. The discarded dress lay on the floor, in a dark olive-green mass. Above the graceful column of her neck a faint rosy glow lit her cheeks from the dying sunlight outside. The air was warm for the time of year. Only a frail flutter of breeze stirred the lace curtains at the slightly opened window. Adelaide always insisted that the heavy velvet ones should not be pulled across until daylight had really faded. She liked the tang of moors and heather which in autumn mingled so nostalgically with distant wood-smoke and drift of brine from the sea.

She found, rather to her surprise, that her interview with Elizabeth had stimulated and freed her from a number of small annoyances arising from the other woman's maddening passivity. She'd been firmly put in her place now, and it was hardly likely she'd make the mistake again of descending upon Trenhawk unless expressly at the invitation of herself – its mistress, Mrs Rupert Hawksley.

In a wave of self-satisfaction, Adelaide took a deep breath and lifted both slender but firmly rounded arms above her head. She sighed, yawned, let her hands stray in luxurious contentment through her tumbled thick hair, and then – there was a knock.

She looked round quickly as the door opened. Rupert stood there momentarily before closing it quietly. His face was faintly flushed, lips set, and eyes – why were they so narrowed and looking at her so intently? Could it be that someone – Mrs Pender perhaps – had unwittingly revealed Elizabeth's visit. With her heart racing Adelaide realised she should have thought of the risk earlier. She'd never seen that particular expression on Rupert's face before. He looked almost – dangerous. And the odour of brandy was strong in the air.

She clutched her under-bodice closer above the white breasts.

'What – what do you want, Rupert?' she asked, trying to control the trace of nervousness in her voice.

'What *should* I want, dear wife?' he queried, 'except an explanation perhaps, and my reasonable due.'

'I don't know what you mean.'

'Don't you, my love, *don't* you?' He came slowly yet purposefully towards her. She drew away, but his hands were on her shoulders from behind, his eyes burningly upon hers through the mirror.

'Rupert –'

'Get up,' he said suddenly.

'But I'm not dressed I –'

'Get up,' he repeated. 'And forget the frillies. You were quick enough to forget them before when that bastard had you in the bracken. So stand up if you please and let me see you as you really are for once. No lies, Adelaide, no more mock modesty. *Get up.*'

With her knees trembling she raised herself to her feet. He pulled her round with such sudden force the layers of petticoats were wrenched from her waist, falling in an abandon of

starched frills and lace to the floor. Instinctively her hands
went protectingly to her stomach and thighs encased in their
long drawers. He laughed a trifle desirously, then snatched at
the disordered bodice, which fell apart revealing the rosy-
tipped breasts above the slender waist.

'Oh!' he said, in light sarcastic tones, 'that's better – much
better.'

'Rupert, if you'd only –'

'If I'd only explain my gross bad manners and violation of
your virgin privacy – yes, that would be nice, for *you* –
wouldn't it?' he said. 'But you've had things your own way
long enough, Adelaide. It's high time we had a proper understanding, don't you agree – ?'

'I thought –'

'You thought we'd continue for ever as we've done since the
very first day when you promised to love, honour – and obey –
or didn't you? No, of course not. Ours wasn't that kind of
marriage. But a marriage nevertheless, with the same impli-
cations.'

She didn't reply.

'How amazing,' he said after a pause.

'What?'

'Adelaide Hawksley lost for words! Well – I'm not surprised, not really. Damn you – how dare you Addy? How *dare*
you send Elizabeth off with some trumped-up tale without
telling me she was here? I'd asked her to come; and she told
you, didn't she? Elizabeth isn't like you – she's straight, direct,
and doesn't lie her head off whenever the mood takes her. But
you – you little hypocrite – you got her out of the way conveniently for your own satisfaction either by lying or damned
rudeness, letting her think I'd forgotten. My God! you've a
nerve. If I had any sense I'd give you the beating you deserve.
You see, my dear wife, even a gentleman has his limits. And
I'm not that, am I? Not a "gentleman" like your two ex-lovers.
Or were there more? How do I know? What guarantee have I
of your virtuous life in London – ?'

'Stop it – stop it –' she cried.

'Why should I?'

'Because it's not true, and you know it isn't –' she flashed,
'I'm not that sort of person –'

'I know very little about you except your moods and tempers and selfish ways – your calculating sordid little plans for
being the only woman in the picture. Always Adelaide Hawksley – Adelaide Drake that was, – the spoiled rich young heiress
who takes what she wants and be damned to the rest –
including Elizabeth – '

'I didn't realise she was so important,' Adelaide managed to
persist breathlessly, 'and you'd no right to ask her here after –
after – '

His hands tightened so fiercely on her shoulders she broke
off wincing with pain.

'I've every right, madam, and after today there'll be no
more talks of "rights" between you and me – ' she strained her
head away and managed to free her hands, beating with her
fists against his chest. One arm tightened round her waist. She
could feel his hard body close against her own. She kicked his
shin and sent her slipper spinning off across the floor. He
laughed. In a tantrum of fury she bit his hand. He slapped her
lightly against one cheek, then swept her over an arm and
spanked her. She was astonished rather than hurt. Her face,
when she looked up, was hot, amazed and indignant, giving
her the appearance momentarily of an outraged child.

'You've been asking for that for nearly twenty years, Addy,'
Rupert said, lifting her up, 'and for more time than I care to
remember I've imagined this moment – ' he was breathing
heavily. His eyes, burning down on her own, were dark and
intimidating, filled with purpose and desire. Her heart jerked
to sudden painful life. She struggled ineffectually and then lay
still, her cheeks gone suddenly pale, the cloud of fair hair
tumbled in a golden stream from her face.

Her body was limp, but trembling with frightened exhilaration as he carried her to the bed and took her, not in lust, but
with an abandonment of passion that was darkness and light to
her – a revelation of all the secret sensual awareness that had
lain dormant and unacknowledged for so long. She had known
romance and affection for David, but nothing like this, which
held the darkness of death, and thrust of being born again; of
subjugation and union with a force utterly beyond her power
or wish to stem. When it was over she lay for a timeless period
on her back, eyes closed, as her pulses gradually died to peace.

She was hardly aware when he eased himself from her side, got up and tidied himself. At the door he turned and said with a nonchalance he was far from feeling, 'I'm sorry if I've inconvenienced you, Mrs Hawksley. To save any embarrassment I shall be away for a few days.'

She could hardly believe her ears. Away? After what had just happened. But why? Was he still trying to punish her over Elizabeth? Or could it be he was testing her reaction?

Pretending indifference she asked casually, 'When are you going?'

'Tonight. Plymouth. I've business waiting.'

'I see. Oh well – I hope it's a success.'

'It's got to be.' There was a short silence, then he added, 'Good-bye then. See you soon.'

'Good-bye.'

She turned her face away, and heard miserably the click of a door followed by the sound of his receding footsteps along the landing.

When at last all was quiet she buried her face in the pillow with heavy sobs tearing at her throat; sobs of disillusionment, loss, anger, and a wild uncontrollable longing. Then, after a time, she got up and went to the mirror. Her naked body, still flushed in parts from his ravishing, was both a condemnation and a pride. She let her hands stray briefly over curves of breasts and thighs; then in a sudden rush of indignation reached for her clothes and hastily dressed.

She waited until all trace of distress had left her eyes, applied rice powder to her complexion, and a touch of rosy lipsalve to her mouth. Then, forcing herself to a semblance of composure she did not feel, she considered herself critically through the mirror, recalling descriptions she'd read concerning the French Empress Eugénie whose fine eyes were always emphasised by a liberal artificial darkening of lashes and brows.

Well, she thought, lifting her head proudly, for looks she could vie with any foreign empress; and the next time she went to a town she'd purchase what cosmetics were available. If Rupert chose to treat her like a – a cast-off mistress – used and left coldly immediately afterwards for some stuffy business deal, she'd contrive somehow to present a fitting exterior.

Should he comment or make objection she could always point out that some of the most exalted young matrons in the country had set the fashion.

This tit-for-tat mood relieved something of her affront and disappointment, and when she went downstairs later a secret little thrill of anticipatory triumph was already reimbursing her self-confidence.

Rupert would soon be back, and then she'd show him. In a few days he'd return. His business, whatever it was – couldn't last long.

But it did.

It was a full fortnight before he appeared again at Trenhawk, and by then without a line from him or a word, her zest for proving herself and paying him out had died into depressing anxiety under a veneer of assumed boredom. Whether any of the servants were aware of the scene preceding his departure, Adelaide didn't know, though she'd had an uncomfortable sensation sometimes that Mrs Pender's eyes frequently held a speculative look in them.

The afternoon of Rupert's return was chilly holding already the intangible quality of winter to come. Genevra, well wrapped, was in her pram near the front porch when he walked up the path from the drive. He glanced down at the small quaint face peering up from its absurd frilly bonnet, and a wave of quick anger seized him. She looked cold. Though the cheeks were rosy with health, her button nose had a blueish tinge. He reached down, picked her up, wrapping the shawl closely round her, and strode into the house. Adelaide was in the parlour seated by the fire thumbing through some fashion magazines.

She looked up, startled to see him carrying the baby.

'What do you mean leaving her out in this weather?' he demanded sharply. 'Or aren't you aware of the first thing about children? It's cold out there.'

She was astounded that after a period away he should ignore any greeting to her personally except at an argument over the child. His sudden appearance had set her heart fluttering. Now cold annoyance swept through her.

'I don't want her cosseted,' she retorted curtly.

'Not much chance of that – with you,' Rupert told her.

'Fresh air's good for babies,' Adelaide insisted. 'They have to be hardened up –'

'Like most women of a certain type,' Rupert said pointedly.

Adelaide flushed. 'If you want to quarrel, Rupert, I certainly don't. I've had a tiring day.'

She jumped up abruptly, took Genevra from him, and confronted him with a dangerous glint in her gold-flecked eyes. 'There's quite a lot to do here,' she said. 'You may not have noticed any difference in the house nowadays – that it's tidier and more – more attractive. All the same –'

'Yes, yes,' he agreed in calmer tones, 'but you have servants now. Mrs Pender and Lucy had the whole lot on their shoulders before.'

'Lilian isn't for the hard work,' she pointed out, 'and the governess expects quite a lot of running and carrying for her. The baby too, and Julian. I'm not sure Miss Venables is right for him. He's had several rebellious fits. Do you imagine I spend the whole time just sitting about?'

The grieved look on her face which made her suddenly appear so much younger and more vulnerable softened him.

'I'm sorry. I apologise. I didn't mean to snap. It was seeing little Genevra. Anyway – ' his manner changed, became a little awkward, 'how have you been keeping?'

At last, she thought, he'd become aware of her existence.

'I'm quite all right. Thank you for asking.'

He suddenly laughed, took two strides towards her and kissed her cheeks. There was a hint of mischief in his eyes when he said, 'What's the matter, Addy? Jealous – of a baby?' She drew away quickly. 'Don't be ridiculous.'

He winced.

'It would have helped if you'd let us know you were going to be away for so long,' she said shortly.

'In what way?' His voice was sharp again, ironic. 'I can't flatter myself you were exactly languishing for my return surely?'

The brief flame in his eyes which she did not see – died completely when she retorted, 'What a stupid thing to say.'

'Yes.'

'It's just that menus and things have to be thought out,' she added hurriedly. 'A man makes a difference. Miss Venables doesn't like meat, and – oh I don't expect you to understand –'

'Good,' he said lightly. 'Then I won't waste the effort in trying.'

He went to the chest and poured himself a whisky.

'Have one?'

'No, thank you. I'm taking Genevra to her cot. It will soon be feed time anyway. There – ' as the baby started to cry ' – if you hadn't disturbed her she'd still be sleeping.'

'She wasn't asleep,' he said pointedly. 'She was chilled to the bone.'

'I don't believe you,' Adelaide retorted, carrying the child to the door.

He sprang after her and opened it wide. 'By the way,' he said casually as they passed through, 'there are a few flowers for you in your room. I had Carnack deliver them to Mrs Pender.'

She stopped for a second. 'Oh – thank you. I – I didn't expect anything.'

The mischievous glance returned to his eyes again. 'Ladies sometimes get what they *don't* expect,' he remarked, 'which makes life rather more fun, don't you think?'

At that moment she could think of nothing but that Rupert by his thoughtful act had once more contrived to get the better of her.

Rupert retreated again into the parlour. By the time Adelaide was nearing the foot of the stairs Genevra was screaming lustily. At an opportune moment Mrs Pender emerged along the hall. Adelaide thrust the baby at her. 'Try and soothe her,' she said, 'you manage her better than me. We shall really have to get a nurse – ' her breathing was quick, her voice excited. The housekeeper stared at her questioningly. With the colour bright in her cheeks, and a few strands of hair escaped over her forehead, ten years seemed to have dropped away from her young mistress's face in a matter of minutes. 'I shan't be long,' Adelaide went on breathlessly, '*please*, Mrs Pender.'

Before any reply was forthcoming she had turned the curve of the wide stairway, and with her skirt held above her ankles in both hands was taking the stairs quickly, to the landing above.

Mrs Pender, with the white bundle in her arms stood nonplussed, shaking her head thoughtfully. Then she turned, peered into the infant's face, rocking her soothingly, and hobbled back towards the kitchen. 'There now – there now – ' she murmured, ''tes no way to carry on, es it? Hush you now. An' what a funny lil thing you are to be sure – more like a little monkey than your mama's babe.'

It was true.

With the frilly bonnet off, the small face, though rounding and better-featured, was still quaint and puckish under the crop of red hair. She hadn't lost it as most children did – instead it had thickened, emphasising oddly, the wise look in the round dark-greenish eyes. Like no one else in the family, Mrs Pender thought with a stirring of compassion in her old heart. Who'd sired her she'd probably never know or anyone else, except Miss Adelaide and perhaps the father himself – who certainly wasn't Mr Rupert. She had her own suspicions, but they couldn't be proved.

The monkeyish look though – and that hair – as she rocked the little thing on her lap in her own sitting room, Mrs Pender recalled a certain afternoon years ago when the St Clare chaise had broken down outside St Rozzan. She herself had been shopping at the time, and as she'd passed the carriage she'd caught a glimpse of a fierce, haughty raddled face staring imperiously through the window. One coachman was on the box controlling the horses, another was examining the wheel. Mrs Pender had paused briefly, intrigued by the flashing display of jewellery and ornate hat perched like some exotic flower-basket on the elaborately arranged flaming red hair.

Then the imperious countenance, after one contemptuous look, had turned the other way, and Mrs Pender had walked on, thinking, 'Well, I'm sorry for anyone working for *you*, milady.'

Sorry! yes, and she was sorry for *this* little thing too she decided grimly, fully aware of Adelaide's attitude to the unwanted Genevra. But she had Mr Rupert anyway. Mr Rupert, bless him, had more compassion in one little finger than his wife had in her whole body. There was another side too. When Genevra grew up she'd back her to manage the whole lot of them if necessary. Only one thing really bothered her – that Mr Rupert's feelings should be so open to be hurt by his wilful

selfish young wife. Anyone with any sense could see he doted
on her. But Adelaide! All she thought of was herself and
mooning over Mr David – or so she made out. And a lot of that
was no more than a show of sentimental fretting. If it hadn't
been, she wouldn't have demeaned herself with another man.
So soon too, after being widowed.

Mrs Pender still felt outraged when she thought of it.

She tried to be charitable for Mr Rupert's sake. And now
the baby had arrived there was nothing else to be done about
it. She only hoped Miss Adelaide would learn sense before it
was too late.

Roses. Red roses – and so many of them. If that wasn't a
sign of love, then she didn't know what else was. But Adelaide
Hawksley had never been one to show gratitude – or even love
for that matter. If she'd been her daughter she'd have taught
her what was right and what was wrong from the very beginning, even if it meant taking a stick to her back.

Or was there *any* way of teaching the good things?

'There now – there now,' she murmured again to the fretful
baby. 'It's all right, my chicken – you've got me an' your da –
who's more of a father to you than any real one – hush now,
hush.'

And presently the wailing ceased.

Adelaide took the roses from the crystal bowl on the dressing-
table and buried her face in the velvet mass. Their perfume
was heady. For a second her senses were drowned in sweetness. She breathed deeply, and for some stupid unknown
reason tears from her eyes mingled with the fragrance of the
damp soft petals. Then slowly, she put the flowers back in the
water. She glanced round. There were others on her bedside
table – of so deep and rich a red her whole being seemed to
melt in glowing response. She moved to the bed and took a
single bloom from the vase. It was not yet fully open and half
consciously she lifted it to her lips, where a petal rested briefly,
soft as the brush of a butterfly's wing.

It was at that precise moment that Rupert came in quietly,
without knocking. He stood just inside the room until she
turned and saw him. He looked uncertain and hesitant with an
odd expression of anticipation mixed with fear in his eyes. But

she was not aware of it – only of his tall dark figure outlined against the door.

'Oh Rupert,' she said, 'thank you – *thank* you.'

She went towards him instinctively lifting her mouth to his. He bent his head. His arm encircled her waist; she could feel the warmth of his cheek on hers. A moment later he had released her.

'How did you know?' she whispered. 'However did you know, Rupert?'

He stared at her, puzzled.

'Know what? The roses do you mean – that you liked them? Well – most women do, don't they?'

She smiled. 'Red roses,' she remarked dreamily, 'they were David's flowers – and you knew, didn't you? Every week until – until he went away – there was a bunch of them, in my room. Somehow you must've – but how? How did you know – ?' She broke off, unaware of her blunder, as he released her suddenly, turned on his heel and went to the door. The single flower fell from her hand, to the floor.

Before he went out he shrugged and said casually, 'I'm a very smart man, I suppose, Addy; it's my nature to be perceptive about such matters. One has to be – in business.'

Business? She thought in bewilderment when he'd gone, what did he mean by that? And then, in a wave of disillusionment the answer hit her. Of course – he was probably trying to get her into a good mood over the mine or something. The business in Plymouth might not have been so successful as he made out, and he needed money. In a way, then, the roses had just been a kind of bribe. She felt flattened and unreasoningly depressed. If he'd asked her straight out she wouldn't have objected. Anyway, as he'd pointed out when he first proposed marriage, in law he had access to her fortune. He really needn't have tried any softening-up process at all. She went to the window and stared out. The light was fading quickly, giving an encroaching uniformity to to the sombre moors under the grey sky. The air was still heavy with the perfume of roses, but their scent had lost allure. On impulse, hearing Lilian's light footsteps on the landing, she went to the door, opened it, and said, 'Lilian, just a minute – ' the girl hurried towards her.

'Do you mind taking these roses away?' Adelaide said. 'Put the vase on the hall table and the other in the dining room. I'll have the bowl up again tomorrow, but it's not considered good to sleep with flowers in the bedroom.'

Lilian took the vase first then returned for the second larger container. She had a puzzled surprised look on her face. Later she said to Lucy, 'I can't understand, Mrs Rupert. Fancy saying flowers were bad to have in a bedroom. If a fine gentleman like the master brought *me* such a lovely present I'd thank him proper, and show gratitude. You know, Lucy – there's something – "odd" about them two.'

'How do you mean odd?'

'Well – ' Lilian glanced round first to see no one else was about, especially Mrs Pender. Then she resumed in significant whispered tones, 'to begin with they don't sleep in the same room. Oh I know the gentry are different – separate dressing rooms and all that. But it isn't as if they have connecting door or anything like that. And so far away from each other too. I mean at opposite ends of the corridor. You can't say *that's* natural, not for a newly married couple.'

'P'raps widows are different,' Lucy observed.

'What do you mean?'

'She *was* a widow,' Lucy said smugly. 'Surely you did know. Mr David, her first, was killed in that there war – only last year. Didn't your aunt tell 'ee?'

Lilian nodded.

'Yes, I'd heard.'

'Well then, that explains et, doan' et?'

'Oh *yes*,' Lilian replied knowingly. 'But I wish I knew the answers to the rest.'

'What rest?' Lucy enquired innocently.

Lilian shrugged.

'Use your loaf,' she said sharply. 'Better still, forget it. It's not our business to poke and pry. And don't you let on to that old besom Mrs Pender that we've been gossiping, or we'll both get our come-uppings quick as a fly can wink it's eye. Oh, and another thing – '

'Yes?' Lucy's voice had a surly note.

'Make sure you've seen Miss Venable's bed's properly turned down before you leave. She's a complainer, that one.'

'It isn't *my* job to turn down beds,' Lucy retorted. 'I'm late getting back as 'tis. There's work to do at the farm, and last time I was here overtime me da said he'd take his belt to me if it happened again.'

'Oh well then, I'll do it,' Lilian told her grudgingly, adding as an afterthought, 'What a lark it would be to put the roses in her room – Miss Venables' – the sly bitch.'

Lucy's jaw dropped.

'You'd *never*!'

Lilian laughed, 'I might at that. No one would know who, providing you kept your mouth shut. And you would – wouldn't you Lucy? It'd be a pity if I had to tell your father of your little carryings on with young Nick. It's more than the belt you'd be getting then.'

Lucy paused before saying, 'You're a wicked one. Real wicked you are.'

Lilian shrugged.

'No. Just playful. And high time I'd say. To put the cat among the pigeons'd brighten things up a bit in this dreary old house.'

Lucy scurried away leaving Lilian mischievously considering a project she'd not seriously thought about until a moment or two ago.

Dinner that night was a subdued affair for Adelaide and Rupert. Contrary to her expectations no mention was made by him concerning finance or the mine, which mildly discomforted her.

The bowl of roses had been placed on the table, and when Rupert said casually, 'Oh. I see you've had the flowers brought down,' she replied equally casually, 'Well, it's such a pity to waste them hidden away don't you think – in the bedroom, I mean?'

'Perhaps.'

She wondered where the others were. Lilian had been told to put them in the hall, and she supposed she'd have to tackle her about it. But perhaps she'd bunched them altogether. Anyway, it wasn't important. The flowers by then had lost significance for her. Rupert seemed so quiet and pre-occupied, almost glum, and had not even complimented her on the new dress she was wearing, which was of gold satin, low-breasted, tight-waisted with voluminous frills falling to the ground. If only he'd say *something*, she thought, playing with her fish. Surely the present of the roses had meant that he'd been thinking of her – had forgotten or put aside the disgraceful episode concerning Elizabeth Chywanna. The memory of their passionate love-making following the incident, still returned at intervals to stimulate her senses and excite her. During the days he'd been away she'd been on edge waiting for his return.

Now everything seemed to have gone wrong. He was once more the curt aloof Rupert she recalled from childhood. The mere suggestion that he could be in love with her was absurd. Rupert Hawksley cared for no one but himself, and perhaps, ridiculously the baby Genevra, and the bumptious cow-like Elizabeth.

She went to bed early, on the pretext that she had a headache.

'Oh,' he said, half absently. 'I'm sorry. Have a good night then, I hope you sleep well.'

Sleep? How could she?

She lay for a long time that night in bed, wakeful and restless, with her ears keyed to the silence, wondering if Rupert would come. She'd left the door conspicuously ajar a little, hoping irrationally to hear his footsteps emerging louder down the corridor. But there was no sound of them. Nothing but the uneasy tapping of a branch from outside on the window, followed eventually by the sharp snap of a latch closing.

It was past two before she drifted off into restless sleep.

And when she did, it was to dream.

She dreamed she was walking along a straight dusty road with nothing on either side but black barren land. There was no breath of wind, and she was alone. It was the aloneness that was so terrifying, because everything else was dead; everything but her own creeping fear and the knowledge of something threatening beyond the bleak horizon. And then she saw in the far distance ahead a tiny figure hurrying away from her, getting smaller every moment, and she knew she had to reach him. She began to run, calling 'David' – or was it 'Rupert', but he didn't hear or look back, simply receded further into the gaping nothingness of land and sky.

She gasped and choked for air; her feet felt heavy and weighted with lead. The sky above her darkened. Immense black creatures with outspread wings like those of giant bats or birds swooped down in a thick cloud, blotting out all trace of lingering light. There was a whirring and high-pitched crescendos of sound in her ears and brain – a furring of the cloying air as her arms went out in futile defence. The breath was torn from her throat and lungs. Burning dots of reddened eyes glared from the darkness. Her own went blind and useless suddenly – her limbs were crushed beneath the smothering blanket of feathered wings. She tried to force herself up and couldn't.

And she knew she was dead.

There was no sound or movement anymore. Only the never-ending void of horror-without-end.

It was then she screamed and screamed, shrill and high, with her own voice shattering the silence.

'Addy,' someone shouted, 'Addy – Adelaide – Adelaide – wake up, what is it? What's the matter?'

She came to herself with a shock. Perspiration streamed from her face and body. Her teeth were chattering; she was icily cold. Great shuddering sobs tore at her as Rupert drew her into his arms. His eyes were filled with compassion and concern, though she did not see it – her face was pressed so close to his chest.

'It's all right,' he was saying, holding her and trying to comfort as though she was a child. 'You've had a nightmare that's all – nothing else – just a *dream* –'

She clung to him with her hands clutching his shoulders. 'Don't leave me –' she said, 'oh, Rupert, don't leave me –'

His arms tightened as his lips brushed her hair. 'While you need me, Addy, I'll always be there –' he told her. 'Always.'

'Oh, Rupert.' Her breathing eased, and the sobs gradually died. After a time, when he'd brought her hot milk and biscuits she tried to explain.

'There was no one there. I was all alone, with everything else dead except some awful black things like – like vampires –'

'Oh! you've been reading too much Edgar Allan Poe,' he said half jokingly.

'No. It wasn't that. There was someone I was trying to get

to – but he went too fast and I couldn't catch up – it was David I think – ' Rupert turned his face away so she could not see the sudden hopelessness, the futile disappointment in his eyes. He became aware half consciously that she was still speaking – 'and then *they* came, smothering me. It was – '

He took her hand.

'Don't think about it, forget.'

'Will you stay with me, Rupert? Will you?'

'Of course,' he answered, 'if that's what you want.'

A little of her own natural glow returned to her cheeks. With her fair hair spilled over her nightclothes she looked like some gratified child suddenly released from fear, and it was as a child he comforted her, and later lay by her side, that night. No desire struggled in him to possess her. Her unthinking reference to David had temporarily dulled sensual awareness into acceptance that her need of him was as protection only; a role that however chilly it would be distasteful, under the circumstances, to violate.

So they lay for the rest of the night hours, as strangers, with the world between them.

And when she woke in the morning, he had gone.

Before setting off for the farm and Wheal Tansy Rupert caught sight of a slim figure carrying a glass vase at the foot of the back staircase. She had a cluster of roses pressed against her thin chest, and one bloom was held close to her chin as though any moment she might bend her prim head and kiss it. When he passed her, for a word with Carnack who was in the kitchen, she glanced up at him with an expression of gratitude discomfortingly personal on her pale rather nondescript face. He hadn't noticed before how fine her eyes were, or their intent almost devouring quality. He knew the look though – recognised it, had learned to fear in the past, that certain consuming adoration of the weaker sex for men of his type.

But why Miss Venables? And why on earth was she carrying so possessively some of the flowers he'd surely given to Adelaide the day before?

'They're so lovely – ' she whispered, in a shy conspiratorial voice. 'So beautiful. I do so *love* roses.'

Then with a quick fluttery movement she hurried on and up

the stairs, looking back once to where he stood momentarily staring after her with a bewildered frown puckering his forehead.

He went into the kitchen. Carnack and Nick were at the table with mugs of tea before them. Lucy was busy at the grate, and Lilian, looking as though butter wouldn't melt in her mouth was preparing Adelaide's breakfast tray. She gave him an innocent glance that didn't deceive him for a moment. The pert baggage, he thought with a touch of amusement, she'd obviously had a hand in the incident. But he was annoyed.

'Did you give my wife's roses to Miss Venables?' he asked sharply.

'*Me*, sir?' she looked astonished. 'They were there on her dressing table when I turned down the bed. I thought –'

'Hm!' he didn't believe her implication for one moment, 'Well, no matter. Perhaps your mistress put them there as a gesture.'

'Yes, sir.'

He was fully aware of the withheld smile on her provocative lips and Lucy's knowing half-fearful glance as she turned her head for a quick glance. Rupert, ignoring the girls further, spoke to Carnack.

'I shall be away for the day,' he said. 'An unexpected meeting at the Count House.'

'Ridin', master?'

Rupert shook his head. 'No. I need a walk to clear my brain. Send Nick to the farm though. There's a wagon load of stuff to get to the Ram.'

'I'll do that, Mr Rupert, surr.' He paused before adding, 'No trouble at Wheal Tansy, I hope?'

'No more than usual – except of Ben Oaks' making,' Rupert answered. 'When the unions got properly started I thought everything would be better for the men and owners alike – especially the men. But one discordant voice can start the dry rot in no time, once suspicion's there. Loyalty can be the first casualty. Power – that's Oaks' trouble. And when the pocket's pinched the greed and danger of it increase. Sometimes I wonder –'

Carnack waited.

Rupert gave a short laugh and went to the side door. 'I wonder what the hell life may be like in a hundred years from now,' he said. 'But then that won't worry us will it? Only our children, and those that come after them.'

'If any,' he thought morosely, not waiting to hear Carnack's reply. His whole being was dejected and ill-at-ease, reason telling him he'd acted illogically in shouldering Adelaide's problems and marrying her with all the additional expense entailed. His first duties had been to the mine and its workers, and being able to cover debts before his meagre capital was eaten away. At first the exploitation of Wheal Tansy's new lodes had appeared a gold mine, a certainty. Now he knew the certainty was diminishing day by day to a mere taunting shadow.

He could no longer blind his eye to the truth – that so far the fresh levels had petered to negative proportions. The expense of new equipment was considerably in excess of what had been scheduled for. Families trusted him for what – unless a miracle occurred – he could see no chance of supplying – decent wages and a future. Already their trust, was beginning to wear thin through Oaks' insinuations. He didn't blame them. His only consolation was that if the worst happened he'd either have to launch into some decidedly tricky and daring contraband scheme, or sell Trenhawk. The latter was so distasteful as to be unthinkable. He was damned if he'd give any gloating St Clare the chance of jumping and confiscating property that had been the Hawksleys' for centuries.

As for Adelaide! Longing, irritation, and a confusion of bewildered emotions swept over him as he recalled the highly-charged incidents of the past few weeks. Probably he'd been foolish to marry her, but the deed was done – and as his wife, whether she liked it or not, she'd have to face the consequences.

If she loved him the prospect would be easier. But she didn't, and he doubted that she ever would.

For the first time the memory of David seemed to sour and embitter his very soul.

As he walked sharply across the moors to Wheal Tansy, dislike that was almost hatred of his dead cousin consumed him, steeling him to purpose and action.

He had still one card to play where his exasperating wife was concerned, and if necessary, he would play it. Anything to wipe the ghostly image from her heart.

As it happened he didn't have to, because other larger and far more terrible events occurred that dispelled personal issued to negation.

In the middle of November there was an accident at the mine.

XII

Ever since the night following her terrifying dream Adelaide had done all in her power to tempt Rupert back to her bed. If she'd been asked why, she wouldn't have known the answer. Or if she had – she wouldn't have admitted it. She just wanted him there. Yet he made no response, even though she made it quite clear her door wasn't locked.

She felt hurt and humiliated, though she knew she shouldn't have been. She'd known he married her mostly for Genevra's sake and because of financial possibilities. He'd been honest about things from the beginning. But the past seemed at times to have been swept away by the new fiery emotion that day by day was deepening in her.

Even David's image became sometimes so pale and blurred she could hardly remember what he looked like. Then she would take out his photograph and refresh her memory. But the poignancy had gone.

Rupert had somehow spoiled the past by his dominating presence and unpredictable behaviour. Part of her responded and desired him passionately. The other side of her rejected and resented him. Yet she was beginning to realise she'd never again get him quite out of her blood. The knowledge that he could treat her so casually filled her with a sense of failure.

Couldn't he tell? Didn't he realise what he was doing to her?

Perhaps he was paying her out, she reflected, trying this way and that to find a satisfactory answer – doing his best to humiliate her because of Genevra and Anthony.

Genevra.

After the first shock of seeing the child was over she'd made an effort to simulate the affection a natural mother should feel for her first baby. If there'd been the slightest resemblance to the Hawksleys on its puckered little face the effort would have been easier. But all she saw was a quick-silver brightness in the dark green eyes proclaiming her alien ancestry – that of the hideous old creature Lady Serena who'd broken so disastrously into her meeting with Katherine that unfortunate afternoon at Carnwikk.

Genevra's red hair affronted her; the occasional elfin smile disturbed her. There was nothing plump, pretty or lovable about the tiny girl to Adelaide, though Rupert at times seemed to find her irresistible.

'She'll turn out quite a character when she's older,' he predicted more than once, not adding 'like you', though he thought it.

'A pity she wasn't a boy,' Adelaide said once. 'Looks don't matter so much with a man. Men can get by anyway if they're strong enough. But a plain girl doesn't have much chance.'

'I shouldn't have thought you'd know anything about that,' he said pointedly.

Adelaide laughed shortly. 'I've seen them sitting with dowagers and chaperones in ballrooms getting hardly a dance all evening, looking so stiff and erect you'd think their backs would break. It must be terrible. I'd hate a daughter of mine to have to go through that.'

'I don't think you need worry,' Rupert told her drily. 'As things are at the moment it's hardly likely there'll ever be balls or a coming-out season for Genevra.'

'What do you mean?' Adelaide asked sharply.

'I mean that Genevra's more likely to be baking bread or churning butter when she's old enough, than collecting beaux for a London season.'

Adelaide frowned. 'You mean there's something wrong – at the mine? Are you in difficulties financially, Rupert?'

He regarded her thoughtfully before answering bluntly, 'Not yet, but we're spending way ahead of our income, what with new machinery, additional labour, the governess, cook, housemaid, and all the extra fallals and household expenditure.'

She flushed.

'Well, that's not my fault. I economise where I can.'

'You don't economise at all, Adelaide,' he told her shortly. 'Not that I blame you. You've a right to your little luxuries. All the same – '

'Yes?'

'Watch it.'

'Of course,' she said assuming false brightness. 'I didn't know you were worrying exactly. I can always dip into my capital – I told you before, and I don't mind, Rupert. It's what the money's there for – '

'But it *isn't*,' he said bluntly, 'not as much as you thought. That's why I've mentioned it.'

'What do you mean?'

He sighed. 'I suppose you've got to know. Those shares of yours – the shipping investments – '

'Yes?'

'They're down, Addy.'

She stared.

'*Down?*'

'Defunct almost.' His voice was dry, emotionless.

The colour drained from her face leaving it set and tense.

'I don't understand. How *could* they be? They're good shares – they always have been – '

'Maybe. But these things sometimes happen in business. A false judgement or project – a chairman of a company with too much ambition and too little sense, or a new rival concern with a better eye to the future, and the whole thing can go bust like a pricked balloon.'

'I see. Well – ' she paused to get her breath, then said calmly, 'I've other – what is it it's called – collateral? Assets?'

'Some,' he admitted ambiguously.

'Then use it,' she said, getting up abruptly and facing him with a challenging tight little smile on her lips. 'Put it into the mine or do what you like with it. I know you don't need my

consent – but it's best for you to know I agree – absolutely.
Anway – ' her voice faltered – 'who needs balls and fine
dresses, and – and parties and things? *I* don't. Not as long as
I've got – '

'Go on.'

'Trenhawk,' she answered, not adding, 'and you', though
she meant it.

The sudden expectancy died from Rupert's eyes.

'It's very generous of you,' he said stiffly. 'But that would
only be as a last resource – to allay any unnecessary human
suffering.'

'For the miners.'

'Yes.'

'Don't forget anyway.'

She walked from the room with a queer feeling of having
bungled things. She'd tried hard to show him something of her
true self for once, reveal subtly without loss to her own dignity,
her changing emotions of the past few weeks. But the response
hadn't been there. Perhaps he simply didn't care about her
anymore. He had – on that wild night when he'd taken her so
forcefully and then so tenderly following their scene over Elizabeth. But ever since then a cold wall of reserve had risen
between them. It was as though he was doing all in his power
to pretend nothing had happened.

Nothing?

But that was ridiculous, when something so incredible had
occurred that her whole being was out of gear – disorientated
to such an extent there were moments when she felt all her
past was an illusion, a kind of blundering through an immense
emotional maze to this one focal point: Rupert.

Did she love him? She didn't know. Love was so difficult to
understand. But she longed for him with an ache that
swamped any lingering feeling for David into a mere shadow,
a frail ghostly memory as intangible as the phantom presence
she'd so frequently sensed about the Tower Room.

She recalled her secret visits there, and the vague face
glimpsed through the shadows.

Had she really seen one? Or was it all imagination – the
product of her own mind under stress?

One late afternoon in November obeying an instinct stimulated mostly by curiosity, she made her way up the narrow staircase to see. The door wasn't open, neither was it locked. She went in. The light was poor, and the cold air struck icily through cracks between floor and granite walls. Near her foot she saw a dustpan and brush pushed by the stone. Her heart jerked when frail faint movement against the window drifted into the whiteness of hair blown in the wind. Then she realised it had started to snow. She shivered, and waited, aware only of intense deepening loneliness and quiet. It was as though the silence itself was whispering, 'You must face the truth. Life is for the living – '.

She stared through the fitful light, still waiting. But nothing materialised. No dark eyes in massed hair; no trembling smile or ghostly outstretched hand – nothing but the shadows of the small room and a gradual deepening resolve in her to somehow make her life with Rupert worth while.

Wild and stubborn she might be, passionate and selfish and wanting things her own way. She couldn't help it – it was her character; she'd been born like that. But she needed him. Somehow she had to make him understand, make him see that all the rest – Anthony, even David, didn't matter any more. How she'd do it she didn't know; he'd seemed recently so withdrawn from her, so cool and business-like. But then that was because of the worries; the mine. She'd make up to him for it all, work like any servant if he'd let her, send Lucy and Lilian packing and ruthlessly cut down on clothes and personal finery. She even had jewellery she could sell if necessary – diamond ear-rings and a necklace from Aunt Matilda. A ruby and diamond brooch given to her by her father that she'd been told was worth a little fortune. And pearls too – a whole set, genuine antique, that had belonged to her great grandmother.

She didn't want them. David had liked to see her wearing them, telling her she looked like a princess when they'd attended the Opera or other social functions in London.

But who wanted to be a princess? She didn't. She'd thought it might be quite fun, during her first early days of marriage – had imagined how exciting it would be to have crowds cheering and waving and bowing when she passed in some glittering Royal coach. But that had been just childish nonsense.

Only Rupert counted now – to have his arms round her, with the pumping of his strong heart against her own, and the pulsing rhythm of their two bodies merged into one.

Unthinkingly her heart had already quickened. She was no longer conscious of the cold air or the dank darkening light of the confined space. Her imagination was alight and glowing, and filled with purpose. Tonight it would be different. Tonight she wouldn't sleep alone. Rupert would be with her. If he didn't properly love her yet, she'd somehow make him. Everything in the future would change. And she'd do her best for Genevra; be the kind of mother Rupert wanted her to be.

Then there could be other children –

In a daze of excitement, she turned with a flurry of skirts and ran more quickly than was safe down the narrow stone steps. When she reached her own room her eyes were brilliant in a face flushed to glowing rose. Her lamp had not yet been lighted, but candles and matches waited on the dressing-table. She lit two, and studied herself critically through the mirror. What should she wear: Subdued grey? Blue? White, or pink? The deep rose-pink one had been a gift to her from Aunt Matilda for special occasions before her marriage to David. But it was still fashionable – low on the neck and shoulders, tight-waisted, with voluminous frilled skirts over layers and layers of petticoats, and hoops. And anyway, fashionable or not, who cared? Rupert had not seen it. It still lay between tissue paper in the wide drawer of her wardrobe.

She took it out and held it before her, noting with satisfaction how the colour added to the pearly translucent quality of her delicately flushed skin. Her hair, in the quivering light, appeared a more lustrous gold. Her eyes held a wilder, richer fire, more amber than hazel, with the darting emerald or gold lights intensified.

She could hardly wait to wash, perfume herself, see that her hair was arranged provocatively high at the back with a few curls loose on her cheeks, before seating herself on the bed and stepping into the dazzling creation.

She could have called Lilian, but she was so slim again, lacing herself was no problem, and Lilian wasn't yet expert at dealing with coiffures. Anyhow she wanted to surprise the household that night – pause on the stairs perhaps, with a flower raised elegantly to her nostrils for the benefit of any servant who might be about. And of course – for Rupert.

Before going down later, she hesitated for a minute below a bend in the staircase, one hand on the rail, head bent pensively towards her right shoulder where a single white Christmas rose nestled in the froth of pink. But no one appeared.

Presently she strolled languidly down again, crossed the hall, and went into the parlour. The single chandelier already glittered over the table; logs burned welcomingly from the fireplace. She walked over, and stood with her hands outstretched to the flames. Her ears and senses were alert, listening for Rupert. She hoped he wouldn't be late. It would be too disappointing if the powder faded or left her nose shiny, or if the carefully arranged curls got out of place. The lip-salve, too, could so easily rub off or disappear from contact with her tongue. She didn't want to sit, either. A standing posture was so much more elegant, and likely to impress.

Impatience, with the niggle of a back-ache began to gnaw her nerves. She was about to pour a sherry for herself when she heard footsteps.

Her heart quickened and missed a beat. She recognized the tread, and knew Rupert was coming. As the door opened she turned. He had changed, and was looking smart in a pale grey suit with a white winged collar and yellow waistcoat. But his face was strained and grim. He looked tired, and older than usual.

'Hullo, Rupert,' she said, giving him her sweetest smile, 'I'm so glad you're not late. I – I –'

'Yes, Addy?' he answered as though hardly seeing her, 'What is it? Nothing wrong, I hope?'

She went towards him, and lifted her face to kiss him. His mouth touched her forehead dutifully. There was no word from him about her dress, or perfume, or any slight indication he noticed anything different about her.

Her heart sank like a stone, to be followed a moment later by a quick rush of irritation.

'Well?' she demanded forgetting her determination to be subtle and cajoling. 'Do you like it?'

His eyes, which were heavily ringed, look momentarily puzzled. 'Like what, Addy?'

'*Oh*!' Her faced clouded with disappointment. 'My dress, of course. *This* dress – the pink. You haven't seen it before.'

He tried to amend matters by saying, 'Oh yes, it's very – charming.'

She sighed. 'It really doesn't matter to you, does it?'

'What?'

'How I look? What I wear? That I'm here at all?'

His expression darkened. He regarded her steadily for a brief interval, then he said, 'Having anything to wear is the important thing. I've got workers on my hand that soon may find it hard to clothe their own children.'

'Oh. I see, the mine.'

'Yes.'

'You sound rather – prim, Rupert.' Adelaide could not help saying a little tartly. 'It isn't my fault that Aunt Matilda gave me a pretty dress, I put it on to please you.'

His lips softened slightly. 'Of course. You're not to blame, Adelaide. Forgive me. And you know – '

'Yes?' The word was breathless with expectancy.

'You really *do* look very smart. Pink is certainly your colour.'

What she would have said in answer to his half-hearted rather impersonal compliment she didn't know, because at that point there was a knock, and Lilian entered with a tureen in her hands for the table.

The evening, following dinner, was a somewhat morose unrewarding affair for Adelaide. Rupert remained unduly quiet and withdrawn, and after sitting for an hour drinking rather more whisky than usual, while scanning the daily papers, bid his wife a perfunctory goodnight, telling her not to wait up as he had business matters to attend to in the study, and that if he didn't get on with it he'd be very bad and boring company.

When he kissed her cheek she turned her face away coldly. She didn't notice his sigh or the worry knitting his brow. All she knew was that he'd snubbed her by not recognising the trouble she'd gone to on his behalf.

Or was it for her own?

She went up to bed a little later, defeated and miserable. She no longer liked the pink dress. Something about it affronted her. It looked mildly vulgar lying there on the floor where she'd thrown it.

She lay in bed for a long time wakeful and uneasy, telling herself how unkind Rupert was – how mean, and thoughtless, and quite without imagination, yet secretly longing for him.

When at last she recognised he would not come, she got up, and closed the half open door. Snow was falling steadily outside; it was cold.

So she snuggled down into the sheets, and presently slept, little dreaming what the next day would bring.

XIII

The weather was bitterly cold next morning. Rupert, with too much on his mind for comfort had slept badly, and got up early to make a visit to the farm before going on to the mine. The old question had risen to niggle his mind whether he sell the manor or not. From a recent intense study of profit and expenditure it had become obvious to him that financially the house was a liability rather than an asset. The Merryns' wages were higher than Elizabeth's had been. The yield from crops only just covered cost in labour; The small dairy herd was not sufficiently productive to make any substantial profit; more vegetables could be grown in the kitchen garden near the stables.

When it came to the point Trenhawk could be almost entirely self sufficient. Retaining the farm had become a matter of principle and vanity rather than necessity. With things at the mine as they were, the unpleasant truth was clear. He should get rid of the manor.

He'd miss it; he'd been born there. It had long been recognised as a part of Hawksley Heritage. But Wheal Tansy came first. It wasn't as if Tom and Elizabeth had to be considered any more. The Merryns, comparatively, were strangers, but the miners were not. He'd been to the homes of most of them, attended weddings, and done what he could for them in sickness and through the bad times. He knew most of their children by their names; the families had given him their trust, which so far he'd not abused. Whatever the loss to him personally he was not going to betray them now.

So his mind was quite clear when he tapped the farm door that morning, and without waiting for an answer went in. Mrs Merryn came out of the kitchen rubbing her hands on an apron, and met him in the hall. She was a thin, ginger-haired, capable-looking woman in her early fifties, sharp featured, with a pleasant smile and shrewd eyes.

'Good morning, Mr Hawksley, surr, you're early. I didn' expect to see you so soon – nothing wrong, is there?'

'No no,' Rupert told her. 'Just a thought I had, about business. Is your husband about?'

'I'm afraid not. He had to go to St Just early. Something to do with cattle food. But if I can help – give him a message – or shall I tell him to call when he gets back?'

Rupert shook his head. 'Oh that's all right, Mrs Merryn. I'll see him some other time. By the way – '

'Yes, surr?' An anxious look suddenly clouded her face as though she sensed something unpleasant was coming.

'Are you happy here?'

Her brows lifted in surprise. 'Happy, Mr Hawksley? Why yes. Has anythin' happened to make you think otherwise? Or isn't our work satisfactory? There could be a few things we have to learn still I suppose – but then it's very early days yet – '

'Your work's excellent,' Rupert told her. 'In fact you've seemed to settle so well here I've been wondering if you and your husband were in a position to consider a longer termed policy concerning the farm.'

The eyes narrowed, the smile completely died from her lips.

'Longer term? I don't quite understand.'

'No. Well, forget about it for the moment,' he said, disappointed and yet relieved to delay the issue for a little longer.

'I'd like to know, surr,' she said persistently.

He shrugged. 'Very well, but this is only an idea, mind. It may be that at some future time, not too far off – I shall think of selling the place – '

'*This* place? The farm?'

'I'm afraid so. I may have to. But when, and if I do – I should like you to have the first chance, on easy terms, of purchasing.'

She laughed ironically.

'Us, surr? Will and me? Where would we find the money for such a thing? You'd get a high sum for it, wouldn't you? And we've practically nothing put by. Oh *no*. If that's what you're thinking I can tell you now, straight out, there's not a chance of it. I only wish you'd said before we came that things were like that with you – so uncertain we'd have to think of getting out before we was properly settled in – ' the colour was rising and fading in quick successive waves over her face. Her breathing had quickened, and sparks of anger lit her eyes. Rupert realised she could be a virago when roused, and wished he'd said nothing.

'Calm yourself,' he said, placatingly. 'Nothing's settled. I hope it won't come to selling. Even if it did I've no doubt your services would be retained in some way. Please, Mrs Merryn, try and forget what I've said. I'll call later in the week, and talk to both of you about it. Will your husband be in tomorrow morning?'

'If you're coming, I'll see he is,' she said tartly. 'The sooner we get things clear the better to my way of thinking. Not knowing where you stand is no good for anyone – *or* for the work. I've done the best I can for this place, Mr Hawksley. There was a lot that wasn't right here when we moved in, in case you didn't know. The cleaning had been let go in the upstairs rooms, and the dairy wasn't even all *that* sparkling. But then I've heard that Mrs Chywanna had other interests.' Her voice was acid, her eyes narrowed and expressionless. Rupert was not only startled, but affronted. What did she know? Had she been listening to gossip or was her allusion to Elizabeth merely the chance criticism of a frightened woman afraid of the future?

He gave her the benefit of the doubt, and a few minutes later was cutting briskly across the moor towards Wheal Tansy. A thin layer of snow still covered the short turf, which appeared likely to remain all day. There was no sign of sun coming up, and the sky was leaden holding the threat of further falls. This was the kind of weather so hard on the Bal maidens and

those working 'at grass', he thought, as he pulled his coat
round his chin. Poor things; no wonder men clamoured for
better wages and conditions. And children too – it was all
wrong that necessity should drive them to such hazardous
employment. He agreed completely with Ben Oaks over this
point. There'd been far too many accidents in previous years
to boys and girls whose longing for fresh air and momentary
escape at break, had driven them into dangerous contact with
machinery, resulting in terrible death.

Boys not more than eight years old had lost their lives
through their own daring and unpredictability of rods and
wheels. Rupert had himself witnessed the outcome of one such
accident when the child's body had been caught up and
mangled to an unrecognisable state. It was a sight he'd never
forgotten, and never would, to the end of his life, and if it had
been within his power he'd have banned child labour from
Wheal Tansy. But it was not. Surface work had to be done,
and families needed what their children could earn. It was
a matter of surviving at risk, or not surviving at all.

Such thoughts passed sombrely through his mind that
morning as he continued along the track to the mine. Later he
was to wonder why. He wasn't the type of man given to
feelings or superstition. Premonitions of disaster had never
troubled him. He'd never seen a 'bucca', or 'knacker' for
instance, or even heard one, though he knew many miners
who said they had. According to legend they were spindly-
legged small people – the spirits of the ancient Jews who had
crucified Christ and been sent forever to work the mines,
mostly to the disadvantage of humans. 'A grizzled lookin'
critter,' one old man had told Rupert, 'all gnarled with wicked
squint eyes.'

Rupert accepted such stories as nothing more than ancient
folk-lore. But there were times when even he himself had a
discomforting inner sense that all was not well. It was with
him that day, and had nothing at all to do with the fact that
he'd seen what appeared to be a white hare lolloping before
him when he first set off for Wheal Tansy. Most miners would
have sent up a prayer for protection – a white rabbit, hare, or
even a snail glimpsed before early shift near the precincts of a
mine were generally taken as a token of ill-luck. Rupert had no

belief in such things, but his uneasiness persisted.

So he quickened his pace, and it was only a hundred yards or so from the mine when it happened. Suddenly there was a tremendous explosion of sound – a thunderous impact followed by a shower of bricks, stones, and earth against the grey sky with a giant cloud of hot black steam momentarily blotting out the immediate landscape and taking the mine and boiler house into oblivion. There were screams and shouting. A seething roaring, dying into a fitful drawn-out moaning of human misery and tumbled gaping ground where the injured and dying lay.

Rupert waited a second or two rigid with shock, then started running. The big boiler and the pumping engine had burst, and bodies were scattered in the rabble over the torn earth. There were two children, two 'bal' girls, and four men who'd been changing there and warming themselves for the next shift. One girl had her arm blown off, a man, Jesse Beal, had lost both legs, and was hardly recognisable from his blackened face. The others were mostly dying or dead. Only one man was saved and when help arrived was made as comfortable as possible in the Count House to await the arrival of the doctor.

Somehow Rupert got through the day doing what he could to help. He was aware at times of distressed relations crowding to the scene, weeping and reviling in turn, cajoling and praying, moaning the loss of the victims, while he tried desperately to comfort and ease the agony of the dying. 'War', he thought bitterly, 'they make their wars in the Crimea and all over the world, but the real war is here – caused by human impotence to protect defenceless workers.'

At one point Ben Oaks confronted him, eyes blazing in his white face.

'So now you do know – ' he muttered – 'it's all there for 'ee to see et, edn it? – The proof of et – why we ask for rights an' sustenance for our bellies. Go on, master – don't be feared – look, *look* – so you never forget how we earns our right to live, an' the cost of et.'

He turned away lunging clumsily into the huddled crowd, and Rupert, looking away, retched.

*

It was already early evening, and the light was fading, when Rupert arrived back at Trenhawk. As he entered by the side door he was aware of hushed conversation from the kitchen. By then, of course, everyone had heard. Mrs Pender opened the door of her room. Her expression was torn by pity and anxiety at the sight of his drawn haggard face, his slumped shoulders, and something dazed in his eyes that told more than any words could have done what he'd been through.

'Oh, Mr Rupert, surr,' she murmured, 'you look so tired. Come to my room surr an' rest a bit. I'll get you a pick-me-up. Et's a terrible thing to happen. But you musn' blame yourself. Not ever – you've bin a good master, an they all know et. These things happen –'

She put out a hand. He glanced at her, shaking his head slowly, and then went on, up the main hall.

Adelaide came out of the parlour to meet him.

'Rupert – ' she cried, ' – Rupert – I'm so sorry – ' her lips were trembling, her eyes bright with unshed tears. He noted vaguely she was wearing red, and thought with a quirk of bitterness now befitting it was – red, the colour of blood.

She touched his arm hesitantly, gently, 'Please – please – ' she pleaded, 'don't look like that. Can't I help? Isn't there anything I can do?'

He didn't reply, just pushed past her as though she wasn't there and went upstairs.

When he came down again she was still wandering about the wide corridor, wondering how to comfort – how to penetrate the defence of steel armed against her. At the foot of the stairs he paused. She saw he'd changed into riding kit, noted how cold and hard his eyes were – relentless as though the spirit behind them was frozen ice.

'Rupert –'

'Yes?'

'Can't you talk to me? Surely you're not going out – now?'

'That's what I'm doing. *Out*,' he said, 'and if you take my advice you'll do the same. There's nothing for you here any more, Adelaide – neither money, background, security, or hope for it. Face the truth, for God's sake. Pack up and take the child with you. You have your aunt in London. She'll look after you and be glad to –'

'Don't talk like that – perhaps I can help. I'm your wife. I need you too –'

He laughed. Not a pleasant sound.

'It's too late, I'm afraid – because I don't need *you*. So for pity's sake – ' he pushed past her roughly, 'do as I say. You have still sufficient in the bank to see you through.'

He strode savagely down the hall, through the side door and into the drive leading to the stables. She stood helplessly with a hand lifted to her breast, trying to calm the painful thumping of her heart.

A minute or two later she heard the sound of hooves clattering past the house towards the lane. She rushed to the front door, flung it open, and stood watching as Rupert's figure astride the grey galloped at unreasonable speed to the main high moorland road. *Where*? she thought desperately. Was he trying to kill himself? Had life become so terrible he couldn't bear to contemplate another day? And was her presence so repugnant to him he could feel only the frozen bitter contempt that had blazed from his eyes when she'd offered herself and her sympathy – all that she had to give?

Suddenly, unable to stand the torment of indecision and inaction, hearing still the echo of his biting voice in her ears – seeing only the frenzied shock and fury of his stare, she rushed to the stables and found Carnack there.

'Saddle Ebony for me,' she cried shrilly, grabbing an old coat of Rupert's from the peg, 'and hurry about it. Where's he gone, do you know? My husband – tell me – tell me –'

The man stared at her shaking his head slowly as though he too was in some kind of nightmare that had struck him dumb. Adelaide grabbed his shoulder, shaking him with all the force she had. 'What's the matter? You heard what I said – get on with it then, damn you – he'll kill himself –'

Carnack pulled himself away and reluctantly saddled the mare. 'How d'ye think *you'll* stop him then?' he said as Adelaide swung herself into the saddle. 'What do you know of men when they've bin through hell as he has? An what chance d'ye think a wumman has – of catchin up – you in skirts too an' not knowin' the moors proper? None at all, ma'am. You'd far better bide here with a doctor at hand for if he appears agen –'

'If – if – ' she screamed. 'That's what you believe, isn't it?

That he *won't* – '

'No, no, I didn' say that, but – '

'You haven't said anything at all to help,' Adelaide told him. 'Where – what direction – ?'

'I doan' know. No one does. An' if you break your neck it'll be to no purpose, I'm tellin' 'ee that. But ef you're so dead set on killin' yourself try the Ram, ma'am. Ais. Et's there he'll be – drinkin' his head off I shouldn' wonder, unless he lands up down one o' they tin shafts first.'

Adelaide shuddered.

'Right. I'll try the Ram.'

She was about to kick Ebony to a fierce gallop when Carnack reached and pulled the reins. 'Best let *me* go or accompany you, ma'am. Come on now, he's well away by this time. It's a man's job, this – '

Adelaide raised her crop, hardly aware of it.

Ebony reared, snorting from excitement as her hooves pounded the ground.

'Get away, you fool – 'Adelaide cried.

'But your clothes, ma'am – '

She laughed, a shrill high sound, as Carnack watched the absurd young figure break away, riding astride in her white bloomers, Rupert's coat round her, the red frills of her dress disarranged to her thighs, her hair already tumbling about her shoulders. As the horse and girl cut towards the lane a silent prayer went up from his heart; he was not by nature a conventionally religious man but if ever a body needed God's help, he thought sombrely, this poor young madam did now, and in the state she was in, too.

'It's a sad day, this, Nick,' he said to the youth, as he appeared round a corner from the stables. 'All those poor scorched bodies down at the mine, and the maister mad as a coot. Her too – his wife. Gone off her head proper she has, ridin' off like a circus clown in her underwear. Heaven knows what'll be the end of 'et all.'

The boy shrugged. 'Tedn' our fault. An' et's far wuss for them – the dead uns. Zacky Traill's gone, I've heard – Maggie's Zacky – burnt black as a cinder, an' Jack Treen an that pretty girl o' Will Richard's. Awful, edn' et? They say – '

'Oh, shut your mouth, lad,' Carnack said sharply. 'Keep the

horror to yourself; there's too much of et for my taste, an' you sound like a real ghoul you do. Now get on with your work. There's plenty to do still with what's happened this day, an' et won't end tonight either.'

Sullenly, Nick turned away.

Meanwhile, a wind was rising, and the air from the moor was bitter as Adelaide spurred Ebony along a narrow track that cut half way along the base of the hill, saving two miles of lane before joining the Penjust road again. Flecks of dry snow feathered her cold cheeks and lips from the lowering night sky, but her mind was ablaze, her will relentless as she kicked her mount to an ever-increasing gallop, riding by instinct rather than sight. Nothing was clearly visible until a shaft of pale moon slipped through a gap in the clouds. She drew the mare to halt for a minute, and straining her eyes scanned the cold landscape.

There was no sign of Rupert or any living thing – only the gaunt ruins of Castle Tol standing stark on the far left horizon, and a vista of rocks streaking with black shadows above small stone-walled fields. Scattered granite cottages were huddled in dips between frozen furze and undergrowth, but the view was mostly desolate of habitation.

She started Ebony off again, trying to subdue her fears by the thought that what Carnack said must surely be true – Rupert was at the Ram, drinking himself to forgetfulness. Oh pray heaven he was, and wasn't lying lost and maimed somewhere at the bottom of one of those awful gaping shafts. She had a nightmarish memory of inadvertently stepping over one herself when she was a young girl. The hole had been covered by thick brambles and weeds that had miraculously born her light weight until she'd sprung to the other side. But later, when the truth had registered, she'd known moments of blackest terror. To be maimed and dying at the bottom of one of those derelict traps – what could be worse? And supposing it had happened to Rupert?

Waves of dread colder than the icy air swept through her. 'On, Ebony – come on now – on, on – ' she cried recklessly forcing the animal to painful speed.

When she reached the Inn there was already a good company in the bar, tinners mostly, and a few farmers. She sprang from Ebony's back, handed the mare to the ostler in the yard, and went through the building from the back. All heads turned her way as she entered, disarranged in her already torn red dress, with bramble scratches on her face, and her fair hair loose like a gipsy's round her shoulders. One or two ribald comments were made, and gestures from men already heated and fired from liquor following the day's hard work. But something in her eyes — something desperately wild and chilling — silenced them to an awkward uneasy watchfulness. Of Rupert there was no sign.

'Have you seen Mr Hawksley here?' she demanded in a harsh strained voice, 'Rupert Hawksley — of Trenhawk?' There was whispering and nudging, while her heart steadied although her senses still reeled from the ride, the cold outside, and the thick heavy air of the bar which was redolent with the odour of sweat, male bodies, and liquor.

'Well?' she demanded, 'can't anyone speak? Did you hear? — Mr Hawksley?'

Then someone shouted, 'Ee edn' 'ere, Missis. Left 'ee 'as 'ee? Gone a-whoring?'

She stared, with her lip curling contemptuously, her hand instinctively tightening on her riding crop.

'Leave her be, Cam,' another voice said placatingly. 'The lady looks fair done up. Want a tot, Missis?'

Adelaide ignored the remark. 'Where's the landlord? Fetch me the landlord, or the barman — '

'Oh I see,' a third voice muttered scathingly. 'Fetch this, fetch that — all ladi-da, edn' we? Who d' ye think y' are, anyway? Ef you was *my* madam I'd — '

What he'd have done was left to the imagination for at that moment the proprietor came in. Having met her before, he recognised her immediately.

'Mrs Hawksley of all people. And in such a state — What's the matter, midear? Had an accident or something?'

Adelaide tried to explain, but was overcome by a sudden feeling of faintness.

'Here — ' the man said, taking her arm, 'come to the back ma'am. You need a bit o' something to steady 'ee, now do as I say, an' maybe somethin' can be done to help.'

Adelaide followed him through a door at the back into a

small private parlour where his wife, a comely kindly-looking woman, was preparing food on the table. Despite her tiredness and distress Adelaide noticed mechanically quite trivial details – a shining aspidistra in a pink pot near a small lace-curtained window overlooking the yard, an oleograph of the Battle of Trafalgar on the wall, and a glass case with a stuffed bird in it.

A drink of something strong laced with rum, was forced on her, with a slab of home-made cake. After that she felt better and was able to explain. When it was all over she sat back, and after a pause in which they both regarded her thoughtfully, Adelaide asked again, 'Well have you seen him?'

'An' if we have my dear, the woman said, 'what difference do it make? A sad story it is, an' no mistake. But you can't be goin' off on your own again on such a wild night an' dressed as you are, too. Tedn' right. Best let our lad get someone to go along home with 'ee – or mebbe he could find someone like Jesse Andrews – '

'No.' Adelaide's voice was firm. 'You can't stop me. I must find my husband myself. Don't you understand? Anything could have happened, and I'm all right. It's my affair. Only – ' she glanced at the landlord, 'tell me. You know something, don't you? He was here?'

The man nodded. 'Ais. And real proper in his cups he was before he took off.'

'Which way? What direction?'

'Now how would I be knowing that? An ef I did how'll 'ee catch up? He was fair mazed, with the spirits of Old Harry in 'en, I'd say. You'd best leave en to his own ways for a bit, Mrs Hawksley. A man in his state doan' want women round. You take my advice an' get back to the house. Or maybe – '

Adelaide jumped up. 'I'm going to find him, and if you won't help I'll have to do it on my own.' Her eyes blazed. 'I'll search every hill valley – every cove, and kiddeywink from here to Land's End. He must be somewhere '

'Here now, don't run on so,' the man told her. 'There are places I reckon where a man so low in spirits as you say he is, might go. Many times when I was troubled in my younger days I'd take off to Castle Tol or the Maidens for a good old think and to straighten myself out. An' I *do* happen to know Mr Hawksley cuts back that way when round these parts.'

'Castle Tol, did you say? Castle Tol?'

He nodded.

'That's right. But 'tedn' a proper place for a wumman alone on a night like this, an' like as not he won't be there. Ef you – '

Adelaide didn't wait to hear more. The next moment she was out of the door and in the yard shouting to the ostler for Ebony. He brought the mare to her, grumbling under his breath, realising there was little hope of a tip that night from such a wild creature as she seemed to be.

As she swung herself on to the mare's back, Adelaide called, 'I'll pay you some other time. I've nothing on me now – ' and before he fully realised what was happening she was away over the cobbles and on to the road making for the moor.

The snow had stopped falling, and fingered shadows clawed the moon-swept landscape when she reached the base of the hill. The track cut upwards to the left, winding through bent black trunks of furze where lumps of granite crouched half hidden like the slumbering forms of legendary beasts trapped by the centuries. Once the mare, with senses strained, half stumbled and halted momentarily, ears pricked and alert, neck arched apprehensively. The steam of animal breath curdled in a frozen cloud with Adelaide's on the harsh air. 'Steady,' she said, patting Ebony's sleek coat. 'Come on, now–on–on–'

Her voice became rhythmic with the soughing sounds of wind and creaking underneath, of thudding hooves and distant screaming of gulls wheeling. Ahead the stark primeval outlines of Castle Tol loomed gradually nearer, tumbled stones and ancient walls lit fitfully by the pale moon against the wild night sky. In spite of the cold, Adelaide like her mount, was drenched now in her own sweat. Her tangled hair blew in a damp cloud behind her, her pulses raced, her heart thundered against her ribs painfully though she was only half aware of it. 'Rupert – Rupert – ' she cried intermittently – 'hullo there – Rupert – '

There was no answering cry. Nothing but her own voice echoing in her ears with the constant dying and falling of the wind as though a host of ghosts from the past had risen to torment her.

When she reached the ancient site, she drew Ebony to a halt, and paused for a time before dismounting. How lonely i

was; how bleak and cold, and empty seemingly of life. Unearthly, with the sullen distorted shadows skimming menac-
ingly across the sweep of moors. Just for a brief time her own
anxiety was swallowed up by a tremendous sense of awe in
which time died, and it seemed the spirits of those who'd once
lived there moved and spoke again. Castle Tol took shape in
her mind as it had been centuries ago – more than three
thousand years – a fortress and village armed against invasion by the late Celts and those that followed. Wild broom
and heather thrived there now, and only granite monuments
remained as guardians of forgotten bones beneath the wild
soil.

Adelaide closed her eyes briefly, rubbed a hand across her
face to dispel the smart of frozen tears, then jumped from
Ebony and tethered her to a tree. She shuddered, feeling
suddenly strangely cold.

'Rupert –' she called again.

But as before, there was no answer. She climbed a little
higher wending her way between the grouped standing stones
to the central ruin, which gave now only a suggestion of
one-time walls. Her legs felt heavy. Hopelessness was intensifying. Rupert was not there – nothing was there but chilling
relics of the forgotten past. She was about to turn and go back
when something caught her attention – an odour at first – a
mere suggestion of smell, but unmistakable – that of spirits,
rum perhaps or whisky, carried intermittently on the wind.
Grasping the undergrowth, with the breath tearing at her
lungs, she started to run, shouting as she did so, but unaware
of what she cried. And then there was a sound – the whining
of a horse. She screwed her brows together, peering through
the fitful light. As she stared a flood of moonlight caught the
silvered coat of Rupert's grey. The horse had its head raised,
nostrils flared sending coils of steam into the freezing air. By
its feet on the ground was a figure – the dark figure of a man.

Rupert.

Adelaide rushed forward, and bent down.

He was lying on his back half hidden by the shadow of the
broken wall, but his face was white and staring in the moon's
glare.

A trickle of blood coursed from temple to chin, but he

was quite conscious. When he saw her his eyes seemed to darken. They closed for a moment then opened again. An ironic smile twisted his lips.

'*Hullo,* Addy, how *extremely* pleasant to see you –'

'Rupert –'

'But how really embarrassing, in such a situation – ' he eased himself up, and she saw he was still clutching a bottle in one hand. It was broken.

'Rupert –'

'What the devil are you doing?' he shouted roughly with a sudden change of mood. 'Can't you leave me in peace for one single moment, damn you – isn't a man allowed to drown his own sorrows in solitude without some heedless woman for ever on his track? Haven't I gone through enough already, without – without –'

'Oh please – *please* – ' she choked back the tearing sob in her throat. 'I was so worried – don't you understand? *Can* you? Won't you try – ?' When he didn't answer she continued in a rush, 'I love you, Rupert. Can you take that in? When you rode off I thought – I didn't know what to think, but I had to find you. I went to the Ram, and they said you'd been there –'

'You went to the Ram? Like that?' He started to laugh, and his laughter angered her to a frenzy of abuse that was relief after the prolonged strain.

'How did you expect me to come? All neat and tidy and elegant like you – your –' she broke off, lost for words.

'Go on, Adelaide,' Rupert said with a dangerous undercurrent in his voice. 'Please continue. My – what?'

'Never mind,' she cried. 'Why should I explain? Why?' her voice rose shrilly against the moaning wind. 'As if you care what I think or do. I don't matter, I never have – to you. It's only the mine and those others –'

'What others?'

'I said never mind,' she shouted, 'it doesn't matter –'

'Oh but it does, and I *do* mind,' he yelled, sitting up quickly and pulling her down by both arms. 'I mind very much, and I'm quite aware of what you meant. I'm not drunk, Adelaide – not any more. I can, as they say, hold my liquor. And the worst was over some time ago. Now if you please – this love affair. What were you saying about love?'

'You heard. And let me go – '

He freed her quickly as though she'd been shot.

'Certainly. I don't want you here – go on, – forget it. Go home, Addy.' His head drooped. 'Why you came, heaven knows –'

Ignoring the rebuff she knelt down again and pulled the bottle from his hand. Then she straightened and flung it yards away into a thick clump of furze. A thin trickle of blood scarred her hand. He jumped to his feet and caught her fiercely by both shoulders.

'And that was a fool thing to do, wasn't it, Addy? A damned wild foolish thing –'

'Yes, yes, yes,' she shouted, 'and so are you wild and foolish. We both are, both of us. Oh Rupert, please — please. Don't hate me –' her eyes glowed bright and pleading in her white face.

Caught by the wind her hair was a silvered stream in the moonlight – her torn skirt a fury of swirling darkness about her thighs. Her lips were rich and glistening, holding such longing and abandon he was startled to sudden comprehension. Around them the elements moaned and screamed; the very earth it seemed, rocked and pulsed with a new wild urgency, taking them to its own deep heart.

'Addy,' he cried as his mouth came down to hers – 'I didn't know – I never dreamed – ' his hands were about her breasts, and thighs, and buttocks, his lips savage yet adoring against her cheeks, neck, and hollow below the firm throat. He pulled the coat from her shoulders and lifted her up in his arms. Then in the shadowed darkness of a great stone he took her to him, with only his body above hers as protection from the biting wind. It seemed, as the clouds cleared, that the world sang. Moon, earth, and fiery stars were alight and glorified. They lay together as countless others had lain before in centuries long past and forgotten. Passion claimed them. Whatever might follow, this night was theirs, something both knew, that had been ordained from the first moments of their lives.

When they got up later, he held her tenderly for a moment before wrapping the discarded clothes round her white body. Then he said – 'You're a witch – I love you.'

'And me. It's the same with me. You're all that matters – everything – '

'Oh, Adelaide.'

His lips touched a bared nipple reverently, before pulling the rough jacket suddenly tight over her breasts. Then he untethered the two horses, and they started back.

She rode before him on his grey, with Ebony's bridle in his other hand. They travelled, slowly, negotiating the rough ground carefully, and when they reached Trenhawk it was late.

No one saw them arrive. No one heard them go upstairs quietly to Rupert's room. Carnack had fallen asleep in the harness room, and Mrs Pender's head was nodding accompanied by heavy breathing, in her rocking chair.

For a time Adelaide and Rupert lay wakeful saying little, content merely to be close and together. Then he remarked when she was on the verge of sleep, 'I never thought it would end like this?'

'What?' she murmured.

'The terrible day – the explosion,' he answered.

Her fingers touched his lips. 'Sh – sh, you mustn't, Rupert. Don't think of it. It does no good. It wasn't your fault.'

'It was the fault of something,' he said, 'men, machines. – the system – whatever it was, human beings weren't meant to go that way – '

She stirred and drew closer to him. 'I know I can't do much, Rupert, but always I'll be here for you to talk to; and when you can't stand remembering, just tell me, and we'll try somehow to get through it. I'm overbearing and stubborn often, and I expect we'll have rows sometimes, but they won't mean anything, because – because you see I love you so much – '

He said nothing, he didn't have to.

A great storm had swept through their lives, but it was over, and he knew that in the future things were going to be very different.

They'd found each other.

XIV

When Adelaide woke up it was past nine o'clock, but Rupert was still sleeping. His face, though relaxed, looked pale and drawn, and she had a deep longing to press her own against it, letting her lips soften the strain and bring him somehow back to consciousness and the warmth of her arms. Although she couldn't fully understand his terrible shock and concern over Wheal Tansy's bereaved families, she realised the explosion was something he would never forget and that he'd be inwardly scarred for the rest of his life. In time, like all tragedies it would recede from his conscious mind. Through loving him, and in mutual passion the shadow would lift. But the grim experience would always be there – a haunted memory to be revived at a chance word or incident to sudden startled clarity.

'Oh Rupert,' she thought, staring down at him that morning, 'I'll do my best to be a help and not a worry to you. I'll try. I really will.'

She spoke no words aloud, but it was as though he'd heard. Very slowly one eye opened, then the other. 'Addy,' he said, lifting his arms to her, 'Is it really you?' She looked so young, with both hands clasped over her breasts, he smiled.

'Come here, my love – my sweet wild wife – '

She fell upon his chest, and his lips were on hers. 'What were you doing?' he questioned. 'Praying?'

To his astonishment she nodded. 'In a kind of way – for you – for both of us.'

His mood changed.

'Why this sudden conversion?'

'Conversion?' she laughed. 'I'm afraid I'm not that kind. There's nothing saintly about me. But you looked so – '

'Yes?'

'So tired, Rupert.' Her voice held conpassion.

He didn't speak, just stared at her as though he'd never really seen her before.

237

'Mentally, I mean – ' she added hesitantly, 'in spirit.'

'Yes.'

She got up. 'I wasn't going to wake you. I didn't quite know what to do.'

'Well it's a good thing you didn't have to,' he told her. 'I've got to be at Wheal Tansy as soon as possible. There'll be enquiries and officials there already, and any number of relatives.'

He jumped out of bed suddenly and started to dress. 'Yesterday morning was the worst time of my life,' he said, 'but today's going to be hell. What am I going to say to them – women with burnt out corpses for their sons – fathers with their daughters gone? Wives trying to identify masses of cinders?'

'Don't, please, don't – '

He touched her forehead briefly with his lips. 'Sorry, Adelaide. Oh my love! – what a grim new beginning – '

'But we're together. That's the important thing,' she insisted. 'All the rest is terrible of course. I know I don't feel it in the same way as you – because I can't; I wasn't there, and I didn't know the men who died. But I can imagine it.' She paused before adding, 'They'll understand one day. They'll have to. It wasn't your fault – '

'I know it wasn't, directly,' he said. 'I shan't be blamed – officially. But it makes you think, doesn't it? Makes you wonder what bloody right human beings have to go messing about the earth with machinery, digging great holes to be worked, only at the cost of men's lives? At the moment there's nothing I'd like more than to see Wheal Tansy levelled to dust.'

'And what good would that do?' she asked, frightened by the wild despair clouding his eyes. 'More families would suffer then, because there'd be no work. You must go on, Rupert. There's money in my name yet – you've said so. You must use it, and not be – '

'Not be what?' His voice had sharpened.

'Not be self-pitying,' she said resolutely, 'or try to shoulder the blame. That's not – not commonsense.'

'Hm!' he pulled his breeches on with a savage gesture. 'You're taking a lot on yourself, aren't you, Addy? Telling me what to do?'

She nodded, went up to him and touched his head with her lips. 'Yes, I am. And another thing – don't think you're going out without eating. Breakfast will be ready. I'll put a wrap on and we'll go down together. *Please* – darling –' it was about the only time she'd ever used the word to him and for a moment faint colour tinged her face.

His expression softened. 'All right. But don't expect me to go into lengthy explanation with the servants. I'll leave that to your own clever little mind. They'll know I was drunk of course,' he added. 'Carnack will already have enlightened her about your mad ride to The Ram. So we'll both have to leave our reputations as decidedly – unconventional – to say the least of it. Still – as a legally married couple I'd say that was unimportant, wouldn't you?'

'Absolutely,' she answered, relieved to have brought him to a lighter mood.

When they went downstairs a few minutes later, breakfast as Adelaide had anticipated was already waiting.

Mrs Pender wore a grim expression. Her voice was tart when she said, putting bacon and eggs before them.

'I thought you might've told me when you came back. Sat up more'n half the night I did, watchin' an' waitin' with my ears an' eyes strained.'

'Oh dear,' Adelaide's tones were contrite. 'We came in quietly, Mrs Pender so as *not* to disturb you. It was a pity you worried. I know I rode off suddenly to find my husband – I had a message though, about the mine –'

'*Suddenly?*' the word came scathingly and without thought from the strained old throat. 'All dressed up like a circus wumman Carnack said, with those – those – unmentionables shewin' under them frills. Up to the waist he did say. I'm sorry, Miss Adelaide – ma'am – maybe I shouldn' be speakin' like this, an' with Mr Rupert present too. But it's my duty, an' ef you want to dispense with my services then I'll go.'

She stood, hands folded primly before her, mouth screwed into a small tight button, waiting.

Then Rupert spoke.

'Nonsense, Mrs Pender, I agree with you absolutely. My wilful young wife deserved a good – well, we'll try and forget it, shall we? Now please don't say another word about the disgraceful episode. It's over and done with. Yes?'

'Ef you do say so, Mr Rupert,' Mrs Pender agreed grudg-ingly, but with obvious relief. 'I'll leave you to your meal then.' With her head up she marched as quickly as she could manage to the door, where she turned and said, 'An see you do eat every bit of what's there. Cooked et myself I did, not knowin' what to expect, an' how long you'd be. Had to put et in the oven, an make the toast fresh. So doan' you waste et.'

When she'd gone Rupert smiled at Adelaide. 'We must be thankful for a little light relief,' he said. 'And no doubt we've provided considerable entertainment for the rest of them.'

'Entertainment?' She was aghast. 'For the servants?'

'Why not?' Drily. 'You surely don't imagine they've not known what was happening recently?'

'I don't under –'

'Now, now, Addy.' He took her chin in his hands. 'Don't overdo the innocence, darling. You understand perfectly.'

'Not perfectly,' she contradicted him. 'But I suppose noth-ing's really secret in this house, except – ' her voice changed subtly, became quieter, more withdrawn, yet puzzled.

'Yes?'

'The Tower Room,' she said. 'That's a secret place. I used to think when I came back here just after David's death – there was something, someone there. Once I saw a face, or thought I did. Even now, I – '

Rupert put an arm round her shoulders. 'Look, Adelaide, you're remembering old legends and letting your imagination play you tricks. You're not supposed to go up there, no one is. In any case the stairs aren't safe.'

'They felt perfectly firm to me the last time I was there,' Adelaide said thoughtlessly.

'The *last* time? Do you mean you've been making regular jaunts up those tricky steps? Do you realise that in damp weather they can be slippery? You could break your neck if you fell.'

'But I wouldn't fall,' Adelaide said stubbornly. 'I'm not the kind. I never go giddy.'

'There's always a first time; and I don't want you climbing up there again. Understand?'

'Yes, Rupert,' she agreed, meekly, although he guessed

whenever she felt like it she'd change her mind and completely disregard his orders. The safest thing to do, he told himself, was to have a solid door placed at the bottom that could be padlocked and barred even to Mrs Pender. It unnerved him when he thought of the ponderous old body clambering up to clean. The trouble was that Lucy was frightened to go there, and had by now no doubt informed Lilian of Trenhawk's ghost and lurid tales – much exaggerated – of the past.

However the Tower Room would have to wait for the moment in view of the other sordid business ahead. The inquest had been fixed to take place that morning at eleven o'clock in the Count House, and he was dreading it, although he doubted any verdict of negligence would be involved. A young 'Bal' maiden outside the boiler house had seen the engineman stoke up the fire and turn the gauge cocks to make sure everything was working properly. Owing to the bitter cold a number of men and one or two girls had been standing near when the boiler exploded. They hadn't, of course, had a chance of survival – which perhaps was a mercy in the condition they were.

'If I hadn' run for my life I'd have bin' took too – ' the girl had said, 'but et wasn' pore Ned's fault – ' referring to the boiler-man, ' – he'd done everythin' as usual. *Everythin'*.'

Rupert was sure of this. The whole tragedy seemed a mystery. The boiler itself had been checked only a week before, and installed again after a minor repair. So what was the answer?

As he walked across the moor shortly after ten towards the Count House, questions and conjectures zig-zagged in an endless refrain through his head. Borlaze had assured him there'd been no human error. 'Only the good Lord knows the truth,' he'd said sombrely, 'an' in my opinion there are many families in these parts that won't be askin' the Lord for anythin' again.'

And who could blame them? Rupert thought, as the square building came into view. And who'd care for the bodies and livelihoods of those that were left, with no man to feed or house them?

'Him? He'd do what he could. But means were limited, and tin was thin. He couldn't provide what wasn't there. God! how he loathed the sorry business. And how was he going to face the sorrowing half-accusing looks of the women – or the two fathers who'd lost their daughters? Girls weren't meant for mining work, he told himself with savage intensity. No – nor boys either, nor children. A mine – what was it after all, but·a savage hungry beast unleashed by lust from the bowels of the earth to kill and devour?

If, at that moment he'd been offered a price, he'd have said, 'Take it – and for nothing if you like. I want none of it any more.'

But of course such moments always passed. Eventually he knew he'd have to come to grips with the problem, utilising every penny he had, every ounce of energy for its sustenance and production.

Five minutes later he was distastefully contemplating the procedure of identification, with Borlaze, Oaks and others, while waiting with the police for the Coroner's arrival.

He got there strictly on time, and the sordid business began.

Ever afterwards Rupert, at intervals, was to recall the scene – the blackened corpses, of which some could only be named by certain articles and possessions – the witnesses – especially the Bal girl haggard-faced, who'd lost her own brother and father. The drawn-out questioning leading to no satisfactory conclusion – the whole sordid atmosphere of human misery overhanging the scene.

He managed to present a stoical front, although his stomach wanted to retch. And in the end the verdict was what he'd expected: 'Death from Misadventure.'

So no one would ever know how, or why. And in a short time when repairs were completed, men would be back once more and the pumping rod again in motion under the winter sky.

But never again Rupert decided, would workers be allowed in the boiler house at all except for the man attending it.

However cold it was, however frozen and stiff limbs and hands became, there must be other means of warmth supplied, though heaven alone knew how it would be done.

Adelaide was waiting for him in the library when he got back to Trenhawk. It was a quiet subdued room, dim and shadowed except for the leaping firelight playing across the floor and round the shelves of ancient books; a refuge from prying eyes and chance encounters with servants. There, more than anywhere else, even his study, he found comparative peace in troubled moments. It was as though the minds and thoughts of those from past centuries provided unseen escape from torment and unrest. If any ghosts really haunted the house, he'd told himself on more than one occasion, it must be here – where so many secrets lingered between the yellowed pages of parchment and vellum bindings. Rupert had never had a great deal of time for reading, but the atmosphere had always been comforting, diminishing current problems to smaller proportions.

Adelaide, wearing a brown dress that somehow highlighted her hair, rushed towards him into his arms as the door closed behind her.

'Oh Rupert,' she said, 'was it very bad? Was it?'

He drew her close against him before he spoke with his mouth on her hair and then her lips. His skin felt cold; she could feel the tension ease slowly from his body as her hand instinctively clutched his. They walked together to the alcove by the fire.

'Pretty bad,' he said. 'Most of them were unrecognisable.'

She shuddered.

'Why? What happened? What was it – they didn't blame you did they? Or Borlaze?

'Oh no. No human error. Misadventure,' Rupert told her, adding bitterly, 'Maybe the Almighty slipped up.'

'You mustn't say that,' Adelaide said. 'There's got to be a reason for things somewhere.'

Rupert's tired eyes stared at her intently.

'Are you trying to tell me you believe in God, Addy?'

She hesitated, then shrugged. 'I don't know. But there must be something. I've been thinking more lately.'

His lips softened. 'Have you? And what conclusion have you come to?'

She moved to his chair, perched on the floor beside him, with her head on his knees.

'There's a pattern in things,' she said in a strangely quiet voice for her. 'You do lots of things in life you don't exactly know why, stupid mad things at the time, that send you off in all sorts of directions you'd never thought of. Then, suddenly quite unexpectedly something happens and you see it makes a kind of picture. Like us – d'you know what I mean?'

'You tell me. Go on.'

'Well – when David was killed –' she paused '– I thought at first everything was over. Everything except Trenhawk. I meant to get it for myself because it seemed it really was mine and I was going to fight you and bribe you until you gave in. I was going to live here and run the place and be a sort of –'

'Queen? Chatelaine?'

'I suppose so.'

'A sterile role, Addy.'

'I know. But I didn't then. I suppose it was just I wasn't seeing straight. Perhaps I didn't want to. You'd always annoyed me, you see, even when we were children. You never noticed me except to scold and try to order me about. you –'

'I never gave in to you, or flattered, that's true,' Rupert agreed. 'I considered you got rather more than your rightful share of adulation. You had David by the ears, but I was damned if you'd get me that way.' There was a pause, then he added, 'For a bright girl you were surprisingly unastute, my love. If you'd known what a hell of resentment I'd suffered sometimes, you might have been kinder.'

'Resentment?' Her brows met over her pert nose.

He nodded. 'From your earliest visits to Trenhawk as a child it was always David. David so fair and handsome and charming. I suppose I shouldn't have blamed you, but I did. And it's taken a whole lot of unhappiness to find the truth, hasn't it?'

She nodded. 'That's what I mean about a pattern. If David hadn't died I wouldn't have found you. I was *in* love with him of course, but –'

'Go on.'

'Well, loving's different. It can't be compared; the thing that matters now is that we can talk about him together. Do you agree?'

'Only up to a point. There comes a time, Adelaide, when the past should be laid aside. You can't erase it, but you can put it into proper perspective. For myself, I'd rather forget.'

'There,' she exclaimed. 'That's what I mean.'

'What?'

'The past. The forgetting,' she said. 'That's just what you've got to do about the mine and the accident. You can't undo what's done. But how do you know the effect it's going to have on the families that are left – '

'I can imagine,' wrily.

'Yes – but you don't *know*. How do you know what the backgrounds of these poor people were? They mayn't have been happy. They may – '

'Have been given the chance to start new lives from now on?' Rupert finished for her, with heavy irony. 'Oh, no, Addy. Don't try to make me accept such a rosy point of view. Be as stoical as you like but don't pretend. Pattern there may be to things, but from any angle the pattern can be bloody awful sometimes.'

'Rupert – '

'Sorry. But only some words are appropriate at such a time.'

She sighed, and got up. 'I know. I suppose I sounded rather – puerile and preachy.'

He shook his head, half smiling. 'No, just very young.'

'Which I'm not,' she said quickly. 'In experience of your kind I may be. But I want to learn, Rupert. I want to have a share in your problems of dealing with people and disasters, so we can do things together. Do you understand?'

'Yes.'

'And agree?'

'We'll have to see,' he told her ambiguously. 'There are certain matters I wouldn't want you embroiled in for the world. So let's leave problemising, shall we? Let's not talk any more. There are other things.'

'What other things?'

His eyebrows shot up over his fine eyes, a habit they had when he didn't intend to be provoked into answering.

'I don't mean to spell it out. You know very well. By the way, to change the subject, I've a rather important guest – or guests – coming next week on the Friday. They'll stay overnight. Sir John and Lady Swiftley. I'm telling you in time so you can have the new cook – what's her name – Cole – primed well beforehand.'

Adelaide was surprised.

'Oh. This is something new. Who are they?'

'Business acquaintances, or rather *he* is,' Rupert told her. 'Very important to me at this time. So do your best, won't you, Addy? I don't like having to woo the rich. But sometimes it's necessary.'

'I suppose you hope he'll invest in the mine. Is that it?'

'Yes.'

'But I thought you said – I thought you said the other day there wasn't sufficient tin or copper.'

Rupert's lips tightened. 'There are whole new levels, a complete area still be explored. With enough expenditure I still believe tin's waiting. Even Borlaze agrees, although he can't see ever being able to exploit it.'

'And do you expect these people – this Sir-something-or-other to invest a fortune in something as doubtful as Wheal Tansy?'

'Don't expect. I hope. Yesterday and this morning I wished a landslide could have swallowed the whole damned mine up. But I was wrong. We've got to go on.'

'Why?'

'The men. The families. Myself. I don't like giving up, Addy. So there's one practical way you can help – be nice to Sir John, not too nice, mind – and to his wife. She comes from the North I've heard – her father made a million out of mills and cotton, a sort of rags to riches story; and although pandering for profit isn't exactly my line or to my liking, I'm sure you can be trusted to make the lady feel good. You understand? A little flattery can work wonders with a woman not yet accepted by society. And I can assure you she's the power behind the throne.'

There was a pause. Then Adelaide said a little more coolly, 'Very well, Rupert. I'll see the house is at its best, and a good dinner put on. But I hope you know what you're doing and you don't get into a muddle – financially, I mean.'

'There'll be no muddle,' Rupert said, 'and if the deal doesn't come off it will be a matter of another little experiment in contraband – which I can assure you is far more risky.'

The matter ended there, leaving Adelaide conjecturing over the visit which was already looming as something of an ordeal in her mind.

The next day before Rupert had arrived back at Trenhawk for lunch, something quite unpredictable occurred. Adelaide was in the small parlour when Lilian knocked to say there was someone – a woman – wanting to see her.

'Woman?' Adelaide queried, 'who? Did she say – give her name?'

Looking faintly embarrassed, Lilian replied, 'Well, yes – she called herself Mrs Hawksley, ma'am, and asked if she could talk to the lady of the house. She said she'd come to see her son, Master Julian.'

Adelaide let a book she was holding fall to the floor. 'Her – *what?*'

'Her son, ma'am.'

'And Mrs *Hawksley* did you say?'

Lilian nodded. 'I thought it was rather funny. But I couldn't contradict her, could I? After all, ma'am, what *is* Master Julian's surname – none of us know, not the servants anyway.'

Nor me either, Adelaide realised with a shock. She'd steered clear of asking that one pertinent fact from Rupert, simply because she didn't *want* to know. As it had never arisen there'd really seemed no point. Possibly Mrs Pender was aware of it. But she'd never said; she wouldn't, naturally, being so loyal to Rupert. Oh how negligent she'd been, Adelaide told herself with a sudden burst of annoyance. To have gone on all these weeks – months a whole year – disregarding because of a gnawing secret fear – the young boy's identity. His ward Rupert had said, the orphaned son of a friend. And she'd asked no more. Anyway, if he was Rupert's son, his name still wouldn't be Hawksley. Or – would it?'

The fear, beginning after the first shock as a mere niggle, intensified slowly into acute dread. Yet her voice was calm, even hard and formal, when she said, lying firmly, 'What a strange thing for you to say, Lilian. Of *course* I knew Master Julian's name. You'd better show Mrs Hawksley in here.'

'Very well, ma'am.'

Lilian withdrew, but not before she'd thrown a cynical glance towards Adelaide who noticed, and was fully aware of the implication.

A moment or two later there was a knock on the door,

followed by Lilian's voice saying, 'Mrs Hawksley, ma'am.'

Adelaide, with stiffened spine and a swirl of skirts, turned.

The woman who entered hesitantly, had an air of bewilderment – almost fear on her face. She was slim, fair, rather fragile looking, and rather over-dressed, although her clothes were of the cheap kind. In her younger days, she must have been pretty; her eyes were large and very blue, Julian's eyes. But her voice, when she answered Adelaide's formal greeting had an accent and edge to it more reminiscent of Cockney London than of Cornwall.

Adelaide touched the gloved hand briefly, noting that the tip of one finger was darned. The perfume exuded was too strong to be good. Everything about the visitor emitted an air of poverty striving to be something better.

'Do sit down,' Adelaide said indicating a chair, 'and tell me how I can help you. You say Julian is your – your son? And you are Mrs Hawksley?'

The woman nodded. 'Oh yes, that's true. Reely it is. I – I haven't called before because – because things weren't too good with me, you see. I hadn't much money, and I was ill – and then – well, I thought, I ought to see how he was. Just once I mean. It's natural, isn't it?'

'I'm afraid I don't understand,' Adelaide answered. 'I didn't worry my husband about Julian, because it didn't seem to be my affair. I accepted him as his ward. But – '

The tired face confronting her drooped. On the lap of the fitting faded blue coat the hands clasped and unclasped themselves nervously.

'You didn't know then – about – about his father, and me?'

'Rupert?' Before she knew it the name was out.

There was a gasp. 'Oh *no*. He's not Mr *Rupert* Hawksley's son. David, I mean. David Hawksley was his father. I'm sorry if – if the news is a surprise. But you see – '

Adelaide's sudden relief was followed by such extreme shock that for a moment the room seemed to revolve round her. Then she managed to say trying to keep her agitation under control, 'How can you be Mrs David Hawksley? He was married only – only last year. Didn't you know?'

'Oh yes – yes. It wasn't quite like that. It was – '

Adelaide waited.

'Well?' In the silence following small sounds registered that she'd not been aware of before – ordinary everyday muted sounds like the ticking of the grandmother's clock in the corner, and from somewhere outside the crying of gulls across the sky. Then she heard the tired voice continuing, 'We were together for three years, David and me. He always said one day he'd marry me – but I didn't reely believe it. I think he *meant* to – but then you see, I was nothing, nobody. So in the end until he got on his feet and all his debts paid, that's what he said – got on his feet – I had my name changed from Purdey to Hawksley. Done all proper it was, and I had an apartment near Camden Town.'

'After Julian was born things got difficult. Money – you know. But we loved each other – never think we didn't, because it wouldn't be true. If I'd been a high born lady with prospects everything would've been all right. But I wasn't. And when he told me there was someone else I understood. So I went away for a time – to Bristol. David thought it best. He sent us money of course, for a time. And then I got a job. It wasn't easy, with Julian as he was. But I managed. Then when I got back to London it was all over. He'd married her. She was a real lady – the proper sort, I suppose, for a wife in his station. He didn't forget me though. His solicitor wrote to me and sent twenty pounds. That helped. But when he was killed in that awful foreign place I got this note –'

'What note?'

'From Mr Rupert, telling me he'd take Julian and see he had a good home and all he needed for a proper start in life. Well, I ask you, what'd you have done? I was grateful. And that's how it was. I said I wouldn't interfere or anything; and I *won't*, honest, even now. But – I thought, seeing how things were better with me, I do sewing you know, that sort of work, and – and – ' her words faded significantly.

'I understand.'

'Well – just to see him, it wouldn't hurt anyone, would it?'

Still bemused and inwardly fighting for composure Adelaide said gently, 'I don't see how it could.'

A faint smile crossed the other woman's face dispelling the years briefly into a more youthful image – a suggestion of the girl David must have known and loved. Adelaide didn't question her integrity for one moment. Her statement was obviously guileless and straightforward, the selfless admission merely of a mother's natural affection for the child she'd born. But David! how *could* he?

Through the confusion of her thoughts a sudden swift stab of anger and disillusion swept over her. She was outraged that the young husband she'd trusted so implicitly could have kept his involvement with the pathetic figure confronting her so deliberately secret and pushed away. David, who'd appeared so gallant and brave and honourable, so passionately in love with her and willing to sacrifice his army career – everything – so he could live with her quietly at Trenhawk, helping her rear a family and carry on the name of Hawksley with dignity in the old tradition. David of all people. Why; was *any* of it true? Had their marriage actually counted anything to him except as a conveniently romantic commitment for helping to pay his debts and ensure an easy existence ahead? How could it have – when all the time there'd been another woman tucked away with a child of his – a handicapped child, unacknowledged and insecure?

In that brief pause any lingering attachment she felt for David seemed to disintegrate and fade. A wave of giddiness clouded and blurred her eyes. She put a hand to her head, and through the fleeting darkness heard the other woman say, 'I'm sorry, ma'am – Mrs Hawksley – it's been a shock, it must have been I know. But, believe me I don't want to make any trouble. It means a lot to me knowing Julian's reely cared for. And seeing as Mr Hawksley, Mr Rupert – your husband's been so kind – '

'Oh yes, yes.' Adelaide said, quickly recovering herself. 'I'm not blaming you. And it's not been such a shock, really – ' obviously David's ex-mistress had no idea that she, Adelaide, had been the woman responsible for his desertion – the 'real lady' concerned. That, anyway, was something to be grateful for.

'How did you get here?' she found herself asking automatically after the short pause.

'By poste-chaise, and then I had a cab from Penzance. I'd saved up,' the woman answered with a pathetic attempt at pride.

'And is the cab still waiting?'

'Oh no. I couldn't afford that. Besides, I like a walk. Especially on a day like this. Cold isn't it? It gets you warm.'

'Well, first you must have some hot coffee,' Adelaide told her practically, 'then I'll tell Mrs Pender – our housekeeper – to bring Julian in. Afterwards, if you want to see my husband, then –'

'Oh no, no, that's not – not necessary, ma'am – Mrs Hawksley –'

'Then our man shall drive us both back to Penzance.' Adelaide continued practically. 'The walk would be far too long, and you look tired already.'

'I'm stronger than I look,' came the answer. 'And – and about Julian –'

'Yes?'

'I don't want to upset him – if you know what I mean. He'd remember me. I thought p'raps I could just see him, from a window, or – or – ' she turned her head away, but not before Adelaide had caught the glitter of tears flooding the blue eyes. She touched one gloved hand lightly.

'Now don't upset yourself, Mrs – ' the word faltered on her lips. 'What's your other name? Your first? Hawksley's so – formal isn't it?'

'Elise,' came the reply.

'I like that,' Adelaide commented quickly. 'Now come to the fire, Elise, make yourself comfortable, and I'll arrange things with Mrs Pender.'

When the visitor had been settled in a comfortable chair near the welcoming blaze of logs spitting above lumps of coal, Adelaide went to the kitchen, ordered the coffee, and after a brief private explanation to the housekeeper concerning Julian, returned to the parlour.

Matters then went comparatively smoothly. Coffee and sandwiches were served by Mrs Pender herself, and half an hour later Adelaide took Elise to the drawing room window which had a fine expansive view of the gardens. From there they watched presently Mrs Pender's broad figure emerge from a side-path on to a wider one cutting between bushes and flower beds. She had the small boy's hand in her own, and he was looking up at her confidently as she pointed at intervals to something of interest – a bird, a particular shrub in its ornamental winter foliage, or a cluster of Christmas roses starred white against the brown earth.

The little boy was well wrapped up in a thick jacket over calf-length trousers reaching to his boot tops. He had a flat brimmed hat on his fair curls, but even that couldn't hide the glitter of gold where the pale light caught it.

Elise stood perfectly still for quite a minute. Glancing at her once Adelaide noticed the thin throat struggling with emotion. Then turning abruptly the slender figure straightened. A hand lifted a screwed-up handkerchief to the tilted nose.

'Thank you,' Elise said. 'I'm glad I've seen him. It'll be the last time I'll intrude, and I'll know now he's in good hands.'

'You're not intruding,' Adelaide told her impulsively. 'There's no reason at all why you shouldn't come to see Julian here any time you feel like it – '

'No, ma'am. That wouldn't do at all. Upsetting it would be – for him as well as me. It's better to have things as they are.'

'Very well,' Adelaide agreed reluctantly. 'But you must leave an address – '

'No, not that either,' the woman said, with surprising firmness. 'Julian's got a reel chance now of growing up a gentleman as his father would've made 'im. An' that's how I want it to be. His uncle, Mr Rupert, has taken him in, and let that be an end of et. A clean break.'

'I think you're very brave,' Adelaide told her. 'It can't be easy for you.'

'I can get by, ma'am. Things'd be a lot worse if I held on to the boy. What would he get from me but worry an' fret with no proper education, and me having the feeling all the time I'd let him down?'

Adelaide saw the point. 'Very well, if you want it that way, I can see there's nothing we can do about it,' she agreed doubtfully, but with a feeling of relief. 'As long as everything is properly settled – '

'Oh it is, it is. All legal. That's why I shouldn't have come reely. I wasn't supposed to. But not having to see Mr Rupert has made it so much easier. I'm grateful to you, reely I am.'

'There's no need to be,' Adelaide remarked slightly discomforted. 'And as you know our address you can always get in touch if necessary. Any help I can give you – ' she stopped abruptly. What right had she to make philanthropic offers when she might need any penny she had for Wheal Tansy?

'I shan't ask help', Elise said. 'What I want I can make – somehow.'

The last word had a bold almost defiant ring about it that betrayed all too obviously its true significance. The cheap finery, the strong perfume and over-use of rouge – these alone were the trademark of a profession as old as time itself.

Later, in the landau on the way to Penzance, Adelaide said, 'I hope you'll find something congenial to do, Elise. Something – work in a store perhaps, or fashion house. You have a good figure and – '

The bitterness of Elise's smile escaped her. 'Oh I *did* have, ma'am – the figure I mean before I was ill. I had a few weeks off this summer – a cold that's all. It pulled me down. But I shall pick up again. There's plenty of jobs if you look all right. I had two months in a summer job at Brighton earlier on.'

'Really? Acting, do you mean?'

'Well, sort of. Dancing more, and showing off. Making eyes – you know the sort of thing. And as I said, I'm good at sewing. I can always take up again for the seamstress. Tiring it is though, makes your neck ache.

When the interview was at last over, and Adelaide had seen Julian's mother safely away from the station, she was surprised how exhausted she felt. Her body, from tension, slumped wearily as Carnack drove her back cross-country, along the winding Cornish lanes. Though the full significance of the encounter had not yet completely registered, one fact was clear, and still numbed her when she thought of it. David's deception and emotional treachery. If he'd been honest about Elise she might still have been able to forgive him. But she knew now however hard she tried, she'd never really be able to. All the long months of anguish following his death, the treasured mementoes so revered and carefully hidden away to be taken out at lonely moments in memory of past times, the bundle of letters tied up with blue ribbon, the heart-ache and longing, all an illusion based on a lie. The David she'd married had been a myth, a picture of her own imagination, no more.

And Rupert had known all along.

Why hadn't he told her?

'My dear girl,' he said later, when she confronted him with the sorry story. 'I'm not quite that kind of bastard, I hope. You'd married David. To destroy the illusion in that particular way wouldn't have gone down very well with myself or you. Call it "noblesse oblige" if you like.'

'You mean you didn't want me to *know*?' Her voice was incredulous.

'Maybe I did,' Rupert told her, 'but not from me. I wanted the impossible, I suppose – just to have you forget him. But I can tell you this, I was getting to the end of my tether. I'm not set exactly set in the heroic mould, love. If you'd gone on forever yearning and mooning over your precious David it's quite likely I'd have let the cat out of the bag, just to make you see sense. He wasn't a bad sort, though, Addy – just a romantic young idiot sometimes, with more than his fair share of good looks and charm.'

'Yes.'

'Probably he could have made you happy – for a time,' he continued speculatively, 'but it wouldn't have lasted. David wasn't by nature the faithful sort. *I* knew that, so did his own father, Uncle William. He had the Hawksley name, but he wasn't born one, Addy. In looks, nature, everything, way back in the blood he was a St Clare.'

She was silent, then she remarked, 'Like Genevra.'

Rupert took her by the shoulders, shook her slightly and said, 'Not like Genevra at all. Get that into your head, will you, once and for good. Genevra's of stronger stock – like that old madam Lady Serena, and you, yourself. She's *yours* Adelaide, and I'm damned well accepting her as mine too, understand? Oh we'll have others, a whole brood of them possibly, but young Genevra's to have her rightful place here legally, in my heart, and yours too, I hope.' He paused, adding seriously, 'If not there'll be trouble. So just you remember it.'

'And Julian? What's *his* position?' Adelaide queried with a hint of tartness.

'My nephew of course,' Rupert answered equally. 'Come to think of it – ' his dark eyes twinkled for a moment, 'we've done quite well for such a newly married couple, haven't we? – A whole ready-made family in the course of just a few months.'

'That you didn't really want,' Adelaide reminded him.

He suddenly swooped her up into his arms. 'Don't you ever say anything like that again. Adelaide Hawksley, or I'll – I'll –'

'Yes?'

'Beat the daylights out of you,' he said, before his lips came down on hers. He held her for an ecstatic moment pressed against his chest one hand straying to the soft breast under the blue satin bodice, then dropped her quickly to her feet as Mrs Pender's footsteps sounded outside. There was a knock, the sound of the door opening, and the housekeeper's voice saying, 'Oh, I'm sorry to bother you, I'm sure, but – '

'Yes' Adelaide queried, straightening her dress, 'yes, Mrs Pender?'

Rupert trying to appear nonchalant was smoothing his hair, wondering why on earth the old biddy couldn't choose her moments more opportunely.

'It's that Mrs Cole, Ma'am,' the old woman said, 'she's all determined on having mutton pie for dinner, and she says she doan' mean to do a savoury as well – '

'Who wants a savoury with mutton pie?' Rupert said testily.

'That Miss Venables,' Mrs Pender told him with a tightening of her lips. 'Et's difficult, with her not eating meat. But I can't blame Cook. Makes twice the work she does – that theer governess. – '

Adelaide thought quickly.

'Tell Mrs Cole the pie will be admirable,' she said placatingly. 'I'll attend to Miss Venables. She can have a salad. I can make it myself – with *her* help. That will perhaps show her that her humanitarianism or whatever they call it, makes extra work domestically. She's entitled to her opinions, but certainly not to upset the cook. Don't worry, I'll get things sorted out.'

'Very well, Miss Adelaide, ma'am, that's all I wanted to

know. They're both of them, Cook *and* Miss Venables, a bit set in their own ways. O' course, with Cook comin' from the North, there's things she wants to put her hand to, an' one o' them's mutton pie.' She sniffed 'I must say I doan' fancy et much myself. Still –'

'If it pleases her,' Adelaide said, 'we must fit in sometimes. You get on well together, don't you?'

'Oh yes. She's a sensible enough body most ways, I do admit. Very willing too. No airs 'bout her like that theer governess –'

'And Lilian?' Adelaide intercepted quickly.

'Oh – she does well enough, in her own place,' Mrs Pender conceded. 'Mind you – she's got 'nuff sense in that toffee-nosed head o' hers to know not to take liberties with *me*. Lucy's gettin' a bit above herself, though. Jealousy, I do s'pose. An' when the young man comes – the one took on for Master Julian, it'll be wuss. I can see trouble theer, sure 'nuff.'

'Oh I don't think so,' Adelaide said, 'Mr Clemis won't be mixing with the girls. We've got it all properly arranged. Julian and his tutor will have their meals in the Bay room when they're not with us. Rupert – my husband – and I thought it would be useful to use it as a kind of schoolroom, being so sunny. I hope you agree. Do you think it's a good idea?'

Mrs Pender's first reaction was obviously negative. Then, complacently aware her opinion was being asked for, she agreed grudgingly, 'As you say, it's sunny, but half a flight o' them stairs up – an for carrin' trays too –'

Adelaide smiled. 'I'm sure Lucy will manage. If not, any tray can be left by the hatch for Mr Clemis to collect himself.'

'I hope it works out, ma'am,' Mrs Pender said. 'An I hopes that poor little mite gets on with the young man. Being as he is makes him sensitive, sort of. I've got to know him well durin' these last months, an' one thing I would *not* stand, pardon my sayin' so, is seein' him lonely or not treated right.'

'You needn't worry yourself over that,' Rupert interposed. 'Now set your mind at rest, Mrs Pender. Master Julian will be perfectly happy and well looked after. I shall see to that – and you too, naturally. You'll still be able to keep an eye on him.'

'Hm. I hope so, I do indeed, Mr Rupert. To think of that

woman – his own mother too – givin' him up just as though he was a passel o' tay or something. It makes my blood boil.'

'She's done what she thought was right,' Adelaide remarked gently.

'What *was* right,' Rupert added. 'And I know we can trust you to keep what you know of the matter to yourself.'

'There's no need for you to point out my duty to me,' the housekeeper retorted sharply. 'I was never under any 'llusions 'bout his parents or how he did come into the world. An' I knowed from the very start you wusn't his father, Mr Rupert, though many think different.'

Seeing the flush on Adelaide's face, Rupert remarked more sternly, 'The subject's closed, Mrs Pender. To all intents and purposes the boy is a son of the house and to be treated as such. So with the question of the mutton pie solved perhaps you'd better go and put Mrs Cole's anxiety at rest.'

The old woman turned and left the room muttering under her breath.

As soon as the door closed Adelaide couldn't restrain a giggle. 'Mutton pie!' she echoed. 'After all the tragedy and everything – to end up with that.'

'I know.' Rupert smiled back. 'I suppose we should be grateful for the light relief.'

Adelaide was. And during the following weeks she had to call on every ounce of inherent optimism she possessed to counter-balance Rupert's alternating moods of depression and anxiety over the inevitable problems of compensation for the survivors and relations of Wheal Tansy's victims.

XV

Adelaide had been prepared for a north country accent, a certain arrogant ebullience from the Swiftleys, combined with a hale-fellow-well-met manner masking inner insecurity concerning the social graces. The truth, as she discovered from the first moment of the couple's visit, was very different.

Instead of the large overdressed figure sailing in on her portly husband's arm, Adelaide was confronted by a thin brisk woman with only a trace of Yorkshire in her brittle voice, and a shrewd assessive quality in her bird-like eyes that was distinctly disconcerting. She must have been about fifty years old, and despite her husband's loud voice and overwhelming physical presence it was quite clear that, as Rupert had predicted, she was the power behind the throne. She was dressed quietly in brown silk, high at the neck, tight-waisted, with a full skirt having no hoops, but suggesting a draped effect to the back, indicating the new fashion lines ahead. Her only touch of ostentation was in the diamonds she wore – two rings, a flashing brooch, and a necklace composed of a pendant and chain.

Her smile was thin, and over-sweet.

'How pleasant,' she said over dinner, 'to be able to eat without those ridiculous finger-bowls everyone in society seems to think so necessary. Of course I'm always one for hygiene – but as I've said to my husband John time after time – "What's the use of dipping your fingers in water when likely as not it's already messy from the first time." '

Adelaide agreed. 'We live very simply here, Lady Swiftley.' she said.

'And I'm glad you admit it. So do we. I've no patience with a lot of show just put on to impress. I suppose really Cornwall's fairly unsophisticated compared with London. In the North it's the same. Values count more than fancy manners.'

'Do you know Cornwall well?' Adelaide asked.

'Oh no. But we visit Plymouth sometimes – being so in-volved with shipping.'

'Shipping? Oh I thought it was –'

'Cotton, of course. Well that's our bread-and-butter, or "jam", you could say,' Lady Swiftley replied. 'But my hus-band always says – and I agree with him – better to have more irons in the fire than one.'

'Now, now, Sarah,' Sir John said from across the table, 'over such an excellent meal thee knows better surely than to talk business –'

'His small eyes in their bags of flesh were upon Adelaide appraisingly. 'A damned handsome woman,' he thought. Style, too. She could be a duchess sitting there in her grey silk. Never had to work hard, he could see that. Not like his Sarah. You could always tell real 'aristos' from their shape. Only the thoroughbreds wore their flesh properly; women of his wife's class who'd not had the chance to develop easily during their young days either became ram-rods later, or put on weight in the wrong places. This one never would. If he was a younger man – but one glance at Hawksley's face told him there'd have been no hope in that direction. A queer customer, Hawksley. Astute enough to have his eye on the main chance, but a bit of a dreamer too. That sort were hard to judge. Unpredictable. And he'd have to know a lot more about this mining venture of his before he risked investing a packet. Sarah would be a help there. She had a strange knack of knowing a winner from a loser. More use there than any man he'd ever met. Warmed by the good wine he chuckled inwardly as he took his napkin to his lips. The fish, followed by excellent pheasant, fruit pie, and very good cheddar, had been admirable. He'd have to com-pliment the cook. Even Sarah couldn't have done better. He caught his wife's eye over the tastefully arranged flowers in the crystal bowl. They were enigmatic, yet knowing – the eyes of a politician.

This was the one quality he found, on occasion, slightly disturbing about Sarah – her capacity for unfeminine mental tricks. Oh it could be a great help in the business world, but there were times when it seemed to him her mind overstepped its proper boundaries. 'You wait, Jonathan Swiftley,' she'd said only recently, 'one day us women are going to take a real proper place in running the country. Oh mebbe you and I won't see it, but it'll come. We'll have the vote an' all.'

She'd meant it too, and with a rush of quick amusement he'd pitied any who came under her thumb. It would never happen of course – not in his lifetime, so as the possibility didn't arise he'd been content to shrug it off and forget such a highly improbable state of affairs. That night though, at Trenhawk, he recognised she was in one of her calculating moods, and wondered how her mind was running.

Actually Sarah was concerned almost completely by Adelaide. She'd been quick to notice during the meal the fleeting expression in those very beautiful hazel eyes each time they wandered to her rugged-looking husband, Rupert Hawksley, and the answering glance in his own. If ever she'd seen a couple in love, they were the ones. And Adelaide, she'd heard, had money. Then why weren't they using it instead of trying to get her John interested in some pig-in-the-poke deal? If it *was* a pig-in-the-poke?

She meant to find out.

Later, when the men had retired for drinks and smokes to the library, and their mutual business discussion, Sarah and Adelaide, having tidied up and refreshed themselves with cologne, went downstairs to the drawing room.

'A really nice place you've got here Mrs Hawksley,' Sarah said glancing round appreciatively.

'Yes,' Adelaide conceded. 'I always liked this room.' And she liked it even more, now. The familiar gold curtains had been cleaned and re-hung, a new cream carpet – at her own personal expense had been laid. The valuable Louise Quinze furniture was sparkling and polished, and the French clock was once more ticking on the mantel-shelf. The general impression was again of luxury and a defiance of time and leaner years. Crystal winked in the candlelight. There was not the slightest sign of poverty here, Sarah thought, and a man – or woman for that matter – a woman like Adelaide, would obviously go to a great deal of trouble to retain it.

Deciding to take the bull by the horns, Sarah said bluntly, 'A pity you're having trouble with that mine or your good man's – tin an' copper's a chancey business these days and can run away with a lot of capital unless you're careful.'

Adelaide thought quickly. 'I'm not an expert,' she said ambiguously, 'but I don't think Rupert's unduly worried.'

'No?'

'Not about finance anyway,' Adelaide replied rather shortly. 'The accident's upset him naturally. And there'll be some delay in restarting. But I'm sure he's certain Wheal Tansy will be extremely profitable once it's properly on its feet again.'

'Hm. And if my husband – or others – don't choose to invest what then?' the thin demanding voice queried. I've heard some shipping magnate or other's already making things difficult. Oh now – don't be riled, I'm just trying to get things clear, seeing as that's why we're here – '

'I don't – '

Sarah lifted a finger disapprovingly. 'Now don't try and tell me you'd have had John and me down here if it wasn't to get something out of us, my dear. There's one thing I've learned fairly well in my life – and that's to know folk. What would your sort and ours have in common *except* that – just one thing, brass?'

Adelaide felt herself colouring. Before she could answer, the other woman continued, 'And there's no need to get on your high horse, though many would. But I think you've more sense.' She paused before adding, 'You love that husband of yours, don't you?'

'Yes,' Adelaide said abruptly. 'But I really don't see my personal relationships are anything to do with you, Lady Swiftley.'

Sarah laughed, a genuine sound, completely without rancour.

'That's right – put me in my place. I like a woman of spirit. But believe me, you're wrong. The sort of person John and I have dealings with is important, *very* important, and don't you make any mistake about it. In a way you see, I'm a bit of a gambler – '

'A gambler? You?'

'Aye. Willing to take a risk now and then, provided I like those concerned. And I like you. Another thing, though you may find it hard to believe – what I say goes – with John, I mean. Now supposing you tell me how the land *really* lies, as far as you know. What your plans are, and what you mean to do if my husband doesn't put his hand in his pocket?'

Adelaide's first reaction was of amazement, followed by a rush of anger that this rather common, unattractive, but exceedingly sharp-minded woman should attempt tying her down in such an unsubtle manner. She had a quick reply on her lips when better judgement took over. Rupert certainly wouldn't approve of her making an enemy of Lady Swiftley at such early stages of the visit, so she managed to answer after a pause, 'Well, we have a farm you know, the Manor Farm which is quite a valuable property and would fetch a large sum if capital was necessary. But I know my husband isn't contemplating it at this stage. It's part of the inheritance you see – very old – '

'Ah. I see – a manor house.'

'Actually yes.'

'I've always fancied having something of the sort,' Sarah said reflectively. 'It might be that if I took a liking to it and your husband was willing John'd buy it for me – at a good price – far more mebbe than it's worth. In fact – ' her small bright eyes became conspiratorial. 'I *know* he would if I said so. Cornwall's got character. I think I'd like it here – just for visiting now and then. And old places are always an investment. Perhaps while we're here you could take me up there and give me a look round. What do you say?'

Knowing that Rupert was already contemplating selling the farm, and realising that Lady Swiftley meant what she said about giving a good price for it if it appealed to her, Adelaide agreed.

'Certainly,' she said. 'We can take a walk up there tomorrow morning – if you don't mind tramping over a patch of rough moors.'

Sarah laughed.

'Why should I? I was bred on them and rougher than anything round here I can tell you. My father worked in a mill, Halifax way. So did I, for a time when I was a girl. So you don't have to tell me about wild country.'

'Oh. I see.'

'You don't, you know,' Sarah said with a more serious note in her voice. 'It must be hard for you – '

'Hard?'

'Placing us – knowing where we stand and how our lives work. How we got where we are? Well, I'll tell you. Grit and damned hard work. That's how John got his brass, and the brass got the handle to our name. Not for nothing, mind you. We *paid*, oh yes – the price was stiff. But we didn't grudge it. Thousands benefited. There's hardly a charity in the land that hasn't got John Swiftley's name in it somewhere.'

'That must be very rewarding,' Adelaide remarked, for want of something better to say.

'It is.' The words jerked out like a snap of a box lid. 'So don't you go thinking my John's mercenary, either. He's got a heart under that bluff exterior.'

From this point Adelaide managed to steer the conversation into less personal channels, and presently the men appeared. How successful Rupert had been during their limited conversation together Adelaide couldn't guess. Rupert's face held its enigmatic withdrawn expression and though Sir John was smiling it told nothing. Still, nothing could have been settled in such a short time, Adelaide told herself reassuringly. The next morning, Saturday, would probably decide the issue, when Rupert was going to introduce Joe Borlaze, and one or two miners on the engineering side, including Ben Oaks, to the tycoon, and a master engineer from Redruth. At first Rupert had been doubtful about the wisdom of including Oaks; then a matter of tact had won. Ben, who'd guess very shrewdly what the business was all about, would appreciate being included. A 'man of the people' all for the new unions and rights of the under-dog he might be, but vain of his skill and fundamentally responsive to flattery.

The next morning, luckily, was fine. The two men set off for Wheal Tansy about ten o'clock, and half an hour later Adelaide wearing a warm cloak over a dark skirt and bodice began the walk with Lady Swiftley to the manor farm. Both women had veils draped over their small bonnets and tied under the chin to secure them against the wind. They held their skirts well above the toes of their boots, as they trod carefully over the narrow track up the slope. It had rained in the night, and the ground was squelchy in parts, but Sarah wasn't concerned. 'This is like old times,' she remarked, 'and a real gradely sight it is to see such heather agen. Is yon the

farm?' All unthinkingly she'd relapsed into her native Yorkshire accent.

Adelaide nodded. 'There. Half way up. It's a crock house,
very unusual for Cornwall.'

'That's a rum way of describing a place.'

Adelaide smiled.

'Just a term. Something to do with using so much timber.
Most places round here on the north coast are built only of
granite – because of the weather; the gales and storms we get.
Of course the manor's sheltered on one side in a slight dip.'

'Yes, I can see that. It looks a pleasant place.'

Adelaide thought so too. Under the lifting sky, pale rays of
winter sunlight already caught the roof and upper windows of
the house, casting a warm glow over the eastern walls.

When they reached the farm Mrs Merryn was in the dairy.
She came to the door looking faintly flustered, and more than
a little suspicious at such early callers.

'This is our housekeeper, Mrs Merryn,' Adelaide explained
hurriedly, to Sarah, 'or rather – our tenant. She's – she's very
valuable, and runs our dairy excellently – Mrs Merryn, Lady
Swiftley.'

Sarah held out her hand, 'Glad to meet you,' she said
affably. Mrs Merryn mumbled something in reply. She was
clearly ill at ease, and did not relax until Adelaide, apologising
for the early intrusion, informed her ambiguously that her
ladyship was merely interested in buildings of the period and
that as her time at Trenhawk was so short they'd had to take
the first available opportunity of looking over it. Even then it
was clear Mrs Merryn did not entirely believe her, something
Sarah sensed immediately.

She flung a shrewd glance at the other woman before saying
abruptly, 'I'm looking for a place round here, and this is the
kind I like – for holidays and visits now and agen. I've been all
for tempting Mr Hawksley to sell, but with no luck so far.' She
paused, adding appreciatively, 'I like the way things look, Mrs
Merryn. You keep it grand, I can see that. Nothing would
please me better than to have such fine useful tenants in a place
of mine. We're particular in Yorkshire – very particular. And
you'd fit the bill to a T. I can see that.'

Mrs Merryn was obviously gratified.

'You haven' seen much yet, ma'am – m'lady – now if you'd care for a drink o' somethin' – coffee, or tay? I'll nip upstairs in the meantime an see that man o' mine hasn' bin littern' things about they bedrooms.'

Altogether the visit was a success, and an hour later when they arrived back at Trenhawk, Sarah confided that as far as she was concerned the deal was settled provided Rupert was ready to sell. The sum suggested to Adelaide made her inwardly gasp, being twice the amount she'd anticipated.

'It'll depend on John though in the end,' Sarah told Adelaide confidingly. 'But as I'm so dead set on it there'll be no trouble there, providing – '

'Yes?'

'You butter him up a bit lass, when you get the chance,' Sarah said shrewdly. 'Men are like great babies really. Vain. Every one of them.'

The chance for the 'buttering up' process came a good deal earlier than Adelaide had anticipated.

Before dinner that evening, Adelaide, having a few minutes to spare, had gone to the conservatory to pick a particular posy for her bodice. She was wearing a gown of blueish green satin, a shade particularly becoming to her clear complexion and fair hair. She stared round reflectively at the assortment of exotice out-of-season blooms – roses, lilies, orchids, and all manner of geraniums and trailing greenery. The old familiar steamy smell of ferns and luxuriant verbage filled her nostrils in an overwhelming fit nostalgia. She lifted an arm automatically. touching a pink bloom with spotted heart shaped leaves that had been originally imported from somewhere abroad. It had a delicate fragrance about it, and had been one of Uncle William's most treasured blooms. She was about to pick it when she heard footsteps behind her.

'Allow me,' a voice said from behind her shoulder, 'thou'll prick thysen.'

Looking round she saw Sir John's bland, large, rather sensuous face looking down on her. She was too surprised to say anything, but allowed him to snap the blossom off and hold it beneath her nose.

'Where's it going?' he asked.

She held out her hand. 'Oh – it was just an idea. For my

bodice. If you give it to me —'

'Now now, you leave that to me, lass. Thee don't want to soil thy hands —'

Unaware how lovely she looked, how subtly inviting was the shadowed dip of her breasts, faintly perceptive above the green satin, or of the quickened breathing of the large figure so embarrassingly close, Adelaide allowed him to peel the stem and place the flower in a convenient froth of lace near her left shoulder. She waited for him to withdraw his hand, but he did not. Instead, it lingered, before travelling subtly between flesh and satin to one soft breast, where the large fingers tightened and pressed suggestively.

Adelaide made an attempt at disengagement. 'Sir John Swiftley — please — 'she said, fighting hard for composure. 'You mustn't —'

There was a low throaty laugh. 'Nobody says that to me love,' he muttered, close against her ear. 'Besides, thou don't mean it.' Before she knew quite what was happening, the other hand had slipped from her waist to the buttocks. She could feel his body — his thick animal body tight and breath-less against her own, and repulsion filled her. She forgot Sarah's advice about 'buttering him up', and of Rupert's anx-iety to have this man on his side. If she'd thought for a moment she could probably have made him see sense in time. Most probably he'd have realised it himself and been satisfied with, in common terms, a slap and a tickle. Seduction was out of the question; there were servants, Sarah, and Rupert in the offing, and the conservatory was far too public a place for any serious indulgence. But Adelaide *didn't* think. With a sudden wrench she tore herself from his grasp and delivered a hard slap across his face. Then, while he stared, watching her, with the blood rising in a blue-ish mottled tide to his florid cheeks she adjusted her bodice saying, 'Get out of here this moment. How *dare* you touch me. Get out this instant or I'll call the man.'

She hadn't heard Rupert approach as she struggled, hadn't seen Sarah behind him, staring in hard astonishment at the uncomely scene. She rushed past them through the parlour in to the corridor, down the hall and up the stairs to her room, and she flung herself on the large bed. She lay face down, a fury of crumpled green satin with her honey gold hair spreading in a cloud over the quilt.

Rupert came up five minutes later. What sobs there'd been had died. Her breathing had eased, she looked up at him apprehensively.

'I'm sorry about what happened,' she said in comparatively controlled tones. 'That he acted the way he did, I mean. Everything seemed to be going so well, Lady Swiftley was going to make an offer for the farm and – and everything. But – ' she sat up abruptly, 'if you expect me to apologise for smacking his beastly cheek you're wrong Rupert. I'm not sorry. I'd do it again.'

There was a short silence in which no flicker of expression crossed his face. Then, suddenly he laughed.

'I wouldn't want you to apologise. If you hadn't tackled him yourself I'd probably have knocked him flying. But why, Adelaide, *why* do you manage to get yourself into such damned difficult situations?'

'I don't mean to. I was simply taking a flower for my bodice and he came up behind and – ' she hesitated before adding, 'a horrible man.'

'Oh I don't know, Addy. You probably looked very provocative. Anyway, you've settled everything very decisively. No Swiftley money for Wheal Tansy.'

'Do you mean – ?' She was aghast.

'What did you expect?' he asked. 'They're off tonight. Lady Swiftley's already packing.'

'Oh dear.' She got up, walked to the mirror and surveyed herself ruefully. 'I suppose I should have been more tactful.'

'*Could* you have been?'

She shook her head. 'No. He didn't give me the chance.'

Adelaide saw Sarah briefly at the foot of the stairs before their departure. She shook her head with mild reproof.

'I told you, lass,' she said with a touch of irony, 'butter him up. I thought you were cleverer than you are, seemingly. Still, no hard feelings. and good luck with the mine. Happen you'll need it.'

A minute or two later there was the sound of carriage wheels and horses' hooves, as the Swiftley chaise rattled along the drive towards the main road.

It was only later that the full implication of the disastrous meeting penetrated Adelaide's mind, and she realised Rupert still had the problem of the mine's future to face.

XVI

Wheal Tansy survived for a few months with the help of certain 'side-lines' of Rupert's and financial aid from Adelaide who insisted on more than half of her remaining financial holdings being sold, much against Rupert's wish. He was grateful for the money, but inwardly ill at ease for fear the mine eventually failed altogther, and Trenhawk had to rely on its own resources and the farm's. Because of the uncertain future he hung on to the manor and even increased the number of sheep. The Cornish short-necked breed were sturdy and fetched a good price on the market. His anxiety however affected Wheal Tansy's workers. Tributers left, and even Borlaze had lost enthusiasm. The ore lodes were by no means dry, but they were thin. The richness expected didn't mature, and insecurity bred ill-tempers from miners and investors. There were, in fact, very few of the latter left. If it hadn't been for Adelaide things would have looked bleak. But because she was happy, she refused to be depressed. She was expecting a child in the winter of 1857, and was overjoyed, envisaging him as a second Rupert who would eventually reign as master of Trenhawk, begetting sons to follow.

The general restlessness of the world outside did not concern her, although news from up country was frequently grim – especially matters concerning the Empire and India, where mutineers had marched on Delhi and murdered many British soldiers and their families at Cawnpore. Reprisals had been terrible. But the House of Commons passed the matter off with fatuous apparent ambiguity, although opinion in political cir-

cles was concentrating to transfer power from the East India
Company to the Crown, incorporating the Company's troops
with the British Army.

Aunt Matilda who had not yet managed the difficult journey down to Cornwall, wrote to her niece in anticipatory
excitement of one day being able to visit Trenhawk to see her
darling great niece and great-nephew-to-be. She was sure it
would be a boy this time, and that he would grow up in a
wonderfully stable war-free Empire, thanks to the moral ever-
growing influence of the dear Queen. It was so gratifying, she
added, that Prince Albert had at last been proclaimed Prince
Consort by his wife herself, and shameful that the government
had not thought fit to do it earlier.

She added titivating bits of gossip concerning London society, including the declining reputation of Vauxhall which
was becoming sadly demoralised by the presence of loose
women who flaunted their charms outrageously for the benefit
of their own pockets and sensual indulgences of *men*.

It was all most regrettable, she wrote, and although the
Cremorne Gardens offered entertainment such as puppet
shows, and masquerades, etc, Vauxhall as it had been in its
heyday, would be sadly missed.

Such news items were of only passing interest to Adelaide.
London was a world away from Cornwall. She could hardly
believe there had been a time only a few years ago when the
tittle-tattle of society had meant so much to her. Everything
she now cared about seemed here in the wild landscape sur-
rounding Trenhawk and the gaunt coast of granite rocks, wild
gales and pounding tides.

Frequently during the months before the baby's birth she
made her way down to the cove, although Rupert was strongly
against such jaunts.

'You could fall,' he said. 'It's not safe. Have sense,
Adelaide –'

She smiled tauntingly and replied, 'What about you?'

'Me?'

'Your little adventures, Rupert? When you vow to me
there'll not be another, I'll promise anything you like.'

'Blackmail?' he asked, staring deep into the golden flame of
her eyes.

'If you like. But you needn't worry, I really don't take risks; and in your own words once, though I may not look it, I'm strong as an ox and nimble as a goat.'

So the matter was left undecided, and gradually as the days passed from autumn towards winter she stopped the rough descent to the cove on her own initiative, realising the climb back was getting too much for her. Her walks then became confined to the gardens or the lanes running towards the moors above. Sometimes she took Julian with Genevra in her push-chair. The little girl by then had improved in appearance, and gave promise of decidedly individual good looks later. But her character was stubborn, and although she could be all charm and sweetness to Rupert she was frequently aggressive to Adelaide as though resenting she was her child.

Julian she adored, and the boy, despite his deafness, doted on her. Partially due to the young tutor's interest he'd lost a good deal of his reserve, and was beginning to speak more clearly and with confidence. Although she tried not to be jealous Adelaide couldn't help feeling occasional resentment at the obviously close bond between the two children. She was fond of Julian, fonder than she was of Genevra, and the glance of criticism in his blue eyes when she scolded or tried to control the rebellious small girl disturbed and affronted her.

'She needs discipline,' she said to Rupert one afternoon, following a particularly stormy interlude. 'And I don't seem able to do it. She's too young to spank, and too wilful to bribe with sweets or kisses. She's more like a boy than a girl. I just don't know how to manage her.'

'Maybe if you tried love it would work,' Rupert told her, cryptically. 'You really *should* work on that, Adelaide.'

Adelaide did not reply, because she knew he was right.

Towards the end of November she was longing desperately for the birth to be over. Her body normally so slender felt cumbrous and heavy – far heavier than it had been when she was carrying Genevra. The lusty kicking of the unborn infant in her womb frequently disturbed her at nights, and she would heave herself out of bed and go to the window staring across the barren moors through the darkness, picturing herself un-fettered and free again, riding Ebony fiercely through the heather. Occasionally she recalled the visit to Carnwikk following her fall, Katherine St Clare's gentle solicitude, and the keen-eyed stare of old Lady Serena under her ridiculous red wig.

She had seen Katherine only once since the incident, and the ancient madam not at all. There had been something frightening about her – a 'knowing' quality due to her great age perhaps that had suggested to Adelaide in some shrewd instinctive way she'd guessed the truth, and would be quick to recognise her own macabre self mirrored in the dark green eyes of the turbulent red-haired Genevra. Adelaide, therefore, was determined to avoid any chance encounter with the 'malicious old creature', and what walks she took mostly led away from Carnwikk in the opposite direction. In any case they could hardly be called walks any more. She seldom got to the end of the lane leading to the main road, and met no one but an occasional farm labourer or worker from the manor on routine visits with vegetables to the house.

She didn't mind the solitude, although the lean black branches of the hedges under the grey sky, the desolate stone-walled fields with the bleak moors beyond, and the gulls' mournful crying from the sea were a constant reminder of how cut-off she was from her past. It didn't matter – she was content and glad for it to be so. So long as the baby was strong and well none of the rest mattered. This much loved child to come – although a torment to her body – was a symbol of the future and her passionate love for Rupert. She had no doubt in her mind it would be a boy. And if in unguarded moments an echo of the past, and of the gipsy woman's allusion to the ancient curse invaded her mind, she discarded it as stuff and nonsense.

As the days of her confinement drew near, she stopped wheeling Genevra, and took her short strolls alone. From a bend of the lane one afternoon she was startled to see a gaunt figure in a bedraggled red skirt and shawl walking purpose-fully towards her with several baskets slung over an arm. Her face was thin and brown, and lined. Her small black eyes were bright under a tangle of black wind-blown hair.

'So we meet again, lady,' she said with sly sweetness in her rasping voice. 'I seed it all, gorgio dear. Thy hand now, lady, thy hand for a mite of silver –'

Adelaide drew her cape closer at the neck.

'No, thank you, no. I told you before – I don't believe in it – not fortunes nor hand-reading. And if – '

'Oh, but you should, my lovely,' the woman interrupted. 'You should – because – ' her head came forward, with a darkening of the eyes and fading of the smile. 'We have the sight, lady, our kind *know*. We have the blood, lady. True Romanies we are, and the blood doesn't lie. Last time there was darkness around thee, but the shadow lifts, lady.' As Adelaide stared she felt a hand grasped in strong fingers, was aware momentarily of nothing but the strange burning eyes obscuring everything else into swimming negation. 'Thy son shall be strong and beautiful and wilder than thine old wild heart, gorgio. No curse shall destroy him, though thy soul may weep for many days. But as rain waters the earth lady, so do tears ease the heart's pain. An' now gorgio one – ' her hand fell away, the thin figure straightened, 'a basket will thee take from a hungry gago woman, or a dozen of fine pegs – ?'

Automatically Adelaide's hand went to her pocket where she kept her reticule. She took out a coin. 'We have plenty of baskets,' she heard herself saying, 'and don't need pegs. Take this, and go away, go quickly. My husband doesn't like – '

'Romanies?' The woman laughed, showing a glimmer of white teeth as she took the silver. 'He has no cause to, gorgio one. No cause at all. There's nothing we could tell him that's good. But thee an' thine will be all right. My blessings on thee, lady, and a thousand blessings in the years to come.' She lifted a hand, speaking, a jargon of words in her own strange tongue. The next moment she'd turned swiftly, with the speed of a panther, and had cut round the bend of the lane leading upwards towards the moors.

Adelaide paused, while the pumping of her heart eased, then, slowly she made her way back to the house.

That night there was a storm. By early evening Adelaide's pains had started. Rupert rode horseback through the fury of rain and wind to St Rozzan for the doctor and midwife. Doctor Maddox, who'd predicted the baby's birth to be due three weeks later, set off in his own carriage, collected the woman, a Mrs Pertwym, and arrived at Trenhawk only a quarter of an hour after Rupert.

By then claps of thunder rolled ominously from the west. Rivulets of water streamed down windows and walls; lamps and candles flickered and died fitfully. Through zig-zagged flashes of lightning the wind moaned constantly round the walls of Trenhawk.

In the large bed Adelaide lay racked by increasing attacks of pain that left her each time gasping with weakness and bathed in sweat. Rupert stood by her most of the time, holding her hand. His face was ravaged, torn with anxiety and compassion.

When the child was born three hours later, he was still there; the compassion on his face and the lusty cry of the baby – a boy – were the last things that registered with Adelaide's mind before exhaustion took her into its deep sleep.

In the buzz of activity no one noticed the small figure of a boy – Julian – creeping up the stone steps leading to the Tower Room. By then the sky was clearing, and watery moonlight streamed between massed black clouds, casting elongated strange shadows from the window above. The door was half open, and it seemed to him a figure stood there, waiting.

Half way up, Julian paused. For a moment he imagined he saw a face looking down on him – a very pale luminous face with pools of eyes staring from massed shadowed hair.

He was not at all afraid. His impulse was to climb further until he was enclosed by the welcoming gentle presence that for a moment seemed more real than the cold floor and stone walls of Trenhawk.

Then, suddenly, because it was something he could not understand, he turned and ran back the way he'd come, only looking back when he reached the corridor below.

There was nothing there any more. Nothing but darkness and a fitful thin stream of moonlight filtering beneath the door which had somehow closed.

At the end of the corridor he ran into Mrs Pender who was moving ponderously, but as quickly as possible, with a jug of steaming water in her hand.

She stopped abruptly.

'Now what are you doin', Master Julian? Sakes alive, with a new Hawksley just come into this world why es it another has to get into mischief at such a time?' Her face softened seeing the puzzled expression in his very blue eyes. She took his hand.

'Come along now, when I've got rid of this, I'll take 'ee to my room for a biscuit an glass o' milk. What the stuck up pie-faced Miss Venables is doin' to let 'ee wander 'bout this time o' night I can't begin to think. Seems to me things were better before she did come.'

Julian went along her with confidently.

Soon all was quiet.

Even the fitful crying of the baby had died, and in the morning frail sunlight spread its layer of pale gold over the garden and winter landscape.

Adelaide woke feeling refreshed and looking almost her old self again.

Rupert was jubilant.

The baby, dark like his father, even that early stage gave promise of having Adelaide's fine features. There was no question about his name which had already been discussed and decided.

He was registered the next morning in Penzance as Rupert Mortimer Hawksley, named after his father and Adelaide's own grandfather.

Aunt Matilda wrote to Adelaide and Rupert congratulating them on the birth of her great-nephew, Mortimer. Her hopes now, she said were to be able to visit Trenhawk in the early summer, when the weather would be more conducive to her visiting Cornwall. 'The journey, I'm afraid, would be far too arduous for me to undertake in our cold winter months,' she wrote.

What a pity, my dear, we are so far apart. That wild Cornwall of yours seems like another country to me. And of course my bronchitis and rheumatism get no better with age. I am only hoping I shall be fit enough to enjoy watching the Royal Wedding procession with the Bentworths on 25th January. As you know their house overlooks the Park and should have a fine view from their balconies. Great crowds are expected. It seems *so* romantic, although seventeen to my mind is rather young for a girl to take such an important step. But according to general opinion and social gossip, Princess Victoria is very much in love with Prince Fritz. I do hope, though, we are not going to become *too* Prussianised? And all this bother over the Hanoverian jewels too – I am thankful, I must say, that I was born an ordinary mortal away from Royal problems and political intrigue –

Reading the letter which went on and on, Adelaide felt faint amusement through her boredom. Even against the grim down-to-earth problems of Wheal Tansy, Aunt Matilda's sophisticated tittle-tattle held an unreal quality that made her wonder if they would ever actually meet again.

They didn't.

That same spring Aunt Matilda's chest condition developed into pneumonia from which she died, leaving the whole of her considerable fortune in trust to her great nephew Rupert Mortimer Hawksley, the income of which was to be her niece Adelaide's for life.

Adelaide was furious.

'What does a young baby want with a lot of money like that?' she demanded of Rupert, with her amber eyes flashing to brilliant gold. 'It's quite ridiculous. I think we could contest it, I really do. *We* need the capital, Rupert, for – for the mine and keeping the estate going without having to worry. And Genevra! what about her? She's a girl and will need a dowry later if she's going to get married – I can't understand it, I really can't –'

Rupert took her hands, drew her to him, and kissed her.

'Calm down, Addy,' he said. 'It's not too bad. Your income will be quite large, and it's a relief to me knowing you're properly provided for. As to the boy – our boy – he won't come into his inheritance until he's twenty-one, and by that time I think you can trust me to have dinned a little sound common-sense into him. As for Genevra –' he laughed.

'Yes?'

'Genevra will get by without a fortune behind her,' he said. 'You wait, my love, you're going to be proud of that young lady in the end. It's Julian I'm bothered about.'

'Why should you be? He's got a good home, He's – he's attractive, in spite of his deafness, and he's not your son, not really.'

'No,' Rupert said, 'and that's the trouble. That's what worries me.'

Adelaide felt her colour rising.

'He's a Hawksley, anyway, David's child.'

'Yes.' He did not add 'of the wrong strain,' though he thought it.

Eventually under Rupert's persuasion, and when she realised how considerable her income was going to be, Adelaide forgot her disgruntlement, stipulating that half of it went annually into reimbursement of Wheal Tansy. Although his conscience niggled, Rupert had to agree for the sake of the miners and future cost involved. The new levels though still below original expectations of tin yield showed indications of improvement and he clung to the hope of still striking it rich.

Meanwhile life at Trenhawk continued on a comparatively easy keel, highlighted by occasional domestic storms and passionate interludes which were always resolved to Adelaide's satisfaction by proof of Rupert's consuming love for her.

Genevra indeed seemed at times to be the only thorn in the flesh. She was an independent child, who at the age of four had developed an irritating habit of worrying her elders by wandering off on every available opportunity towards the moors and was consequently scolded and punished for it. Adelaide blamed Miss Venables. 'Surely it's not too much to ask you to keep an eye on the child,' she said more than once rather pettishly. 'She's not five yet. It isn't as if you have to trouble over Julian – '

Jane Venables' fine eyes glowed with dislike. 'I can't be everywhere,' she said. 'I've quite a lot to do for little Mortimer these days. Perhaps you should have a nursemaid, Madam?' She did not care for Adelaide who in her opinion was overbearing and vain, thinking more of her appearance and displaying her airs and graces before her husband, than of her own children. He of course doted on her, the silly man – it was all too obvious. But one day, Miss Venables consoled herself, Madam Hawksley would go too far. She couldn't see a marriage like theirs continuing forever. Why, she'd even caught them kissing in the dining room one evening, and Mrs Hawksley showing far more of her white bust than was decent at any time. The love in her husband's dark eyes had been – upsetting – to say the least of it. And she shuddered to think what went on behind the closed door of their bedroom.

There'd been times when the sound of their hushed voices, odd little whispered noises and throaty comments had quite *revolted* her. It didn't occur to her she could be jealous. But ever since the strange incident of the roses she had found it difficult to get Rupert Hawksley out of her mind, and seldom missed a chance of appearing on some trumped up excuse however flimsy, when he was about. She even resented his affection for little Genevra, though she did her best to suppress it. It was not the child's fault if he made more fuss of her than of Julian or baby Mortimer. Men were said to prefer daughters. The trouble was that Genevra was such a handful. On that, the whole household agreed. And she was certainly outstanding to look at. Not pretty. Her hair was too wild and red, her chin too stubborn below a mouth far too mobile or wide for beauty. And those green eyes of hers – they were intimidating somehow; so direct and searching in her heart-shaped face, and such a strange shade, neither green or blue, but holding the darkest tones of both.

Miss Venables simply could not make her out. Of course she had a lot of her mother in her, poor little thing. And because of this the governess did her best to bring her to heel.

It was impossible.

Genevra seemed to delight in tormenting her elders, especially by her ridiculous games of hide-and-seek when she'd tuck herself away in some remote spot of the garden or house, having them look for her for hours on end if necessary. Nothing made any difference; she'd been pleaded with, scolded, even on occasion spanked, but the next day it could easily happen again, and on the first opportunity Genevra would be missing.

Actually the little girl didn't mean any harm. She had a quick mind, and vivid imagination, which with a strong inborn theatrical sense tempted her into becoming a dozen different characters during the day, a princess from one of her favourite fairy tales, Snow White perhaps, or a young queen escaping from the wicked dragon, and even a toad if she wanted to. But mostly it was the wicked witch she was running away from, and that's why she had to find a hiding place. At others she simply wanted to wander off on her own thinking of nothing in particular, happy to be free under the wide Cornish sky, with the foxgloves and bluebells round her, and the white gulls flying above.

On an afternoon shortly before her fourth birthday she slipped out of the house when Adelaide and Miss Venables were occupied upstairs with Mortimer, and the servants were busy in the kitchen. It was a quiet day of summer sweetness, with only a trace of wind, and the lush smell of curling bracken, gorse, heather and wild flowers carried down from the moors above.

Genevra, tired of adults, of 'don't do this,' and 'don't do that,' cut swiftly and lightly across the drive to the lane, from where she made her way half dreamily yet purposefully towards the main moorland road. There was no one to see. The farm labourers were busy in the fields, and her small form in its green cotton frock was unnoticeable through the thick foliage of hedges and lush long grass.

When she reached the moor above the road she sat on a rock, listening, enchanted, to the chirping of a bird from a thorn tree, her eyes transfixed by the lolloping gait of a young rabbit as it moved from behind a clump of furze to its hole. Then, presently, she went on again, tickling her chin at intervals by a long feathery grass she'd picked, imagining she was a queen of some magic dell escaped for ever from the stupid world of grown ups like her mother – a queen able to work spells, and do wonderful things like changing a green frog into a handsome prince who'd put a golden crown on her head.

Soon she forgot even about queens and spells, and was content merely to walk among the great stones and heather, resting when she felt like it and then going on again. She was surprised, after a time, when she eventually came to a ribbon of lane cutting up over the moor towards the distant towers of a great house that looked to her like a fairy palace against the shimmering blue sky. She wondered how far it was, and her heart sank a little. Her legs were suddenly tired, she was hungry, and wished the blackberries were ripe. But when she picked a red one and put it between her teeth it was hard, and sour and she spat it out. She sat on a granite boulder, wondering what to do, whether to go on to the big house which seemed then a very long way off, or to turn and try and find her way home. They would be very cross, of course. Mama might spank her, because her dress was torn, and it was a new one. If she waited till her papa was back from the mine, though, it would be all right. He wouldn't let Mama hurt her. He was kind, he loved her and she loved him. So she decided to wait a little longer.

It was then that the carriage clattered up the lane from the valley below. It was a very fine one painted yellow, with some funny letters in gold on the side. Two men sat in front, behind the horses, in tall hats, wearing far handsomer uniforms than Carnack's best. And someone was inside – someone with very bright red hair and a lot of twinkly things in it. There were feathers too, masses of them looking like a parrot on top.

Genevra stared fascinated, as the coach slowed down. A very old lined face with a hooked nose and jutting chin was pressed to the glass.

'A witch,' Genevra thought with a bumping of her heart. 'She must be a witch.' But she was too enthralled to move. There was the sudden shrill cackle of a voice, and rapping on the window. One of the footmen got down and opened the door. The old head leaned forward, and the thin drawn mouth gaped in a smile. One twisted finger beckoned to the little girl. 'Come here, child,' she croaked, 'here – here – do you want a lozenge, eh? – '

Unable to resist the thought of a sweet, Genevra moved cautiously forward and took a sweet from the bag. The old creature grasped her wrist, and then let go saying, 'I shan't hurt you, child. What are you afraid of, eh? I like children – ' her eyes narrowed, became cunning, ' – especially your sort. Like as two peas in a pod, aren't we? Aren't we, child?'

Genevra half swallowing the lozenge, nodded.

'There, there, now. That's a good child, come in, my dear, sit beside me. I've a whole bag full of these, *and* cachous. You're hungry, aren't you, my dear?'

'Yes,' Genevra managed to say.

'Well then.' The old creature sat back, saying irritably to a

younger woman who looked a little like Miss Venables, 'Move
up, Graves. Stir yourself. This poor little girl needs rest and a
good meal I'll be bound. Or if you *can't* stir your stumps – give
a good roll and fall out. A walk'd do you all the good in the
world. Get a bit of the fat off your rump. Well, girl – '

Her voice ended in a shriek.

The poor companion, attendant, maid, or whoever she was
– shrank against the far window, pulling her skirts tightly
round her thighs. Genevra trembled. But when the old lady
turned, the smile was broad on her face again. 'Well, my dear,
you're not afraid of poor old Lady Serena, are you? Now now –
just come and talk to me, and we'll have a nice little ride back
together to Carnwikk, and something to eat.'

With her fears receding at the thought of food, Genevra
allowed herself to be lifted into the chaise by one of the men,
and a moment later the horses were off, and the vehicle
moving smartly towards Carnwikk.

Anthony's wife, Harriet St Clare, was in the hall when her
mother-in-law entered with one hand on her stick the other
grasping the little girl's hand. Harriet was wearing a blue
velvet dress that did not suit her. In spite of tight corseting
beneath, the thick material only emphasised her generous
curves. 'A magnificent figure of a woman' would have aptly
described her. She moved stiffly and without grace. Her skin
was good; her brown rather nondescript hair, thick, but pulled
too severely from her face which though well-featured was
broad and rather bovine looking.

Genevra, who had never seen anyone so large and imposing
before clutched at the old lady's hand.

Harriet didn't speak for a moment. Her fairish eyebrows
lifted and almost disappeared before she said, 'Who's this?
Who have you there, Grandmama.'

'Who do you think?' Lady Serena snapped, adding after a
second or two irritably, almost maliciously. 'Who does she
look like, eh?' The old head jutted forward, becoming almost
on a level with the child's. Glancing up at her, puzzled,
Genevra saw that she had hairs on her chin. 'And don't call
me Grandmama,' the irascible old voice continued. 'I don't
breed 'em like you.' A senile little chuckle escaped her, but her
eyes were shrewd.

Harriet flushed. 'Very well, if you want to insult me I can't stop you,' she said coldly. 'Perhaps I'd better call Anthony to deal with the matter.'

'Anthony? *Anthony*?' Again the harsh laugh. 'Where is he? You tell me that. Nowhere about here, I'll be bound. More likely bedding some tarty bit in a hay-loft – and a more fruitful one at that. You should look to your guns, girl. Leave horses alone for a bit and look to your rightful job of begetting an heir – '

'When you've quite finished,' Harriet remarked coldly, yet inwardly burning with anger, 'perhaps you'll kindly explain *who* this is, and *why* she's here?'

The old lady momentarily diverted, glanced down again at Genevra.

'What's your name, child?' she asked more gently.

'Gemma,' Genevra said in her light clear young voice, using her own abbreviation which came more easily to her than the proper version.

'Gemma? Oh I see. Celtic, and very pretty. A very pretty name my dear. I like pretty things, so do you – I can tell that.' She stooped down even closer to the little girl, then raised her raddled face to Harriet's looming figure. 'Like as two peas in a pod, ain't we?' she said maliciously. 'One a bit browned and wrinkled at one end – the other all young and juicy for ripening?'

Harriet sighed, turned, and went to the door. 'I'm going to call Crawford to take you upstairs to your room, or Graves if you prefer it. I'll deal with the child.'

The young woman who'd been in the chaise with them stepped forward from the shadows. 'Oh yes, Lady Serena, do let me help you. You must be tired – '

'*Tired*? Fiddlesticks.' She shook so much her walking stick fell to the floor. 'Pick that up,' she screamed, 'and tell someone to get tea. I'm having it in my *own* sitting room with my little friend here. And see there's cream and plenty of jam, or I'll have the skin off your backs – '

Genevra drew back, frightened, but also awed by the old woman's fierceness and by the fact that everyone started immediately scurrying about to do her bidding.

'Now,' Lady Serena said, leading the little girl down a maze of corridors to her own chosen domain. 'You said your name was Gemma. What about the other, my dear, Gemma what?'

'Hawksley,' Genevra told her. 'Do you like it?'

The old woman was temporarily shocked and lost for words. Then she answered, 'No. But I'm sure it's not *your* fault, child. More the fault of – of – ' her face went blueish red while she struggled for words. 'Never mind,' she spluttered, with a trickle of saliva running from her mouth to chin. 'We'll let that be. But you remember, my dear, if you ever need me, I'm here. That house of yours – that hell house of a place ain't right for the likes of us. It's here *you* belong. Look at me, child. A long long look –'

'Like – like *Beauty and the Beast*?' Genevra queried, because for a moment she really thought the old creature was something like the Beast in a picture book she had, and she wondered if she could try very hard and love Lady Serena she'd change suddenly and miraculously into a handsome prince or princess. Or a queen, yes, perhaps a queen, she decided wistfully, with long golden hair and a crown on it.

The bony hand tightened on the slender young wrist. 'Something like that, my dear,' the old voice answered, and Genevra, with the perception of youth detected sadness beneath its grating sound – something that made her want to cry, not knowing why.

Afterwards, looking back over the following hour, everything was to appear as a dream more than reality – the grey and blue room filled with crystal and glistening silver – the delicate china tea service patterned with roses and elegant gilt furniture shining like gold from the firelight, the musical-box that played a tune while a china shepherd and shepherdess danced, and the gold clock with its pendulum swinging from the wall; – above all the iced cakes and sweetmeats with sugar fairies on top! Oh it was all a magical new world for Genevra who was so hungry and at the same time so fascinated, she did not even have time to wish hard that the strange old woman in the lop-sided red wig could be disenchanted and turned back into the noble good queen she really was.

Just how the adventure really ended she never quite knew except that Lady Serena suddenly seemed to become tired and not want to talk. She lay back and began to snore. Genevra was wondering whether to wake her or not when the large woman in blue velvet entered and led her out of the room. She asked the same question as the old lady had, about Genevra's real name, and when the child told her, drew her lips together primly and said, 'I think you're a very naughty little girl. And when you get home I hope you receive a sound whipping. You certainly deserve it.'

Soon after this chilling remark Genevra was being driven in the St Clare chaise back to Trenhawk. Harriet sat stiffly beside her, hard and uncompromising. Stealing a glance at her from time to time the child wondered why the 'big lady' hated her so much. She was sure she did – her mouth was so pursed up, like a big button, drawing lines from her noise to the hardened lips. Besides, she'd said she hoped she'd he whipped. That wasn't a nice thing to wish, and it wouldn't happen anyway, because by the time they got home Genevra was sure her father would be back.

He was. And his words made Genevra far sorrier for her adventure than any spanking could have done.

'You've caused us a lot of worry,' he told her quite severely for him. 'Both your mother and I have been very, very upset. Carnack and Nick have been searching for you everywhere, and I've been out on my horse scouring the moors for hours. You must never do such a thing again, Genevra, do you understand? Sometimes you've got to think of other people. Supposing *I* went away and didn't come back when I said I would? Supposing I never came back at all?'

'Oh, Daddy, you wouldn't run away, would you? You couldn't.'

'I don't suppose I would. But I easily could. Like you. Now will you promise?'

Genevra hung her head. 'Yes,' she said in a subdued quiet little voice. 'I promise.'

'Good. Then see you keep it. Promises aren't made to be broken, remember. Now run upstairs Miss Venables is waiting to make you tidy. Then afterwards come down and say you're sorry to your mother.'

This little scene could have ended the Carnwikk episode, but it didn't – quite.

A fortnight later Lady Serena St Clare died. When her will

was read, much disgust was felt by her family to learn that she
had bequeathed a very valuable pendant to her young friend
Genevra Hawksley. It consisted of a single extremely large
emerald in a setting of diamonds, and was valued at fifty
thousand pounds.

'Of course it must be sold,' Adelaide said promptly. But
Rupert was adamant. 'Certainly not. It belongs to Genevra,
and will remain hers. Superstition, as you know, isn't a
characteristic of mine, but I'm going to take this overture in
the spirit it was made, as a gesture of goodwill.'

Adelaide smiled.

'You'll never stop surprising me, Rupert. At one time you
seemed to me so hard and overbearing, whereas at heart
you're quite the reverse.'

His hand touched her breast softly. Love flowed between
them, gentle in compassion, warm with desire. As his lips
closed on hers she knew that nothing in the world mattered –
either poverty, riches, the future or the past; only the present
in which they had each other and belonged.

Rupert.

He was her world, and she was his.

XVII

In spite of Wheal Tansy's reprieve, the mine during the next
few years showed only a minimum of profit; and Rupert was
still frequently gnawed by anxiety for its future. Mines
throughout Cornwall were closing and families taking off to
America. He had not the money to expand further or invest in
new property. Adelaide had spurts of economy when she
refused to have new clothes and made it her mission to install
more frugality into the running of the household. Servants
were made aware of the need to consider expense. She had
even tentatively considered dismissing Miss Venables. But the
idea remained theoretical. Jane Venables, after all, was gene-

ral help to her, as well as becoming governess to Genevra. And
little Mortimer liked her. Despite her prim exterior, the woman had a way with children. So only Genevra defied her, and
when this happened Adelaide had her own method of dealing
with her rebellious daughter. Rupert would not have approved, but Genevra was not a tell-tale, and when punishment
was over it could be forgotten as far as she was concerned. She
wished though, that Mama could love her more, as she loved
Mortimer and even Julian. But then Julian was quiet and
clever and liked to be by himself at Trenhawk. When he was
not in the schoolroom with Richard Clemis, his tutor, he could
generally be found in his own patch of garden near Mrs
Pender's rooms, either feeding his rabbits or watching his fish.
Sometimes he took paper and paints there, and made sketches
of the pets.

Mrs Pender, who was too old now to do much about the
house, and left most of the responsibility to Mrs Cole, said he
was very bright. 'You mark my words, Mr Rupert,' she said
one day, 'that boy'll mek a name for 'eself when he's grown up.
His pictures are real handsome.'

Yes, Rupert agreed wrily, wondering at the same time
where would the money come from to keep him? Artists were
notoriously poor, and he didn't see any possibility of leaving
David's son more than a very meagre legacy, if that. Under the
circumstances he felt he had to explore every channel of collecting money due to him from whatever source. Elizabeth
Chywanna, for instance, still owed him a tidy little sum concerning her bakery. She'd offered repayment of the loan several times during the past two years, but he'd refused to accept
it, partly through vanity, partly philanthropy, and a lingering
rather discomforting feeling that he still owed her something.
He'd heard she'd never married, which had increased the
irritating conviction that her feelings had been far deeper than
his own during their brief affair.

However, much water had run under the mill since then,
and it was obvious the time had come to sink his pride and
accept what was owed materially, providing she was still in the
position to repay.

That last point he had to decide for himself.

So one spring morning having told Adelaide he'd be

away for the day on business, he set off by branch train to Truro, arriving there about noon. The bakery, which was situated at the corner of a cobbled narrow side street, had CHYWANNA printed boldly across its front under the slanting eaves. He had not seen it since Elizabeth first took over the property, and he was impressed by the new window where confectionary, cakes and home-made bread were displayed to effective advantage. The business looked prosperous, and Rupert's heart lifted, not only for his own but Elizabeth's sake.

A girl in a white apron over a black dress was serving bread to a customer when he went in. After she'd gone he gave his name and asked if he could see Mrs Chywanna. He realised he should have arranged the meeting earlier. If Elizabeth was out it would be a wasted journey; besides, women liked to be prepared for a male visitor. But he didn't see her putting on finery for his sake; Elizabeth had always been a perfectly natural unassuming character, with an innate sense of dignity that made her fastidious at all times, both in private and public.

The girl returned after a minute or two saying that Mrs Chywanna would see him in the parlour if he went in. Before he was through the door at the back of the shop, she was already half-way up the passage, wearing her favourite colour blue, with a small white frill of a lace cap on her head.

'Mr Rupert,' she exclaimed, 'how nice, how very nice to see you, surr.'

Relief swept through him. The voice was the same — full, warm, the tones welcoming. He blamed himself for not having called before. 'Come with me,' she continued. 'Come and see for yourself what a nice tidy place I've got now –' she broke off with a hint of shyness.

'You sound in top form, Elizabeth,' Rupert said, 'and look it.'

'Oh, I am. Thanks to you, surr, I've made a new life for myself.' She led him to a small room on the right, and opened the door. It led into a neat parlour where the faint tang of polish mingled with the tempting smell of cooking from the back of the house. The room was homely and pleasant though a little overcrowded, with a round oak table, two spindle-backed chairs, a leather upholstered one with an antimaccassar draped carefully at its back, a china cupboard in one corner, and an old chest along one wall. A carved clock with its pendulum swinging hung above, and an oleograph of Queen Victoria stared majestically from its frame, opposite another of Tom above the velvet covered mantelpiece. A small sofa filled the only available space left. Rupert remembered most of the furniture, and realised with a pang that she had clung to it because of the past, and Tom.

'Sit down, Mr Rupert, do,' Elizabeth said, indicating the armchair. 'It's nice to see you.'

He took her hands briefly, then dropped them saying, 'And you, Elizabeth. You haven't changed much.' In one sense this was true. The comely looks, the friendly personality remained, but she had aged. There was grey in the fair hair, and she had put on considerable weight. The age-gap between them was now emphasised. He found it hard to accept that this over-plump woman was the same he'd taken in friendly passion those years ago. She could have been his aunt rather than a contemporary, and he felt she realised it.

'The years pass though,' she remarked a little wistfully. 'Time doesn't stop – and for a woman they make a difference. But what about you? How are things with your family, and the farm? An' what about the mine, Mr Rupert? I heard 'bout all the trouble you had, and I was very sorry.'

'Yes.' Rupert paused, then gave her news of whatever was relevant concerning Trenhawk and the estate, ending with the frank admission that keeping within financial limits had been a problem at times.

'Then perhaps now you'll oblige me by taking what's owing to you from the loan you was so generous with in the past,' Elizabeth said briskly at the first chance she had of breaking into the conversation. 'It's worried me you refusing to take it before. Tom wouldn't have liked it, either, as you must know, being the proud man he was.'

Rupert gave her a slow, contemplative smile.

'Very well, Elizabeth. If you remember I always said when the right time came I wouldn't hesitate in taking it – providing it meant no hardship to you. Well – Wheal Tansy's a bit tight at the moment and if things are going well for you I'm ready to sink my pride and accept your offer.'

Elizabeth laughed. 'Offer? What a way to put it, Mr Rupert. You'll have what you so kindly gave, in full and what's more with interest – no, don't try an' stop me. I'm a business woman now, an' I know what's what. I shall write you cheque here an' now, an' after that we'll have a cup of something, or a glass of wine if you prefer, while you sample some of my sweetmeats.'

An hour later Elizabeth saw Rupert to the door, where they stood for a few moments in the bright spring sunshine chatting amicably before parting.

As he walked down the street to the main thoroughfare Rupert was conscious of a tremendous relief, not only because the affair had been settled so easily without loss of face on either side, but because no lingering or faintest desire for Elizabeth had risen to unsettle him. He hadn't expected it, feeling as he did for Adelaide. But talking to Tom's widow had proved to be no more than a placid business interlude between past acquaintances. It was extremely unlikely, he thought, that their paths would ever cross again.

The weather was still fine the next day, and Rupert set off early for the farm first, informing Adelaide he would not be back until the evening as he had an important meeting at the Count House in the early afternoon.

'You're so busy these days, Rupert,' she complained when he told her. 'Yesterday, and now today. It would be nice to have an afternoon together sometime. I mean, we could take the children and go for a picnic occasionally.'

'All in good time, Addy,' he said a little abstractedly. 'And why on earth picnics? Flies and jam and sticky fingers, with young Mortimer bawling his head off? I can think of pleasanter occupations.'

'So can I,' she said tartly. 'Only it just happens I'm loaded with a family and have to consider them.'

'You have our very capable Miss Venables,' Rupert reminded her. 'And the servants, Don't – please don't picture yourself as a domestic drudge, my darling.'

'I don't. But Miss Venables isn't exactly stimulating,' she protested. 'Genevra's a little horror, and even your son Mortimer's becoming a handful. Sometimes I wish –' her voice ended in a sigh.

'Well? What do you wish?'

'I wish we could be married all over again, properly,' she said impetuously. 'in a church with bridesmaids and a reception, and no encumbrances.'

His face darkened. 'Don't call the children encumbrances, Adelaide, and don't go yearning over the past.'

'I'm not.'

'Aren't you? Weren't you dreaming of wedding veils and iced cakes and – David perhaps?'

She flushed.

'That's a wrong thing to say, and you know it. I was only wishing for us.'

'Well, please don't, in that particular way,' he told her, more harshly than he'd meant. 'I can understand there are certain things you miss that you had with Aunt Matilda. But as I can't provide them it would be better not to look back, for both our sakes.'

He turned to go. She caught his arm 'Rupert – '

'Well?'

'What's the matter with you this morning?'

He turned and drew her briefly into his arms. 'Nothing, Addy,' he said. 'Forget it.'

'Business, I suppose.'

'There's always business,' he answered abruptly, 'but that's not your worry – except to understand occasionally when I feel edgy.' He kissed her lightly, and the next minute was on his way to the stables.

She watched him ride away later with a queer feeling of restlessness in her, due partially no doubt to that particular season of the year when all nature seemed inducive to strange moods and yearnings for the unobtainable, for life, adventure, and gaiety, and partly to the irritable misunderstanding between Rupert and herself. Mostly there was no disharmony in their relationship these days, but just occasionally their temperaments clashed, and although open quarrelling was extremely infrequent, she recognised the danger signs when they arose, and she knew that, if Rupert had not gone when he did that moment, tempers might have flared.

He generally won of course, simply because she knew she had no chance against him once his mind was made up.

Usually she gave in as suddenly as the trouble had started, revelling in the sweetness of making up. But that morning being thwarted emotionally, she felt strangely resentful. It was easy for Rupert, of course, she told herself, he could just take off whenever he liked on the pretext of business, leaving her alone at Trenhawk with difficult children to manage, and never a day with anything exciting happening. It was unfair.

She felt suddenly she could remain in the house no longer, and decided on the spur of the moment to take a walk to the Polvanes – a mining family living near St Rozzan who were generally in need of food or new clothing, having a large family to support on the meagre wages.

Yes. She'd do that. Take a chicken from the larder if there was one to spare, and a few goodies in a basket. This would please Martha Polvane, release a few of Adelaide's own inhibitions and in the role of Lady Bountiful make her feel better in herself and with life in general.

Mrs Cole, though a kindly woman, was thrifty. A *chicken*!' she exclaimed, when Adelaide appeared in her grey visiting outfit with a braided shoulder cape and wearing a small grey bonnet trimmed with veiling on her fair hair. 'Well now, ma'am, there is one – two – in the larder. I was thinking o' one for tomorrow. What about a bit o' mutton now? Them families is used to mutton, an' it goes further for stews an things. *Chicken*!' Her voice deepened with disapproval. 'Once you start a thing it gets to be expected with the poorer folk.'

'Poorer folk have the same tastes as the rest of us,' Adelaide retorted sharply. 'I'll take a chicken, Mrs Cole, and some of those small buns and pastries you cooked yesterday.'

'My buns? But ma'am – '

'That's what I said.'

Adelaide's eyes flashed, her tones were final. Muttering to herself, the cook went to the larder, packed two baskets, and brought them back filled with the food.

'You'll find them heavy,' she said, dumping them on the table.

Adelaide picked up the largest. 'Yes. Well – I haven't far to go, only the Polvanes – less than half a mile. Let Lucy come with me to the cottage. It won't take her more than ten minutes there and back.'

Obviously Mrs Cole was annoyed by the suggestion, but Lucy, glad to be free of domestic ties for a bit, willingly set off with Adelaide, carrying the largest basket.

The air was clear, and fresh, faintly stirred by a soft wind blowing down the moor from the hills above. Young curling bracken shone pale green between clumps of pink bell-heather and bushes of flashing golden gorse; small wild things scuttled through the undergrowth, seagulls wheeled against the blue sky. As they neared the Polvanes' cottage – a small granite place huddled behind a dejected vegetable patch, a blackbird trilled sweetly from a nearby May tree.

'Thank you, Lucy, Adelaide said, taking the basket from her, 'you can leave me now, and – ' she smiled, 'don't take too long about it, or Mrs Cole will take umbrage.'

Lucy nodded and hurried away.

Adelaide knocked on the wooden door which she noted needed repainting, at the same time catching the drift of an unpleasant smell from the far end of the cottage. Her nose wrinkled. A cesspool – the usual thing of course. No wonder these poor families had been so inclined to catch cholera and typhoid in the past. And things didn't seem much better now. She decided she'd make a point of bringing the matter up with Rupert. Surely better toilet facilities could be installed at a minimum of cost. To have such unhealthy conditions so near living quarters were dangerous – not only to occupants there, but other families as well. And epidemics spread so easily. Why, even Trenhawk could be at risk.

She was still debating the matter when the door was opened by Anne Polvane. She was a thin anxious looking woman in the early fifties, with nine children and a husband working at Wheal Tansy who recently had been troubled by his chest. Two of the elder sons were also employed at the mine, and the elder daughter 'at grass' as a Bal maiden.

'Oh ma'am – Mrs Hawksley. I didn't expec' you,' Anne said, rubbing her hands hastily on her apron and pushing a strand of hair away from her eyes. 'Ef I had, I'd have bin' lookin' better than this, surely.' She paused, adding doubtfully, 'Will 'ee come in, ma'am – 'et's a small place we've got here, an' a lot of us to fill et, but – '

'No thank you, Mrs Polvane,' Adelaide answered, not wishing to embarrass the woman, and anxious to be away as quickly as possible from the unpleasantly smelling air. 'I've simply come to bring you a few things – well, a chicken and some buns. Our cook sometimes over fills the larder, and – anyway I suppose you can find use for it –' she uncovered the larger basket, displaying the plump bird, already plucked and ready for cooking.

Anne Polvane did not speak at first. Her eyes simply stared as though riveted by the sight. Wondering if her manner of speech had been tactless and somehow wounded the other's dignity, Adelaide continued quickly, 'We don't need it you see – it seems such a pity to waste it. My husband has often spoken about you and said how hard your husband and family work at Wheal Tansy. So I thought, well I – ' she broke off hesitantly. 'Oh dear! have I said the wrong thing?'

Anne looked up, slowly shaking her head. 'The wrong thing, ma'am? How could 'ee. My dear soul! 'tes a godsend. We may be proud folk, us tinners, ma'am, but not such fules as to turn away good food for our childer's stomachs. Thank 'ee Mrs Hawksley. 'Tes real kind of 'en.' She was lifting the chicken and bags of goodies from the baskets when a small child, followed by a tiny toddler emerged from the shadow at the back of the cramped room. They both huddled themselves behind their mother's skirts, peering shyly from dark eyes at 'the lady'. Adelaide saw that though they wore no shoes they were cleanly though thinly clad and she had a pang of guilt when she thought of her own stock of Genevra's half used frilly dresses and underwear. Still, such fancy things would obviously be quite unsuitable for the Polvanes. On her next visit to Penzance or Penjust she'd see what woollies were in the shops, and insist the family had presents at Christmas.

As she walked down the track to the road a few minutes later something of Rupert's philanthropy stirred in her. He was right to fight for the welfare of his men, straining somehow for better conditions. Right in his efforts to keep Wheal Tansy at least alive. But why wouldn't he share more of his business problems with her? Why did he persist in imagining her only possible help could be with finance or by charming lecherous old men into investing?

Her brain was seething with questions and ideas when she

came to the main lane and saw Doctor Maddox's gig standing by a gate leading into a field. A path from there led to another cottage about a quarter of a mile from the Polvanes'. The doctor's wife Emilia was seated placidly waiting, with the horse's reins in her hand. She was a stout, rosy-faced woman wearing a purple woollen cape over a black dress, though the weather was comparatively warm. Her old fashioned bonnet was high and liberally trimmed with violets, ribbons, and osprey feathers.

'My dear Mrs Hawksley,' she gushed, 'how *very* nice to see you. Been visiting, have you?'

'I've just paid a call on Mrs Polvane,' Adelaide told her a little shortly. She did not really care for Emilia Maddox who she thought a rather nosey interfering woman with a lot of silly tittle-tattle always ready on her tongue for those who cared to listen.

'How very thoughtful of you, my dear,' Emilia said. 'You must be a great help to your good man. He's such a kind man I always say to my husband. Not a great talker, but then it's deeds that count, not words, isn't it? That poor Mrs Chywanna for instance – ' Adelaide's nerves froze as the fatuous voice continued, 'he was so thoughtful for her wasn't he, after her husband's terrible end? And that's a funny thing. Coincidence – isn't it strange? – I saw them yesterday.'

'You what?' Before Adelaide knew it the question was out.

'Your husband, my dear, and Elizabeth Chywanna. In Truro. They were coming out of her bakery – quite a pleasant looking little place I must admit, and I thought she looked very well, oh very well indeed.

'I see,' Adelaide tried to keep her voice from trembling. 'You were there then?'

'My husband had an important patient to visit, so I accompanied him. I do like a change now and again. But it's so odd, isn't it, how one can meet the most unexpected people at the most surprising times?'

Yes Adelaide thought with an ugly confusion of emotions quickening her heart and breathing. So that had been Rupert's business the previous day – a secret visit to his exmistress Elizabeth, if she *was* ex. Without knowing it the colour had deepened to crimson in her face before receding to a

curious dull pallor. For a moment she thought she might
faint. Then she pulled herself together and heard the other
woman's maddening smug voice continuing placidly. 'They
didn't see me of course, I was on the other side of the road. I
should have bought some confectionery if I'd had time, but
my husband was anxious to get back as soon possible. Doctors
you know –'

Adelaide did not wait to hear the rest of the oration. Hardly
aware of what excuse she made, she managed to extricate
herself from listening to further details, and in considerably
less time than she'd taken on the journey to the cottage, was
back again at Trenhawk.

Her whole being was in a tumult. Rupert had lied to her.
Had lied and deceived her probably all the time – ever since
he'd married her. All that talk of business and having to
economise – of professing to love her had been nothing but a
half truth. To think she had been so gullible as to believe him for
one moment – to accept that Elizabeth Chywanna meant
nothing to him. He was a cheat – worse than David, because
David had been so young, and had never been forced into facing
things.

Hardly knowing what she was doing she rushed upstairs to
the small sewing room where a trunk was stored containing a
few relics from her London days. At the bottom carefully
folded and almost forgotten was a pair of David's riding
breeches. She took them out and carried them to the bedroom.
They were pale grey, appearing almost as new.

With savage intensity she tore off her dress and cape, pulled
the breaches over her stockings, and hooked them at the waist
below her embroidered underbodice. Then she found suitable
boots, tugged them on and fastened them. A black cape was
lying over a chair. She flung it over her shoulders, and tore the
small grey bonnet from her head, flurrying it across the room.
Tears were bright in her eyes, tears of confusion, and anger.

'Rupert,' she thought, as she sped down the stairs, 'Rupert,
oh, damn him, I'll show him – somehow I'll make him sorry –
somehow I will,' Mrs Pender was in the hall when the wild
figure rushed by and out of the side door to the stables.

'Miss Adelaide – ' she called, amazed by the sight – 'my
dear soul – what are you about now – ?' She turned cum-

brously, making her way with difficulty towards the kitchens. 'Did your mistress come this way?' she demanded from Lilian who was polishing some silver. Lilian shook her.

'No. I heard a clatter in the yard and Carnack shouting, that's all.'

Breathlessly Mrs Pender heaved herself to the back door and was just in time to see Adelaide hatless, with her hair tumbled down her back, riding Ebony, astride like any heedless boy, up the side drive to the lane.

'Sakes alive,' she muttered, 'she's mazed. Must've gone right off et. An' those poor little children. God bless my soul what's goin' to happen to us now?'

Lilian, not liking the look on the old housekeeper's face, forced her into a chair. 'Now you just sit there, Mrs Pender, while I get you a stiff toddy. Don't talk for a bit. You can tell us all about it later.'

By the time Mrs Pender had recovered, Adelaide was well up the moor, heading all unawares in the direction of Carnwikk. She rode furiously, kicking her mount to its limit, hair blown back in a golden stream, cape flying behind her. Her eyes were hard in her white face, her mouth set above her stubborn chin. From the west sullen clouds massed over the horizon. The horse reared several times almost throwing her; then, spurred by the sting of the crop on its flanks, galloped on again. The air darkened and chilled as the sun dimmed behind the rising cloud-shapes. Near the summit of the moor, suddenly aware of her direction, Adelaide cut abruptly to the right, leaving Carnwikk far below to the left. By a group of standing stones she halted Ebony and wiped the sweat from her own brow. Exhaustion both emotional and physical overcame her. She dismounted and flung herself on her back in the heather, gazing blankly at the open sky. The mare snorted belligerently and took off on its own; Adelaide did not mind or care; all that registered was her own despair – the conviction that Rupert whom she'd loved more than all the world, had betrayed her. Tears clouded her eyes coursing over temples to the ground. Gradually they ceased, and dried in the breeze.

Time passed.

The sun came out again, bathing the wild landscape in a flood of patterned light and shade that dappled her lonely form with gold one moment, and the next took her into the brooding darkness of ancient stone and twisted undergrowth. The sound of hooves roused her. She sat up, thinking it was Ebony returned. But there was no Ebony – only a fair-haired rider on a black stallion.

He reined the horse, sprang off lightly, and stood a moment staring. She jumped to her feet, clutching her riding crop to her side.

Anthony.

He had a faint smile on his puckish mouth, his eyes gleamed greenish blue in the fleeting spring light.

'How surprising to see you here, Mrs Hawksley,' he remarked, 'especially in that – rig-out. I thought it was some gipsy boy trespassing on Carnwikk land. Never mind. I'll overlook the liberty – as it's you.' She didn't answer, merely turned her back on him and started walking down the moor. He caught her up, and stood confronting her.

'You're going the wrong way,' he said. 'Trenhawk's to the left, and a considerable distance.'

'Get out of my way,' she replied in a cold voice.

'No. This is my property. And I'm wondering why you're here. You seem to have a liking for roaming our land.' He paused, adding after a moment, 'What are you after? Have you missed me?'

She flushed. Her eyes were furious.

'Don't be insulting. Missed? I wish I'd never seen you. You're a – a – '

'Rogue and seducer of women?' he asked lightly. 'Oh but you're mistaken you know. I haven't the slightest wish to touch you, Adelaide.' His eyes had narrowed, but though the voice was contemptuous a flicker of desire crossed his face. 'You really *have* let yourself go, you know. That's unwise of you. You may have netted a husband of sorts to father our – mutual offspring – but keeping him may be a different matter. Another thing – ' he moved closer, 'don't send that child of yours trying to inveigle herself into my home again. She was extremely successful with my grandmother, which no doubt you intended. But Harriet has no weakness for red hair and Hawksley bastards. Keep her out of my sight for your own good and hers. Do you understand?'

Before she properly realised her intentions, Adelaide raised the crop suddenly and struck him on the cheek. It almost missed, but was sufficiently well aimed to leave a short red weal near his chin. He put his hand to it, while his eyes changed from blue to sullen darkening grey.

'My God,' he said, 'if I wasn't a gentleman or you a woman, I'd have the skin off your back for that. One day you'll be sorry though. I'll break the whole damned lot of you if it's the last thing I ever do – '

Breathing heavily, with a sick feeling round her heart and at the pit of her stomach, Adelaide rushed away down the hill, blundering through furze, and heather, tearing her hands and face against projecting thorns and branches. She didn't look round or pause; the network of narrow paths eventually receded into a mere wilderness of bracken and small stunted trees. She stopped against a bent May tree to get her breath. The world was dark and spinning round her. The breath tore at her lungs. Her heart was thumping as though it would burst against her ribs. When her mind could register she looked round disconsolately for Ebony, but there was no sign of a horse any more against the landscape; no thud of distant hooves – only the wild hillside under the changing sky, and the crying of a single gull wheeling overhead. She put both hands to her mouth and called – 'Ebony – Ebony – here – Ebony –' but there was no response. Turning desolately, she went on again, searching for a path, for some sign of a cottage or landmark to guide her back to Trenhawk.

There was nothing.

And then, as the land dropped into a dip below a further ridge of the moors, the distant cry of a man's voice was carried thinly on the air.

'Hullo there – hullo – Addy – ' the tones rose and died fitfully, ending on a drawn out echo of sound that seemed to reverberate through bushes and undergrowth, valleys, rocks, and undulating patches of boggy earth. She stood tense, listening. The voice had faded, but with her ears and senses alert she caught the unmistakable approaching thud of hooves from somewhere below. A minute later the figure of a man astride a horse appeared dark against the tangled undergrowth. A shaft of sudden sunlight caught the unruly black hair. He was riding with purpose, chin up, scouring the brilliant horizon against the sky.

Rupert.

For a brief interim she forgot her own unhappiness in the relief of seeing him. She waved her arm, feeling suddenly weak from loneliness, exhaustion, and her confrontation with Anthony. At first he appeared not to notice her; then the slight movement and flap of wings from a bird disturbed caught his attention. He urged his mount to a gallop, and in less than a minute was confronting her torn bedraggled figure. He stared at her without speaking for a drawn-out moment of time. Then he took her by both shoulders, staring down into her scratched face.

'What are you doing here?' he said. 'What on earth's got into you? When Ebony arrived back alone I was worried sick. My God, Addy, if you didn't look such a weary spectacle I'd – I'd – ' he broke off for a moment shaking his head. Then he continued – 'Dressed like that too – aren't you ashamed? Aren't you?' He shook her fiercely.

'Don't speak like that. Let me go – '

'Why should I? You've some explaining to do. What the devil do you mean by it? Taking the first chance of meeting St Clare too – on Carnwikk land. But of course you knew that, didn't you? Knew he'd returned. What sort of woman are you –'

'And what sort of man are *you*?' she flashed, 'sneaking off to Truro to see your mistress? Oh I heard all about it, Rupert, Mrs Maddox told me. And don't accuse me of meeting Anthony. I never gave him a thought. I was just sick at heart to find how you'd deceived me. All that paltry talk about business – ' her eyes blazed, contempt filled her voice. 'Another thing – ' she added, with the words tumbling over each other' – I did see Anthony, but not as you think – it was by chance – ' the wild colour flooded her face. 'And if you must know I hit him – with *this* – ' she held the riding crop up dangling it before his face. 'So perhaps now you'll curb your temper, leave me alone, and just show me the way. That's all.'

He was so astonished he could not at first speak, then, freeing her, and shaking his head slowly, he said, 'You struck St Clare, did you say?'

'Yes. And I wish I'd aimed better. Still – it got him nicely by the chin.'

She would have pushed past him, but he caught her arm and swung her round. Her amber eyes were bright with unshed tears.

'Oh, Addy,' he said, 'what fools we are. You thinking I still hankered after Elizabeth, and me believing for one moment you were after that lascivious St Clare – '

'Weren't you though?' Adelaide said, 'Hankering after Elizabeth, I mean? Mrs Maddox did see you. She wouldn't make it up, you know.'

'Of course not. Why should she? Yes, I visited Tom's widow for the sole business of collecting a loan lent to her years ago. Quite a considerable one, which will be useful at the moment. That's not the point, though. The fact is – '

'Yes?'

'I shouldn't have to prove myself to you, not after these years we've had together. Don't you think the time has come to trust me, Adelaide?'

'Yes, But – you didn't trust me, did you?'

'Well – ' He waited before slipping his arm round her waist and adding, 'Women are different; especially your kind, love. To be quite honest, however faithful you might be – and I believe you, Addy – I wouldn't trust a man within inches of you alone – especially his kind, Anthony's.'

'Or Sir John Swiftley?'

'Ah. Yes, the old reprobate.'

'So that's something for you to remember isn't it?' she queried. 'Not to lure me into being 'nice' to fat old philanthropists just to get your own way.'

He laughed.

'Trust you to have the last word, Mrs Hawksley.' His grip tightened round her waist. 'All the same it's time we got back now. Come along – ' he fetched his horse from a nearby clearing, and when she was hoisted behind him on the mount, they set off again for Trenhawk.

There was no one about when they reached the stables. The hall too was mercifully empty. He hurried her to the foot of the stairs, picked her up in his arms and carried her to their bedroom. Before taking off his habit he laid her on the bed and loosened her clothes, then fetched a cloth and wiped her face and hands clean of scratches and soil. He undressed her gently, and stood for a moment or two staring down. Her pale body was licked to golden flame from a beam of sunlight filtering through the window, the breasts shone rosy-tipped and ripe for love. With desire intensifying he slung off his shirt and breeches and took her to him. The thrust of love was rich and strong between them, culminating in a climax of utter joy and completion.

So it was, that on that wild spring day, twins were conceived to further Trenhawk's pattern of life ahead.

Meanwhile the bad blood between the Hawksleys and St Clares intensified. Rupert could not forget Anthony's insulting behaviour to Adelaide, neither could Anthony forget or forgive Adelaide's provocative act on the moor, which combined with his grandmother's rash bequest to her red-headed offspring swamped any lingering desire he'd had into hatred.

And in Hook's valley a black eyed gipsy woman hugged what dark secret knowledge she had to herself, although she sensed disaster ahead.

The children, a boy and a girl, were born three days before Christmas, the girl half an hour earlier than her brother. She was small, dark, perfectly formed, with none of the wrinkles generally attributed to very young babies. A touch of furry – almost black hair – crowned her head. Her skin had an olive glow. Her eyes too were dark – Rupert's eyes. The bedroom, like the rest of the house, had a bunch of holly and Christmas roses arranged near the window.

'We'll call her Holly,' Adelaide whispered to Rupert, catching his hand. 'She reminds me of holly somehow.'

The boy was quite different – fair, a little smaller, but showing from the first moment a curious resemblance to Adelaide's father whom she'd loved very much and lost as a child.

'He can be Drake, if you don't mind, Rupert,' Adelaide said, the next day, 'Drake Hawksley, or *Rupert* Drake Hawksley. We could call him Drake though. Drake and Holly – doesn't that sound rather nice?'

Rupert smiled, and planted a kiss on her forehead. 'Anything you want pleases me,' he said.

So Holly and Drake they were.

Julian was enthralled, even a little awed by the babies, but Mortimer screamed.

'He's jealous,' Adelaide said.

'Not at all. That young man merely means to steal the show whenever possible,' was Rupert's comment. 'A little later on he'll have a few things to learn from me, strictly for his own good of course.'

'No one's going to bully *my* children,' Adelaide told him. 'I want them to grow up free, and strong and – and – '

'Selfish and a damned nuisance when they feel like it?' He laughed wrily. 'Oh no, my love, I don't think so. I've seen you pretty stern on occasions with the youngsters.'

'With Genevra perhaps.'

'Yes. Especially Genevra. And she loves you, Adelaide. Look how she dotes on the babies. One day, you mark my words – she'll be more comfort to you than all the rest. Unless of course you've driven her to run away by then through your fierce tempers.'

Adelaide gave him a long hard stare, then remarked, 'I can't understand why it is you always stick up for her. It seems quite – quite illogical, under the circumstances.'

He shook his head.

'No. A man doesn't get so emotionally involved with children as women do. I've often thought – looking at things objectively – you're apt to give Genevra a pretty raw deal. So I do my best to level things out. That's all.'

When she faced the question squarely Adelaide knew that what Rupert said was true, and after their brief conversation she tried to react more gently to the little girl's vibrant personality. The trouble was that the past lay between them. In spite of all her efforts, deep in Adelaide's mind the knowledge persisted that the child had been foisted on her as the unfortunate outcome of a bitter relationship. However bright and loving she was, her unfortunate begetting was against her, and could never be eradicated.

XVIII

On an afternoon in late summer when Adelaide was choosing plants in the conservatory for the house, Lilian came to the door saying there was a chaise at the door, and a lady had come to see her. 'She looks all dressed for travelling, ma'am, and I thought –'

Adelaide sprung round.

'Did she give her name?'

Lilian looked a little uneasy. 'Yes. She said it was St Clare.'

'Do you mean – *Mrs* St Clare? A *large* woman?'

'Oh no, ma'am. It's the little one – the sister I think.'

Adelaide was conscious of great relief.

'Katherine. I haven't seen her for – months – ages. It must be over a year. Do show her in, Lilian.'

'Here, ma'am?'

'Why not? It's quite nice with all the flowering things.'

'Very well.'

Lilian went out.

Half a minute later Katherine entered the conservatory. She was wearing a black suit with a matching shoulder cape, and a small black bonnet on her demurely dressed hair.

Adelaide held out her hands. 'Oh Katherine, how nice to see you, I've tried to contact you once or twice during the last year, but you know how difficult it is.'

'Yes.'

'Do sit down – or is it too hot in here? I can open the door –'

'No – no. I rather like the smell of plants.'

'Then let me take your cape.'

Katherine allowed the cloth shoulder garment to be removed, and when she was seated comfortably on a curved backed wrought-iron affair liberally padded with cushions, Adelaide said curiously, 'You look as if you're going somewhere. Travelling or something.'

'I am. I'm leaving.'

'Leaving? What do you mean? Carnwikk?'

'Yes. My father's died. Didn't you know?'

Adelaide was astonished. 'No, I hadn't heard. When was this?'

'Last week. He was buried quietly this morning in our family vault. Father Mago came from Polcrane to conduct the service in our own small chapel.'

'Oh. I'm sorry.'

Katherine smiled gently. 'I'm not. I'm glad he's at peace. His life was rather – turbulent you know. Since my mother died he didn't seem to find much worth living for. And it will be easier for me.' She paused, continuing calmly, 'There's no point in being a hypocrite, is there? I did what I could for him while he was alive. Now – ' she shrugged, 'I can follow my vocation.'

'What do you mean by that? Nursing?' Adelaide asked. 'With Miss Nightingale? I remember – '

'Nursing, yes. But not with Miss Nightingale. At one time during the Crimean war it was my one ambition. But lately, I've changed, Adelaide. There's been so much bitterness, and quarrelling, and jealousy at Carnwikk I – I just want peace and the chance to get on with my work quietly with other women who think like I do. The sisters run a hospital – there'll be a training and testing period before I'm accepted, but I know it's the right thing for me. You see – '

Adelaide could not wait to let her finish. 'You said sisters. What do you mean – *Nuns*?'

Katherine nodded. 'Sisters of St Christopher's – the convent and cottage hospital near Gilverryn.'

Trying to collect her thoughts and get a clear picture of Katherine attired in long robes and coif as a nun Adelaide asked, 'Do you mean you're really going to spend your life praying and looking after other people without any fun for yourself? Is that it? Giving up any chance of marrying and having children and happiness just to live in a cell and do penances? You'll have to have your hair shaved, won't you? Oh, Katherine, I can't believe it.'

'It's true; and really – you're exaggerating. The nuns are very ordinary kindly women, and the convent has beautiful gardens. You know how I love growing things – '

'Yes. But – ' Adelaide paused swallowed nervously, then resumed, 'when are you going?'

'Now. I'm on my way.'

'*Now?* But – but what's the hurry?'

'Oh, I think it's best to make the break as soon as possible,' Katherine told her. 'I'm not needed at Carnwikk – in fact Harriet positively resents me.'

'She would,' Adelaide observed cryptically.

'I don't blame her really, you know. My presence is superfluous. And perhaps when I've gone she and Anthony will be able to work things out better for themselves. It hasn't been easy for them living there, first with grandmother, and then my poor father's – moods – on top of everything else. They have the two children as well, you see – '

'I didn't know,' Adelaide said abruptly. 'What are they? Boys or girls?'

'Both boys, and quite undisciplined. Still, if I said anything I only put my foot in it, so for all concerned it's better for me to be away without any shilly-shallying.'

'Well!' Adelaide's voice was a gasp more than an exclamation. 'I didn't believe in Saints before, but you really are one, Katherine. And they don't deserve it, not any of them.'

Katherine sighed. 'Oh no. In my own way I'm being quite selfish – doing what I want to escape family quarrels, and feuds and all the wretched wars that seem to be brewing through the world. There's just one thing I'd like though, before I leave – '

'Yes?'

'Could I see Genevra?'

Adelaide's heart quickened uncertainly; the colour deepened in her face. Why Genevra? How much did Katherine know?

'Well – yes, if you want to,' she said hesitantly. 'But – '

'My grandmother was very fond of her,' the quiet voice continued.

The pendant. Of course, Adelaide thought, with her nerves relaxing.

'I'd forgotten that your grandmother had met her,' she said, 'I shouldn't have, when I think of it. If I'd had my way – I hope you'll believe me when I say that I – that Rupert – both

of us – would have sent that jewellery back as soon as possible
if your brother hadn't made such a fuss. But he was so beastly.
I'm sorry, Katherine, the way he behaved, the things he said
were quite intolerable.'

Katherine's lips tightened perceptibly. 'I quite believe it.
You don't have to tell me anything about Anthony.'

'No.' Adelaide got up. 'Well – I'll go and see if Genevra's
about. She's got a naughty habit of wandering away whenever
there's the slightest chance. I used to spank her, but it had no
effect at all. She's just incorrigible.'

She left the conservatory and presently returned with the
small girl who was wearing a blue frock tied by a wide sash,
with a ribbon round her deep red hair. Her dark jade-green
eyes were solemn under the thick brows, her mouth wide and
unsmiling above the stubborn little chin. Yet the general
effect, somehow, was of a personality that by a single word
could be stimulated to laughter and warmth.

'Genevra?' Katherine said softly. 'Hullo, I've been wanting
to meet you –'

The child paused only a moment, then she stepped forward,
held out her hand, and said, 'Hullo.'

'You don't know me,' Katherine resumed, 'but you knew
my grandmother, didn't you? Lady Serena?'

Genevra nodded. 'The old lady like a queen, in that big
coach?'

'Yes.'

'She was nice,' Genevra said, 'she had twinkly things in her
hair, and she gave me lozenges. Three I had, and a ride to the
big house. And she sent me a present, didn't she, Mama?'

Adelaide nodded. 'Much too fine a present for a little girl
like you.'

'I don't agree,' Katherine remarked firmly, and rather annoyingly to Adelaide. 'My grandmother could be very wise
sometimes, especially to those who recognised her good
points.'

Genevra thought for a moment then said quite irrelevently;
'Her hair fell on one side.'

Katherine laughed, but Adelaide said sharply, 'Don't be
rude, Genevra; run away now, I want to talk to Miss St
Clare.'

When the child had disappeared, Katherine said, 'I'm glad I've seen her. My grandmother asked me to. I know now that she was right.'

'Right?'

'To send her the pendant. And about other things too. Oh, Adelaide, don't look so – outraged. Does it matter? She's a lovely little girl. I think you should be proud of her.'

Whether the words were meant as a rebuke or not Adelaide couldn't quite tell, but as the carriage drove away she renewed her own promise for making an effort to be more patient with Genevra.

XIX

In the autumn of the following year Rupert had to go to London ostensibly on business to meet a shipping acquaintance, although he was determined for once, in spite of Wheal Tansy's problems which were still considerable – to make it also a pleasure trip for Adelaide.

She was delighted. Although she loved her own children she was not by nature the exclusively 'mothering' type possessing no ambitions beyond rearing a family. Alone with Rupert at Trenhawk she would have been happy; but there were times when the company of young children and babies got on her nerves and tired her. Having borne them she would have fretted if they were not there. The fact was though, that to be able to spread her wings a little, with a breath of social life, away from endless maternal duties would be stimulating in the extreme.

'Can we afford it though? Really?' she asked Rupert when he first suggested the break.

'No,' he answered, 'but we're going all the same.'

So they set off in the middle of September, travelling by postchaise to Truro, and from there by steam train to London, crossing the Tamar from Saltash by Brunel's famous Royal Albert Bridge. They did not arrive at Euston Station until late in the evening, but Adelaide was not too tired to feel the old thrill of excitement at entering the capital. The station, which had been built in 1838 never failed to impress her by its size and magnificent structure. London was really very wonderful after all, she thought, as Rupert hired the cab to take them to their hotel, and in her eyes no man of fashion appeared quite so handsome as Rupert that evening. There was only a faint fog. It could easily become a 'pea-souper' the following day, but the effect on their arrival was one merely of blurred lights and an ever-changing mystery vista of shapes and traffic passing accompanied by clatter and the clip-clop of horses' hooves.

Their hotel in Kensington, was not large, but sufficiently élite to enable Adelaide the vanity of displaying her 'wardrobe' to effect. Rupert had smiled to himself when he'd seen the assortment of dresses she'd managed to pack, but amusement had soon turned to pride in the face of the admiration she evoked. Her beauty – unlike that of many women – was emphasised by her ripening maturity. It seemed on that brief holiday together he could not have enough of her to himself.

Over dinner at nights the provocative allure of her white rounded shoulders above the low cut gowns she wore, drove him almost to distraction. They went out most evenings, either to the opera, theatre, or ballet, but before setting off he never failed to make love to her – an indulgence to which she responded with all the passion of a wife combined with the experienced art of a delightful cocotte.

This was an Adelaide he'd never quite known before. David perhaps? But he dismissed the thought of David instantly. He had no power any more to shadow their lives. She'd been a girl when she knew him. Their mutual life together had been no more than a romantic episode, painful in its effect, but brief. He knew it would not have lasted.

During the few days they were in town, they seemed to go and see almost everything – Tower Bridge, the West India Docks where tremendous vessels carrying sugar and hardwoods were constantly berthing and setting sail again – the immense Port of London itself with its numerous smaller docks

– and of course the Tower. They drove and walked along the embankment where plane trees lifted their delicately networked branches over the water, looking southwards towards Lambeth Palace. They saw too, the stock exchange constructed in 1854.

Adelaide was familiar with most places of interest, but in Rupert's company she saw everything with new eyes.

They visited Hampton Court and Kew's famous Botanic Gardens, with the wonderful orangery and pagoda designed by William Chambers. When Rupert explained the history of the Palm House built from 1844-1848 to the design of Decimus Burton, she listened entranced, although she had heard it all before. The large glass houses interested Rupert, and the tropical plants which included one or two varieties similar to Trenhawk's collection.

The day's passed so quickly Adelaide lost count of time, and would gladly have stayed in London a little longer. But on their last evening Rupert became more subdued.

'I love you, Adelaide,' he said, before taking her to bed. 'Not just – with my body. My heart too. You know that don't you?'

'Oh, yes, Rupert – my love, my only love,' she whispered, 'And it's the same with me.'

He kissed her. 'Whatever happens in the future – we've had this,' he said. 'Nothing can change it – not one moment –'

A faint shadow crossed her face. 'What do you mean? What *could* ?'

'Nothing. I said so.'

'Is anything wrong, Rupert?' she asked quietly. 'If there is, I'd like to know. Was that business meeting you had yesterday a flop? When I was at the hairdressers, I mean – ? Tell me, please. I didn't like him much – that man we had to lunch. It was him, wasn't it?'

Rupert did his best to allay her fears. 'He didn't exactly come up to scratch, financially speaking. But that's not your worry, or mine particularly. We're not too flush at the moment, Addy, but we'll get through.'

Rupert spoke more confidently than he felt, and the following week, following their return to Trenhawk, the grim truth really registered.

Wheal Tansy, with proper luck should have had its head 'above water' by then. But it hadn't had the luck. Instead, small mishaps and delays, unexpected difficulties, had eaten away any profit made during recent years. Profit, in any case, was hardly the word to use when so much of Adelaide's income had been taken in the process. The copper levels had not proved nearly so productive as had been optimistically expected, and were already showing signs of pinching out. Prices for the ore were dropping due to the cheaply worked deposits found on Lake Superior and in Chile. Tributers were leaving, many to go abroad, and the working miners of Wheal Tansy were becoming restless again, sensing that the Trenhawk mine had already seen the writing on the wall. On top of this worry, for Rupert, was the fact that all unknown to her, Adelaide's income from her aunt's estate was meagre compared with what it had once been. The trustees, suspicious of the future of some of her shares, had sold a large number and invested in safer holdings for security reasons. This meant they had very much less coming in. Obviously, unless a miracle happened there would have to be ruthless cutting down somewhere, and Rupert no longer believed in miracles.

He turned his thoughts to other possibilities – smuggling, or, in more polite terms, further dealing in contraband. But the exercise would have to be on a large scale to make any considerable difference, and although it was in his nature to take risks when necessary, having a wife and four young children made the whole idea, now, seem impractical. He went so far as to invite a friend of his – a Captain Blanchard to dinner one evening. In the past Rupert had been able to give him a leg-up in the Revenue Service, having one or two contacts in high places, and now Blanchard himself was in a position of authority it occurred to him the man might be willing to co-operate in an ambiguously negative way.

Rupert abandoned the suggestion in their first hour together. Blanchard, proud of his achievements, had become quite obviously a fanatic to duty. To try and bribe him would not only be impractical but unfair.

Adelaide did not care for him. He was pompous, she said, and vain. 'He was watching all the time, she said, 'to find out what effect he was having.'

Rupert threw her a quizzical look. 'Oh? And how did you know that, Addy? Your eyes must have been on him quite a bit.'

Adelaide frowned. 'You can't help being jealous, can you, Rupert?' she said. 'You only see things one way.'

'Yes, where you're concerned, my love.'

'Then it's very stupid of you.'

'You shouldn't be so beautiful,' he told her, and was both gratified and amused to see her blush.

One evening in mid December Ben Oaks called at Trenhawk, demanding to see Mr Hawksley!

Mrs Pender who'd heard his voice at the side door talking to Lilian, went to speak to him herself.

'Tisn' the time for workers to call,' she said pointedly. 'You shud' wait till the mornin'.'

'I'll be seein' him now,' Oaks answered. 'Since I've come all th' way from St Rozzan. Ef you doan' like et wumman, let me by an' I'll find the way for meself.'

'You'll do no such thing, Ben Oaks.' Mrs Pender retorted with her jaws snapping. 'You just wait an' I'll go and see.'

Mumbling under her breath she made her way down the hall to the parlour where Adelaide was stitching at a piece of embroidery and Rupert was thumbing through some bills, with a brandy and soda by his side.

''Et's that Ben Oaks,' the old housekeeper said without any preamble. 'Wants to see 'ee, he do. *Demands* et, if you please, an' not even askin' for 'master' either. Just Mr Hawksley. I'll be seein' him now,' he did say. Without so much as by your leave – ' she broke off, gasping, with a dry cough rattling her lungs, then added scathingly, 'Rabble he is. No manners, nuthink. All for hisself and they Unions. *I'd* give 'en unions.'

Rupert got up. 'Yes. Well, – things are changing these days. I'd better see him. Show him into the library and I'll be there in a minute.'

The old housekeeper sniffed. 'Ef you do say so, o' course.'

She withdrew, and in a matter of moments the two men were facing each other by the library fire. Oaks wouldn't sit, but stood there, cap in hand square-jawed and ruthless looking, staring Rupert straight in the eye. His expression was belligerent.

'I doan' want to mince words,' he said, 'this edn' no social call. Et's to tell 'ee we've had enough at the mine. Things is worse now than they ever was. Livin's goin' up all th' time, while wages is more down than up. Et's not right. For months, years now – you bin tellin' us like that Borlaze, that everythin'll be grand. Ef we do stick et and work our guts out there'll be plenty to fill our bellies an' pockets next week, or the week after or mebbe the week after that. But 'et doan' come, do et? Tomorrow's just a lie an' a trick edn' et, Mr Hawksley, *surr*!' the word was spat out. 'An, you know et. That there Wheal Tansy's dyin', an when et' gone *we'll* be gone too. So jus' you put your hand in your own pocket, Mr Bloody-owner, before et's too late. Et's not our plan to end up without a rag or penny to our name. A little in hand now'll help to ease the break when et comes – so jus' you see we have et, mister. Life's changin'. There's laws now, oh, yes. Things is changin', an doan' you fergit et.'

'Have you quite finished?' Rupert asked in a dangerously quiet voice when the threatening oration was over.

'I've said what I came to an' what was needed.'

'Then get out,' Rupert said from between his teeth, 'and stay out. You're out of a job from this moment, Oaks, so you can tell Borlaze or not, it will make no difference. I shall. You've been a good engineer, I'll say that for you, and I'll see any-one who takes you on knows it, but where I'm concerned you're finished. Now – off with you before I throw you out.'

The man's jaw tightened. For a moment Rupert anticipated a punch-up. Then, suddenly, Oaks thought the better of it, turned on his heel and a minute later was plunging through the door into the cold night air.

Rupert sighed, drew a hand over his forehead wearily, and went back to the parlour. Adelaide's expression was startled.

'What was all that about?' she asked. 'An argument obviously.'

'More than that – a threat,' Rupert answered heavily, 'and he meant it. There'll be trouble, Adelaide. I shall have to see Borlaze immediately and put him on the alert. Oaks has been a pain in the neck for a very long time and he won't give up easily. I've sacked him, but in all probability that will only make things worse.'

'But not tonight,' Adelaide begged. 'Surely the morning will do – '

'*Tonight,*' Rupert insisted. 'The miners are already restless and uneasy – frightened even. Somehow Borlaze and I have got to put their minds at rest.'

'But how? Money? Have you got it? You must draw on mine more. I've got a little upstairs, then tomorrow we can go to the bank – '

Rupert shook his head. 'No, Addy. It's up to me now. Besides – you haven't got it any more. Not what's needed.'

She stared blankly before asking, 'Then what will you do?'

He put his hands on her shoulders, kissed her forehead, and managed to say in comparatively light tones, 'I shall think of something. Don't worry. When I've seen Borlaze I expect we'll work out something.'

With that she had to be content, but she knew Rupert's optimism was only assumed, and the truth was likely to be very different. It was late when he returned that night, and from his face, as he entered the bedroom Adelaide knew her premonitions had been proved correct.

'It wasn't any good, was it?' she asked. 'Borlaze is worried.'

'Naturally. We shall get through the next week or two – with luck over the Christmas period, and there's a bit in the Welfare Fund for extras. After that – ' he shrugged. 'Well, it's all in the lap of the gods – if you believe in such things.'

As matters turned out the gods did not have to be tested, because in early January shortly following the New Year, something happened that was to alter the whole course of their lives and Wheal Tansy's future.

No one would have expected the gale to rise so suddenly. The day had been quiet until about three-thirty in the afternoon when a wind quite unpredictably rose over the sea from the North West. Within half an hour the incoming tide was pounding savagely against Trenhawk's coast-line. Tremendous breakers crashed over the rocks, drenching the cliffs in a fury of flying spume. The walls of the house echoed from the thunderous impact of the elements. Rain was driven torrentially from the darkened sky. With each great wave stones were caught and flung in a battery of sound against the granite. A lower window of the house was smashed.

Mrs Pender threw up her hands shaking her head ominously.

'Let us pray to the good Lord no poor souls be caught out there on the sea,' she said fervently. ''Twas just such a storm like this took poor Zacky Trevellyan an' his crew. I do remember et clearly though I was but a child at the time. A dozen set off and not one came back.'

She was still shaking her head and muttering to herself when she went into her own room to pray.

Her prayers were needed.

An eight-hundred-ton vessel *The Fair Grace*, an East India trader, was in difficulties on her way up the channel for Bristol with a cargo of gum, hides, and wool. When the coastguard spotted her she was already in a dilapidated condition, five miles off the coast, and drifting helplessly towards the rocks. As the crippled ship drew nearer it was seen that her sails were torn and fallen, her bottom breaking up and her bulwarks practically gone.

Rescue teams were hurriedly assembled, and Rupert rallied all the men he could find for the operation, including Carnack, Borlaze and most of the miners. By the time the vessel struck the rocks her sides were nearly gone, the valuable cargo smashed and floating in the water. Dark shapes of bodies could be seen floundering in the swirling mass of rubble and foaming waves. The local lifeboat was helpless against the storm's fury. There were screams as timber crashed and gasping heads were sucked under. On shore men came rushing from villages and moors to plunder what they could of the lost cargo, followed by their womenfolk. They were embittered men – many hungry and in need of what could be salvaged. There was no question of wrecking or conscious disregard for human life. But the scene of the wreck was a vortex of impersonal destruction. The light had quickly faded; it was almost night, and the battle was one of 'every man for himself'.

Rupert was already waist-length in the water when Adelaide arrived, screaming his name. She had ropes under her arm. Her hair was wild in the wind, her face white and desperate.

'Come back – ' she shouted, 'Rupert – Rupert – ' She plunged wildly after him flinging the ropes towards him. He looked round once, and she saw in a flash of sudden lightning, a stream of blood coursing from temple to chin. He had a man's head over his arm and was struggling to free him from an ugly cross section of jagged timber. He tried to shout, to compel her to go back, but the words were silenced on his lips. Before he could turn his head again a remaining portion of ship's mast crashed down on him crushing his chest, so his broken body with that of the one he'd tried to save were taken as so much flotsam and jetsam beneath the ugly tide of swirling sea.

Adelaide screamed and screamed. She was still screaming, struggling vainly to reach Rupert when strong arms encircled her waist from behind and dragged her to the shore. Rolls of thunder split the sky; gulls wheeled and cried mournfully over the water darkened with the reddened foam from men's blood. Like hungry birds the small figures of men and women picked and clawed among the wreckage. Others pulled what dead and dying there were to be found, to the rocks.

Adelaide lay unconscious with her eyes closed on a slab of granite near the cove where she'd wandered so often in the past. Borlaze was wiping her forehead when she opened her eyes.

'It's all right, m'dear,' he said. 'We'll get 'ee home. Rest now – '

'Rupert – ' she managed to say. 'Is he – '

'Mr Rupert's free of 'et,' the kindly voice told her. 'All right he'll be – better un many this night.'

Adelaide relaxed, misunderstanding him, as he'd meant she should.

It was only later when she properly recovered consciousness in the bedroom of Trenhawk, that she learned the truth. She would never see Rupert alive again.

And then she wanted to die.

Epilogue

Somehow winter passed to spring, and Adelaide day by day learned to live again. Not with happiness or passion, but stoically, accepting the inevitable.

'But you have the children,' the servants, vicar, doctor, and everyone she met, told her. 'They'll be such a comfort to you later. You're lucky to have them.'

She said, 'Yes, of course,' politely, because she knew they meant to be kind. But she didn't really believe it. What use were children when Rupert wasn't there? If it wasn't for them she'd be free to walk away – to walk and walk forever, not caring where she went, until she dropped of exhaustion into forgetfulness. She wanted to die.

But life went on. While breath remained there was somehow always something to do, some duty or mundane occurrence to keep one chained to loneliness and the inevitable daily routine.

Meanwhile nature changed and blossomed; celandines starred ditches and hedgerows, followed by the first daffodils in the garden, and white froth of May blossom. She became aware one day of Julian and Genevra watching her from a path, as she stared over the green and violet expanse of moors, remembering – always remembering. The pale sunlight licked the boy's fair hair to gold, and Genevra's to burnished copper. But it was their eyes that caught her attention – something solemn and static in their gaze – hurt and troubled, that caused a lurch of her heart.

The little girl came forward followed by Julian.

'Are you better, Mama?' Genevra asked staring up at her. 'It's a lovely day, isn't it? Look what I've found.' She half opened one small hand, and showed a baby field mouse peeping from her palm. 'I shall call him Bobby,' the young voice continued.

'Bobby? Why?' Adelaide heard herself asking, with a clutch of tears at her throat.

'Well – I think it's a nice name. Even if it's a girl it's nice,'
Genevra said. 'But Julian says I must put it back near its nest,
I just thought – I thought p'raps you'd like to see it.'

If it hadn't been for the fear of crying, Adelaide would have
obeyed her instinct to take the small girl into her arms. Instead she merely said, managing a smile, 'Yes, I'm sure
Julian's right. Thank you for showing me, Genevra. He's a
very nice little mouse.'

When she got upstairs to her room, reaction, after the long
strain, claimed her at last, and she was able to ease some of her
distress by the merciful release of tears.

That evening, as the sun was setting, just before the older
children went to bed, Adelaide had an impulse to go up to the
Tower Room. The fading light spilled through the long window on the landing in a golden stream across the foot of the
narrow stone steps, and looking up she saw the door was ajar.
She climbed the stairscase with her head lifted, watching with
curious intensity the fitful movement of light and shade from
the small room above.

At the top she paused, before pressing her hand against the
door and going in.

Dim light streamed down from the high window, falling in a
circular pattern on the floor. A young figure stood there staring upwards. He had his back to her, but the stance was
unmistakable. Mortimer. He appeared not have heard her.
His posture was very still. And as she watched a shadow
seemed to spread and grow about him, assuming at first the
shape of a blurred dimly defined woman with open arms. A
sense of well-being encompassed Adelaide, almost as a physical presence. Then that too changed, and became a man's
form.

Rupert's.

For a moment or two there was no sound, no movement,
only the guardian shape encompassing that of his son and
hers.

Then she knew.

The spirit of the house had spoken, giving the first glimmer
of hope through despair. By the children she would survive,
and somehow make the best of the years ahead. The ghost of

Trenhawk was not death, but love itself, of which there was no end – only peace and a long sleep.

Presently she said quietly, 'Mortimer you'd better come down with me now.'

The little boy turned. His face was radiant.

'Yes, Mama.' He came towards her obediently, and she took his hand. What he'd seen she never asked. Perhaps nothing at all, perhaps everything. With the passing of childhood much would inevitably fade into merely a half memory – a kind of dream in life to be recalled only at rare interludes under stress or heightened awareness.

And that was as it should be, she told herself later.

Real life was for the living.

Something she, too, was prepared to face at last.

Barbara Riefe

SO WICKED THE HEART

Snatched from safety and her husband's harbouring
arms by the lawless corsairs of Algiers, fiery but tender
Lorna Singleton is forced to obey a pirate captain's
bold lusts. But Ahmed's animal passion does not lack
barbaric splendour. As a Christian slave in brutal
Muslim hands, Lorna must find a protector to save her
from the torment and degradation that awaits her in
the casbah . . . even if the price of salvation is her
virtue.

SO WICKED THE HEART is a gale-force story of
surging passion and turbulent love, an unabashed tale
of a woman's struggle to defend the storm-wracked
fortress of her heart against an onslaught of
unparalleled savagery and betrayal.

HISTORICAL ROMANCE   0 7221 7363 6   £1.95

Blood Red Wine

Laurence Delaney

Alicia Orsini was beautiful, even as an unripe peasant girl.
Which brought her to the notice of the old *Padrone*, feudal
master of that backward part of Italy. He used her – and
paid. Alicia's brother, Rafael, was forced into a grotesque
act of brutality to save his family honour.

To escape retribution, Rafael fled to California, where he
built up a prosperous wine-producing dynasty, a shining
example of immigrant success. But the simmering feud
pursued the Orsinis even there – over decades, turning
Rafael's dream into a nightmare of savage vendetta that
only one supreme stroke of destruction could bring to its
dramatic end . . .

Moving from poverty-stricken, turbulent Italy of the
1920s to ruthless big-business in contemporary America,
BLOOD RED WINE is an authentic, hugely compelling
story that seizes and grips to its last, power-packed page.

HISTORICAL ROMANCE   0 7221 2994 7   £2.25

A selection of bestsellers from SPHERE

FICTION

THE STONE FLOWER	Alan Scholefield	£1.95 ☐
TWIN CONNECTIONS	Justine Valenti	£1.75 ☐
YOUR LOVING MOTHER	Deanna Maclaren	£1.50 ☐
REMEMBRANCE	Danielle Steel	£1.95 ☐
BY THE GREEN OF THE SPRING	John Masters	£2.50 ☐

FILM & TV TIE-INS

THE PROFESSIONALS 14 & 15	Ken Blake	£1.25 ☐ each
E.T. THE EXTRA-TERRESTRIAL	William Kotzwinkle	£1.50 ☐
E.T. THE EXTRA-TERRESTRIAL STORYBOOK	William Kotzwinkle	£1.95 ☐
THE IRISH R.M.	E. E. Somerville & M. Ross	£1.95 ☐

NON-FICTION

THE HEALTH & FITNESS HANDBOOK	Ed. Miriam Polunin	£5.95 ☐
ONE CHILD	Torey L. Hayden	£1.75 ☐
GARBO	A. Walker	£5.95 ☐
BEFORE I FORGET	James Mason	£2.25 ☐

All Sphere books are available at your local bookshop or newsagent, or can be ordered direct from the publisher. Just tick the titles you want and fill in the form below.

Name _____

Address _____

_____

Write to Sphere Books, Cash Sales Department, P.O. Box 11, Falmouth, Cornwall TR10 9EN

Please enclose a cheque or postal order to the value of the cover price plus:

UK: 45p for the first book, 20p for the second book and 14p for each additional book ordered to a maximum charge of £1.63.

OVERSEAS: 75p for the first book plus 21p per copy for each additional book.

BFPO & EIRE: 45p for the first book, 20p for the second book plus 14p per copy for the next 7 books, thereafter 8p per book.

Sphere Books reserve the right to show new retail prices on covers which may differ from those previously advertised in the text or elsewhere, and to increase postal rates in accordance with the PO.